RANDOM
HOUSE

LARGE
PRINT

dreams
of
falling

ALSO BY KAREN WHITE
AVAILABLE FROM
RANDOM HOUSE LARGE PRINT

The Night the Lights Went Out

dreams *of* falling

KAREN WHITE

RANDOM HOUSE
LARGE PRINT

All rights reserved.
Published in the United States of America by
Random House Large Print in association with Berkley,
an imprint of Penguin Random House LLC, New York.

Cover photos: hand and ribbon © twomeows/ Getty Images;
woman © Elisabeth Ansley/ Trevillion Images
Cover design by Rita Frangie

The Library of Congress has established a
Cataloging-in-Publication record for this title.

ISBN: 978-0-5255-8919-8

www.penguinrandomhouse.com/large-print-format-books

FIRST LARGE PRINT EDITION

Printed in the United States of America

10   9   8   7   6   5   4   3   2   1

This Large Print edition published in accord
with the standards of the N.A.V.H.

To Claire

acknowledgments

Thanks to my amazing team at Penguin Random House in editorial, marketing, publicity, sales, and art. I just write the books, and you all make the magic happen by ensuring they wind up in the hands of my readers. A thousand thanks for your support and friendship over the past eleven years.

No acknowledgments would be complete without a shout-out to my first readers, partners in crime, and BFFs, Susan Crandall and Wendy Wax. Thanks for being kind enough to tell me what I'm doing right—and what I'm not!

And, of course, thanks to my readers who faithfully buy each book. Your enthusiasm and kind words really do make all the agony of each deadline worthwhile. You truly are the best part of this writing gig—right up there with my two favorite words: The End.

Thanks to the lovely town and residents of Georgetown, South Carolina, for your Southern hospitality and kindness during my visits. You made the research part of this book nothing but fun. Thanks also to former resident Marilyn Barnhill, who was a treasure trove of information about Georgetown in the fifties. I wish I could have seen it then!

Last, thanks to the unsung heroes who fight for the preservation of old buildings, who understand that our collective history is inexorably tied to these witnesses of time and that once they are gone, they are gone forever.

Caol Ait: Thin Places. Gaelic for where this world and the next are said to be too close. According to legend, heaven and earth are only three feet apart, but in thin places, that distance is even less. Carrowmore, in County Sligo, Ireland, is one of many such thin places found throughout the world, a place where time stands still and the secular world brushes against the sacred.

dreams of falling

one

Ivy
2010
GEORGETOWN, SOUTH CAROLINA

I think I am dead. Yet I smell the blooming evening primrose and hear the throaty chirps and creaky rattles of the purple martins flitting home across the marsh. I see their sleek iridescent bodies gliding against the bloodred sunset sky, through the blackened Corinthian columns and crumbling chimneys of Carrowmore. **The house is named after a legendary thin place, far away in Ireland.** I can hear Ceecee's voice again in my head, telling me what the name means, and why I should stay away. But as with most things Ceecee has ever told me, I didn't listen.

Carrowmore and I are both in ruins now, with wrinkles in our plaster and faults in our foundations. It's oddly fitting that I should die in this house. I almost died here once before, when I was a little girl. I wonder if the house has been waiting for its second chance.

The thrum of Ellis's 1966 Mustang rumbles in the distance. If I could move, I'd run out the front door and down the walk before he can honk the horn and irritate Daddy. There are no things Daddy dislikes more than Ellis's long hair and that car.

But I can't move. All I remember is stepping on a soft spot in the old wooden floor, then hearing the splintering of ancient rotten wood. Now I'm lying here, broken in so many pieces.

My brain reminds me that Ellis has been gone forty years. His precious car sold before he shipped out to Fort Gordon in 1969. Still, the acrid scent of exhaust wafts over me, and I wonder with an odd hopefulness whether it's Ellis, coming for me after all this time.

There's something soft and silky crumpled in my fist. My fingers must have held tight when I first felt the ancient floor give way beneath my feet.

A hair ribbon. I'd pulled it from Larkin's dresser drawer. My sweet baby girl. The daughter who'd always desperately wanted to be just like me. Almost as desperately as I wanted her to be different. I wanted her to be happy. Not that Larkin is a girl anymore. She's too old for ribbons, but I kept everything in her room just the same as she left it, hoping one day she'd come home for good. Decide it was time to forgive all of us. To forgive herself.

I remember now using a black marker to write down the length of the ribbon, the letters bold and big, shouting my anger with silent strokes. But that's the only clear memory I have. I can't feel that anger anymore. Nor remember the reason for it. I must have driven here, but I don't remember. Just my writing on that ribbon, and then here, falling. My brain is playing tricks on me, recalling things from long ago with the clarity of hindsight, yet leaving what happened only thirty minutes ago in a dark closet behind a locked door.

Bright pops of air explode inside my skull. Streaks of light like shooting stars flit past my line of vision. I think they're the purple martins of my past, constant as the moon and stars in my memories. And then the pain comes, white-hot and precise, settling at the base of my head, then traveling upward, a large hand slowly constricting my brain.

Then darkness covers me like a mask and everything fades away. Except for the engine fumes of an old car, and the raucous chirp of a thousand martins coming home to roost.

two

Larkin
2010

The introductory notes to an old song distracted me for a moment, causing me to glance up from my computer and look around with an oddly satisfying appreciation. I loved my desk. Not because it was beautiful or rare—it was neither—but because of its simple functionality.

It was no different from the metal desks of the other copywriters at Wax & Crandall, the ad agency where I'd worked for the past five years, except mine was devoid of all personal effects. No frames, no kitschy knickknacks or rubber-band balls. Nothing tacked up on the walls of my cubicle, either, or mementos of my four years spent at Fordham earning my undergraduate degree. My one concession to my past was a gold chain with three charms on it that I never removed but kept tucked inside my neckline.

I loved that nobody asked me why I seemed to have no past. This was New York, after all, where people seemed to care only about where you were going, not where you'd been. They just assumed that I had no husband or significant other, no children or siblings. Which was correct. The people I worked with knew I was from somewhere down south only because every once in a while a long consonant or dropped syllable found its way into my sentences. I never mentioned that I was born and raised in Georgetown, South Carolina, or that if I closed my eyes long enough, I could still smell the salt marshes and the rivers that surrounded my hometown. My coworkers probably believed that I hated my home and that was why I left. And in that assumption they'd be wrong.

There are reasons other than hating a place that make a person leave.

"Knock, knock."

I turned to see Josephine—not "Jo" or "Josie," but "Josephine"—standing at the entrance to my cubicle. The lack of a door meant people had to improvise when they wanted to enter. She was one of our account executives, a nice enough person if she liked you but someone to avoid if she didn't.

"Are you busy?" she asked.

My fingers were at that moment poised above my keyboard, which made her question unnecessary, but Josephine wasn't the type to notice such things.

She was one of those women who commanded attention because of the way she looked—petite, with sun-streaked brown hair, and perpetually tanned—so it had become customary for her to get what she wanted with just a smile.

I was streaming Pandora on my computer, and the song playing would distract me until I could name it. It was an old habit I'd never been able to break. "'Dream On.'" Aerosmith. I smiled to myself.

"Excuse me?" Josephine said, and I realized I'd spoken aloud.

I thought back to her question. "Actually . . . ," I said, but as I began, the vague feeling of disquiet that had been hovering over me since I'd awakened exploded into foreboding.

Ceecee would have said it was just somebody walking over my grave, but I knew it was the dream I'd remembered from the night before. A dream of falling, my arms and legs flailing, waiting to hit an invisible bottom.

Ignoring my body language, Josephine stepped closer. "Because I wanted to ask you about a dream I had last night. I was running, but it felt as if my feet were stuck in glue."

I let my wrists rest on the edge of my desk but didn't swivel my chair, hoping she'd take the hint. "You can Google it, you know. You can find out a lot about dreams on the Internet. It's handy that way." I kept my hands poised near the keyboard.

"Yes, I know, but I just thought it would be quicker

if I asked you. Since you're the expert." She beamed a smile at me.

With a sigh, I turned around to face her. I wasn't an expert—only well-read on the subject after years spent trying to analyze my mother's dreams in an attempt to understand her better. As my delusional childhood self, I'd thought knowing what was in my mother's head would help me unlock the reasons for the sadness and restlessness behind her eyes. I'd hoped she would be so grateful, she'd include me in her various quests for peace and beauty. I'd failed, but in the process, I'd discovered an avid interest in these windows into our subconscious. It gave me something to talk about at the rare parties I attended, a parlor trick I could pull out when conversation faltered.

"There are probably a million interpretations, but I think it might mean that some ambition in your life, like your career or love life, isn't progressing as you'd like it to be, and you feel as if something is holding you back."

Josephine blinked at me for several seconds, and I wasn't sure whether she either didn't understand or was in complete denial that anything could ever hold her back. "Thanks," Josephine said, smiling brightly again, any self-doubt quickly erased. "You going with the group from sales to the Hamptons for the weekend?"

I shook my head, eager to get back to work. I was at the gym every afternoon at five thirty, meaning I had to leave at five. Though it kept me in shape, the habit didn't allow for much after-hours socializing. Not that I didn't like my coworkers—I did. They were a fun, creative, and young group, including a smattering of millennials who didn't act too much like millennials. I just found that I preferred socializing with them in an office setting, making it easier to escape back to my desk if any question went beyond which apartment I lived in and whether I preferred the subway or cabbing it.

"No," I said. "I think I'll stay in the city." It never ceased to amaze me that people who complained about the crowded city always seemed to gravitate toward the same beaches at the same time with the same people from whom they were trying to escape. "The water will be ice-cold, anyway. It's still only April."

Josephine scrunched up her nose, and I noticed how nothing else wrinkled. She said she used Botox only as a preventative measure, but from what I could tell, she was well on her way to looking like one of the gargoyle women I saw shopping in the high-end stores on Fifth Avenue. As Ceecee would say, it just wasn't natural.

"Not any colder than usual," Josephine insisted. "Come on. It'll be fun. We've got a huge house in Montauk. There're two queen beds in my room, if you don't mind sharing with me. You could analyze everyone's dreams."

I was tempted. I'd never been part of a group or

hung out with girls who rented houses together and took trips on the weekends. For a brief time in elementary school, I'd had a cluster of friends my age, but by the time we reached middle school, they'd formed their own smaller groups, none of which included me. I'd always had Mabry and her twin brother, Bennett, though. Our mothers were best friends, and we'd been bathed in the same bathtub when we were babies. That right there made us best friends, regardless of whether we ever acknowledged it. At least until our senior year in high school, when we'd stopped being friends at all.

The memory made it easier for me to shake my head. "Thanks for the invite, but I'll stay home. I might rearrange my furniture. I've been thinking about it."

Josephine gave me an odd look. "Sure. Oh, well, maybe it's for the best. I don't want to be the one standing next to you wearing a bikini—that's for sure."

"For the record, I don't own a bikini." I was more a T-shirt-and-boy-shorts type girl. "But thanks for asking. Maybe next time, okay?"

My cell phone buzzed where it lay faceup on my desk. I didn't have a picture or a name stored in the directory, but I didn't need to. It was the first cell phone number I'd ever memorized. When I didn't move to pick it up, Josephine pointed to it with her chin. "Aren't you going to get that?"

It was oddly telling that she didn't excuse herself

to give me privacy. I reached over and silenced it. "No. I'll call him back later."

"Him?" she asked suggestively.

"My father." I never took his calls, no matter how many times he tried. When I'd first come to New York, the calls were more frequent, but over the past year or so, they'd tapered down to about one per week—sprinkled across different days and times, as if he was trying to catch me off guard. He wasn't giving up. And neither was I. I'd inherited the Lanier bullheadedness from him, after all.

"So, you have a father." Josephine looked at me expectantly.

"Doesn't everyone?"

The phone started buzzing again. I was about to toss it in my drawer when I noticed it was a different number, another number that I knew and received calls from frequently, but never when I was at work. It was Ceecee, the woman who'd raised my mother, who was pretty much my grandmother in standing. She was too in awe of my working in New York City to ever want to interrupt me during office hours. Unless there was a good reason.

I picked up the phone. "Please excuse me," I said to Josephine. "I need to take this."

"Fine," Josephine said. "Just know that if your body is ever found behind some Dumpster in Queens, we won't know who to call."

Ignoring her, I turned my back to the cubicle opening. "Ceecee?" I spoke into the phone. "Is everything all right?"

"No, sweetheart. I'm afraid it's not." Her voice sounded thick, as if she had a cold. Or had been crying. "It's your mama."

I sat up straighter. "What's wrong with Mama?" I tried to prepare myself for her answer. Ivy Lanier was anything but predictable. But anything I could have imagined couldn't have prepared me for what Ceecee said next.

"She's missing. Nobody's seen her since yesterday morning. Your daddy said when he got home from work yesterday that she and her car were gone. We've called all of her friends, but nobody's seen her or heard from her."

"Yesterday morning? Have you called the police?"

"Yes—the minute I heard. The sheriff has filed a report and he's got people looking for her."

My mind filled and emptied like the marsh at the turning of the tides, enough stray bits clinging that I could form my first question. "Where was she yesterday morning?"

A pause. "She was here. She's been here just about every day for the last month, refinishing her daddy's old desk out in the garage. She'd come inside—I only know that because she left the kitchen a mess, the drawers yanked out. Like she was looking for something."

"And you have no idea what?" The thread of panic that had woven into my voice surprised me.

There was a longer pause this time, as if Ceecee was considering the question. And the possible answer. "I thought she might have wanted more spare rags for the refinishing. I keep a bag on the floor of the pantry. It's empty, though. She must have forgotten she'd used them all."

"But she was looking through the drawers and cabinets."

"Yes. When I saw her car pull away, I thought she was just running to the hardware store. But the police have checked—she didn't go there. Your daddy and I are beside ourselves with worry."

I closed my eyes, anticipating her next words.

"Please come home, Larkin. I need someone here. I'm afraid . . ." Her voice caught, and she was silent.

"Ceecee, you know Mama is always off in one direction or another. You've always called her a dandelion seed—remember? This wouldn't be the first time she's run off without explanation." The words sounded hollow, even to me. My dream returned to me suddenly, jerking me backward as if I'd finally hit the ground, the air knocked from my lungs.

"She always comes back the same day," Ceecee said fiercely. "They've checked all the roads within a hundred miles of here. Your daddy's driven Highway Seventeen all the way up to Myrtle Beach, as far south as Charleston." She paused again. "I wasn't going to tell you this, but I had a dream last night. I dreamed I was falling."

I stared at the black letters against the white background on my computer screen, lines and symbols that suddenly meant nothing at all. "Did you land?" I asked.

"I don't remember." There was a long silence and then, "Please, Larkin. Something bad has happened. I feel it. I need you to come home. **We** need you to come home."

I closed my eyes again, seeing the place I was from, the creeks and marshes of my childhood that fed into the great Atlantic. When I was a little girl, my daddy said I bled salt water; it was in my veins. Maybe that was why I didn't go back more than once a year, at Christmas. Maybe I was afraid I'd be sucked in by the tides, my edges blurred by the water. There was more than one way a person could drown.

"All right," I said. I opened my eyes, disoriented as I imagined the brush of spartina grass against my bare legs, but saw only my metal desk under fluorescent lights. "I'll take the first flight I can find into Charleston and rent a car. I'll call you to let you know when to expect me."

"Thank you. I'll let your daddy know."

"And call me if you hear anything about Mama."

"Of course."

"Have you called Bitty?" I asked.

Her voice had a sharpness to it. "No. I'm not sure if she's really needed—"

I cut her off. "Then I'll call her. If something's happened to Mama, she'll want to be there."

"She'll just make a fuss."

"Probably," I agreed. But despite her own flurried wind, Bitty always helped me find the calm in the eye of whatever storm I found myself. "But she loves Mama as much as you do. She needs to know what's happened."

I could hear the disapproval in Ceecee's voice. "Fine. Call her, then. But please get here as soon as you can."

Immediately after I hit the "end" button, my phone buzzed with another incoming call. I recognized the 843 area code, but not the rest of the number. Thinking it might have something to do with my mother, I answered it. "Hello?"

A deep male voice, almost as familiar to me as the sound of rain in a flood-swollen creek, spoke. "Hello, Larkin. It's Bennett."

I quickly ended the call without answering, and put my phone on "silent." I felt as if I were back in my dream, falling and falling into a dark abyss and wondering how long it would take before I hit the bottom.

three

Ceecee
2010

Ceecee stood halfway between her kitchen door and the detached garage, retracing Ivy's steps and trying to figure out what Ivy had been searching for. She'd studied the antique desk, now stripped of its finish, the drawers pulled out and stacked—a gutted fish with only skeletal remains. She reexamined the pantry and the open kitchen drawers, trying to see whether anything was missing. To find any message Ivy had been trying to leave her.

The more Ceecee didn't see, the more worried she became. She'd turned to head back into the garage when she heard the cough of an exhaust pipe and saw a plume of black smoke billowing down her long driveway. She knew who it was before she caught sight of the outrageous orange hair reflecting the afternoon sun, or the faded and peeling paint of a once–powder blue Volkswagen Beetle, circa 1970.

Bitty had been too old to own a Beetle in the seventies and was definitely too old for one now. She'd always said it was the only car built to her small scale, but she looked ridiculous, especially with that hair and her penchant for rainbow-hued flowing robe things that made her look like she'd been in a pre-school finger paint fight. Perpetually single but with a swath of brokenhearted suitors left in her wake, retired art teacher Bitty lived her bohemian lifestyle on Folly Beach, earning her living as a painter, with occasional intrusions into Ceecee's life.

They'd known each other too long for the intrusions to be all unwelcome. Once, according to Ceecee's mother, they'd been thick as thieves, she and Bitty and Margaret, inseparable since they were schoolgirls in smock dresses and patent leather Mary Janes. But time changed all things, oxidizing friendships like old copper pots, so they no longer saw their reflections in each other's faces.

As Bitty drew near, the clownlike horn of the car beeped twice, making Ceecee jump, as she was sure Bitty had intended. She heard the crank of the parking brake, and then Bitty was running toward her, nimble as a teenager, her arms outstretched. It wasn't until she was in Bitty's embrace that Ceecee remembered the security of an old friendship. Like an ancient sweater with moth holes that you still wear because you remember how it once kept you warm.

Bitty looked up into Ceecee's face. "You look tired," she said.

"And you smell like cigarette smoke." Ceecee frowned at the bright blue eye shadow and round spots of rouge on Bitty's cheeks. Her makeup hadn't changed since the sixties. "If I wore as much makeup as you, I'd still look awful, but I'd at least cover up my tiredness."

Bitty dropped her hands. "Good to see you, too. What do you think has happened to our Ivy?"

Our Ivy. Those two words stirred up the old anger. Ivy didn't belong to Bitty, no matter how much she wished she did. Some would argue that Ivy didn't belong to Ceecee, either, but Ceecee disagreed. She'd raised Ivy, and Ivy called her Mama. That was as much proof as she'd ever need.

"You'll be wanting coffee, I suspect," Ceecee said, walking back toward the kitchen and leaving Bitty to handle her bags. Bitty was the only person their age who still drank fully leaded coffee and could fall asleep and stay asleep at will. She'd been that way since high school, when they'd all started drinking coffee just because Margaret did, and it was as irritating then as it was now. "And no smoking inside."

She was at the kitchen door before she heard the sound of another car. "It's Larkin," she said, although it was obvious from Bitty's vigorous arm waving that she'd already recognized the driver. Ceecee said it again, as if to claim ownership, and moved to stand next to Bitty. When Larkin's tall form unfolded from the driver's side, she wished she'd kept walking toward the car so she didn't seem to be making Larkin choose between them.

Then Bitty was running toward the beautiful young woman with the honey gold hair that was just like her grandmother Margaret's, and both Bitty and Larkin were laughing and crying, as if at a joke Ceecee hadn't been part of.

But then Larkin turned toward Ceecee and smiled, and Ceecee put her arms around her before holding her at arm's length and shaking her head.

"You're too thin," she said. "A strong wind might blow you away. I'm going to make some of your favorites while you're home—my sweet corn bread and fried chicken."

"It's good to see you, too, Ceecee. Any word from Mama?"

Her bright blue Darlington eyes searched Ceecee's face, and again Ceecee felt like she was looking at Margaret. Dear, sweet, impossibly beautiful Margaret. Never "Maggie" or "Mags" or "Meg"—always "Margaret." Margaret Darlington of Carrowmore, the former rice plantation on the North Santee River. The Darlingtons were as shrewd as they were good-looking, their luck legend. Until it wasn't.

Ceecee squeezed Larkin's shoulders, feeling the bones, sharp as blades, beneath her hands. "No, honey. I'm so sorry. Nothing yet. Let's go inside and get you something to eat, and I'll call your daddy to let him know you got here safely."

"I've already eaten, but can I have some coffee?"

Bitty came up on the other side of her and slipped her arm around Larkin's waist. "A girl after my own heart. I knew I taught you something."

Larkin leaned her head against the top of Bitty's. "You taught me a lot. Like how to drive a stick shift—remember?"

Their strained reminiscences did nothing to hide the worry they all felt about Ivy. **Her** Ivy. Without checking to see whether they followed, Ceecee let herself into the kitchen and made a pot of strong coffee. Then she picked up the phone to call Mack to invite him to dinner. She knew Larkin would stay with her and not with her daddy. Not that she blamed her. It was hard to forgive a father who'd fallen rapidly and spectacularly from hero status in the eyes of his only child.

She held the phone absently, still scanning the tidy kitchen counters and her pretty antique teacup collection, which she dusted daily. She bent to straighten the dish towel on the handle of her oven, but stopped.

An unidentifiable object had fallen in the space between the oven and the edge of the cabinet and was peeping out at her from where it had wedged itself near the floor.

Ceecee left a brief voice message, letting Mack know about Larkin's arrival, then ended the call. Her knees popped and cracked like breaking glass as she squatted. Reaching her fingers into the small space, she grasped the object and pulled it out.

"Are you stuck?" Bitty asked, standing over her, one of the rare occasions when Ceecee had to look up at her friend.

Ceecee started to say something but stopped, the thought lost the moment she realized what she held in her hand. Holding the counter, she pulled herself up, ignoring Bitty's outstretched hand.

"What is that?" Bitty asked.

They both looked down at the white cardboard spool, the Hallmark price tag faded but still legible. A small section of gold foil ribbon was stuck to the inside, held in place by yellowed tape. Their eyes met in mutual understanding.

"What are you looking at?" Larkin asked.

Ceecee and Bitty turned toward Ivy's daughter, unable to speak. Larkin stepped forward and took the spool. "Is this for ribbon?"

Finally, Ceecee found her voice. "Yes. I think it might have been in the kitchen junk drawer. Your mother must have dropped it."

Larkin screwed up her face the same way Ivy did when she was confused or angry. Margaret had done the same thing in her day. "So, **what**? Why are you both looking like that?"

Bitty spoke before Ceecee could. "We think we know where your mama is."

"Come on," Ceecee said, grabbing her flip phone

and the keys to her Cadillac off the counter. "We'll tell you about it on the way."

"On the way where?" Larkin plucked the keys from her hand. "I'll drive—you talk. Just tell me where we're going, and I'll get us there as fast as I can."

Ceecee
APRIL 1951

The three girls—or "women," as Ceecee's mother insisted on calling them now that they were all eighteen—sat on top of the eyelet bedspread on Margaret's four-poster rice bed, a fluffy tulle petticoat and three manicure scissors between them. Graduation from Winyah High School was only a month away, and Margaret had invited Ceecee and Bitty to Carrowmore for the weekend, promising a big surprise.

"Won't your mama mind?" Ceecee asked, knowing with her whole heart that **her** mother would mind— very much. As the wife of the Methodist church's pastor, Mrs. Tilden Purnell was all about doing her best to be an example of piety, propriety, and poverty. Not that they lived in poverty—Ceecee's father never would have allowed that—but Ceecee and her two younger brothers knew their mother took frugalness to a level her Scottish ancestors would have admired greatly. Her proudest achievement was reusing the same soup base for an entire week, adding scraps from previous meals each day. Lloyd, the older of Ceecee's brothers, insisted that only their father's position with God allowed all five Purnells to get through that particular week without dying of food poisoning.

Her frugalness extended to her shows of affection toward her children, although Ceecee and her brothers never doubted that their mother loved them fiercely. She simply had a quiet way of showing it—a squeeze of the hand, a smile behind their father's back as he was sermonizing after some small infraction, an extra slice of cake when no one was looking.

Margaret arched her left eyebrow—she was the only one of the three best friends to accomplish that feat. They'd practiced for hours in a mirror after watching **Gone with the Wind.** It made her appear even more regal and aristocratic than usual. "Mother wants me to do whatever makes me happiest. Even if it means cutting up a petticoat I haven't worn yet so we have something to send to the Tree of Dreams."

Ceecee and Bitty exchanged glances, then picked up their scissors and began cutting the undergarment into strips. Nobody—including Margaret—knew when or how a narrow opening in the trunk of an old oak tree on the river at the edge of the property had become known as a special place for storing dreams, a kind of thin place that acted as a conduit to the other side. All Margaret knew was that it had been called that since the Revolutionary War, when the first Mrs. Darlington had placed a ribbon with messages for her absent soldier husband in a small opening in the tree's trunk. It had been used in the Civil War—their history teacher refused to let them refer to it by any other name, even if this **was** South Carolina and Margaret's recently passed grandmother had refused to call it anything besides the "Late Unpleasantness"—and ostensibly for any crisis in which the Darlingtons had found themselves since.

Margaret's mother called the tree divine, placed on the property as a gift from their Creator, a symbol of the family's good fortune. After all, the Revolutionary War ancestor had come home to father fourteen children, and the family and property had seen nothing but good health and good fortune ever since, even being spared during the Civil War because the Darlington owner at the time was a Mason.

Ceecee's father called it pagan, this writing notes on ribbons as a sort of good luck token, instead of good on-your-knees prayer. But Margaret stubbornly called it the Tree of Dreams, the place she went when she needed some of the Darlington good fortune to shine on her.

Whatever people called it, it seemed to work. Everything the Darlingtons touched turned to gold. Their men were handsome, their women beautiful, their children brilliant. They were always a little bit **more** than others. If Ceecee hadn't loved Margaret so much, she might have hated her.

And Ceecee's mother knew that, and that was why

she'd tried to discourage their friendship. Jealousy was one of the seven deadly sins, and even if you disguised the green-eyed monster with admiration or friendship, it would always be a sharp-toothed beast waiting to pounce.

"I brought my paints and brushes like you asked," Bitty said. Her father was the school principal, and her mother the art teacher. Ceecee was pretty sure that neither her parents nor Margaret's approved of their friendship with a girl whose mother worked, but the bond that had formed in first grade couldn't be broken, no matter how much their parents tried.

"Good," said Margaret, sliding off the side of the bed. "After we've thought long and hard, we need to paint our dreams on our ribbons. Whatever you want your life to be."

She smiled beatifically. Ceecee looked at the ribbon in her lap and frowned. Bitty's parents were allowing her to study art after graduation, and Margaret had been bombarded with marriage proposals from eligible young men with pedigrees and social standing since her debut the previous season. She'd been accepted at Wellesley, too, but only because a senator's wife (her goals at least were hand in hand with her parents') needed a good education.

But Ceecee's future hadn't been discussed. Not because it didn't matter, but because it was a forgone conclusion. She would marry, hopefully someone she could tolerate, someone who wasn't too hard on the eyes—and not the overeager, Brylcreem-slicked Will Harris, who was ten years older and already giving her meaningful glances during Sunday church services. But so far, he was the only potential candidate, any other possible suitors being shy of approaching the pastor's daughter and passing muster under the hawkish eye of her mother.

Margaret must have seen Ceecee's frown. She leaned forward, put her hand over hers, and squeezed. Ceecee's mother called Margaret superficial, but at times like this, Ceecee knew it wasn't true. Just because a person was born perfect didn't mean she didn't see or sympathize with the imperfections in others. "Don't think of the realities, Ceecee. Think of possibilities and dreams. Of things you can't even imagine yet. And write those down."

"That's easy," Bitty said, uncapping a jar of red paint and settling herself on the wide-planked pine floor, a ribbon stretched out in front of her. They watched as the tip of her brush formed precise red letters: **I dream of being a significant artist.**

"Don't you mean a **great** artist?" Margaret asked, the bridge of her perfect nose wrinkling.

"No," Bitty said. She was never afraid to disagree with Margaret. Despite her stature, she'd been raised to have an opinion and not to be afraid to voice it. And Margaret was smart enough to realize that she needed someone like that in her life.

Bitty continued. "'Great' is subjective, and I'd never know if it was true. But if my art has meaning to me and to others, then it will be significant." She balled up two blank petticoat strips and slid them away from her. "That's all I want."

Margaret turned to Ceecee. "Then it's your turn. Think hard. Remember—consider the possibilities of the rest of your life."

Ceecee stared at her friend, pinpricks of anger tightening her jaw. It was so easy for Margaret. She was a Darlington. Their world was a tidal basin full of oysters, each containing a perfect pearl. Ceecee, no matter how much she might choose to dream, had been born into a life as predictable as the tides.

With a smug burst of defiance, Ceecee began to paint the words with the brush Bitty handed her, keeping the letters only as big as her dreams allowed.

I dream of marrying the perfect man— handsome, kind, and with good prospects, and my love for him will be endless.

Ceecee placed the brush in the empty jar Bitty slid in front of her, then glanced up at Margaret. Her friend gave her an odd look but didn't criticize. "It's your turn," Ceecee said.

"I've already done mine," Margaret said with a sly grin.

She waited until Bitty and Ceecee were once more sitting on the side of the bed, the painted ribbons drying on the floor. When she was sure she had their full attention, she cleared her throat dramatically. "And now for my big graduation present for both of you."

She watched their faces with her bright blue eyes, until Ceecee couldn't take the suspense anymore. When the three of them went to the movies, she was always the one with her hands over her eyes during the scary parts.

"What, Margaret? Tell us!" she shouted.

"I've gotten permission from Mama and Daddy and my aunt Dorothy for us to stay with my aunt and my uncle Milton for a whole two weeks at their house in Myrtle Beach the day after we graduate! Mama said she'll smooth it over with your parents—you know how good she is at that—and we can take her Lincoln Cosmopolitan convertible!"

They squealed with excitement and jumped around the room, avoiding the wet paint, their arms thrown around one another. This would be the trip to say good-bye to their girlhoods, Ceecee thought. To embrace the women they'd someday become. And maybe have some fun along the way.

Margaret ran to her dresser drawer and pulled out a rolled-up ribbon. "Hurry, y'all. It's going to rain, and we need to get this done before Mama makes her phone calls." She stopped, facing them with a solemn expression. "This marks the beginning of the rest of our lives. I want you both to always remember this moment."

They raced down the curving front stairs, through the wide central hall to the back door, which had been left open, a screen filtering in the scent of rain and the tidal river at low tide. Angry clouds sat on the horizon, casting out the sun and dulling the colors of the river and marsh.

As they ran, Ceecee looked back—just once. She loved seeing the great house of Carrowmore from a distance and never tired of its graceful lines and perfect symmetry. But the clouds had dimmed the vivid brightness of its white paint, making the old house and familiar landscape appear as a fading memory.

Hollowed-out gourds hung from the limbs of the river birches, elms, and oaks that dotted the lawn past the formal gardens. It was near sunset, and a large flock of purple martins dipped and swirled as they returned to the gourds, their nests for the night. Ceecee stopped for a moment to look up, hearing the chirps and rattles. She realized she'd never hear them again without remembering right now, this threshold they were all crossing.

The ancient oak tree, with its sweeping drapes of moss, waited at the end of the lawn near the river, its arms seemingly outstretched in welcome. Margaret walked right up to the opening in the trunk and stuck her ribbon inside.

"Hurry—the rain's going to start any minute, and I've just washed and set my hair."

"But won't somebody be able to reach in and take ours out and read them?" Bitty said.

Margaret shook her head. "The birds will come and take them and use them in their nests. Granddaddy used to say they were the go-betweens from this world and the next. You want them to take your words and bring them where they need to go."

"What does yours say?" Bitty said.

As she spoke, a streak of lightning flitted across the sky, and a fat drop of rain landed on her cheek.

"Hurry," Margaret said, already taking two steps back toward the house.

Bitty and Ceecee rolled up their ribbons and stuck them inside the tree, neither indicating how crazy this was. Margaret Darlington had the kind of power that made sane people do insane things.

The sky opened up with a sudden, drenching downpour as they ran back across the lawn to the old white house.

"What did you put on your ribbon?" Ceecee called again, her voice nearly drowned out by the loud bark of thunder above.

Margaret laughed her laugh that always turned heads, throaty and melodic like a movie star's. "The same thing you did!" Her long legs helped her overtake her two friends, so that she made it to the back porch first, her blond hair darkened by the rain to the color of sea oats in autumn.

A strong wind pushed at Ceecee's back, and an odd sound floated through the rain toward her. She stopped and turned, saw the birdhouse gourds swaying from their tethers, their round holes like tiny mouths opened in surprise as they keened in the wind.

Shivering, Ceecee began to run again, spotting Margaret on the porch, dripping with water. She looked more beautiful than ever, her hair slicked back, revealing the fine bones of her face. Ceecee felt anger again, at the "more" Margaret always seemed to achieve without trying. Angry, too, that the wish she'd carefully written on the ribbon had to be shared.

It didn't occur to Ceecee until much, much later that all legends and myths have a drop of truth in them. And that she should have listened to her mother about being careful what she wished for.

four

Larkin
2010

On the hour-and-a-half drive from the Charleston airport to Georgetown, I thought I'd get acclimated to being home. I listened to the radio, eventually settling on a station playing mixed rock hits, songs I could identify before the first chorus. There was something reassuring about that, a reminder that I hadn't completely shed my skin.

It had been nearly a year and a half since I'd been to South Carolina, having skipped the past Christmas visit. I'd said I had plans to go skiing with friends. It was a lie, but sitting home alone in my Brooklyn apartment was so much easier than returning to my childhood. Each visit was like slowly peeling off a Band-Aid, and my pattern of avoidance was now a habit.

After landing in Charleston, I sped up Highway 17, worry over my mother pressing my foot a little harder on the gas pedal. I made the mistake of rolling down the windows. As soon as I caught the redolent scent of the marsh and saw the first roadside sign advertising butter beans and bait, I knew I'd traveled much farther than the six hundred or so miles separating me from New York. Whoever said you could always go home again had never met my family.

Both Bennett and my daddy called twice while I drove, but I didn't answer, citing road safety as my reason. Like I needed one. At least by the time I pulled into Ceecee's front drive, I'd managed to stop crying and pretend I had it all together. I'd had a lot of years to practice.

Now, not ten minutes after I'd arrived, I was heading down Ceecee's driveway again. Ceecee had promised to tell me where we were going while I drove, but she and Bitty were too busy interrupting each other for much of the story to emerge intact.

"One at a time," I shouted, the long travel day and my lack of coffee catching up with me. "You first," I said to Ceecee, knowing she'd expect that.

"We're going to your grandmama's old house. The place where your mama was born."

"Carrowmore? I thought it burned years ago."

Ceecee shared a look with Bitty. "It did. But the ruins are still there."

I glanced at Bitty in the rearview mirror. "I don't understand. The land was given to the state before

I was born. We don't even own it anymore. Why would my mother be there?"

Bitty's eyes went wide. In the passenger seat, Ceecee bent her head, studying her hands. The nails were clipped sensibly short, but she wore pale pink polish on them, the same shade she'd worn ever since I could remember. It never ceased to amaze me how little things changed.

"What?" I said. "What am I missing?"

Bitty leaned forward and placed her hand on my shoulder. "Your family still owns Carrowmore and all the property down to the river. It's a dangerous place, so everyone agreed we'd make sure you understood it wasn't a place for you to go."

"I don't understand," I said again, the shock of Bitty's words hitting me. Not for the first time, I found myself wishing that my family wasn't so complicated. That I wasn't so ignorant. That I was the orphan I pretended to be in my new life in New York.

"I wish I hadn't come back," I said under my breath, the way a child does when scolded.

Ceecee frowned at me, and I saw her as the old woman she was, seventy-seven, her face lined and sun-spotted from too many years on the beach and in her garden. "Don't talk like that, Larkin. Your mama could be hurt and needing you. Or worse."

Bitty squeezed my shoulder. "And if she is hurt, just tell yourself that there will be a better day, honey. Don't you forget that."

She'd said that before—the day I'd left Georgetown for good and she'd given me the gold chain necklace with a thin circle from which dangled three gold charms: a quill pen, a palmetto tree, and a pointed arrow. Bitty had told me that she was proud of me for embarking on this new adventure, but she wanted to give me something to always remind me of my dreams and of the place I'd always call home, whether I believed it or not. When I'd asked her about the arrow, she'd just said that I'd have to figure that one out. I hadn't taken off the necklace since and wore it tucked securely under my clothes so no one would ask me about it.

"Your mama is special, Larkin," Ceecee said. "Just like you. She'll get through this, like she's gotten through everything else in her life."

I stole a glance at Ceecee, all anger and tenderness rolled up together like a sweet gum tree seedball, impossible to separate. She'd let me, from an early age, plow through my life with the belief that my Darlington birthright meant I was without flaws, that I was the smartest, the most talented, and the most beautiful. That despite all evidence to the contrary, I was destined to be a star.

My desire to be like my free-spirited mother, who was never afraid to try something new and who never worried what other people thought, fueled the illusion. For most of my growing-up years, I thought that running roughshod over my peers and loved ones could be excused because I was on the path to greatness.

My attitude actually won me friends at first, girls who wanted to be swept up into the stratosphere of stardom, until they tired of my false air of superiority and my mastery of the humble brag. Everyone except for Bennett and Mabry. They'd stuck with me up until the moment I discovered they were just like everybody else.

I turned my head to focus on the road, feeling the weight of Bitty's hand on my shoulder. It was as if she were helping me hold in the words that threatened to spill out of me.

As we drove, Ceecee spoke about Carrowmore and the origins of its name. There was an oak they called the Tree of Dreams, and once, when Ivy was a little girl, her father had brought her to Carrowmore to put her own ribbon inside the ancient tree.

"Just that once?" I gripped the steering wheel tightly, frustrated and angry. "Just that once, and you think for whatever reason that that's where she must be now?"

Bitty spoke up from the backseat. "She went more than once—quite frequently, actually, as soon as she learned to drive and could get there by herself."

Ceecee looked sharply at her old friend. "How do you know that?"

"Ivy told me. She said she went there to feel closer to her mother. To Margaret."

Crossing her arms over her chest tightly, Ceecee said, "She never told me that."

"She didn't want to sound disloyal to you."

I sensed Ceecee stiffen beside me. She leaned forward, bracing both hands on the dash. "Slow down—you need to take the next right. It's a small road and easy to miss."

"I'm surprised you remember how to get here," Bitty said softly.

"Maybe Ivy's not the only one who visits."

Scrubby pines crowded together on each side of the two-lane highway, blocking from sight everything that lay beyond. It had never occurred to me before that parts of the Lowcountry preferred to remain hidden from outsiders, keeping their secrets like an evening primrose before dusk.

"Turn here," Ceecee said.

"I know." I'd already begun to turn the car, knowing this road, this break in the trees. The crunch of car tires over sand and loose rocks brought back memories I hadn't known I had. I felt both of the older women watching me, and said, "I've been here before. Not in recent memory, but I've been here."

Without being told, I curved left at a Y in the road, noticing how the trees and undergrowth huddled closer, like children whispering.

I want to show you a secret. It was my mother's voice. I could see her in the driver's seat, and me as a little girl, sitting next to her, the shoulder strap of the seat belt digging into my neck as I strained to see over the dashboard.

"I've been here before," I said with conviction now,

unable to determine whether the recalled scents of an overgrown garden were remembered or real.

Two brick posts stood sentry on either side of the narrowed road, appearing to hold back the vegetation. Large black iron hinges clung to them, ghosts of a once-imposing entrance. Missing mortar and broken bricks told of a losing battle with the elements.

The sun dipped behind a cloud, casting us in shadow. My cell phone rang. I glanced at it in the cup holder. "It's Daddy. Please answer it, Ceecee. Tell him where we are just in case we lose our signal."

As she did, I pressed my foot harder on the accelerator, hearing the rocks spit out behind us. Mama was here. I knew it. I felt it. I was back in my dream again and falling, waiting to hit bottom.

"He's on his way," Ceecee said. "He's bringing Bennett."

I almost slammed on the brakes. "Why?"

She gave me a sidelong glance. "Because we might need help."

I pressed harder on the accelerator, the car lurching forward. The overgrowth moved away from the road, now two strips of sand with a grassy line between them, and then the pines and Chinaberry trees gave way to a long line of elderly oaks, their arthritic backs hunched over the road while their geriatric shawls of moss hung listless in the humidity.

I wanted to ask why Bennett would be with my father, or why both had been trying to reach me.

But I was distracted by what seemed to be hundreds of gourds hanging from poles and tree branches, their man-made holes appearing to stare at me with rounded eyes and mouths of surprise. I remembered them. I remembered being afraid and my mother telling me about the purple martins and how they relied on humans for their homes, because after hundreds of years of human intervention, the little birds had forgotten how to build their own nests.

And I remembered my small hand tucked into my mother's as we headed toward the oldest tree, down by the river, its trunk wider than our car. I hadn't forgotten, and the sight of the gourds brought it all back.

She'd let go of my hand, then taken a rolled-up ribbon from her pocket and held it against her heart.

"What's that?" I'd asked.

"A dream. I wrote it on the ribbon."

"Can you tell me what it says?"

Mama knelt down in front of me, and I recalled that part because it was the first time I'd noticed how her eyes focused on me without really seeing, the way a person might pretend not to have seen a ghost. "It might not come true then," she said. "It's like making a wish before you blow out your birthday candles—you're not supposed to tell anybody what you wished for."

She'd stood and shoved the ribbon inside a skinny opening in the tree's trunk. The sky had darkened for a moment as a flock of martins flew overhead, coming home, their calls and chirps echoing in the sky.

"It's time to go, Ivy." Mama walked away quickly without reaching for my hand like she was in a hurry and couldn't wait to leave.

Without hesitating, I stuck my hand inside the trunk and pulled out the ribbon, holding on to its edge until it had completely unfurled. There were words written on it, words I hadn't yet learned to read.

I'd looked up at Mama's retreating back and curled my hands into little fists. Ceecee would have told me what it said. Ceecee didn't believe in keeping anything from me because, she said, I was mature for my age. Mama only ever told me to stop pushing so hard and to just enjoy being a little girl. But I couldn't. Because I wanted to be like her.

I'd shoved the ribbon into the elastic waistband of my pants and run after Mama, climbing into the backseat and buckling my seat belt without being told.

"What's wrong?" Bitty's hand brushed my shoulder, and I realized I'd slammed on the brake.

"It's . . ." I turned to Ceecee, the one person who knew my mother better than I did. "She's here. I feel it."

We had reached the end of the oak-lined lane and found ourselves facing the ruins of Carrowmore. The old Greek Revival mansion loomed like a prophet in front of the bent trees, its partially missing roof

and gaping window openings doing nothing to de-
tract from the impression of a grande dame greeting
her guests. Brick chimneys protruded from the second floor like raised fists. The Corinthian columns
looked out at the ruined trees with calm acceptance,
despite their crumbling bases and missing plaster.

"Go around to the back," Ceecee instructed, leaning forward in her seat as if to move us faster. "She
wouldn't have gone inside the house."

I wondered why she sounded so sure, so convinced
that Ivy would have thought first before acting. As if
she'd ever done that in her fifty-eight years. Then I
realized that Ceecee was reassuring herself, the way a
child does when hearing a noise in a darkened room,
unable to bear any other possibility.

I grimaced as the car ran over uneven terrain,
the sound of a branch scraping the undercarriage
abrupt in the silence, and stopped near a ruined
wooden gate that had once protected a garden. I
peered through the windshield, covered now with
the carcasses of insects, and looked toward the river.
The infamous oak tree stood where it had been for
more than two centuries, as regal and impassive as
the house, as aloof. And alone.

"I don't want to get stuck," I said, turning off the
ignition. "You two wait here while I go check things
out."

As if I hadn't spoken, both women were already
opening their doors, rocking slightly to get the mo-
mentum to exit the car. "You wait here, Larkin, for

your daddy and Bennett," Ceecee said. "Bitty, you go to the tree, and I'll go inside. If you see Ivy, give a shout."

I'd opened my mouth to argue when I spotted my mother's navy blue Cadillac. Ivy had always driven the same car, just a newer model each year. Daddy bought her one annually, on the same day as his dental exam. He always said both were important to his well-being—keeping his teeth in shape and knowing that Mama was safe out on the road. If I hadn't known any better, I might even have thought they had a good marriage.

The back end of the car protruded from the other side of the house, making me think she'd been on her way out before deciding to stop. Or maybe she'd thought she'd missed something.

"Mama!" I ran toward the car, knowing how it would smell (new leather and Mama's Aqua Net hair spray) and how it would look (scrupulously clean, since Daddy vacuumed and washed it just about every day). "Mama," I shouted again as I reached the car, running to the driver's side to yank it open.

I stared inside, waiting for the sight of my mother's purse on the passenger seat and her keys in the ignition to register. Then I looked in the backseat and popped the trunk, just in case.

"Is she here?" Bitty asked, panting with exertion, as she reached me, her face dewy with perspiration. Several yards behind her came Ceecee, pressing a tissue to her forehead and looking like she might pass out.

I shook my head. The panic I'd been pushing back ever since I'd received Ceecee's phone call in New York was rising up in me. "Did you bring your phone?" I asked Ceecee as she caught up to us, wheezing.

She nodded.

"Good. Call Daddy. Tell him I found Mama's car and that I've gone inside to find her. You two are going to wait right here."

The brick steps, more holes now than bricks, led to a wooden door that might once have been painted black. The four window rectangles at the top were broken, and a hole gaped where the knob should have been.

Ceecee found her voice. "Where did you learn to be so bossy and opinionated?"

Without responding, I climbed the steps, carefully placing my feet on whichever brick looked more permanent than its neighbors.

"She was raised that way," Bitty said, and I couldn't tell whether her tone was full of admiration or condemnation. Not that it mattered. It had been the ruin of me and not something from which someone could easily recover.

I pushed open the door and listened as the hinges protested. Inside, it smelled of smoke, and damp wood, and the passage of time. Splinters of smudged light came in through broken windows, the remaining glass covered in grime. The room I'd entered was open, most likely a sunroom once, surrounded by windows and filled with plants, the view of the oak tree and the river the only art and window treatments. I moved forward carefully, stepping over moth-eaten rugs and broken furniture, and found myself in what must have once been an impressive central hallway.

A curved staircase crept up one side of the wall, its banister solid and elegant despite the mildew-covered wallpaper and the missing risers, the wood having long gone to termites. I looked up and saw a darkening sky, the edges of the ceiling peeled back in charred lines, the floor around me covered in old soot and ground-in ash.

"Mama?" I called, my voice too quiet, as if I were afraid to wake whatever was left there. "Mama!"

Only the scurry of unseen animals rippled through the dusty silence. **What happened to you?** I turned slowly, taking in the scorched and ruined house, wondering why my mother had come there. And why she'd brought me there when I was a girl.

Then I stopped, teetering off balance, and grabbed the banister to keep from falling into a gaping hole I'd thought was a shadow on the floor. The wood appeared fresh and dry, the pale blond color a garish smear against the blackened and soiled floorboards.

"Mama!" I shouted. I dropped to my knees and peered into the utter blackness beneath me. With shaking hands, I pulled out my cell phone and turned on the flashlight.

The circle of light illuminated the prone figure of a petite woman wearing purple sandals and a pair of jeans, her wavy blond hair matted with red and covering her face.

"She's here, she's here!" Not wanting to turn my attention away from my mother in case she moved, I yelled, "Call an ambulance—she's hurt!"

But my mother wasn't moving. Her eyes were closed, and one of her arms was bent the wrong way. I couldn't hold the flashlight steady enough to see if she was still breathing, and I was glad, because if she was dead, I didn't want to know. I didn't want to believe that I wouldn't have the chance to talk to her again, or that all of the years spent not talking had been filled with "laters" that wouldn't ever get here.

I heard Ceecee and then my daddy's voice telling her to stay back. Two sets of footsteps made their careful way toward me.

"I'm in the center hall—be careful," I shouted. "Mama fell through the floor." I still wasn't crying, my brain somehow shifting to survival mode. But I could taste tears, hot and metallic at the back of my throat. Tempting me to be less of the person I wanted people to see.

Then my daddy's hands were on my shoulders, dragging me backward, and another set of arms was holding me back.

"An ambulance is on the way, Larkin. It's going to be okay."

It was Bennett, and if it had been anybody else, I would have relaxed into his arms and let myself cry. But I couldn't. Not then, not ever. I remained stiff, my gaze focused on the hole as we waited for the sound of an approaching siren.

I was led out of the house and stood with Ceecee and Bitty as we watched my mother being taken out on a stretcher and loaded into a waiting ambulance. I felt one knee buckle when Daddy told me she was alive but hurt real bad, that they were taking her to the hospital and I should meet them there.

I began walking toward my car, but Bennett pulled me back, forcing me to look at him. He was just as tall as I remembered, his face achingly familiar, his muddy green eyes as wary and unreadable as the last time I'd seen them on the banks of the Sampit River.

"You shouldn't be driving. Leave your car here, and I'll drive you all to the hospital."

Knowing he was right, I nodded, unable to thank him. That would have meant speaking, and I wasn't sure I could.

He held open the passenger door of my dad's car before helping us all inside, then followed the ambulance down the unpaved road, its screaming sirens making a mockery of our slow progress.

It began to rain, heavy drops beating down on the car and the ruined house, darkening the ground and wetting what remained of the roof and the exposed floors, a final insult and ignominy for what had once been a place of beauty and pride. A place that had been kept hidden from me. Except once.

I turned my head to get another glimpse of Carrowmore, seeing the surprised faces and sightless eyes of the hanging gourds, and I remembered my first trip there, as a girl. The ribbon my mother had placed inside the trunk of the old tree; the words I'd finally read:

Come home to me, Ellis. I'll love you always.

Hot tears slid down my cheeks. I wasn't sure if they were tears for the mother I didn't really know, or for a stranger my mother had once promised to always love.

five

Ivy
2010

The pain that radiates through my body tells me I'm not yet dead. But I'm not exactly alive, either. Maybe I'm a ghost, if that's what being half in this world and half in the next is like. Or maybe this is all a dream and I will awaken and everything will be like it was before.

Except I'm not sure that's what I want.

All I remember now is the desperate need to be at Carrowmore. And I remember the pain, different from the pain that throbs in my head and echoes through my back and my limbs. Pain that presses on the heart and makes me forget to breathe. Like what I felt when they brought me the news about Ellis. My heart hurts, but it's not about him. Not this time.

Ceecee. It's something to do with her, but I can't think of what it could be.

I had something in my hand. Yes. I'd needed to bring something to Carrowmore. I hadn't been there in years, visiting it only in my dreams. The same dream, over and over. I'd be in the house, and it would have a roof and floors and furniture. I'd be standing at a door with my hand raised to turn the knob. Ruffles covered my wrist and hand, a much smaller hand, like that of a little girl. But it was mine. I was sure it was mine.

I never knew what happened after I turned that knob. Those were the nights I woke up screaming, Mack trying to calm me down, his words like a teaspoon trying to bail out the ocean.

My nightmares are why Larkin's so obsessed with dreams. It's why she's such an expert at analyzing them. She always believed that if she could figure out what they meant, they'd go away. I wish that she could have, for both of us. That together we could have vanquished whatever it was that haunted me in my sleep. It would have been something for us to share, besides the color of our hair and the shape of our noses. Something that would have made her happy. Or at least happy enough that she'd stop wanting to be like me.

I hear her voice, and my chest lightens. She's here, and I want to think she's come to see me, but I can't be sure. There's something about mothers and daughters, I think, that makes us always want to hold close at the same time we try to push each other away. I think she blames me, too, for what happened with Mack. And for that, I couldn't disagree.

I don't deserve her, this daughter of mine. God made a mistake when he gave a perfect child to this imperfect mother, and I think Larkin's always known this. Even as a baby, she'd cry when I held her, quieting only when placed in Ceecee's or Bitty's arms. It was as if she knew there was something missing inside me, something I was looking past her to find. That's the other thing about mothers and daughters—we always know where it hurts.

"Mama? Can you hear me?"

I try to open my lips, but it's like somebody else's body is attached to my brain. Still, I know it's my Larkin. I can tell by her scent. Since she was a baby, she's always smelled like sunshine and salt air. Not something a person can shake is what I told her when she said she was headed to New York City for college instead of the University of South Carolina. She and Mabry had already picked out matching bedspreads for their dorm room.

I should have expected it. Should have known she was never mine to keep. I'd spent most of her childhood letting other people raise her. She looked and acted too much like me, and it scared me.

So I stood back and watched, trying to distance her from me, mothering behind the scenes, filling in the missing pieces. Ceecee and Bitty were so good at mothering, anyway; I let them take all the credit.

A warm, soft hand folds over mine, and I know it's Larkin's. Her heart has always been as wide as the moon even though it shouldn't be. Her ability to love easily made those who loved her most call her perfect in every way until Larkin believed it.

I want to open my eyes, to tell her I'm sorry, but I can't remember for what. I'm so tired, and I can hear Ellis's Mustang. It's not too far away, and it's coming closer, and all I know for sure is that I'd better have it all figured out before he gets here.

Larkin

I stood outside my mother's hospital room without moving, unaware of people walking past me. I'd stared at the bruised and bandaged woman in the bed, spoken to her, and touched her hand. I'd even willed some kind of emotional response, but it was like squeezing a dry rag.

Until I'd remembered her asking me once if I thought dying would be like dreaming. It had been after one of her really bad nightmares, one about being in the river at night. The memory jarred me, made me wonder why she'd been found at the burned-out ruins of an old house by the river. And it reminded me of how little I knew my mother.

When I was five years old, Ceecee told me that the woman I'd always called Ivy was my real mother. I'd told Mabry and Bennett that I didn't have a mama, and they'd said that everybody had one. So I'd run home and cried to Ceecee, who explained it all to me.

Ceecee was the one who packed my lunch box and drove me to school, who took me shopping in Charleston and planned my birthday parties. But Ivy was my mother, the beautiful woman with hair just like mine who took ballet lessons and sang in various bars and music festivals and who wore colorful clothes she made that matched the watercolors on the walls of our house that she'd painted. That's when I started calling her Mama, so everyone would know she was mine.

My therapist in New York had once asked me if I believed my mother loved me. I'd said yes immediately. Of course she did. I'd always felt it, and she'd told me often, usually right before leaving the house for a class or event or art show. She never took me with her, no matter how much I begged, telling me to find my own dreams, that hers were too sad to share. It made her even more irresistible to me, more mysterious. At least until my therapist asked me what it was in my mother's past that made her so sad, and I couldn't answer. I still couldn't.

But I never doubted that she loved me, any more than I doubted that Ceecee and Bitty did, too. I was still working with my therapist to understand how three such women could love me and still mother me into the disaster I'd become.

"Larkin?"

I jerked my head up.

"It is you!" Mabry was still a head taller than I was, just as slender, her hair just as dark, her skin a golden tan.

I considered ducking back into my mother's room, but that would have been postponing the inevitable. Mabry was never able to resist a challenge. Instead, I attempted a smile and raised a hand in a stupid little wave.

Ignoring my hand, Mabry enveloped me in an unexpected hug, my face pressed against her green scrub top. I remembered my father telling me she was an operating room nurse now, but it hadn't occurred to me that I might run into her here. She pulled back to hold me at arm's length, just like Ceecee, her green eyes scrutinizing me. "You look great," she said, dropping her hands.

"So do you," I said, looking away, embarrassed by her close examination.

"I'm sorry to hear about your mother."

I nodded, wondering when she was going to mention the apology I owed her. I was nine years too late. I found myself looking at the side of her head for evidence of a scar.

She laughed, realizing what I was doing. "Don't worry. My hair hides it."

"I came by the hospital to see you. After . . . Afterward. To see how you were. But you'd already been released and sent home."

Mabry reached out a hand and squeezed mine. "I

know. I understand. I just wish that sometime in the past nine years you'd have thought to call or write or come visit. I have a son, now. He's four and looks just like Bennett, poor kid." She let go of my hand, her face serious. "I never expected what happened to drive a permanent wedge between us. I don't hold on to grudges, you know. They're like expired milk in the fridge."

But I do. I looked at her, so content in her green scrubs, her life as perfect as she'd always planned, and the old resentment curdled inside me. I wasn't the only one who needed to apologize for events she'd moved on from and for which I'd had to rearrange my life.

I jerked my thumb in what I hoped was the direction of the waiting room. "I've got to go. We're still waiting to hear from Mama's doctor . . ." I let my voice trail off, unable to explain that the biggest grudge I held was against my younger self, the girl I'd been trying to bury for almost a decade.

"Sure. Despite the circumstances, it's good seeing you. If you need anything, please let me know. I live on Prince Street—next to my parents. Nothing so exotic as New York for me." Mabry smiled again, and I wanted to cry for the little girls we'd been before the world's glaring spotlight eradicated our childish imaginations.

I began to walk away, but Mabry called me back.

"Have you finished your Pulitzer-winning novel

yet? I've been keeping my eye out for my red-carpet dress. Remember, you said I could go with you to the ceremony."

I thought I might be sick right there on the hospital linoleum, the emotions of the last twenty-four hours finally catching up to me. I wondered why other people's minds chose to remember the most obscure and awful things, the ones you'd prefer they forget. Like a younger version of myself practicing an acceptance speech that would never be given.

"I've got to go," I said without answering, and ran down the hall toward the waiting room sign. I entered without thinking, and both my daddy and Bennett spotted me before I could back out again. Both men stood, making an exit even more impossible, but reminding me, too, of something I'd missed while in New York.

I started to say that I needed coffee, to give me a reason for an immediate retreat, but the doctor who was overseeing my mother's care exited the room, having apparently spoken to my father. I considered rushing down the hallway to ask him to repeat what he'd said, but I decided against it. It was something the old me would have done. The girl who'd thought that being demanding and rude was the same thing as being assertive. I'd been raised on it, and it had been one of the hardest lessons for me to unlearn.

Instead, I sat down across from the two men. Avoiding Bennett's eyes and focusing on my father, I asked, "What did the doctor say?"

My father looked older than his fifty-eight years, his suntan beneath the harsh fluorescent hospital lighting making him look yellow. He actually looked like a man worried about his wife, someone he loved. Yet we both knew that wasn't true.

He cleared his throat. "He told us we need to wait and see. She has a fractured skull, a broken pelvis, and a shattered arm and foot. It's too early to tell what kind of outcome we can expect. I want to move her to an advanced trauma care center, but her surgeon said we should wait. They've got the technology they need here, and the staff is trained to care for trauma victims."

The words hit me like dull darts, finding their target, then falling to the ground. I wished Ceecee or Bitty were there to guide me. But they'd retreated to the cafeteria. Ceecee had pressed a Little Debbie cake from the vending machine into my hands before she left, telling me I should eat something. Some things never changed.

Daddy cleared his throat. "The doctor said he didn't expect anything new before tomorrow and that we should go home and rest." He rubbed the back of his neck like he'd always done when he wanted to avoid meeting my eyes. "I think I'll go home, take a quick shower. I'm not hungry, but I don't think I've eaten since sometime yesterday." He forced himself to look at me. "Why don't you come with me?"

I was shaking my head before he'd finished speaking. "I think I'll stay here—just in case there's any change." I held up the packaged cake. "I have this if I get hungry."

He stood, shoved his hands into the pockets of his khaki pants. "All right. Call me if you need anything." For a moment, I thought he'd come over and kiss my forehead, but to my relief he didn't. He glanced over at Bennett. "You coming?"

Bennett shook his head. "Mabry's almost done with her shift. I'll hitch a ride home with her." He pulled out his car keys and tossed them to my father. "I'll come by later to get my car."

Daddy nodded, then with another good-bye directed somewhere over my head, he left the room.

To Bennett, I said, "I appreciate you bringing me here, but if you're going to wait here for your sister, I'm going to wait someplace else."

I made to stand, but he held up his arm. "Larkin, come on. It's been a long time. Surely long enough for us to be able to sit down like adults and talk about what happened. Or why you didn't say good-bye when you left."

Because you already know. "Not long enough," I said.

He remained sitting. His green eyes stared calmly back at me, as if he hadn't had a front-row seat to the worst moment of my life. Or anticipated its inevitable arrival. "You look great, by the way."

"You mean I'm not fat anymore." The words were out of my mouth before I could pull them back.

Bennett didn't flinch. "I always thought you were beautiful."

His words took me by surprise. For a moment, I couldn't say anything. "You and Ceecee." I looked down at the Little Debbie cake and placed it on the side table. All my life Ceecee had been stuffing me with food, trying to feed my disappointments and insecurities and fill the void my mother's absences left. It had taken me two years with a therapist to figure that one out.

"I'm going to the cafeteria. Tell Mabry I'm planning on heading back to New York as soon as my mother's released. I don't expect I'll have time to stop by."

Bennett's face remained expressionless, but his green eyes were cool and assessing. When I was growing up, they'd been a barometer for my behavior, letting me know when I'd gone too far. At the very least, they'd been my warning that he, Mabry, or both were about to give me a reality check. For a while after I left, I'd found myself looking for his eyes in situations in which I needed them. But I didn't anymore. I was a different person now, finally able to see myself as others did, and not just those who indulged me. But the memories of before still made me cringe.

"I'll let her know. But she's a block away from your parents, so it probably wouldn't be too much of a strain on your schedule to stop by."

I wanted to tell him that despite what she'd said, I knew Mabry didn't really want to see me. If I were she, I certainly wouldn't want to see me, either. Instead, I said, "Well, that's how little you know about me and my schedule."

Again, his eyes gave nothing away. I found myself squirming under the scrutiny.

"Did she tell you who she married?" he asked.

If I'd had any food in my stomach, it would have tried to come back up. "She didn't mention it."

"A nice guy named Jonathan Hopewell. She met and married him while they were both in nursing school. Thought you might want to know."

I knew what he was trying to tell me, what he thought I wanted to know. But I pretended I didn't. I nodded stiffly. "Sure. Thanks."

"Are you seeing anyone up in New York?"

"No. I'm pretty busy with work."

"I can only imagine." He rested his elbows on his knees and clasped his hands between them, always a sure signal that he wasn't done telling me all that he wanted to. "Do you still randomly identify music, artist, and lyrics, or a song that's playing wherever you happen to be?"

I would have laughed if my mother hadn't been lying in a hospital bed in a coma. If I remembered how. "No," I lied. "I don't." I straightened, remembering the question that had been niggling in my brain. "Why were you with Daddy yesterday?"

Approaching footsteps sounded from the hallway. We looked up to see Ceecee and Bitty, the former carrying a cafeteria tray laden with plastic-encased pieces of cake, a doughnut, a brownie, two fried chicken legs, and a single apple. I was pretty sure the apple was Bitty's contribution.

Bennett stood and greeted the two older ladies before turning back to me. "Mabry's shift is almost up—I should find her. I'll check in with you later, see how your mama's doing. I'm sure my mother will be delivering a casserole tonight if she hasn't already."

"You didn't answer my question."

"I'll probably hang out at Mabry's and stay for supper. I can tell you all about it when you drop by to say hello." He gave me a victory grin, then said good-bye and left the room before I had a chance to hit him.

Ceecee began placing the food on the small coffee table in front of my chair, opening up lids and placing plastic forks inside each container. "You must be starving. You need to eat something to keep up your strength."

I picked up the apple and slid the doughnut toward her. "I could say the same for you. I haven't seen either one of you eat since we found Mama."

They looked down at the sugary offerings without enthusiasm. "I don't think I could eat a bite," Bitty said. "But taking care of you takes some of the worry off our sweet Ivy."

Ceecee gave her an odd look, but anything else

she might have said was interrupted by the arrival of a nurse carrying a large brown paper sack.

"Are you Ivy Lanier's family?" she asked.

I stood. "I'm her daughter. Is everything all right?"

"There's been no change. But I have your mother's personal belongings here—including her jewelry and the clothes she was wearing. I thought you might want them for safekeeping."

"Yes, thank you." I took the bag and signed the form on a clipboard she produced. After she left, I sat down again, with Bitty and Ceecee on either side of me. The bag was light, almost as if it were empty. I remembered the sandals Ivy had been wearing and wondered whether I'd find them inside.

"Are you going to open it?" Bitty asked.

"Do you think that's appropriate?" Ceecee frowned. "Ivy is going to wake up, and she might not appreciate us poking around in her personal effects."

Bitty frowned back at her. "Mack took her purse, so there's not a lot of snooping we can do. I thought we should look—just in case there's some clue as to why she was there."

"It's her clothes, Bitty. There won't be any clues." Ceecee reached for the bag as if to put it out of the way, but I clung to the folded-over top.

"Maybe there's some note inside. Or maybe not. Either way, we need to check." I'd always felt like a referee between these two women, which was surprising, considering they were lifelong friends.

"There," Bitty said, taking the bag. "Larkin understands, don't you, sweetie?" Without waiting for a response, she began to unroll the top.

"I should be the one to open it. She's **my** daughter." Ceecee's face was pinched with unshed tears.

Bitty sent her a look that I couldn't decipher. "Then I'm glad I'm here to spare you." She opened the bag and peered inside. "Just her clothes, and her sandals." She leaned in closer, then reached her hand inside and drew something out. "And this."

"A ribbon," I said as Ceecee reached for it, clenching it in her fist before lowering it to her lap and laying it flat so that the words could be read.

I know about Margaret.

A fat tear fell on the ribbon, smearing the letter "M." Ceecee didn't look up or attempt to wipe away the teardrops that were running the letters together in a river of black ink.

"Does she mean my grandmother Margaret?" I asked.

Neither answered for a long moment. Then Bitty gave her head one decisive nod. "Yes. I suppose she does."

I stood, staring down at these two old women. I'd known and loved them my whole life, but suddenly they seemed like strangers. "What about Margaret? What does she know about Margaret?"

Ceecee met the gaze of her old friend before turning to me. "I'm not sure. We always said Margaret was like the moon, glowing and shining light on the world around her. Everybody loved her."

Bitty slipped her hand into Ceecee's and squeezed.

"But why would Mama have written that on a ribbon and taken it to Carrowmore?"

Ceecee smiled weakly. "We'll just have to ask her when she wakes up, won't we?" She released Bitty's hand and stood, using both hands on the chair's arms and looking less stable than when she sat down. "I need to go powder my nose. Please excuse me."

I watched her go. Her hair seemed more gray than silver, her movements slower, her shoulders rounded. It was as if she'd been carrying an enormous burden and had suddenly become aware of its weight.

Bitty stood, too. "I swear, the older I get, the more my bladder shrinks. I'd better go to the little girls' room. If I can talk Ceecee into going home right now, we'll ask Mabry for a lift. I'll check in on you and your mama later."

She gave me a quick peck on the cheek and then left, leaving behind a lingering scent of Youth-Dew perfume and an unmistakable sense of déjà vu.

six

Ceecee
MAY 1951

Ceecee's mother kissed her on the cheek. Deep lines bracketed Mrs. Purnell's eyes, almost as if the word "worry" were written between parentheses. As the wife of the Methodist pastor, she'd seemed torn between raising her children the right way in the eyes of her husband's congregation and raising them the way she wanted to. As a result, her mothering wavered between suffocating strictness and lots of warm hugs, with the occasional blind eye toward minor transgressions.

She gave Ceecee another hug. "You call me as soon as you get to Mrs. Harding's, you hear, Sessalee? I'm sure it's long distance, so leave a quarter by the phone. If you offer to pay, she'll refuse, so this way she doesn't have a choice. You know we don't believe in being beholden to anyone."

Mrs. Purnell fixed the white piqué collar of Ceecee's brown cotton dress, her lips pressed together with worry. Ceecee's girdle dug into her ribs and pinched the breath from her lungs, or else she might have used some of the air to reassure her mother. She'd been nothing **but** worried since Margaret's mother had called to explain what she'd planned for her daughter and her daughter's two best friends. Not that it had really been explaining or asking permission. It had been more of a telling what was going to happen, with the assumption that permission was a foregone conclusion. No one ever said no to a Darlington, and neither Ceecee's mother nor Bitty's was about to be the first.

"Yes, Mama," Ceecee managed, her knees nearly buckling with relief when she heard the car pull up in front of the house. Until she was inside the car and driving away in the direction of Myrtle Beach, she wouldn't believe that her parents were letting her go.

Her mother and Lloyd, her brother, carrying her small traveling case, followed Ceecee out onto the porch. The case was her graduation gift from Margaret, and it had Ceecee's initials on it. Bitty had been given one just like it, but with her own initials. It was the finest thing Ceecee owned, and she couldn't believe it was hers. Her mother and grandmother had worked so hard on a quilt for Ceecee for her graduation gift, but even it had lost its shine when placed next to the soft brown leather of her traveling case.

They walked down the porch steps together, Mrs. Purnell's arm through Ceecee's. Ceecee wasn't completely convinced her mother would be able to let her go. She had to restrain herself from pulling away and rushing forward when she saw Margaret behind the wheel of her mother's convertible Lincoln Cosmopolitan. Dark sunglasses sat on her nose, and if Ceecee hadn't known better, she'd have sworn she was Lauren Bacall. A turquoise silk scarf, the color of her eyes, was tied beneath her chin, but it couldn't completely hide the golden sheen of her hair.

Mrs. Purnell's grip tightened when Margaret turned the force of her smile on them and waved. "Ceecee!" Bitty squealed from the backseat, using the nickname Ceecee's mother abhorred. Mrs. Purnell's worry radiated waves of heat, making Ceecee perspire.

"Hello, Mrs. Purnell. You're looking well." Margaret slid the sunglasses down her nose. "Just put her bag in the backseat next to Bitty, if you would, Lloyd." She turned the force of her smile on Ceecee's brother, making him blush.

Mrs. Purnell put her hands on Ceecee's shoulders. Quietly, she said, "You don't have to go, Sessalee. Just because Margaret Darlington invited you doesn't mean you can't say no."

"But I want to go," Ceecee said. "Please stop

worrying. You've raised me right. And I'm eighteen years old, Mama. I know how to behave." She smiled reassuringly. "Remember last summer, when Mrs. Darlington sent us all to the Junior Home-makers of America Camp Lodge at Ocean Drive Beach? We behaved like respectable ladies—you even received a nice letter from the camp supervisor telling you so. Remember? So, you don't need to worry. Besides, Margaret's aunt and uncle will be our chaperones at all times."

She wasn't exactly sure that was true, but she could sense her mother's resistance growing, most likely owing to the sight of Margaret in that scarf and sunglasses behind the wheel of the convertible. It probably seemed to her mama that the devil himself had pulled up in front of their house to take Ceecee away for good.

Mrs. Purnell frowned, and Ceecee knew she shouldn't have mentioned the aunt and uncle. Margaret's uncle Milton was a friend of the Huntingtons from Connecticut, who'd bought nine thousand acres near Pawleys Island as a winter retreat for Mrs. Huntington's health, as well as a place to display her sculptures. As if it weren't bad enough that the land had once belonged to four large rice plantations, the Huntingtons were Yankees—and rumored Nazi sympathizers during the war. Ceecee had heard a rumor that they'd helped supply U-boats along the South Carolina coast, an easy feat since their land abutted the Atlantic Ocean. Nothing was ever proven, but people like her mother, who didn't understand the concept of "summering" anywhere, were inclined to believe the worst of outsiders.

"They're decent people," Ceecee said in a rush. "Mrs. Harding is Mrs. Darlington's sister. God didn't bless them with children, so they enjoy spending time with their niece and her friends. I'd almost say we're doing a charitable thing by visiting."

Ceecee could see her mother wavering. She refrained from mentioning that Aunt Dot's childless state was most likely intentional, judging by the book by activist Margaret Sanger in her bedside table drawer. Their own Margaret said she'd been looking for a pencil and discovered it by accident, but Ceecee wasn't sure that was the whole truth.

Regardless, they'd done the responsible thing and told Bitty's mother about the book. She'd sat down and explained what it was all about and how the girls should never, ever mention the book to their mothers if they ever wanted to be let out of their respective houses ever again.

"I brought my Bible, Mrs. Purnell," Bitty said somberly from the backseat. "So we can say our evening prayers together."

Ceecee's mother relaxed beside her, then turned to fix Ceecee's hat, a monstrosity of straw and dried flowers her mother had said she'd need to protect her skin from the sun. Ceecee imagined a scarecrow somewhere might be missing its hat, but she wore it to make her mother happy. "That's good of you,

Martha," Mama said. She was the only one who ever called Bitty by her real name. "And I know Sessalee appreciates it as much as I do."

She looked at Margaret, waiting for her to say something, but Margaret was busy refreshing her lipstick.

Using her mother's distraction, Ceecee opened the passenger-side door and slid quickly into her seat. Lloyd gave his sister a cursory wave, his gaze settling on Margaret. Ceecee waved to her mother and brother, facing forward as soon as she saw her mother raise her hand to her mouth like she might cry.

"Don't forget to take lots of pictures!" Ceecee's mother called after them, forcing a smile that didn't fool anyone.

"Did you really bring your Bible?" Ceecee asked Bitty as they pulled away.

"Yes. Just in case your mother needed more convincing. I didn't want to lie to her."

Ceecee waited until they'd turned the corner onto Church Street before throwing back her head and laughing. Margaret pressed down on the gas pedal and headed the car north on Highway 17 until Georgetown was behind them and then, with squealing tires, pulled onto a dirt road and traveled along it until they couldn't see the highway behind them.

After putting the car in park, Margaret turned to Ceecee and slipped her glasses down her nose. "Sessalee Purnell, where on earth did you get that hat?"

"Mama gave it to me. You know how badly I

freckle, and she told me she didn't want me looking like a pickaninny when I get home."

"Well, you look like a nun. I simply can't drive into Myrtle Beach with that on your head."

Margaret reached for the hat, but Ceecee pulled back. "What? You can't be serious . . ."

"Really, Margaret," Bitty said, always the voice of reason. "I think Ceecee will feel better wearing her hat until we get to your aunt's house. We can buy her another before she heads to the beach."

Margaret turned to regard both of her friends with one of her brightest smiles, the ones that always sent alarm coursing through Ceecee. "Are y'all ready for the biggest surprise?"

Bitty and Ceecee exchanged a look. Bitty could take Margaret's surprises in stride, probably because of her parents' uninformed (Mrs. Purnell's word) views on the greater scope of life. But Ceecee was always pretty sure Margaret's surprises would end with her feet dangling over the fire pit of hell (another of her mother's observations).

"As ready as we'll ever be," Bitty said with a tight smile, squeezing Ceecee's shoulder as if to show they were on the same team. Although a team of two was never big enough or strong enough to win against Margaret Darlington.

"My aunt Dot thinks we're coming to Myrtle Beach **next** week! She and Uncle Milton are at their house in Connecticut until the middle of May. Mama doesn't know that, of course, and I'll make sure Aunt Dot is in the know before we leave—she'll love the conspiracy. We'll have the house all to ourselves without having to worry about curfews or chaperones. Isn't that brilliant?"

If it had been anyone else, Ceecee would have mentioned the holes in her plan, as glaring as the craters in the moon. But Margaret was a Darlington—as she often reminded them—and therefore the possessor of a charmed life.

Ceecee and Bitty exchanged a glance, and Ceecee opened her mouth to tell Margaret that this was unacceptable; that her mother trusted her, and this would be the absolute worst breach of trust she could ever imagine. But those words didn't come out, her mind drifting instead to dreams and possibilities. She remembered the ribbon she'd put into the Tree of Dreams, the fundamentally unimaginative wish of an eighteen-year-old girl. **I wish to marry the perfect man—handsome, kind, and with good prospects, and my love for him will be endless.**

In her head, she'd done it to aggravate Margaret. Margaret, whose dreams and aspirations always had a chance of coming true, had wanted her to wish for something bigger. But Ceecee hadn't. Her world was too small for someone like Margaret to understand, too limited and practical. Those were two words Ceecee was pretty sure weren't even in Margaret's vocabulary (in English or French; she spoke both fluently).

So instead of telling Margaret to turn the car around like she should have, Ceecee began unpinning the hideous hat. "I guess I'm never going to have another chance to be wild," she said. "I might as well take it."

Before she could think about repercussions, she tossed the hat onto the side of the road. Margaret squealed and clapped her hands. "And here, put on some color. I don't understand how your mama could be so against your wearing a little bit of lipstick."

Before Ceecee could protest, Margaret had steadied her chin with one hand and was aiming a gold tube of lipstick at Ceecee's mouth. When she was done, she handed Ceecee a linen handkerchief and showed her how to blot her lips. "That's Revlon's Certainly Red—I saw it in Mama's last issue of **Vogue** and asked her to buy it for me. It looks divine on you." Margaret took the handkerchief and replaced it with a pocket mirror. "See?"

Ceecee held up the mirror, wondering who this stranger with the messed-up hair and red lips might be. It was her, but not.

"I think that color might look better on Ceecee than on you, Margaret," Bitty said from the backseat.

"And I think you're right." Margaret placed the black lid on the tube and slid it into Ceecee's pocketbook. "A little gift from me to you."

"I can't . . ."

"Sure you can. And I've got a tube of Stormy Pink so my lips won't look naked."

"Do you want my scarf?" Bitty asked, already untying the knot under her chin.

"No, thanks. I'd like to feel the wind in my hair."

"Wonderful," Margaret said magnanimously. "Glad we're all happy now." Not leaving any room for argument, she took the steering wheel and turned the car around.

Ceecee hated her then. She hated her for making her pretend to be someone she wasn't. And Ceecee loved her, too, for the exact same reason.

It wasn't until much later, when it was too late, that Ceecee remembered Margaret telling her that she'd written the same wish on her own ribbon that day they'd gone down to the river to tell the tree their dreams.

Margaret's heavy foot on the pedal made the drive from Georgetown to Myrtle Beach shorter. Despite Ceecee's death grip on the door, Margaret showed no interest in slowing down for either the sanity of her passengers or fear of getting pulled over. Ceecee had never seen her get a ticket; the police officer usually knew her family or was easily susceptible to Margaret's charms.

Bitty sat up in the backseat, her chin resting on the front seatback so she could be heard over the wind rushing through the car and the radio playing Tony Bennett and Nat King Cole. Ceecee tried to relax, to enjoy the warm sun without worrying about freckling, to revel in a sense of freedom she'd never experienced. She'd never been anywhere without her parents or another responsible adult. It was like running into the ocean in February—the water hadn't yet warmed from the sun, but it was too tempting to just stay on the sand. There was something alarming about how good it felt, but she couldn't help feeling wicked just the same.

"Anybody want a Tootsie Roll?" Bitty thrust a brown paper sack forward. "I brought extras for the trip."

"Bless your heart," Margaret said, taking one and dumping it in her lap. "Mama won't let me eat anything sweet. She says it will ruin my teeth and my figure. I should just have her look at you, Bitty. I don't think there's been a day since I've known you when I haven't seen you eating Tootsie Rolls. I'd be as big as a house if I ate as many as you do."

"It's patriotic to eat them, you know. They saved our marines in the Battle of the Chosin Reservoir." Bitty took a bite and swallowed.

"What are you talking about, Bitty?" Margaret asked, a pucker between her brows.

"Didn't you hear the story? Our marines were stuck in a mountain reservoir between China and North Korea without food or supplies, and when they finally received an airdrop, it was just a bunch of Tootsie Rolls! It was so cold that the candy was frozen, but the men were still able to eat them, so they didn't starve. Even better, when they'd made them into a soft putty by chewing on them, they were able to repair holes in their vehicles, hoses, and other equipment. So they were able to escape to the coast and get to their transports."

"Not to be unpatriotic, but no thanks," Ceecee said, worried about ruining her lipstick. As if reading her mind, Bitty rolled her eyes and slid back into her seat.

As they drove, Ceecee could hear Bitty and Margaret's conversation, even offered the occasional nod of agreement, but she was focused mostly on figuring out who this new Ceecee was, this Ceecee who let her hair blow wild in a convertible and wore bright red lipstick.

They passed farm fields and ramshackle shacks and barns with the occasional bright white farmhouse and fencing that had recently seen a coat of whitewash. The wind rushing through the car smelled of summer, of freshly mown grass and hay heated by the sun. And always, always, the prevailing sent of the nearby rivers and marshes that crisscrossed most of Georgetown and Horry counties.

Lloyd had once joked that the veins on their mama's legs looked a whole lot like a map of the Lowcountry, showing all the tiny creeks and waterways. Ceecee's laughter had gotten her a switch to the bottom and a trip to her room without supper. But even now, she couldn't look at a map without smiling.

As they approached Main Street in Myrtle Beach, Margaret slowed, remembering to use her signal before turning into an Esso station. "We've been practically on empty the last few miles, but I was sure we'd make it this far at least."

Bitty and Ceecee shared a glance as Bitty mouthed, **Of course.**

Feeling flush with Margaret's unexpected gift of the lipstick, Ceecee left the car as the gas station attendant approached. "I'll go get us three Co-colas. Be right back."

At the service station, under a deep overhang attached to the building, the icebox and the red Coca-Cola machine huddled together in the shade. Ceecee was digging in her pocketbook for three nickels when she nearly bumped into someone already there. He—it was definitely a man, a tall young man wearing creased khaki pants—was thumping the heel of his hand on the front of the machine, as if the inanimate object might be a cow he could coerce into stepping aside.

Feeling emboldened by her lipstick, Ceecee stepped around him. "Excuse me," she said, wiggling the small silver lever. After a brief moment, the machine rumbled. A slight clicking noise announced that the small door had been unlatched, and he could take his bottle of Coke.

"Well, don't that beat all," the man said, retrieving his beverage. He turned to look at Ceecee with deep blue-green eyes she was sure a girl could drown in. She thought she'd just smile and walk away, leaving him wondering who this enigmatic girl might be, but she wasn't that comfortable yet with the new Ceecee.

Instead, she said, "My younger brother showed me how to do that. He's real smart."

He smiled, and his smile was as beautiful as his eyes, with perfect teeth and a cleft in his chin. "I'm guessing brains run in the family."

She found herself staring at him, her cheeks heating as she tried to think of something to say. She wished Margaret were there. She could talk to anyone. But she was also glad Margaret wasn't there, because Ceecee was pretty sure this man wouldn't have been speaking to her if she were.

He held out a hand. "My name's Boyd. I'm from Charleston, but I'm on my way home from medical school at the University of Virginia, having just finished a full-year internship in family medicine. Stopping in Myrtle Beach with my younger brother for a few days. He just graduated with a law degree. Guess we both need a break—don't think I've had one of those since I got out of the army in 'forty-five."

His smile lost some of its brightness. "Sorry to go on and on. I can't seem to stop myself when I'm around a pretty woman."

Ceecee blushed. "It's nice to meet you, Boyd." His fingers wrapped around hers, and she couldn't breathe. She pulled away.

He was looking at her closely, as if he could see beyond the lipstick and wild hair and still liked what he saw. "We're staying at a guesthouse for a couple of weeks on North Ocean Boulevard. Maybe you could grab a friend and meet us tonight to go dancing."

She felt suddenly shy and out of her league. Her parents would never have let her go dancing with a boy she'd just met at a gas station, especially if they had never met his parents. "I don't . . ."

"I understand," he said, his voice kind. "You've been raised right, and you don't know me. But I fought in the Pacific, which kind of makes a person forget how they were raised, and I only know one person here in Myrtle Beach, so I'm wondering why I'm here at all. Then I see this beautiful girl, and I lose all my sense. How about I stop by your house and come meet your parents?"

Ceecee thought about him coming to the house and Margaret opening the door. Or about him finding out that they were there unchaperoned. Either way, it would be a disaster.

"I'm sorry," she said. "That won't be possible." She stepped back. "Enjoy your Coca-Cola. And good luck to you."

Ceecee hurried back to the car, turning once, expecting to see him bending down to the bottle opener to open the cap of his Coke. Instead, he was staring back at her with that smile, his blue-green eyes squinting a bit in the sun, but following her just the same.

When Ceecee got back to the car, Bitty looked at her empty hands. "Where'd you put the Cokes?"

"Machine was broken," Ceecee said, sliding into the seat and taking her time arranging her dress so she wouldn't have to look at her friend. Bitty always knew when she was lying. "Let's get to Aunt Dot's house and figure out what we're going to do for supper. I'm assuming none of her help will be there, and we'll have to do for ourselves."

Margaret punched the gas pedal. "Good plan," she said. "As long as it's food my mama won't allow me to eat at home."

As Bitty laughed, Ceecee looked back toward the station, hoping to get a glimpse of Boyd, but he was already gone.

seven

Larkin
2010

Before I moved to New York, I'd spent my whole life within one square mile of the historic district of Georgetown, South Carolina, split between my parents' on Duke Street and Ceecee's on River Street. They were both older homes, Ceecee's built around the time of the Civil War and my parents' around 1900, with lots of creaky floors and nooks and crannies perfect for a little girl playing hide-and-seek. I had my own room in each house; both had walls painted in soft yellow—my favorite color—and had tall canopy beds.

But Ceecee's house was my favorite. It was where I'd go after school for a snack and to do my homework. It was where I brought my friends, mostly

Mabry and Bennett, even though they lived on Prince Street, closer to my parents, and where I went whenever my mama was going through one of her self-improvement phases and decided it was time to try something new. These were the times when she'd turn inside herself and forget things like cooking supper or attending my dance recital. It would make Ceecee mad, but I always knew that Mama was chasing her dreams, and I was okay with it. Because one day I knew she was going to show me how to chase my own.

Mama's phases were sometimes easy to live with, like when she turned the library into an art studio and painted still lifes, or when she took sewing lessons and made new curtains for the living room. Her violin phase had been short-lived, mostly because my daddy said her practicing gave him a headache. He didn't hear the music Mama and I heard beneath the mistakes, the lovely melody hiding just behind her unpracticed fingers. So she'd quit, but it was enough to know that she and I had heard the music anyway.

With no updates about my mother, and none expected for at least another day, I left the hospital and went home with Ceecee and Bitty, despite my father's hopeful glances and Bitty's pointed suggestion that I stay with him.

As a consolation, Ceecee invited him for dinner and fixed a large supper of fried chicken, butter beans, and biscuits that nobody had any appetite for, and set the dining room table with her best china and heirloom silver. She and Bitty kept the conversation rolling. Considering the talk was all about my life in New York and I answered mostly in single sentences, it didn't take long before we were staring at our still-full plates in silence, moving the food around with the occasional scrape of a fork or knife against Ceecee's Limoges.

Finally, I pushed my plate away after just a few bites, my appetite gone while my stomach twisted with worry over my mother. "Who's Ellis?" Out of habit, I addressed the question to Bitty. Of the three, she would answer the most directly.

But nobody spoke. My father looked down at his plate; Bitty shared a long glance with Ceecee, and I knew that I had just inserted a pin in the fragile eggshell of my mother's past. The past I'd selfishly been blissfully ignorant about until I'd seen my mother lying broken beneath a hole in the floor at Carrowmore.

"You really should eat some more," Ceecee said, standing and retrieving the bowl of potato salad. She scooped out a large spoonful and dumped it on top of the untouched pile already on my plate. "I know how much you love my potato salad. And there's my mud brownies—the ones you used to eat a whole plate of, remember? I always make sure I have a batch in the freezer, just in case you ever decide on a last-minute visit."

I shouldn't have been surprised. Ceecee always used food to make things better, to soothe me, like a thick grout to cover the cracks in my life. But grout gets old and crumbles, and the cracks are still there, showing themselves when you least expect them. Like now.

"I'm really too worried about Mama to eat. Maybe later if I get hungry." I turned back to Bitty. "Who is Ellis?"

Again, no one spoke. Finally, Bitty said, "Where did you hear that name?"

"I didn't—I saw it. It was on a ribbon—the one I remembered Mama putting in the Tree of Dreams a long time ago. When I was just a little girl. I took it out to see what it was. I'd forgotten all about it until yesterday. When we . . . when we found her." I didn't tell them what else was on the ribbon. I'd already shared enough of a secret that wasn't mine to share.

"Ellis Alton was your mama's first husband." Bitty said it quietly, as if she didn't really want me to hear.

Daddy was still looking down at his plate. All I could hear was the ticking of the clock in the hall and the rush of blood in my ears. I tried to put into a single sentence all the words that swirled around my head, but they formed a logjam in my throat, and I couldn't speak.

"She was only seventeen," Bitty continued. "And Ellis was nineteen. He was the love of her life."

Daddy took a sharp intake of breath, but Bitty didn't look ashamed for having said it. I was glad he was having trouble with this conversation. So was I. "What happened?"

"He was drafted." That was Ceecee, her back to us as she arranged brownies on a plate. "It was 1969. The war in Vietnam . . . He never thought twice about doing his duty. He went proudly and willingly, and it broke Ivy's heart."

"How long were they married?" My voice was reed thin, like I couldn't find enough air to push out the words.

"Not long." Ceecee put the plate of brownies in the middle of the table. I could smell the chocolate. I remembered what they tasted like, how good they'd made me feel. At least for as long as it took to swallow, and then I'd feel empty again.

"He went MIA only four months after being deployed." Ceecee sat down and reached for a brownie. "It broke Ivy. Cut her in two. Sometimes I think it would have been easier on her if he'd been killed outright. I think it was the not knowing that got to her. Nowadays I would have taken her for counseling, but back in the day, that wasn't something people did. We just sort of said, buck up and suck it in. But that doesn't work when your heart is crushed and you're bleeding from the inside."

"Larkin . . ." Daddy reached his hand toward me, but I didn't take it. I couldn't. And we both knew why.

I folded my arms across my chest and forced myself to look into my father's face. "Why have I never heard about this?"

Ceecee took her time cutting a brownie into small

bites. "Your grandfather and I decided it would be easier to forget if we never talked about him. To let Ivy heal. She'd already had enough sadness in her life."

"You mean because her mother died when Mama was so young?"

Bitty and Ceecee rose at the same time, bringing plates and food back to the kitchen.

"Yes," Bitty said, pausing in the doorway and staring down at the bowl of potato salad as if wondering why it was in her hands. "It was probably the worst thing we could have done, but, like Ceecee said, there wasn't a lot of discussion back then about mental health. So we just swept it all under the rug and pretended we couldn't see the lump."

"Until someone tripped on it." Daddy stood and picked up his plate. Something in his voice made me look at him, really see him for the first time in years. It could have been the overhead lighting or the lack of sleep since Mama's accident, but he seemed haggard, his skin blanched and without elasticity.

I followed him into the kitchen. "Did you know? When you married her?"

He nodded slowly. "Ceecee told me. Your mama and I never really talked about it. Not until the Vietnam War Memorial was completed. It was 1982—I remember because she was pregnant with you. On the news, they were showing all the names inscribed on the wall, and she . . ." He stopped.

"She what?" I demanded.

"She told me that she'd never love anyone like she'd loved Ellis Alton."

His eyes were bleak as I held my breath, waiting for him to say more.

Ceecee came and took the plate from his hands. "It's still no excuse for what you did, Mack." She walked into the kitchen, leaving my father and me alone, his eyes on my face.

"I never thought my actions would cause you to leave. I'm so sorry."

I closed my eyes briefly. "It's not what made me leave, Daddy. But it's one of the things that made it easy to stay away." I stood suddenly. "I need some air," I said. "This is all really whacked, you know. Families shouldn't keep these things secret. Despite popular opinion, it will **not** make the problem go away."

I almost ran to the back door before throwing it open to stand on the porch, my hands on my hips as I sucked in deep breaths of warm river-scented air.

Someone touched my arm, and I knew it was Bitty. She'd always been the peacemaker, the person who could bridge Ceecee's black-and-white world with my own messy one. "Do you need some company?"

"No. I really need to be alone right now."

"I get it." I heard her fumbling with something. I turned, and saw her pulling out a cigarette and lighter.

"Does Ceecee know you still smoke?"

She grunted, holding the cigarette between her

lips. "That woman doesn't miss a thing. She just prefers not to mention it if it's something she'd rather not discuss."

I nodded in the near darkness, feeling the sting of my first mosquito bite since my arrival. I slapped my arm, hoping I'd killed it and that it had hurt. "Like what 'I know about Margaret' means? Am I going to have to wait until Mama wakes up to ask her?"

Bitty exhaled. I smelled the acrid scent of burned tobacco and paper. "That's probably best. Ceecee never talks about Margaret. Never."

I looked up at the **wok** call of a chunky night heron that was swooping low over the water before landing on a dock piling. "Neither does Mama. But she was only two when her mother died. She probably doesn't remember her at all."

I faced Bitty, realizing there was so much to that story I didn't know. I'd never asked. I'd never thought to ask. "How did she die?"

Bitty coughed before drawing deeply on her cigarette, the glowing tip creating small pinpoints of light in her pupils. "Fire." She turned her head to the side and blew out the smoke. "The fire at Carrowmore happened the morning after Hurricane Hazel. The power was out. They say Margaret must have lit a candle or something. So very sad. For all of us, but especially for little Ivy."

I thought for a moment, trying to picture my mother as a baby, trying to understand what it had been like to be a motherless little girl. "Where was Mama during the fire?"

The night heron took off from the piling, spiraled upward over the water, then glided silently over the house and out of sight. Bitty took another drag and coughed again. "These are questions you'd best ask her when she wakes up. It's not my story to tell. Of course, you could ask Ceecee, but I'm guessing she'll tell you the same thing."

"And nobody has ever thought to tell me about all this?" I blinked hard, trying to believe it was the cigarette smoke stinging my eyes, not the imagined scent of a house on fire with a woman inside. My grandmother.

"You never asked." She blew air out of her nose, the sound like a soft snort. "Ceecee always did a good job of protecting you and Ivy, making sure you wouldn't feel any of the pain in life. The jury's still out on whether that was a good plan."

Bitty took a long drag of her cigarette and added, her voice raspy, "I'd suggest you start smoking if I didn't know it was so unhealthy. Ceecee in one of her moods always makes me need a cigarette."

I thought of her coughing and the ragged sound of her voice, and I almost told her that she should quit. But I'd been telling her that since I was a little girl, and it didn't seem to matter. Bitty was one of the most fiercely independent people I had ever known, intent on doing what she wanted.

I turned around and faced the river, listening to the faint clanging of halyards against metal masts from the nearby marina. The sound gave me an unsettled feeling, like an unfinished sentence. A constant reminder of where home was. Even in New York, surrounded by two rivers, I never felt that way. Maybe the salt water that ran through my veins recognized the East and Hudson rivers as foreign entities, incompatible with my blood type.

"I . . . I think I need some time alone to think."

"I get it. But while you're sorting things out, I want you to remember something important. Regardless of how annoying and unsympathetic she can seem, everything Ceecee has ever done has come from a heart so big, you could park a shrimp boat in it and still have room for a kayak or two. Her whole life has been you and your mama, and you can't fault a person for loving too much."

It seemed as if she was warning me against rushing to judgment about some fault in Ceecee's reasoning that I didn't yet know. I wasn't sure I could take one more surprise or disappointment. Not tonight.

"Tell Ceecee I won't be long." I heard Bitty draw on the cigarette again as I moved toward the porch steps.

"Larkin?"

I stopped and faced her in the growing darkness. "Yes?"

"I'm glad you're back. We all are. We all missed you something terrible—your mama most of all."

I took a step forward, then stopped, lacing my hands in front of me. "Yeah, well, she's one of the reasons why I stayed away." I listened to the silence, almost hearing Bitty's unasked question, but unwilling to answer it.

"Good night," I said as I stepped down onto the lawn, then walked around to the front of the house, and headed down Front Street in the direction of Prince Street. Mabry had said she lived next to her parents, and even without knowing the address, I was pretty sure I could guess which house would be hers. The yard would be immaculate, with beds full of multihued flowers that weren't meant to go together, but they would look fabulous and coordinated just because Mabry dictated it.

But I didn't want to see Mabry or Bennett. I'd already reasoned with myself that my mother would be on the mend in the next few days. I could ask my father why he and Bennett were together when they arrived at Carrowmore. The knowledge of whatever it was couldn't possibly be worth the awkward awfulness of knocking on Mabry's door.

It was almost full dark when I set out. The pretty overhead streetlights cast a welcome glow as I passed under live oaks as large and imposing as the ones I remembered from my childhood, as familiar as Ceecee's brownies. A car passed, the windows down, a song trailing in its wake. I recognized "It's My Life" by Bon Jovi. From the album **Crush.** 2000. I rolled my eyes at myself. Some things would never change.

I reached Orange Street and paused. Instead of turning right to go toward Mabry's house, I turned left, heading toward Harborwalk—the wooden boardwalk that ran alongside the Sampit River and traversed nearly the full length of Georgetown's historic district. Even though it was the number one destination for tourists, it was a beautiful spot on the river to shop and eat and people watch for locals and visitors alike. As soon as we'd been allowed to go by ourselves, I'd sat on a bench there with Mabry and Bennett, eating ice cream and making up dramatic stories about the people we'd seen, their hidden lives and dark secrets.

Mabry said I gave her nightmares sometimes, that that was the true mark of a storyteller, to make people believe something made-up was real. It was Bennett who'd first said I should write novels. Mabry said I'd be good at picking out the music when they were made into movies, since I knew every song ever written. Like everything back then, I'd believed it all possible.

There were more people on Harborwalk, mostly tourists, although it was still early in the season. Snowbirds from up north found the mild Lowcountry winters preferable to shoveling snow, though they'd usually head back before the South Carolina sun became too hot.

My feet seemed to know where they were going, and I found myself in front of Gabriel's Heavenly

Ice Cream & Soda, one of many eateries perched between Harborwalk and Front Street, their colorful
awnings like a happy wave on warm days.

I stopped inside the large rear window, smelling
the familiar sugary sweetness. Three small café tables
were still set against the wall, just as I remembered,
two with couples enjoying what I'd always thought
was the best ice cream in the world—not that I'd had
a lot of experience from my limited travels outside
Georgetown County. On the rear wall was a painted
mural of a local scene, the adjacent walls still a pale
yellow, decorated with photographs of dolphins, the
edges beginning to curl around their thumbtacks.

And there, behind the curved glass counter that
covered the bins of ice cream, was Gabriel Jones, his
skin as dark as I remembered, his black hair now
mostly gray. But his smile as he spoke with a cus-
tomer was as large and warm as it had been the first
time I'd come there with my mama and daddy as a
little girl.

The door was propped open to allow in the cool
river breeze, and I stepped inside, waiting against
the wall for Gabriel to finish with his customers.
A tall man peered into one of the cases, his hand
resting protectively on the back of a petite brunette
standing next to him, both focused on their flavor
selections.

I didn't recognize the woman, but there was something about the man, something about the way

his broad shoulders filled out his shirt and the way his sandy brown hair flopped over his forehead as he leaned down, his cheek very close to the woman's.

In the way a person can tell when they're being stared at, he turned his head to look at me. That's when I knew I'd been right. I did know him. Had known him almost as long as I'd known Mabry and Bennett. Except Jackson Porter and I had never been friends. Ever.

His gaze settled on me for a brief moment, long enough for me to see that his boyish good looks had morphed into strong, handsome features, like Christopher Reeve's in the old **Superman** movies. But of course they had. People like Jackson didn't allow themselves to grow soft with age.

He frowned slightly, as if wondering whether he should recognize me, then turned back to the woman. It was stupid, really, the rush of heat to my face, the not-so-distant feeling of humiliation. Maybe I found it hard to believe that someone who was such an important part of the worst day of my life didn't even recognize me.

I waited, my mouth dry and aching for a root beer float to help push down the shame and embarrassment. Gabriel finished their order, took their cash, then waited for them to leave, Jackson holding open the door for his companion.

"Miss Larkin," Gabriel said, beaming as if he'd invented my name. "Just as pretty as you ever were." Before he could make it out from behind the counter, he paused to look up at the ceiling speaker, which was playing something smooth and mellow. He'd only ever played music from the decades right after World War II, saying all the modern stuff was poison to the mind and an affront to his ears.

"'I'll Never Stop Loving You.' Doris Day."

He must have heard the quiver in my voice, because when he reached me, he already had his arms stretched out. "You don't pay him no mind." He jerked his head toward the door. "Some people are too stupid to know any better."

I started to cry—big painful sobs for my mother, for the good parts of the old me I'd gotten rid of along with the bad parts, and for my shallow, weak heart, which was still infatuated with Jackson Porter after all these years.

eight

Ceecee
2010

Ceecee paused in front of the hall mirror before pulling out the top drawer of the small chest beneath it. Several tubes of lipstick rolled forward. She selected Cherries in the Snow, a Revlon classic from 1953 that she'd always loved and had already told Bitty she wanted to be wearing when it was her time to meet Jesus.

She applied it carefully, listening as Bitty and Larkin finished their breakfast and conversed about the weather and the tides and everything except Ivy.

I know about Margaret. Ceecee's hand shook, smearing lipstick above her upper lip. What had Ivy meant?

Her gaze shifted to the side window, to the old

detached garage where Ivy had been allowed to set up shop for her furniture-refurbishment business. Ceecee had gladly given over the space, donated the old horse-drawn buggy that had once been stored there to a local collector. At the time, she'd assumed this would be another of Ivy's phases, but it had lasted longer than most. It had been relatively lucrative, too, considering her work space was rent free and her business came word of mouth from Ceecee's friends.

As Ceecee smudged out the lipstick mistake, she made a mental reminder to go inside the garage when they returned from the hospital. She was fairly confident that Ivy had left out open cans of varnish and paint remover and Lord knew what else. As she'd always done, Ceecee would go behind her, cleaning up, putting on lids, and emptying trash bins overflowing with Diet Dr Pepper cans and cheese slice wrappers. It was all Ivy ate or drank when she was in one of her creative phases, finding the sheer monotony of meal preparation stifling to her creativity.

"Are y'all ready yet?" she called out to Bitty and Larkin, impatient to go now. She had her notepad and pen in her purse, prepared to interrogate Ivy's doctors as to what kind of care she'd need when she returned home. When, not if. Ceecee had already decided she'd convert the library on the first floor to a sickroom. Ivy wouldn't have to navigate the stairs to her old bedroom until she was completely healed.

She hadn't bothered to ask Mack if he agreed. She was Ivy's mother, and considering what Ivy and

Mack's marriage had been like for the last ten years, his opinion simply didn't matter.

"What are those for?" Bitty asked, looking at the bouquet of tea roses Ceecee had placed in a vase.

"They're from my garden, and I'm bringing them to the hospital for Ivy's room. I thought the scent might help bring her around. She's always loved my roses, and they bloomed a little early this year, as if they knew she'd need them."

Larkin appeared behind Bitty in the kitchen doorway. "I'm ready."

Ceecee looked at Larkin's face, scrubbed clean and bare. She had beautiful skin, most likely thanks to Ceecee keeping her out of the sun when she was younger and insisting on the importance of a good skin-care regimen. Although she'd inherited the Darlingtons' vivid blue eyes, Larkin's lashes were pale gold, even lighter than her hair.

"Aren't you going to put on some makeup?" Ceecee asked. "Maybe a little mascara and lipstick?"

"I think Mama will recognize me without it, don't you?"

"Of course, sweetheart." Ceecee smiled tightly. "But if you change your mind, I've got some in my pocketbook."

Ceecee was aware of Bitty and Larkin exchanging a glance behind her back, but she didn't care. She'd kept this family together for too long to mind what other people said about her.

"I'll drive," Larkin said, stepping in front of them and holding open the door.

"Only if you promise to go at a safe speed. I still haven't recovered from yesterday. And we don't need to pick up your daddy. He called me earlier and said he was already there. No news," she added, in anticipation of their question.

They made the drive in silence. Ceecee's tight grip on the door handle had nothing to do with Larkin's relatively sedate pace. She was thinking instead of the ribbon they'd found in Ivy's hand when she fell, and of Larkin asking what it meant. Ceecee closed her eyes and sent a desperate prayer to a God she hoped had a short memory. She needed Ivy to wake up, to be okay. To listen to her story, to understand. To forgive.

For the first time in her life, Ceecee could feel her age, could sense the tightening of her joints and the slowing of her steps. Every so often, when she'd see a gray hair or another wrinkle, she'd have the disloyal thought that Margaret would have hated getting old.

Of course, Margaret would have found ways to still be beautiful and vibrant. If things had turned out differently, she'd have been dancing on all of their graves. Over the past week, the three of them and Mack had taken turns sitting with Ivy, talking to her, or reading articles from magazines, watching a steady flow of trauma nurses and doctors check her vital signs and change her position in the bed. It comforted Ceecee, knowing that even if Ivy hadn't opened her eyes or squeezed a finger or wiggled a toe, things were being done to make her better.

She closed her eyes even tighter, making another bargain with God. If Ivy woke up, she would tell her everything. Of course, the fact that Ivy had been found at Carrowmore with that ribbon in her hand meant that she already knew. **But how? And what?**

Had Ivy been angry when she'd gone to Carrowmore? Angry at Ceecee over what she'd somehow discovered about Margaret? The thought made it so much worse.

At the hospital, when it was Ceecee's turn to sit with Ivy, she set the vase of flowers on the table next to the bed, then pulled out her knitting. It was a skill she'd learned during one of Ivy's phases, when Ivy had wanted to make sweaters for Larkin, living up in New York. Ivy had never made it past one long sleeve, and Ceecee had thought she'd hang up her own knitting needles for good, too. Yet here she was, working on Ivy's unfinished sweater, pretending to be calm enough to remember how to knit one, purl two.

After the nurses left them alone, Ceecee pulled her chair closer to Ivy. "Mama's here, baby girl. Everything is going to be all right, I promise. I brought you some of my tea roses." She slid the vase closer to the edge of the side table so Ivy could smell them. "They just bloomed in the last couple of days. Open your eyes, Ivy, so you can see them. Please. Please open your eyes."

She waited for a response, but Ivy remained still, her skin waxlike and stretched taut over the fine bones of her face. Tubes ran in and out of her, helping her breathe and eat. She looked more like the little girl she'd been, and Ceecee's heart squeezed in her chest, wringing out memories of this child she'd always loved as if she were her own.

Sitting back in her chair, Ceecee let the ball of yellow yarn rest on her lap. "You probably have questions for me. Questions about your mother." Ceecee touched Ivy's hand, the skin cool under her fingers. Leaning closer, she whispered, "Please wake up, Ivy. Please. I need you to look at me and tell me you forgive me."

She sat back again and picked up the yarn and her knitting needles while she thought for a moment of a good place to start.

Ceecee
MAY 1951

Ceecee leaned into the mirror, picked up the red lipstick Margaret had given her, and applied it to her lips, just the way Margaret had shown her. Carefully, she closed the lid and placed it inside the small clutch bag Margaret had loaned her, then smiled at her reflection. She didn't feel like Ceecee Purnell anymore. She was the young, wild woman who'd spoken to a man she didn't know at a gas station and swung her hips as she'd walked back to the car.

"You look divine, Ceecee. You really do," Margaret said, admiring her handiwork. She'd styled Ceecee's hair in shiny, thick waves and loaned her a pale blue eyelet-embroidered batiste dress with a becoming draped bodice and matching shoes. It was the most beautiful dress Ceecee had ever worn, and even with the short bolero thrown over her bare shoulders, she still felt a little scandalous.

"Aunt Dottie says things are a lot more casual at the Ocean Forest than they were before the war, so we don't have to wear long gowns, but I think we look glamorous," Margaret said. "And you really do look lovely, Ceecee. Now, when all the handsome gentlemen ask me who is that divine woman I'm with, I'm going to tell them your name is Sessalee. You look too regal to be just a Ceecee."

Bitty, standing next to Margaret, nodded her agreement. "I agree. And here, take one of these. When one of them approaches, put it between your lips so they'll light it." She took a pack of Lucky Strikes out of her purse and handed one to Ceecee. "Cigarettes make everyone look more sophisticated."

Ceecee frowned at the cigarette a moment before accepting it, trying not to think of what her mother would say. "Thank you, Bitty. I'll try to remember. But from what Margaret has told me about how to sit and smile and flirt, I think my head is almost too full for one more thing."

She giggled, partly on account of the champagne—Margaret had found a bottle in her uncle's basement crawl space, which Margaret said he called his wine cellar. She promised he wouldn't miss it, and if he did, he'd give her a conspiratorial wink and never tell her mother.

"Will they be playing any of that 'dirty dancing' music?" Ceecee asked, half hoping the answer would be yes. She'd overheard her parents talking in the parlor one night about the music some young people were now dancing to, and how some jurisdictions were threatening arrest of any person found dancing to it. Bitty had taught her and Margaret how to jitterbug, but apparently the new dance steps involved "mimicking the act of procreation." Her father had used the word "lascivious," a word he usually saved for sermons involving fornication and adultery. It had sent her right to Bitty, whose family had a library full of books and their own dictionary on account of her father being the principal of the school, where'd they'd learned what "lascivious" meant.

"I certainly hope so," Bitty said, taking a drag from her cigarette and blowing a smoke ring—something she'd spent a lot of time practicing. Her parents allowed her to smoke at home; they considered her an adult and old enough to make her own decisions. Ceecee hoped no one ever mentioned that to her mother, or she'd be forbidden to see Bitty ever again.

"At the Ocean Forest Hotel?" Margaret asked, crooking her eyebrow Scarlett O'Hara style. "I sincerely doubt it." She dabbed some of her aunt's Joy perfume behind her ears before handing the bottle to Ceecee. "They're still strictly old-school. There was a joint on the colored side of town called Charlie's Place where they played all the new music, but the KKK raided it just last year. I'm sure there are other places we can find new music, but it won't be at the Ocean Forest."

"Have you been before?" Ceecee asked, trying not to feel guilty about the perfume. She placed a tiny dab behind one ear before handing it back.

"When we visit my aunt and uncle, we go there all the time. It's very upscale and elegant—they called it the 'million-dollar hotel' when it was built in the thirties." Margaret angled her eyebrow again. "Maybe we'll see a movie star or two. Aunt Dorothy was pretty sure she saw John Wayne in the lobby last season. But he stepped into an elevator, and it closed before she could reach it. She wouldn't even run for a movie star."

Bitty crushed her cigarette in a crystal ashtray. "I say it's time to go. I'm famished, and I want to make sure we have time to eat before the dancing begins. I heard that couples can dance under the moonlight on the Marine Patio, and I swear if nobody asks me to dance, I'm going to do the asking."

Ceecee stared at her friend, the champagne taking the edge off her shock. "Surely you wouldn't, Bitty!

That's what fast girls do. And your behavior will re-flect on us, too."

Before Bitty could reply, Margaret placed her hand on Ceecee's shoulder. "Ceecee's right, Bitty. Which means when you want to ask a boy to dance, whisper it in his ear instead of shouting it across the table."

Bitty and Margaret laughed, and Ceecee, unsure what to do, picked up her champagne glass and took a long sip. Then she picked up her Canon cam-era, a graduation gift from her grandparents, and took a picture of Margaret and Bitty. It was the first photograph of the trip, and she hoped she'd brought enough film, because she imagined filling an album.

The Ocean Forest Hotel was exactly what Ceecee had envisioned, with its impressive white-painted brick façade and red roof, a tall tower in the center surrounded on both sides by long wings filled with arched windows. A Federal portico protruded from the front of the building, as gracious as any mansion Ceecee had ever seen.

As they approached the circular drive, admiring the fountain and the expensive cars parked around it, Ceecee was glad she wasn't alone. She'd never find the courage to go inside such a place. But Margaret's self-assuredness and Bitty's unconcerned attitude gave her the confidence she needed to smile at the gray-and-burgundy-uniformed bellman as he opened their car doors at the main entrance.

Ceecee had to remember to keep her mouth closed at the extravagance of the interior, the gold trim, the rich mahogany, the Persian carpets. She pushed back all the words that came to her, words that her parents would have been saying, about how there were starving people in the world and a rich man had as much chance of getting into heaven as a camel did getting through the eye of a needle. For tonight, at least, Ceecee was going to block out their voices and enjoy herself. She doubted she'd have another chance once Margaret and Bitty departed for college and she would be left alone to rebuke the advances of the eager Will Harris. At least until she gave in from sheer boredom and lack of options, she'd find herself living the sedate married life her parents had always expected.

But this night—these two weeks—was her graduation gift to herself. Not as practical as the quilt her mother and grandmother had made, but more memorable. For the first time in her eighteen years, Ceecee didn't care. It wasn't that she dreamed of living a life where exquisite furnishings and shiny patinas were commonplace, where everyone she knew wore silks and furs, because she didn't. She'd been raised to be far more practical than that. But for a short time, she wanted to be like Margaret, exuding confidence, able to appreciate and enjoy lovely things without feeling any accompanying guilt. She wanted to feel beautiful and to walk across the room and pretend that every man was watching her.

Margaret led the way as if she were a queen and Bitty and Ceecee her ladies-in-waiting, her hair glowing in the light of the large crystal chandeliers that hung above them, the marble floors and columns almost fading into the background as if acknowledging her superior beauty. Her dress, in yellow moiré, made her glow like moonlight, casting everyone else in her shadow. The maître d' in the dining room seemed suitably impressed when she gave her name, and found them a table by the large windows that looked out on the ocean. Although it was nearly eight o'clock, the sun hadn't yet slipped behind the horizon, its rays just beginning to bathe the dining room and its inhabitants in a buttery glow.

Before Ceecee could reflect on the beautiful view, the maître d' appeared at their table with a complimentary bottle of champagne and poured three glasses. Margaret thanked him graciously before leaning in to Ceecee and Bitty. "Rumor has it that there's gambling on the upper floors and my uncle is a frequent participant. Whether that's true or not, I'm happy to use his name to get the best table. It's all about attitude, Ceecee. Remember that."

She winked at Ceecee and took a sip of champagne, and Ceecee felt the sharp prick of anger needle the base of her neck. It was so easy for Margaret to talk about attitude. She already had everything else. Attitude was the frosting on an already perfect cake.

The thing with Margaret, Ceecee thought, was that she insisted on believing they were the same, that all Ceecee needed was a little change to her mind-set. She would never understand that Ceecee didn't have the foundation to support such a thing. It would be like Ceecee wearing Margaret's debutante gown, with her lackluster hair and bad shoes. She wouldn't fool anyone.

Their bottle of champagne was followed by a bottle of wine, compliments of the maître d', and then another, which they all enjoyed with their dinner. Dessert and cocktails followed before they moved out to the Marine Patio, where the orchestra had already begun to play.

It was all so decadent. Ceecee knew she could never tell her parents. But her anger at Margaret had mellowed to a dull throb as she listened to her friend telling stories. She was a good storyteller, always able to keep her audience interested and hold their attention until she revealed the twist. Ceecee couldn't stay angry with her. After all, she was at the Ocean Forest Hotel because of her friend. She wore Margaret's dress and shoes and carried her pocketbook.

Now Ceecee smiled through hazy, grateful eyes as Margaret launched into the story of the ghost of Theodosia Burr Alston, which reputedly haunted Brookgreen Gardens. Ceecee wanted to tell her to stop, that she'd have nightmares, but she didn't want Bitty to call her a scared little girl. That's how it went with the three of them—Margaret suggesting something outrageous, Ceecee cautioning against it, and Bitty goading them all into doing it anyway.

"Excuse me."

The three of them looked up at the young man standing by their table, dressed in a dinner jacket, his hands held respectfully behind his back. He was tall, with auburn hair, and was the kind of handsome that made it seem okay to stop and stare. His hair was neatly combed back from his forehead, but an errant wave sprang forth at his left temple, giving him a boyish look and making him approachable. Ceecee liked him immediately because of that curl, because of that infraction against perfection.

He smiled, and his eyes sparkled. "I hope I'm not intruding. My name is Reginald Madsen, and I'm going to be president of the United States one day."

He said it so matter-of-factly and sincerely that it was impossible to doubt him. He certainly looked the part. Ceecee could sense Margaret straightening in her chair, recognizing a kindred spirit, her attention focused on the young man.

Reginald continued. "I'm visiting Myrtle Beach for a few days with my brother. We're here because we were told that the most beautiful women in the world come to Myrtle Beach, and I can see the rumors are true." His accent was warm and familiar, letting them know he was from the same part of the world they were.

Bitty frowned up at him, as if she might already be guessing his next words. And she'd probably be right. But Ceecee had already made up her mind. She liked this Reginald Madsen, with his outspoken ambition and imperfect hair, and she was already getting ready to stand at his open invitation to dance when he turned to Margaret.

"Yellow is my favorite color, so I'm thinking it's some sort of sign that you're wearing that dress tonight." He held out his hand to her. "May I have the honor of a dance?"

Margaret smiled prettily. "I would love to. Thank you." She placed her hand in his. With a quick glance and smile at Ceecee and Bitty, she left their table for the dance floor.

Bitty put her elbows on the table and leaned toward Ceecee. "I'm glad that's over. Now maybe someone will notice us."

Ceecee wanted to say they probably wouldn't, but Bitty would call her out for the lie. It wasn't that she and Bitty were unattractive. It was just that standing next to Margaret was like comparing daisies to a rose. Not that there was anything wrong with daisies, as Bitty always reminded her. It was just that most people preferred roses.

Ceecee was about to suggest they take a short stroll on the beach, when she felt a presence at her side.

"I was hoping that was you."

She looked up to see a familiar face—the young man she'd met at the Esso. He was dressed in a dinner jacket and tie, and his dark hair was combed back. But she recognized his blue-green eyes, the way they turned down slightly at the corners as if they were used to smiling.

"When my little brother, Reggie, approached your table, I was afraid he was going to ask you for a dance before I could find the courage." He smiled tentatively. "I'm Boyd, remember? Boyd Madsen. We met at the gas station. But you didn't tell me your name."

"It's Sessalee Purnell," Bitty said from across the table. She held out her hand to shake just like her parents had taught her to do, even though she was a woman. "I'm Bitty Williams, and if you're looking for a dance, I know Sessalee would love to dance with you."

He threw back his head and laughed. It was such a nice sound that Ceecee forgot her embarrassment and managed to smile. Boyd held out his hand to her, and she took it. His fingers closed over hers as he led her to the dance floor. When he drew her into his arms for a waltz, she remembered the ribbon she'd placed in the tree and what she'd written on it, and for the first time in her life, Ceecee Purnell began to believe in dreams and possibilities.

nine

Larkin
2010

After successfully avoiding a conversation with my father at the hospital and dropping off Bitty and Ceecee at home, I headed south on Highway 17. I'd told Ceecee only that I needed to run a few errands and make a call to work to extend my leave. I hadn't mentioned that one of my errands was to visit Carrowmore.

Despite Ceecee's badgering questions, neither Mama's doctors nor the brain trauma specialist had been able to guarantee a complete recovery or give us a hint as to when they expected Ivy to wake up. The only thing they could tell us was that some of the brain swelling had come down, which was a good sign. Just not good enough for Ceecee, who'd spent half the night browsing the Internet, searching for related cases. She stopped only when I began to cry, the seriousness of the situation finally sinking in.

I'd spent so many years pretending that my previous life in Georgetown had been permanently relegated to my memory. Actually being here, and being involved with my family and my mother's accident, had seemed like a dream. Until now, with the ugly reality of my mother's condition staring me in the face.

Bitty had taken me by the shoulders and led me down the hallway, frowning at Ceecee as she did. "Don't pay her no mind. She's doing the one thing she knows how to do best, and that's fierce mothering." Her eyes turned sad for a moment. "She's just not always prepared for when it backfires."

I wasn't sure what she meant, and I was too desperate to get out of the hospital and breathe air that wasn't laced with antiseptic and bleach to slow down and listen. Thankfully, the ride to Ceecee's house was short. There wasn't time for any long conversations, or any questions as to why I hadn't considered my mother's possible death before today.

It seemed the old me hadn't completely packed up and left after all. All of my thoughts so far had been about how the accident affected me and the life I had now. It was the same Larkin who'd never asked how her grandmother had died so young. It was as illuminating as it was humiliating, and I needed to be alone, to consider the possibility that I was irredeemable.

I drove past the eyesore steel mill, which had closed the year before, and then past the International Paper plant. I left the windows down, missing the old smell of my childhood, the plant's stench of rotten eggs that had somehow—miraculously, some said—been almost completely eradicated in recent years. Mabry, Bennett, and I used to make a show of holding our breath as we crossed the bridges driving into town, competing to see who could last the longest. It had been a rite of passage, the odor and the breath holding. Knowing it was gone left a hollow feeling in my chest.

An old pickup truck, its paint faded to a powder blue, moved in front of me. I spotted the bumper sticker right away—it was the brightest and newest part of the truck. **Friends don't let friends buy imported shrimp.** Ceecee had told me during one of my Christmas visits that the local shrimping industry was getting so bad that sometimes shrimpers simply abandoned their boats in the harbor. They couldn't see any other option. It made me sad in the same way the abandoned steel mill and the lack of the paper-mill smell saddened me. My childhood had been vanishing bit by bit while I'd been living in New York, trying to pretend it had never existed. Maybe that was what the old saying—that a person can never really go home again—was all about. You couldn't go home because even though home might still be there in brick and mortar, everything else would be unrecognizable.

I found the turnoff to Carrowmore without really looking, bumped over the same road, turning left at the fork. The late-afternoon sun played hide-and-seek with the branches of the overgrown trees, while an orchestra of unseen insects strummed their wings in an undulating rhythm that mimicked the waves of the ocean.

I parked my car at the back of the house, near the ruined garden, wishing I knew what it had once looked like. What the house had looked like. Even in its charred state, the mansion was elegant and grand, an old woman whose beauty shone out past the wrinkles and age spots. Except, of course, the damage to the house at Carrowmore was more than superficial, and no amount of cream or potion could hide that.

Stepping out of the car, I smelled the river and the marsh grasses that filled the space where tidal river and land met. It was the steadfast scent of the Low-country, of my childhood. It was the one thing that hadn't changed, and I clung to it, breathing deep and remembering Mabry, Bennett, and myself kayaking and swimming in the river, and jumping off the dock behind my parents' house.

But I stopped my memories there, before they moved forward in time to a place I never wanted to remember.

Watching where I stepped and slapping at mosquitoes, I approached the oak tree near the riverbank. Purple martin gourds dangled sporadically, forming a pattern recognized only by whoever had placed them there. Something about them wasn't right, I thought; some odd piece of trivia had come to me the night before as I was drifting off to sleep. I stared at them for a long time, wanting to remember what it was, but I couldn't.

A snowy white egret perched on one skinny leg in the tall sawgrass on the edge of the river, each of us keeping a wary eye on the other. Not wanting to startle the bird, I walked slowly and carefully toward the tree until I stood in front of the hollowed opening in its trunk. I saw now how much it looked like a cavernous mouth. I couldn't help but wonder if the opening was trying to hold something in or spit something out.

Before I could talk myself out of it, I leaned forward and stuck my hand inside, my fingers rooting around for anything that felt like fabric. Although I'd been raised fishing on the river with my granddaddy and my daddy, and I was adept at putting all sorts of bait on a hook, I didn't relish the thought of reaching into the unknown and feeling something soft wiggling beneath my fingers. Or getting bitten.

Right away I felt what could only have been a ribbon or piece of cloth, smooth and even with a ridged edge. I moved my fingers and determined there was more than one, both of them crisp and fresh, as if they hadn't been there very long. I grabbed them at the same time I heard the sound of an approaching vehicle, music from the stereo piping softly from an open window. I jerked up, either my movement or the sound of the pickup truck coming to a stop near my parked car causing the egret to spread its wings and fly away, coasting low over the water.

Not really knowing why, I shoved the fabric into the front pocket of my jeans, and turned to see Bennett emerging from the truck. I didn't move as he approached, hoping maybe he hadn't noticed me or my car. Which was stupid, really, considering I was standing in the open and he'd parked right behind me. But the old habit of assuming everything was going to go my way was hard to break.

He stopped about five feet away from me, his face expressionless. "Hello, Larkin."

"'Iris.' By the Goo Goo Dolls." I jerked my chin toward his now-silent radio, and he laughed.

"Still the same Larkin," he said.

"No, actually. Some things are just harder to get rid of than others." I frowned. "What are you doing here?"

"Well, I waited at Mabry's house last night for you to stop by. Nothing. Today, you didn't answer any of my texts, so I figured I'd come and find you. I stopped by Ceecee's house, and she told me you'd practically squealed the tires leaving, you were in such a hurry. So I figured you'd come here."

That was the thing with people who'd known you your whole life. There was no keeping secrets. I sighed. "Did it occur to you that I'd want to be alone?"

"Of course. But you keep saying you're going to

leave as soon as your mother wakes up, so I figured I'd have to take the chance to talk with you while I could."

I started walking back to my car, as eager to end this conversation as I was to find out what I'd shoved into my pocket. "Talk fast, Bennett. I'm sure Ceecee will have supper waiting on the table for me."

"I wanted to talk to you about what your daddy and I were doing the day of the accident."

I made the mistake of looking into his face. It wasn't that I'd never noticed him before, never noticed how his eyes were the color of the ocean or how square his jaw was, how nice he looked when he smiled. I would have had to be blind not to. But he and Mabry had been my best friends, as physically invisible to me as if we'd been siblings. And then we hadn't been friends at all.

Looking into his face now, I could see that Bennett looked different, in the same way Jackson Porter had. Gone were all traces of soft boyhood, replaced with the hard planes and solid stature of maturity. It suited him. Not that I would ever tell him that. He'd never let me forget it if I did.

I always thought you were beautiful. The words he'd said at the hospital came back to me, making me flush. I glanced away. "I'm not sure I care enough to wait, so speak quickly."

I opened my car door, grateful for the annoying tone that reminded the driver the door was open.

He held his hands out, palms up, as if to apologize for the abruptness of what he was about to say. "A few months ago, developers started sniffing around Carrowmore, trying to determine who owned it and how interested in selling the owners might be. Your dad approached me to see what I thought." He squinted up at the back of the dilapidated old mansion. "Just thought you should know." He turned and began walking back toward his car.

I slammed my car door. "Wait! You can't just leave without telling me more!"

He paused, his hand on the door handle. "I don't want to keep you from your supper."

I tugged on his arm, feeling like a child, but desperate to get him to tell me more. "Why would Daddy want to talk with you about it?"

His eyebrows knitted together over his nose. "Have you followed anything that's happened here since you left?"

For the first time in nine years, I felt embarrassed about my abrupt departure and the complete severing of all my ties. My actions had been justified—I was still sure of that. But all the time I'd been away, I'd assumed that everything had remained the same, that people and beliefs hadn't changed. Which was stupid, because I hadn't stayed the same. I felt a little of my old resolve not to look back shift and redistribute itself, like sand in an outgoing tide. That was another thing I'd never admit to Bennett.

"No," I said, focusing my gaze on the old tree by the river and thinking of the ribbons I still had bundled in my pocket.

He paused for a minute, as if expecting me to tell him I was joking. After a brief shake of his head, he said, "I own a small firm in Columbia that focuses on repurposing older commercial and residential buildings for current use. A couple of other engineers and I lay out all the new mechanics in ways that won't destroy the integrity of an older building, and we work with architects with preservation backgrounds to design and oversee the projects. That's why your dad came to me. He told me about the land development company that's been asking about Carrowmore—the same group that built the high-end cluster home community and golf course over by Pawleys Island."

"Sounds lovely," I said, once again eager to leave. "Seeing as how I have barely any memories to connect me to this place, give them my number. I promise to pick up. Maybe I can convince Mama it's a good time to sell."

"Seriously, Larkin? I know the house looks bad, but it's not a lost cause. It's been owned by your family since the seventeen hundreds, and the land, right on the river—I can't imagine them razing all of these old-growth trees and the house and putting cluster homes on it. It's . . . obscene. That's why your father wanted to talk to me. He wanted to know if there might be other options. Like, I don't know, maybe rebuilding it."

"But why would we want to rebuild it?" We could both hear the frustration in my voice. "My parents are comfortable in their house, and I don't live here anymore, remember? And it's not like we have enough money for this kind of restoration."

He fell silent, studying two martin houses hanging from the limbs of a nearby sweet gum tree. "But Ceecee does have the money. She controls the trust. For now, anyway."

"The trust? What is that supposed to mean?"

He narrowed his eyes, as if unsure that I really didn't have a clue what he was talking about. "The house, the land all the way down to the river, and the entire assets from the Carrowmore estate are held in a trust with Ceecee listed as trustee. Apparently, right before her accident, your mother visited a lawyer to contest Ceecee's trusteeship of Carrowmore—even though she was the one who initially set up the trust, right after you were born. She apparently changed her mind, because she was asking the lawyer to transfer it to you now instead of waiting for your thirtieth birthday. That's a condition of the trust. According to the lawyer, Ivy thought you had more right to oversee Carrowmore's future since you're a Darlington descendent."

I could have listed a dozen things I'd expected him to say. That wasn't one of them. "This is all meant to be mine in three years? Shouldn't it go to my mother first?"

He shrugged. "It would seem so, but I don't know the full story, so I don't want to speculate."

I realized I was shaking my head, and made myself stop. "But why would Mama do that now? And does Ceecee know?"

"Your daddy didn't say. Just said Ivy didn't want Ceecee to be making any decisions about Carrowmore. He did tell Ceecee—he thought she needed to know. I don't think Ivy wanted either one of them to know, though. Your daddy found out about your mother's visit to the lawyer accidentally. He answered your mama's phone—it was the day of the accident, and she'd left it behind—and it was the lawyer asking for more details about the trust. Your daddy's distraught enough right now that I didn't want to bring it up with him, which is why I've been trying to talk with you."

I stared back at him, wavering between guilt for not answering my texts and worry regarding my mother's motivations. I shook my head. "I don't know what to say, or think. This is all so . . . unexpected."

"I'm sure it is. Like I said, your daddy didn't explain. I'm guessing—and this is only speculation since I haven't spoken with your mother directly—that she might have been trying to make it more difficult for the developers. Since you're in New York and don't pick up your phone and all." His eyes remained cool and assessing, although I detected a hint of recrimination in his voice.

I continued to look at him, as if he might suddenly blurt out all the answers I was looking for. "I don't know what to tell you, Bennett. I don't know what I feel about this house, other than I don't want it. I didn't even know it existed before yesterday, much less that it's been held in trust for me until I'm thirty. For the time being, its fate is in Ceecee's hands, regardless of whether that's the way my mother wants it to be. I say let's wait until she wakes up and ask her."

"And if she doesn't?"

His words lashed out at me like a whip. "She will. Of course she will." I wasn't a doctor and had no understanding of what would be required for Mama to be okay again. Waking up was the scenario I'd decided upon, and I was moving ahead accordingly, just as I'd always done. Except for one glaring exception, my method had always worked.

"Ceecee . . . ," he began, then stopped.

"Why do you care, Bennett? You don't have any skin in this game."

His face remained expressionless, but a shadow moved behind his eyes. "What do you know about the fire?"

"Besides that my grandmother died here? It happened the day after Hurricane Hazel in 1954. That's all I know, and I just learned that yesterday. I really don't know what's worse—the horrible way that my grandmother died, or the fact that nobody ever thought to tell me."

I could see the war going on behind his eyes, his weighing whether to tell me something. He'd always been easy to read, probably because I'd had years of practice. Finally, he said, "My granddaddy was the fire chief back then. Remember him?"

I nodded, vaguely remembering a gray-haired man who'd looked like a much older version of Bennett. His wife had died years before, and he lived alone in a fishing cabin on the Pee Dee River. He always had a stash of Hershey's chocolate bars in his freezer. It was sad, I thought, that that was the one memory I had of him.

"He was on duty that night. Back in the day, most people didn't evacuate for a hurricane. They just rode it out and dealt with the damage afterward, which is why all first responders were on call. A policeman saw the fire and radioed it in. By then the phone lines were gone and the electricity was out, so it was a miracle that a police cruiser was in the right place at the right time."

He stopped then, and his eyes narrowed. That worried me. It meant he was about to tell me something I probably didn't want to hear. "Larkin, Ceecee was in the house, too. She's the one who pulled your mother out and saved her from the fire. But she couldn't save Margaret."

I reached behind me for my car door to lean against. I wasn't completely sure I could remain standing on my own. "She saved my mother from the fire?"

Bennett walked toward me, and when I waved him away, he ignored me and put his hands on my shoulders to steady me. "Are you okay?"

"I'm fine, I'm fine," I insisted, even though I wasn't. It took all of my willpower not to grab my phone to call Ceecee and ask her to explain.

"I can't believe nobody told you the story. If not your family, then surely it must have come up in conversation at some point."

I almost laughed. "Everybody probably assumed I already knew and didn't want to talk about it. It's pretty awful." A moment of silence, and then I asked, "Did my mother know?"

"I have no idea. You need to ask her when she wakes up."

I looked up sharply, wondering if he was humoring my optimism about my mother's recovery. "Or I could speak with Ceecee today and ask her why the hell all of this has been kept from me." I indicated the empty shell of the old house, a foreboding hulk against the dimming light.

"Talk to Ceecee," he repeated gently. "I'm sure she can explain."

"Oh, I will." I slid into the passenger seat and began to hunt for the keys I'd tossed into my purse.

Bennett leaned into the car. "Gabriel said he saw you last night—and that Jackson Porter was there, too."

I lowered my face even though it blocked the light, making it harder to find the keys in the black interior of the purse. "Was he?"

Bennett pulled back, and I knew I couldn't look at him and allow him to read my face. I'd found the keys and clutched them in my palm, feeling them dig into my skin.

"He's still single, you know. He and Melissa were married for about five minutes before they split up. Now he has a string of girlfriends. Runs his father's insurance business. Just thought you'd want to know."

I forgot that I was trying not to look at him. "Why are you telling me this?"

He studied my face closely, reading every secret. "Guess I'm just trying to bring you up to speed with what's been going on since you left."

"Thanks, but I don't see the urgency. I'll let you know what Mama says about the property once she wakes up. It's been like this for more than sixty years. It can wait a little longer."

"True," Bennett said. "Just remember, once a historic property like this is gone, it's gone forever. There's no bringing it back."

"I'll let you know," I said, putting on my seat belt.

"I'll follow you out." Bennett indicated the path around the house. "Don't want you getting stuck."

I swallowed my disappointment. I'd wanted him to leave so I could read the ribbons in my pocket, but he was right. It would have to wait. "Thanks," I said before jabbing the key into the ignition as he closed my door.

The sun had started its descent, turning Carrowmore into a hulking shadow. I began moving forward, slowly, waiting for Bennett to pull up behind me. I was aware of his truck's headlights in my rearview mirror, and found an odd comfort in knowing he was there.

But as soon as we reached the asphalt of Highway 17, I floored it, leaving Bennett behind. I knew he could have overtaken my car if he'd wanted to, just as I knew he was aware of how much I needed to be alone to think.

I pulled into Ceecee's driveway and turned on the dome light inside the car so I could see. Leaning back for better access to my pocket—and completely unrepentant about my recent penchant for skinny jeans— I pulled out two ribbons, still white and crisp.

I could count on one hand the number of times my mother had ever written a letter to me, yet I knew this handwriting was hers. I stretched out the first ribbon across my lap, flattening it to read it better. I stared at the thick letters, written with what appeared to be a black Magic Marker. **I miss you. I wish I'd been given the chance to know you.**

My heart thumped inside my chest. It reminded me of watching a horror movie with Mabry and Bennett after lying about our ages to get in, the scene where a young girl is about to enter a darkened room without turning on the light.

Almost as if a director were sitting in the backseat, telling me what to do, I stretched the second ribbon on top of the first. It wasn't penned in black marker, and the handwriting seemed different, although that could have been because it was written using another writing instrument. It was hard to see in the fading daylight, but the color of these letters appeared to be crimson.

I blinked several times, just to make sure I was reading it correctly.

Forgive me.

I closed my eyes, feeling as if I were reading someone else's diary. Then I opened them again, unable to stop myself. Gingerly, I rubbed my fingernail against one of the letters, flicking it back and forth to try to determine what it had been written with. Small flakes scattered on the light denim of my jeans. Definitely not marker, then. Something else. Maybe a gel pen or one of those glitter glue pens Mabry and I had been crazy about in middle school.

The porch lights blinked on, and Ceecee opened the front door, her worried expression telling me that she'd been aware of my sitting in the car without coming in. Without knowing why, I tucked the ribbons back into my pocket and exited the car, closing the door behind me with a sharp snap.

ten

Ivy
2010

I see Ceecee talking to me as I lie on the hospital bed. The fat skein of yellow yarn rests next to my leg; her knitting needles stab into a small square of whatever it is she's making. She's talking to me and I can hear her, but I can't see her lips moving.

I'm floating up near the ceiling, looking down at my body. It doesn't even look like me.

I'm seeing the top of Ceecee's head and a spot of thinning hair. She'd just die if she knew anyone had seen that.

A memory pricks at me, a memory of something that happened before I fell. Something that made me angry at Ceecee. Not the familiar push-pull of my anger over our differences in raising Larkin, or over her opinion that I should grow up and move on from my grief over Ellis. Something else. That one slippery worm of memory keeps wiggling past me. It's like the password I need to be released, but I can't for the life of me think what it could be.

I drift higher and higher toward the ceiling every day, but I never leave this room. I've tried. But something is tethering me to this life, to the lives of those who come and visit, who hold my hand and tell me they're praying for me. I think it's the secrets keeping me here. I feel them like a spider's web, sticky and impossible to escape. Maybe this is the purgatory my Catholic friends have told me about, that place between life and death where we have to atone for our sins. Or maybe it's just a chance to come to a place of higher understanding. Of forgiveness.

I keep hearing the engine of Ellis's Mustang, so I look for him, too. But he and Mama are hiding around the corner, waiting for something. I just can't figure out what.

I wish I knew how to let go. And if someone will come and show me the way. Nobody who's already dead has come to wait at the foot of my bed or guide me to the light like I've seen in the movies and read in **Reader's Digest.** I'm disappointed, because I want to see my mama. I don't remember what she looked like, except everybody tells me she was beautiful. Ceecee said that Larkin looks just like her. All of my mother's photo albums burned in the fire, so I never had the chance to look at my daughter and say, "Yes, she has Mama's nose, don't you think?" or "Mama had the same smile." I know Ceecee has photos of the three of them together—Margaret, Ceecee, and Bitty—but when I've asked, she's always told me that some things are too painful to remember and that's why she keeps those photographs in the attic. One day, she promised, she'll bring them down, and we can look at them together. We never have.

Mack and Larkin each come every day and sit with me. Mack doesn't stay long, mostly fidgeting and telling me how sorry he is for any pain he might have caused me, promising to make it up to me when I wake up. I want to wake up just so I can tell him that I don't blame him, that I finally understand what happens when two people love each other in unequal measure. In my defense, I warned him before we were married, but he said he could love enough for both of us. It was my fault for believing him, and his fault for believing it, too.

Whatever our mistakes, creating Larkin wasn't one of them. I float around the room when she visits so I can get a good look at her, admiring her perfection. I'd always known she was beautiful, even during her awkward years, when the only people who thought her pretty besides me were Ceecee and Larkin herself. But now I understand that Larkin believed it only because Ceecee told her, just like how Ceecee hardly ever let me walk on my own until I was almost three because she couldn't bear to see me hurt myself. Same thing, really. Except a person never truly learns how to move past disappointment and pain without going through it at least once. Despite everything, I'm glad Larkin has Ceecee now. For all Ceecee's faults, being short on love is not one of them.

Larkin's changed so much. I see her once a year, at Christmas, and we like to pretend that's enough. And we pretend that I don't know my part in her disappointment that solidified her reasons for leaving and staying away.

My biggest regret is that I've never told her how proud I am of her, how brave she is. There were things she didn't like about herself, so she up and left and changed everything. I'm glad she failed in her lifelong wish to be just like me. I've never been that brave. Never been the kind of mama she needed. We both looked to Ceecee when maybe we should have been looking to each other.

But like Ceecee has tried to tell me a million times, there are no do-overs in life. Would I have wished to never meet Ellis? My life would have been so much easier if I hadn't seen him that first time, speeding down Front Street in that Mustang of his with the top down. He looked at me, and I looked at him, and I knew right then and there that we were meant for each other. Ceecee told me to wait to get married, to be sure. Not about how much I loved him, but how much I could bear to lose. She said it's the sadness that either breaks a person or makes them stronger.

I didn't listen. Maybe I should have. I just can't stop wondering how she could have known that.

The heart is a funny thing. It will love where it wants, and there's not a thing you can do about it unless you're strong. Like Larkin. She just doesn't know it yet. I learned the hard way that you can't spend your whole life facing the wrong way. You'll never see what's ahead of you if all you ever see are the ghosts of your past.

I want to wake up so I can tell her that, so I can spare her the pain of figuring it out herself, but I'm starting to think that I don't have a choice in the matter.

The corners of the room are fading, like my world is getting smaller. I feel tired even though I think I've just been sleeping and imagining that I'm flying around the ceiling. I wish I knew what was happening to me, and how long I'm supposed to be here. What I'm supposed to do or learn to move on. I feel the tugs of all those secrets nipping at me like little fish, and I'm thinking about what I'd found out before I fell through the floor at Carrowmore. Why I was angry with Ceecee. But like the corners of the room, it's out of focus, and as I settle back on the bed, I hear Ceecee speaking, and she's telling me about her, and Mama, and Bitty, and I'm trying to pay attention because I know there's something there that I'm supposed to know. Something important. So I slip back into my body, and I begin to listen.

Ceecee
1951

Margaret's shoes were a half size too small, so Ceecee's feet should have been hurting after the third dance with Boyd. But they weren't. They were dancing on clouds, her whole body cushioned with the warmth of his body so close, and the touch of his hand in hers. By the time he asked if she needed some air, she'd memorized the color of his eyes and the shape of his ears. And the vertical creases along his cheeks when he smiled. She took Boyd's hand and allowed him to lead her away from the other dancers, to the steps leading down to the beach, trying not to think what her mother would say if she knew.

They paused on the top step just long enough for Boyd to help her out of Margaret's shoes before descending into the sand, the gritty coolness beneath her stockinged feet, something she'd never feel again without remembering that night. The round moon sat in the sky pregnant with ivory light, appearing close enough to touch, close enough for her to pinch off a piece and put it in her purse as a memento.

He tucked her hand into the crook of his arm, and she carried Margaret's shoes in her other hand as they strolled along the moonlit beach, and she wanted to keep walking, touching him and listening to his voice for the rest of the night if not forever. He told her about his family back in Charleston, and how he spent a lot of time with his uncle and cousins in Anderson, South Carolina, on their farm, where he'd learned to deliver baby calves and had first decided to be a doctor. His father was a lawyer, and he was glad Reggie had decided he wanted to be a lawyer so Boyd was free to pursue his dream.

"Reggie decided he wanted to be a lawyer when he was about ten when he found out that so many presidents of the United States were lawyers before they went into politics. His greatest disappointment was that he was too young to fight in the war. Apparently, military experience looks good on a presidential résumé, too."

"Well," Ceecee said, "there's the conflict in Korea now if he's still interested."

Boyd was silent for a moment, the sound of their footsteps in the sand adding beats to the music behind them. "Yes, well, our parents have done their best to dissuade him. It just about killed our mother to watch me go fight. Her hair turned gray almost overnight. I can't imagine what watching her baby go to war would do to her."

"So, did they convince him?" Ceecee asked.

"I'm not sure. The call to serve our country is in his blood. We've a long line of ancestors who put on a uniform and fought for their country. Reggie would be the first son not to." He leaned down toward Ceecee. "And you?" he asked. "Besides your parents and your two brothers, who else is waiting for you back in Georgetown?"

She thought about Will Harris with his overly

shellacked hair and his dirty collars and her mother's insistence that Ceecee be nice to him. "No one. My two best friends—that's who I'm staying with—are both going to college in the fall. I suppose I'll be spending a lot of time helping my mama at home, and I sing in my daddy's church choir and play the organ sometimes."

"Sounds nice," he said, and she couldn't detect any sarcasm. She gave credit to his mama and daddy, who must have raised him right. "Tell me about Georgetown—is it a nice place to live and grow up?"

Ceecee shrugged. "I guess so. I've never known any other place. It's really beautiful—and historic, too. Did you know that the Marquis of Lafayette landed in Georgetown the first time he visited America during the Revolution?"

He smiled, his white teeth glowing in the moonlight. "I did not know that."

"It's true. And we've got rivers as far as the eye can see—we're surrounded by rivers, creeks, and marshes, so everybody has a boat and knows how to swim and fish." She looked up at him through her eyelashes like Margaret had shown her, hoping he could see in the moonlight. "I know Charleston's not far from the coast, but if you haven't spent a lot of time on the water, it wouldn't take you long to learn how to do all that. People are friendly there and would show you." She'd wanted to say that **she** would show him, but she'd already been forward enough. "The harbor's so pretty—like a postcard—and we've got lots of old houses and abandoned rice fields right behind town that you can kayak through and see some of the old dikes." She peered shyly up at him. "You should come visit sometime."

"You make it seem so nice, I'm thinking I should. The thing about being a doctor is that you can be a doctor pretty much anywhere. I can either join an existing practice or start my own. My mama would be disappointed if I didn't go home to Charleston, but I like to keep my options open."

"That's nice," she said, a feeling like fluttering wings tickling the inside of her chest.

He looked sideways at her, as if unsure whether she was joking. "The way I see it, the only thing lacking in Georgetown is intelligent, suitable young men. I can't believe you don't have any suitors breaking down your door."

She stopped and looked up at him, the moon framing his head like a halo. "You don't need to flatter me, Boyd Madsen. I've already let you lead me onto the beach and walk far enough away from everyone that if you kissed me, I would probably let you." Ceecee wasn't sure where all those words were coming from. Maybe she'd seen too many movies with Margaret and Bitty and thought that was how women were supposed to talk to men. Or maybe it was the moonlight and the sound of the waves and the distant musical notes sliding their way into the breeze and this man whose presence seemed to make all reason and caution disappear.

"Is that so?" He gently nuzzled the underside of her chin with his finger before tilting her face upward. "Because even though I've been thinking about kissing you from the moment I first saw you at the Esso station, I've been doing my best to be a gentleman at least until tomorrow when I see you again."

"So, you're already planning on seeing me again tomorrow?" she asked, trying to sound provocative the way Deborah Kerr had in **King Solomon's Mines.** Instead, her voice was so soft, she wasn't even sure she'd actually spoken. She'd been keeping her hope that he'd want to see her again wrapped up inside her chest, where it couldn't be seen or ridiculed as being overly optimistic. Her mother was always accusing her of that, so Ceecee had learned to keep her dreams tucked inside a corner of her heart.

He pulled back slightly. "Only if you want me to."

And because she was afraid he might change his mind, she stood on tiptoes on the shifting sand and pressed her lips against his. She'd never kissed anyone on the mouth before, but Margaret had told her and Bitty to practice on their pillows so they'd know how to do it right when it was time.

But nothing could have prepared her for what it was like to kiss Boyd. There was softness, and heat, and soft tongue that made her knees buckle. His large hands came around her waist to support her, and because her hands had nowhere else to land, she slipped them around his neck and held on tightly, pressing herself against him because she had the oddest thought that they were two halves of a shell, fitting perfectly together to become a whole.

Eventually, he pulled back, breathing heavily, his hands slipping from her waist. "Wow. That was a surprise."

"You . . . you didn't like it?"

He cupped her head in his hands. "I liked it a little too much." He pressed his forehead against hers, still breathing heavily. "You're something else, Sessalee Purnell."

"And so are you, Boyd Madsen," she whispered.

"We should get back to your friends," he said. "Before your reputation is completely ruined."

She knew what he meant—as a way to keep Ceecee on the straight and narrow, her mother had been drilling her about what happened to girls who'd lost their reputation. Not that her mother had ever been able to go into the actual specifics of what a girl had to do to lose her reputation. She was fairly sure going somewhere alone with a man and kissing him was pretty close, but she also knew there was much more they could have done that would have sealed her reputation as a loose woman.

He tucked her hand into the crook of his arm again as they walked back to the hotel and the others, the moon at their backs casting long shadows in front of them. The dark sand swallowed their footsteps, hiding them as if they'd never been there at all, making Ceecee shiver.

"Are you cold?" Boyd asked, taking off his jacket

and placing it around her shoulders before she could answer.

"Thanks," she said, pulling the lapel closed over her neck. She was busy thinking of ways to extend the evening, when she spotted Bitty coming down the steps to the beach and running toward them.

"There you are—thank goodness," she said. "Margaret's not feeling well, and we need to get her home."

Ceecee let go of Boyd's arm and began walking quickly toward the steps. "What's happened?"

Bitty leaned toward Ceecee and lowered her voice. "I think too much to drink and too much dancing. Reggie convinced the band to play some jitterbug music, and I think it just shook up Margaret's stomach."

"How can I help?" Boyd asked. "Can I carry her to the car?"

Bitty started to say yes, but Ceecee interjected. "No, but thank you. We can manage." She told herself that she wasn't ready to share Boyd yet, but she knew it was more than that. She wasn't ready for Boyd to meet Margaret. Even the flash of shame she felt at the thought wasn't enough for her to change her mind and ask for help.

She turned to face Boyd, reluctantly handing back his jacket. "Thank you. It was a lovely evening."

"Can I see you again? Tomorrow?"

Ceecee pretended to think, knowing she owed her mother at least that. "All right. Meet me at the Pavilion—say five o'clock?"

"Can't I pick you up?"

She shook her head. "I'll meet you at the Pavilion. At five." She turned to follow Bitty, who was headed to the ladies' room, where she said she'd left Margaret after she'd propped her on a bench with a wet towel pressed to her forehead. Ceecee looked behind her once and found Boyd watching her, a question in his eyes.

But she just smiled, then turned around and kept walking, unwilling to admit even to herself that she wasn't ready to find out whether Boyd Madsen really liked daisies better than roses.

eleven

Larkin
2010

The smell of what could only be breaded and battered chicken frying in the kitchen assaulted me as I ran up the steps to the front porch, the rolled-up ribbons from the Tree of Dreams in my pocket thick against my hip bone. I untucked my blouse as I stepped inside, hoping to cover the small bump. I had so many questions and had decided to start with what Bennett had told me about Ceecee and the fire. All the things Ceecee had never thought to mention to me in the last twenty-seven years.

I rounded on her as soon as I'd closed the door behind me. I stopped midturn and with my mouth partly open when I spotted the figure standing behind her in the doorway to the dining room.

Ceecee smiled. "You remember Jackson Porter, don't you, Larkin? His daddy has always been our insurance agent, and now that he's in semiretirement, he's letting Jackson handle some of his accounts. Jackson is here going over some paperwork, and I've invited him to stay for dinner. It's your favorite—fried chicken."

I had the sudden urge to burst out laughing, the situation so surreal that I couldn't quite adjust my emotions to compensate. The new controlled and mature Larkin fought very hard to overpower the younger version of myself who'd once sat on the bleachers at Georgetown High School, cheering the star quarterback as he burst through the GHS Bulldogs banner surrounded by the cheerleaders' waving pom-poms.

"I . . . ," I started to say, but stopped as Jackson stepped forward and enveloped me in a hug before kissing my cheek. He wore the same cologne, soft with a hint of spice that still made me think of Jackson whenever I smelled it. When I was sixteen, I'd bought a bottle of it with my birthday money to keep hidden in the back of my drawer so I could smell it whenever I wanted to. I cringed at the thought, not just at how stupid I had once been, but at how pathetically stupid I still was. I should have been telling him that he was a jerk, that he had no business hugging me. That he should apologize for ruining my life, even if he probably had no idea that he had. Over the years, I'd told myself that ignorance was no excuse for compliance, yet looking at Jackson Porter now, I forgot everything except how I'd felt watching him burst through that banner on the football field, believing that over all those other girls, he'd picked me.

He stepped back, regarding me with hazel eyes that sometimes seemed more green than brown, depending on what he wore. My high school diary had contained a paragraph at the end of each day listing what Jackson wore to school, and what color his eyes were that particular day.

"You look . . . amazing," he said, grinning that grin that belonged in men's underwear commercials. That's what Mabry had told her all the cheerleaders said in the locker room after games, and then I'd started to say it as if the words were my own.

"Thanks," I said, grateful for the skinny jeans and the spaghetti-strap blouse. And in my stupid, sixteen-year-old heart, grateful that he'd noticed. "You do, too."

He shrugged. "I try to keep fit—still throw a football around with Bennett and some of the guys. But you . . . wow! You're completely different." He must have realized that couched somewhere in between his words was an insult, so he added, "I mean, I always knew you were pretty. I guess I didn't realize until right this moment just how pretty."

I watched Ceecee beam from behind him, and I was grateful yet mortified at the same time. If she had any idea of what my past relationship—if you could call it that—with Jackson had been, she would have thrown him out the door on his ear. But I'm glad she didn't know. Because then I didn't need to excuse his behavior, or mine, and instead could pretend we'd been simply classmates who'd met up again after nine years.

"Come on in and sit down," Ceecee said, motioning for us to follow her into the dining room, where the table was set with Ceecee's best crystal and china, and where Bitty was pouring sweet tea into glasses and looking up at me with worried eyes. **She doesn't know,** I told myself. She couldn't. It's just that Bitty had always been more perceptive than Ceecee, always seeing what was really there. Ceecee only ever saw what she wanted to.

"I had Bitty set a place for Jackson right next to you on this side of the table," Ceecee said, touching the rim of a delicate piece of antique French bone china. She indicated the single place at the foot of the table. "I set a place for your daddy just in case, but he said he'd probably stay at the hospital and eat something there."

"I'm real sorry to hear about your mama," Jackson said, pulling back my chair for me to sit before heading to the front of the table to do the same for Ceecee while Bitty pulled out her own and sat down before Jackson could make it to her side of the table.

"Thank you," I said, placing my napkin in my lap and looking everywhere but at his face. Because every time I did, I was reminded of the last time I'd seen him before I spotted him at the ice-cream shop. And what he'd said. "We're all hoping she'll wake up any minute now. It's given us all a real scare."

"But it's brought you back to Georgetown," Jackson said, accepting the bread basket from Ceecee. "I know your relatives aren't the only ones happy to see you back." He grinned that grin again as he passed the basket to me, and I almost dropped it.

"Bennett and Mabry were certainly excited to see her," Bitty said, stabbing the stick of butter with her knife. "You should ask them over sometime, Larkin—meet Mabry's husband and little boy. Go out on the river or something."

I frowned. "I really don't expect to be here long enough to do much socializing . . ."

As if I hadn't said anything, Jackson said, "I've got a boat—we can all go skiing and have a little party while you're here. It will be just like old times."

I stared at the chicken breast I'd placed on my plate and felt almost physically ill. I nearly asked him whether he was joking. I finally raised my eyes to his, just to make sure. But there was no recognition or memory to dim his enthusiasm.

"Maybe," I said. "Of course, it all depends on when Mama wakes up and how much recovery time she'll need."

"Of course," he said, putting his hand briefly over mine.

Smiling, I found myself relaxing and even managed a few bites of my chicken and butter beans. We talked about old classmates and teachers, about his sister, who was four years younger than we were and who'd graduated from Carolina but was in California getting her graduate degree in physical therapy.

I'd imagined this scene so many times when I was in high school, of having Jackson Porter sitting next to me at dinner, of having him touch my hand and smile at me, that I almost pinched myself a few times to make sure I wasn't dreaming. I tried to push the memory of the last time I'd seen him before I'd fled to New York into the forefront of my thoughts, but years of infatuation superseded my common sense.

When Ceecee brought out her lemon sponge cake for dessert and I helped clear the dishes, Bitty went to the old stereo console in the front parlor and put in an eight-track tape. It was one of those things Ceecee never saw the need to replace no matter how out-dated or how warbly the music sometimes sounded because the tape had stretched in places. If it worked and her supply of eight-tracks lasted, she'd keep the circa 1970 stereo. As I placed the dessert plates on the table, I listened to the opening strains of a famil-iar song, and before the first lyric was sung, I said, "Linda Ronstadt. 'You're No Good.'"

"Excuse me?" Jackson asked at the same time Bitty coughed into her hand.

"The song." I jerked my head in the direction of the parlor. "That's the name of the artist and the song. It's a thing I do." I thought he knew that about me. Or maybe I just thought that he **should** have known that about me.

"Yeah," he said, vaguely nodding his head as he accepted a slice of cake from Ceecee and placed it in front of me before holding up his own plate.

I cut a forkful and put it in my mouth, the taste bringing back memories. I'd always loved Ceecee's lemon sponge cake and had eaten half of one the first time I hadn't made the cheerleading squad. I'd eaten the second half the following day when Mabry had come by to tell me she was going to resign from the squad if I found it too hurtful. I'd smiled and hugged her, then told her she was being ridiculous, that I wanted to focus on the school play and my writing and editing for the school paper. And then Ceecee had come in and told me that I was better than all those girls on the squad, and that it was their loss. I pretended to believe her, and when she'd left to go to the grocery store, I'd finished the cake.

When we were done with dessert, Jackson turned to me. "It's nice outside—would you like to go for a walk?"

As much as I wanted to get Ceecee alone and ask her about Margaret and the fire, I found myself unable to say no. But before I could respond, Bitty said, "We'll need Larkin to help clear the table." She leaned over and took Jackson's plate without asking even though there were still a couple of bites left.

Ceecee gave her old friend a stern look. "Even at

our advanced age, we are more than capable of clear-ing the table without help." Facing Larkin, she con-tinued. "You young people go enjoy the nice evening. It won't be too much longer before the heat and hu-midity arrive and make walking more than a block a miserable experience."

Jackson smiled gratefully at Ceecee, but he gave an even bigger smile to Bitty, who continued to frown at him as he escorted me out the front door.

We retraced the route I'd taken the previous night to the Harborwalk. When Jackson reached for my hand, I let him take it. I felt self-conscious at first, and then held tightly, thinking—misguidedly or not—that I had earned it.

"I saw you at Gabriel's last night, didn't I?" he asked. "I'm sorry I didn't recognize you. I don't think I would have even known who you were if Ceecee hadn't introduced us."

Again, I felt as if there were something vaguely insulting in his confession. "Yes, well, that's all right. You looked like you were busy, so I didn't want to disturb you."

He blew out a breath through his nose. "That was Ashley—she's a receptionist at the agency. We were working late, so I offered to walk her home and on a whim stopped for some ice cream."

I didn't say anything, and he must have taken my silence as understanding, because he asked, "How is it that you're still single?"

I pretended that I hadn't dreamed of this exact

conversation more times than I cared to admit. I felt myself blushing and kept my head down. "I work a lot, and most of my coworkers are female, so not a lot of opportunities to meet guys."

He grimaced. "And I'm working in the same town I grew up in, where everybody knows my family, so it's almost like we're in the same boat. A lot of tourists bring in fresh faces, but nothing permanent, you know?"

The word "permanent" and the sound of the lapping river brought a sense of déjà vu, a reminder of us having been here before, or someplace similar. On his daddy's boat, anchored offshore, the sound of the river pushing against the fiberglass. Part of me wanted him to remember, too, while the other part wanted him to forget. I had made up my mind to ask him when he spoke again, and the moment passed.

"Do you remember Melissa Griffin?"

I did remember Melissa. Ceecee used to tell me we could have been twins. She said it so often that I actually believed her. Melissa was the cheer captain, and the student council president, and she also visited nursing homes as an extracurricular. She was also on the varsity field and track team, which gave her the athletic body that I hadn't had until I started running in college. But I never noticed that she and I were as different as nonsisters could be, despite what Ceecee said.

"Yeah, I remember her." I stopped there, not willing to admit that I'd had my hair cut just like hers and imagined that it made me look even more like her. It didn't, of course, but I wouldn't realize that until years later, looking at our senior yearbook. I'd tossed it in the garbage.

"We were married while still in college, but divorced within a year—no kids, thankfully. We were too young, I guess."

"I'm sorry," I said. "That must have been hard. It's a good thing you figured it out before you had kids."

"True. Still pretty traumatic. I guess I'd bought into that permanent part, and it was shocking to realize how wrong I was."

Permanent. He'd used that word again. I stopped to look up at him, the large gaslight behind us turning the tips of his beard stubble the color of fire. His eyes were green tonight—definitely green because of the oxford cloth button-down he wore in a pale shade—and when he looked at me, I thought I saw a flicker of recognition. A flicker of **something.** Like a shared memory. But then it was gone as he looked at me with the simple expectation of waiting for me to speak. I should have said something then, but the old me wanted to be standing there with Jackson, pretending that the past didn't exist and of all the girls in the world, he'd picked me. So I spoke, but not the words I should have.

"Or maybe," I said slowly, "the word 'permanent'

means something completely different depending on our age. Like how when we're children, the word 'old' means anyone over twenty."

"Yeah, that must be it," he said casually, hurting my feelings a little bit, because I thought I'd just said something profound. He pulled on my hand. "Come on—let's get some ice cream."

I allowed him to lead me back to Gabriel's. I held our seats at a table inside while Jackson got our orders—two cups of vanilla frozen yogurt with granola topping. Gabriel caught sight of me and raised his eyebrows when Jackson wasn't looking. I simply shrugged, not sure how I would explain tonight to myself, much less to Gabriel.

I chiseled out the yogurt along the edges of my cup with my white plastic spoon while Jackson stabbed his right in the middle, taking out a big scoop. "This whole thing with your mother—I'm so sorry. You know, she came to see me recently, asking about various insurance policies."

I lowered my full spoon back to the cup. "Was there anything in particular she wanted to know?"

"She was asking about that old burned-down plantation over on the North Santee. I had no idea your family owned it. My buddies and I used it for years as a party place. Always gave the girls the creeps, which just meant it was a good thing to be a big football player, you know? We'd build a bonfire and bring sleeping bags and a cooler full of beer. Always a good time." He winked as he licked his spoon. "I sure am glad we were never tempted to go inside. Even back then it seemed like a bad idea. Besides, the girls didn't want to go within ten feet of the place, and us guys were willing to keep them warm and safe."

He put another big scoop of frozen yogurt into his mouth, oblivious to the fact that I'd known that he and his friends and the popular girls would go to an old burned-out plantation house and light a bonfire. Or that I'd never once been asked to go.

His smile faded quickly when I didn't return it. "So, what did my mother want to know?" I asked.

"She said she wanted to find any insurance records from 1954, which is when the house burned. Mostly who the beneficiary was. My granddaddy owned the agency then, and I remember him saying that his office and all the records were a total loss because of all the hurricane flooding from Hazel." He took another stab at his yogurt. "She seemed real disappointed, like she was figuring out some big puzzle, and just as she got near the end, she realized there were some pieces missing."

I pushed my cup of half-eaten yogurt away, eager now to go home and speak with Ceecee. "I'm sorry," I said. "I'm pretty exhausted—worrying about my mother, mostly. Would you mind if we head back now?"

"Of course not—I understand. I'd be worried sick,

too, if it were my mother." He stood and picked up our trash, depositing it all in a nearby can before pulling out my chair.

"Thanks, Gabriel," I said as I walked by the owner as he was placing three big scoops of ice cream into a banana split boat.

"You come back soon," he said, his eyes sliding to Jackson's back. "So we can have a chat."

"Will do," I said with a wave before following Jackson, who was holding the door open for me.

His car was parked on the street in front of Ceecee's house, but he insisted on walking me to the door. The outdoor lights were on, creating as much light as deep shadows on the front porch. I felt Jackson looking at me, but the light stopped at his neck so that his entire face was in shadow. I felt a small chill shudder down my spine as I wondered what the symbolism would be if this were a dream.

"I had a nice time catching up," he said, and I heard the smile in his voice.

"Me, too." I shifted my feet, the sense of déjà vu almost overwhelming, and I wanted to ask if he remembered, too. But the memory was nestled like a silk dress between gum tree seedballs, prickling and tearing at the fabric, and I had no idea how to retrieve the dress without ruining it. So I left it where it was and smiled up at Jackson.

"I'll call you about maybe going out on my boat this weekend. Or dinner sometime. Even if your mama wakes up soon, I hope you can stay a little longer so we can get to know each other again."

For the first time in years, I wished Mabry were there as a witness. Or that I knew her phone number so I could call her and tell her that Jackson Porter just said he wanted to get to know me better. Then again, maybe I didn't. Because I wasn't exactly sure she'd be so happy for me.

"I probably won't still be here this weekend, but let me give you my number . . ."

"Ceecee already gave it to me. I hope you don't mind."

"Of course not. I'm usually at the hospital or here, so it's easy to reach me."

"Good." He leaned toward me, and I didn't move, not sure what I should do. He kissed me softly on the cheek, his lips warm and lingering, and I felt an odd sense of relief. "Good night, Larkin."

"Good night, Jackson," I said. I watched as he walked back to his car. I still felt his kiss on my skin and smelled the lingering scent of his cologne, which made me remember things I wished I could forget.

twelve

Ceecee
2010

Ceecee walked around the parlor, unnecessarily rearranging frames and her collection of Limoges boxes and other trinkets while listening to the ticking of the hall clock. She heard Bitty coughing upstairs, then smelled cigarette smoke, even though she'd told Bitty more than once that she wasn't allowed to smoke in the house.

Ceecee had already washed her face and put on her cold cream and pinned her hair, but she couldn't go to sleep until she knew where Mack was and that Larkin had come home. She'd called Mack's cell phone twice already, knowing that visiting hours at the hospital had ended long before, but he hadn't returned her calls. Gritting her teeth, she picked up a silver-framed photo of Ivy and Mack on their wedding day, then rubbed it against her housecoat to remove any flecks of imaginary dust. She had better not find out he was with **that woman,** not while Ivy was in the hospital. Not while Larkin was home. It would be beyond the pale.

Ceecee replaced the photo and picked up another from the mantel, this one taken on her own wedding day. There was Bitty, wearing the bright red dress she'd chosen herself, but which was simply another shade of gray in the black-and-white photo. She looked young and pretty with her wide-brimmed hat, and Ivy, too, wearing a soft yellow dress as befitted a flower girl. Ivy and the groom wore similar expressions of surprise, as if neither one could imagine how they'd gotten there.

Ceecee adjusted her glasses, bringing the photo closer to her face and examining the smudge behind her ivory-silk shoulder. She'd always thought it was a fingerprint the photographer had missed on the camera lens. It was Bitty who'd pointed out that the smudge hadn't appeared on any of the other photos from the wedding, and that it must have been Margaret's ghost, letting them know she was there. Whenever Ceecee looked at the picture, she stared at the blurry mark, imagining sometimes that she saw a face and at other times just a fingerprint.

Carefully, she replaced the frame on the mantel, smelling old smoke and ashes from the fireplace. She couldn't recall whether she'd had the fireplaces cleaned in the last year. It bothered her that she couldn't remember the little things anymore—which was why she now wrote everything down. Bitty said that as long as she remembered the big things, she had nothing to worry about. The ashy scent was particularly strong tonight, and she wondered if the wind might be strong outside, blowing through the old mortar. She hoped that was the reason for her dreams of the past few nights, dreams of this very house engulfed in flames, the fire slowly climbing the stairs to the room where she slept.

Ceecee was on the way to the kitchen and her calendar to make a note to call the chimney cleaner tomorrow when she heard another heavy cough from upstairs at the same time the front door opened. After directing a frown upstairs, she moved to the foyer and found Larkin with her back to Ceecee, staring at the closed front door.

"Is everything all right?"

Another cough from Bitty brought their attention to the stairs. Ignoring her question, Larkin asked, "Has she seen a doctor about that cough?"

"I don't know." Ceecee's answer embarrassed her, made her feel ashamed that she didn't know. "She's a grown woman, so I suppose she has." She watched as Larkin's worried expression turned into a slight frown. "I'll ask her tomorrow. We both know how stubborn Bitty can be." She said it with a smile and was pleased when Larkin looked relieved.

"How did it go tonight?" she asked. Ceecee looked

for any lessening of the tightness around Larkin's eyes, the hollowness in her cheeks, and the slight dip of her head that hadn't been there when she was a child and seemed to get worse every visit home. It made Ceecee think of the chameleons she'd once seen at a zoo, how they changed their colors to match their surroundings. She wondered if Larkin was doing that on purpose, trying to fit in in New York. Or maybe she was trying to disguise herself enough that no one who'd known her before would recognize her now. Which was silly, really. Larkin was perfect in every way, and had always been. She had no reason to hide. Maybe it was simply the stress over her father and now her mother.

"It was fine." Larkin didn't move toward the stairs, but instead stood looking at Ceecee, her eyes now angry. "We need to talk."

Ceecee forced herself not to swallow the sudden lump in her throat, afraid Larkin might hear her. "Of course. Can it wait until morning? I'm simply exhausted . . ."

"No. It really can't. It's about the fire at Carrowmore."

Ceecee glanced up the stairs to make sure Bitty wasn't at the top, listening.

"All right. Come into the parlor and we'll chat. Can I get you a glass of sweet tea or a piece of cake?"

Larkin shook her head. "No. Thanks." She moved into the parlor and dropped her purse, but didn't sit down. Instead, she headed to the mantel and absently picked up Ceecee's wedding photo. "Bennett told me about my grandmother. About how she died."

Ceecee decided she should sit down even if Larkin didn't. "It wasn't his place to tell you."

"No, it probably wasn't. But I suppose we were both wondering why nobody thought to mention it to me before. I'm twenty-seven years old, Ceecee. When did you think I'd be old enough to know that my grandmother died in a house fire? Or that the house she died in still belongs to our family and will belong to me when I turn thirty?"

"I . . ." Ceecee rubbed her arms under her housecoat, feeling suddenly very, very cold. "It was such a horrible thing. And it happened long before you were born. Your mother . . ."

"She was there. Bennett said she was in the house. And so were you. You saved her, but you couldn't save my grandmother."

Unshed tears filled Larkin's eyes, and Ceecee felt her own eyes filling. "It was the worst night of my life, something I never want to think about. I never talked about it to Ivy because she'd been there and I didn't want her to suffer any more than she already had. Not that she ever really forgot. She remembered it in her nightmares. You remember those."

"Her dreams of fire." Larkin moved to an armchair and sat down heavily. "It's why I started analyzing dreams. So I could help her understand them. So I could help her stop. But I only ever thought they were nightmares—not memories from her past."

Ceecee hugged herself, the cold now penetrating her bones. "I didn't talk about it with you for the same reason I didn't talk about it with your mama. Some things are too sad, and best left in the past. I just wanted to protect you both."

Larkin looked up at the ceiling. "That never works, you know." She met Ceecee's eyes. "You saved Mama's life. I would have liked to grow up knowing that."

Ceecee avoided meeting Larkin's eyes, turning instead to look at the photo on the mantel. "Would it have made a difference?"

"Maybe." Larkin's voice sounded less confident than she'd probably intended. "Maybe if I'd known about Mama's first husband, and how she'd lost her mother in a fire, I might have been able to help her instead of dogging her every step." I swallowed. "I might even have avoided the disaster I became."

"You were never a disaster. Ever. It seems to me that the more we try to dissect our pasts, the more we try to go back and relive them. Trust me, it's more important to pick up the pieces and move forward and live our lives the best way we can. I've never been a fan of leftovers."

She pushed herself to her feet, feeling more tired than she remembered feeling in years. "If you're done with your questions, I'm going to bed. Please turn off the lights before you head up."

Larkin stood, too. "Bennett also said that Ivy was trying to challenge your trusteeship so that Carrowmore would be mine now instead of waiting for three more years. Did you know that? Did she say anything to you? And why wouldn't the house be held in trust for Mama instead of me?"

Ceecee heard herself gasp, felt the space around her heart exhale. "She never wanted anything to do with Carrowmore, which is why, after you were born, she and your grandfather set up the trust. But, no, she never said anything to me about changing anything."

"She also went to see Jackson Porter to ask him about the insurance policy on the house when it burned—who the beneficiaries were. In case you were wondering, he didn't know—all the records were lost in the Hurricane Hazel flooding in 1954."

Ceecee began walking toward the bottom of the stairs, each step seemingly interminable. She looked at the heavy carved balustrade, focusing on it. If she could reach it, and hang on to it, she could make it to her bedroom without collapsing. "I don't know. You'll have to ask your mother when she wakes up."

"Mack said that developers have approached you about selling Carrowmore. Maybe Mama found out about that, and that's why she started questioning the trust."

Ceecee leaned against the newel post, all the fight in her gone. "They did, and I didn't give them the time of day. As for the insurance money, it's all in the trust waiting for you. Along with other Darlington assets that belonged to your grandmother at the time of her death. I've never touched a cent." She took a deep breath. "Good night, Larkin. I hope Ivy wakes up tomorrow so we can ask her all of these questions. Because she's the only one who can answer them."

"Good night, Ceecee." Larkin watched as Ceecee slowly climbed the stairs. She paused at the top, then walked toward Ivy's bedroom. When her husband had died, Ceecee had slept in Ivy's empty bedroom, unable to bear the emptiness of her own room, of the cold sheets in the bed next to her. In the beginning, she'd slept on his pillow, smelling his scent, balling up his pajamas so she could press them against her heart. But eventually she'd had to launder the sheets, replacing his scent with that of the detergent. That was when the emptiness began. The search for another place to sleep so she could pretend she was traveling somewhere alone where she wouldn't expect another person in the bed with her.

But tonight, she couldn't. She could almost hear Ivy slamming the door in her face, blocking her out like she'd done so many times as a teenager. **Why, Ivy?** The question burst like a bubble out of her heart, stinging her in the chest. **Why did you go to Carrowmore?**

A loud bout of coughing came from Bitty's room, and Ceecee walked over to the closed door, hovering her fist over a raised panel and preparing to knock. She stayed that way for a long moment before silently lowering her hand and walking toward her bedroom.

She crawled into bed and lay on her side for a long

time before rolling over and grabbing the other pillow, smelling it deeply as if it might still hold his scent. Instead, she imagined she could smell Joy perfume, the cool touch of the stopper on the inside of each wrist. Then she closed her eyes and remembered.

Ceecee
1951

Margaret held the bottle of perfume under Ceecee's nose and laughed. "Come on, Ceecee—like I already told you, Aunt Dot won't mind."

Despite having been up most of the night throwing up, Margaret still looked beautiful. Her hair was unbrushed, her skin scrubbed free of any makeup, and she still looked like she should be on a pinup poster.

"Only if you're sure," Ceecee said, taking the stopper and hesitantly putting a dab on each wrist.

"Oh, for goodness' sakes," Bitty said, grabbing the bottle and upending it on her finger before generously sloshing perfume behind each of Ceecee's ears. "She's got to know him a bit longer to make him get close enough to smell just that tiny bit of perfume," she said around a cigarette clenched between her lips.

Laughing, Ceecee jumped up from the dressing table. She felt self-conscious in the violet pedal pushers she'd borrowed from Margaret, but secretly pleased, too. She had long, elegant legs like Margaret, and the pants showed them off. Her mother would take to her bed with a headache if she could see her, but there was no chance of that, thank goodness. She closed her eyes, concentrating on her resolve to enjoy herself for the next two weeks without regret or self-recrimination. She'd have the rest of her life for that.

There was a knock on the door, and the three women looked at one another with varying degrees of surprise. "It can't be Boyd," Ceecee said with confidence. "I didn't tell him our address, and I told him I'd meet him at the Pavilion."

"Don't look at me," Bitty said. "What about you, Margaret? Did you tell Reggie where you were staying?"

Margaret's blue eyes widened in horror. "Oh, my gosh. I did. But surely he wouldn't . . ."

Bitty dropped to her knees and crawled to the bedroom window that faced their street and moved aside the curtain. "It's Reggie!" she said in a loud whisper. She quickly crawled toward the unmade bed and grabbed the silk wrap from the bottom. It belonged to Margaret's aunt Dorothy, but Margaret had been wearing it, and the matching silk pajamas, swearing her aunt wouldn't mind. "Throw this on," she hissed. "I'll get the door. And I suggest running a brush through your hair. You look like something the cat dragged in."

As Ceecee helped Margaret into the robe, they listened as Bitty opened the door and pretended to be surprised. "Oh, it's . . . I'm sorry, I think I've forgotten your name. From the Ocean Forest, right?"

"It's Reginald Madsen—Reggie to my friends. Is this where Margaret Darlington is staying? I'm pretty sure this is the address."

"Yes, but . . ."

"I wanted to make sure Margaret is all right. She was . . . wasn't feeling well when she left last night, and I feel responsible. I brought her some flowers. Is it all right if I come in? I'd like to see her in person and apologize, and give these to her if possible."

"I really don't think she's in any state . . ."

Ceecee tried to hold Margaret back, but her grip easily slipped on the silk sleeves of Margaret's robe. As she tightened the tie around her slim waist, she slid on small kitten-heeled slippers with soft fur balls at the toes, then walked casually out into the main room like a movie star, Ceecee close behind. "Did I hear somebody at the door?" she asked, feigning a yawn and stretching her arms over her head.

"Just for a minute . . . ," Reggie began, but then stopped when he spotted Margaret stretching, outlining her breasts against the silk of her pajamas and robe.

At that moment another figure stepped out from behind Reggie. Although he was just as tall as his younger brother, Bitty must have missed spotting him because he'd been standing to the side, out of view.

"Boyd," Ceecee said, her voice laced with surprise. "I thought we were meeting at the Pavilion." She moved toward the door, blocking the men's view of Margaret in her state of undress.

"I know, but then Reggie said he was coming here. I knew you and Margaret were together, so I decided to come along. And if Margaret is feeling better, maybe we could all go—including Bitty, of course."

Bitty took a drag of her cigarette and watched the smoke rings rise to the ceiling, dissipating slowly like little dreams. "Gee, thanks. I'm honored."

Ceecee sent her a quelling glance before turning back to Boyd. "Well, I'm already dressed, and I don't think Margaret is feeling well enough . . ."

"Don't be such a wet blanket, Ceecee," Margaret said as she stepped out from behind Ceecee and extended her hand. "I'm feeling fit as a fiddle after such a good sleep. And you must be the same Boyd that Ceecee has been talking about nonstop since last night. I'm Margaret Darlington."

Ceecee watched as Boyd grasped the tips of Margaret's fingers and squeezed. "It's a pleasure meeting you, Margaret Darlington."

Ceecee watched his eyes as he took in Margaret's face and tall, lean figure; she watched at the way his eyes didn't change and how he dropped her fingers quickly. She wasn't ready to let out a sigh of relief quite yet, thinking about how sometimes a person could get exposed to a cold or some other infectious horror and not develop symptoms for a week.

Margaret turned her attention to Reggie, whose eyes darkened as he watched Margaret approach, each curve of her body clearly outlined with each step. As she looked at Margaret standing next to Reggie, Ceecee thought they seemed to have been carved from the same block of marble, each as beautiful and physically perfect as the other. Boyd was decidedly handsome, but Reggie had an air of power and purpose around him that probably affected Margaret like catnip would a cat.

Margaret batted her eyelashes up at him. "And aren't you just darling to bring me flowers." She took the bouquet of red roses from him and delicately sniffed the petals. "These smell just divine." She graced everyone with one of her wide smiles. "Just give me a moment to put these in a vase with water and throw on some clothes, and we'll all head out to the Pavilion and have some fun."

Everyone watched her retreat toward the kitchen except Ceecee, who watched Boyd, noticing how his eyes seemed reluctantly pulled in Margaret's direction before he jerked his gaze back to Ceecee and smiled.

An hour and a half later, they piled into Margaret's car—because Reggie's car wasn't a convertible and the day was too pretty, according to Margaret—and drove to the Pavilion and the attached boardwalk and amusement park. Bitty sat up front with Margaret while Ceecee sat in the middle of the backseat between Reggie and Boyd. After they were settled, Boyd's hand found hers and held it the entire short ride, making Ceecee want to weep with joy or relief—she wasn't sure which.

"Let's go on the carousel first!" Margaret announced as she waited for Reggie to open her door for her and rewarded him with a warm smile. "It's very famous, you know—all hand-carved wooden animals, and they just brought it here from Alabama. There's a blue sea dragon with a gold mane, and I'm riding on that one first." She turned to face Ceecee. "Did you bring your camera? Because I must get a photograph of us all on the carousel."

"Of course," she said, patting it in its case around her neck as they stood in front of the carousel with its red-and-white-striped awning, its short stature nearly eclipsed by the tall Ferris wheel next to it. "I say we start with that instead," Bitty said, pointing to it. "So we can get a bird's-eye view of the entire boardwalk and Pavilion. Not everybody has been coming here since we were children." She looked pointedly at Margaret.

Margaret shrugged. "Fine by me," she said as she tucked her hand possessively into the crook of Reggie's arm.

He offered his other arm to Bitty, but she shook her head. "Before we get on the Ferris wheel, I'm going to get some cotton candy. I'm famished since we had to wait so long to leave the house. Would anybody else like to get some? Margaret, I know how much you love it."

Margaret's face blanched, most likely due to her

stomach not being completely back to normal after the previous evening, despite Bitty's efforts to stuff her full of bread that morning, hoping to soak it all up. "I'm not really hungry, so I'll pass, but I know Ceecee would love some, wouldn't you?"

Ceecee did love cotton candy, but also knew she'd be wearing it all over her face by the time she finished hers. It had never bothered her before, but she'd never tried to impress a boy, either. Her stomach rumbled, but she pressed her hand against it to make it stop. "I'm not hungry, either, but we'll go with you—I'm sure Boyd and Reggie might like some."

They headed over to the vendor, and while they were waiting in line, Boyd turned to her. "I'm guessing Ceecee is your nickname?"

She nodded, her stomach rumbling louder now that she could smell the spun sugar. "Yes, everyone except my mama and daddy call me Ceecee. Sessalee is my real name."

"It suits you." He smiled, his eyes crinkling and his cheeks creasing in a way she already found endearing. "Would you mind if I continued to call you by your full name?"

"Not at all. Especially if it means you're speaking to me." She blushed at her outrageous flirting, wondering what he must be thinking of her.

He threw back his head and laughed. "I like a woman who says what she thinks. My mother would like you. She's never been one for those silly girls who only say what they think you want to hear."

She smiled openly up at him. "I hope you're not saying I remind you of your mother."

He pretended to think. "That wouldn't be a bad thing, but no, I'm not. Unless it's okay if I call you both smart women."

He handed money to the pimply teen behind the counter and received two gigantic cotton candies in return. "I know you said you didn't want any, but I don't think I could stand to hear your stomach grumbling without feeding you something. Besides, Bitty told me it's your favorite."

"Thank you," she said, inhaling the sweet smell but unsure of where to bite it. She would die if she had dried cotton candy stuck to her nose and cheeks for the rest of the day.

As if he'd read her mind, he took a big bite out of his own, the pink confection clinging to the beard bristles on his chin. "There," he said. "Now we'll be even." He handed her a napkin. "I'll keep your face clean, and you can repay the favor." He stood closer and said quietly, "But if you get some stuck to your lips, I have a much more interesting way to remove it."

Looking into his eyes, she moistened her lips, then took a big bite out of her cotton candy and smiled up at him.

"Well, now, if that isn't a challenge." He leaned down and touched his lips softly to hers, his tongue flicking over her lips. Lifting his head, he closed his eyes. "I do think that's the sweetest cotton candy I've ever had."

She laughed as Bitty grabbed her arm and pulled her away. "Don't make it too easy for him, Ceecee," she said as she led them toward the Ferris wheel. They rode it three times, the last time Boyd riding with Bitty so she wouldn't feel left out. Ceecee waited at the bottom, enjoying the smells of roasting hot dogs and popcorn, and the sounds of laughing children and excited young people shouting boasts to one another as they took their chances at Skee-Ball and water gun races. A row of benches had been set up along the boardwalk facing the rides where exhausted parents sat with small children and forgotten stuffed animals as the older children ran from activity to activity.

Ceecee allowed herself to daydream of her future self with her own children, visiting on a family vacation, eating cotton candy, and letting Boyd kiss the sticky candy from her lips. Someone grabbed her hand and pulled her down the boardwalk. "Come on!" Bitty shouted. "We're going on the Comet!"

Ceecee looked back at Margaret to see what she thought about riding the roller coaster that they'd been told was nicknamed the "vomit Comet," but Margaret was occupied staring up into Reggie's eyes.

"Disgusting, isn't it?" Boyd said as he caught up with her and took her arm.

"Absolutely," Ceecee agreed. "Because I can see a whole quarter of an inch between them. If she really liked him, there wouldn't be any space at all."

Boyd chuckled and drew her against his side. "Like this?"

She nodded. "Exactly."

They stayed at the boardwalk for the rest of the afternoon, riding all the rides, including the kiddie rides and bumper cars, and Boyd always making sure that he saved a ride to go on with Bitty. Margaret sat for a charcoal drawing that even Bitty admitted wasn't half-bad. Margaret rolled it carefully and gave it to Reggie with a small kiss.

"We'll have to hang this in the White House when we get there," he said. "I'll be sure to put it in a safe place until then."

It was such a boastful thing to say, but coming from Reggie Madsen, it sounded nothing less than sincere and prophetic. And it made Margaret glow.

They stuffed themselves on hot dogs and popcorn, then went to the photo booth to have their pictures made behind cardboard cutouts of fat and skinny swimmers (Ceecee and Bitty), and behind the half-moon depicting Miss Myrtle Beach (Margaret). Ceecee's favorite was the one of Boyd and Reggie at the Myrtle Beach jail, wearing matching expressions of blatantly false misery.

Afterward, as they sat at an outdoor table finishing their ice-cream cones, Ceecee slid her feet out of her sandals under the table. They were Margaret's and too small, and she thought she'd have permanent scars from where the straps bit into her skin. She almost sighed out loud, hiding it instead in a bite of her ice cream.

Boyd turned his attention to Bitty as she sat back and lit a cigarette. "Sessalee tells me you're going to school to study art. You must be excited."

Bitty nodded, looking surprised but pleased to be the center of attention. To show him how she appreciated it, Ceecee squeezed Boyd's hand where it sat on her armrest.

Bitty turned her head to blow out smoke. "I am. My father thinks I should also get a teaching degree so that I can teach art and have a steady income, so I'm thinking about it." She pointed her cigarette at Boyd and then at Reggie. "What about you two? What are your plans?"

"I'm planning on starting a medical practice in Charleston," Boyd said, looking a lot less excited about it than he had when he'd first told Ceecee his plans.

Margaret sat up and folded her hands on the table. "You know, Boyd, Dr. Griffith has been our family physician in Georgetown since Mama was a baby, but he's getting ready to retire. He always planned to have his son take over the practice, but poor Donny got killed in the war. I think you should talk to him. Just in case Charleston isn't sounding as appealing as it used to." She winked at Ceecee, who looked down at her lap to hide her blush.

Boyd squeezed her hand. "I might just have to do that, Margaret. Thank you."

"And you?" Bitty asked, indicating Reggie. "What are you going to do?"

"He's going to practice law in Charleston," Margaret said proudly, as if she'd been the one to earn the degree.

"Eventually." Avoiding looking at Margaret, he continued. "But I'm planning on enlisting in the army first. I can't sit back and watch what's going on in Korea without doing my part."

Margaret went very still, but Reggie kept talking. "I'm a few years younger than this old guy," he said, elbowing Boyd, "so I didn't get the chance to serve my country in the last war. I feel I need to earn my stripes somehow, to prove myself before I become a public servant. I've got big plans for my future. Very big plans. Which is why I need to do this now."

Margaret stood suddenly and walked away without a word. Reggie immediately jumped up and followed her, leaving the three of them sitting in stunned silence.

"Well, I guess he hadn't mentioned that to Margaret before."

Ceecee grabbed Boyd's hand with both of hers. "Can you talk to him? Tell him it's a bad idea?"

Boyd shook his head slowly. "It's not my place. When I enlisted in 'forty-three, I was just a little bit younger than Reggie is now. I understand how he feels. And I didn't have a sweetheart at the time, but my mother was pretty upset. She thought I should wait until I was called up, to let it be in God's hands.

But once a man makes up his mind to do something, it's too late to change it."

"Don't say that." Ceecee pressed her forehead against his shoulder, imagining herself in Margaret's place.

"They'll work it out," Boyd reassured her. "Reggie is a good man—one of the best. He's smart and ambitious. Our father always said it was like he had two elder sons." He grinned. "Reggie saved my life once, when we were boys. We used to rent a house on Folly Beach each summer. I went out too far and couldn't swim back, and he came out and got me even though I was the stronger swimmer. I thought we were both going to drown. So, yes, I trust Reggie to do the right thing—whether or not it's what we think is the right thing."

Boyd placed his arm around her shoulders. "We have tonight and almost two weeks together. Let's enjoy it." He squeezed her, then let her go before standing up. "You two go find a spot for us to watch the fireworks on the Pavilion. I'll go find Reggie and Margaret and come find you."

Ceecee nodded, fighting the feeling of panic at the thought of his leaving her, even for a short while, then acknowledged the nudge of excitement at the thought of his taking over for Dr. Griffith in Georgetown. Her mother had always told her that if she fixated on something she wanted to happen, it wouldn't because vanity and joy seeking weren't things that God rewarded. Instead, Ceecee pushed the thought from her mind and left the table with Bitty to find a good vantage point along the boardwalk.

By the time they'd found places on a bench to watch the evening's fireworks, Ceecee's face hurt from so much smiling and laughing throughout the day, and she promised herself that she would never regret one single moment. Nor would she tell her mother about any of it, so that she'd never have shadows encroaching on these memories.

While Bitty held their spots, Ceecee walked along the boardwalk looking for Boyd, knowing his tall form would be easy to find even in the diminishing light. She found herself wearing an idiot grin but couldn't make her mouth stop. When she spotted him, she ran toward him, relieved to discover that Margaret and Reggie were with him, Margaret's head resting on Reggie's shoulder, his arm protectively around her waist.

They watched as the evening sky exploded into bursts of red, white, and blue stars of light, the feeling of excitement and euphoria echoing in Ceecee's chest. She was on fire with it, with the heat and longing and brightness of it all. And with Boyd, who kept her hand in his for the entire display, and then when the sky had finally grown dark and silent, kissed her. Streaks of light from the fireworks repeated themselves on the insides of her eyelids, and she knew, right then, what it was to be truly happy.

As they walked back to the car, Ceecee and Boyd, Margaret and Reggie, with Bitty and the tip of her lit cigarette leading the way, Ceecee recalled the ribbons they'd placed in the Tree of Dreams, and she smiled to herself. **I wish to marry the perfect man—handsome, kind, and with good prospects, and my love for him will be endless.** It was only later when she was lying in bed and staring up at the moonlit sky that she remembered she and Margaret had wished for the same thing, and then she laughed out loud.

thirteen

Larkin
2010

A strong breeze followed me into Gabriel's Heavenly Ice Cream & Soda, slamming the door behind me with a bang. A young girl with thick black braids stood behind the counter, wearing a red Gabriel's hat with his trademark halo embroidered in gold in the middle. Her matching apron had the name of the shop in the center, and the devil's forked tail and trident on one strap and a halo on the other. Besides unlimited ice cream, that apron had been the single reason why I'd wanted to work there when I was a teenager.

The girl smiled at me expectantly. I smiled back. "I don't want anything—I'm looking for Gabriel. Is he in?"

Before she could reply, Gabriel appeared from the back room with a wide grin. "Well, look who's here." He turned to the girl. "Erin, would you please get us two small cups with a scoop of vanilla yogurt and granola sprinkles, and bring them to us at the table outside?"

As he held open the front door, which faced the Harborwalk, I asked, "How do you remember everybody's orders?"

He pointed to his graying head. "Keeps me young. Besides, ice-cream orders are like fingerprints. Each one unique. I can tell everything I need to know about a person by what they order. If it's lemon sorbet or peanut butter chocolate chip, or a banana split with extra fudge. Everything I need to know," he said again, pulling out a chair for me before joining me at the table.

I leaned forward. "So, for a young man to order himself a frozen vanilla yogurt with granola sprinkles means what?"

"That he's trying to impress the girl he's with by ordering the same thing she ordered. And she's trying to watch her weight even though it looks to me like it wouldn't hurt her to gain a few pounds."

I rolled my eyes. "I do allow myself ice cream when I want it. I just haven't had too much of an appetite since I got back."

"No change yet with your mama?" His eyes were warm and sympathetic, probably the reason I'd gravitated to his shop during my growing-up years.

And, I freely admitted, the ice cream. It was the one place I could go when Ceecee and Mama were arguing about me where I could get comfort food and understanding.

I shook my head. "There's been no change. My daddy and Ceecee remain hopeful, so I'm trying, too."

"There's nothing more you can do than remain hopeful. Me and the missus, we'll keep praying for her. She's been added to our prayer list at church, too."

"Thanks," I said with a smile, remembering sitting in church with Ceecee and my grandfather and listening as the interminable prayer requests were read out to the congregation. It wasn't that we had so much sickness and misfortune in our community; it was more that people thought the good Lord needed to know about their sick dog or sprained foot. The memory made me smile now, but it made me nostalgic, too.

"So, Gabriel, now that I'm older, maybe you'll tell me why you never hired me. I wanted to work here so badly, and every time I saw your Help Wanted sign in the window, I was always the first to apply."

"Yes, you were. Always dressed neatly, respectful of adults, and you were smart. Yes, missy, you were a real smarty-pants. You would have made a great employee."

"Then why? I'd practically run home crying every time you told me no. It hurt my feelings. Especially when you hired Joe Craigman. He couldn't count change to save his life, and he always got the orders wrong."

"True."

"So why would you hire him and not me? I could calculate change in my head before he could do it on the cash register."

Erin came out with our frozen yogurts, and Gabriel waited until she'd gone back inside.

"Because he didn't have a mother who begged me not to hire him. Your mama didn't think it was a good idea to have you working in an ice-cream shop."

My mouth went dry as if all the air in my lungs had suddenly rushed out of it. "What?"

He shook his head. "That Ivy. Ceecee was always the one coming down and yelling at me for not hiring you, telling me how you were in tears over it."

"I didn't think Mama ever even knew I was interested in working here. And why would she care?"

Gabriel took a small bite of his yogurt, taking his time as if he wanted me to figure things out on my own. I shook my head. "I really don't understand."

"She knew one of the benefits of working here is that I offer all the ice cream you can eat to my employees, that's why."

I took a bite of my own yogurt, just to bring moisture back to my mouth, and because I had no idea of what I should say.

"They both wanted you to be happy. They just had different ideas on how to make that happen." He gave me a contemplative look. "Your mama was always in a difficult place where you were concerned. She didn't think she could be a good mother to you, but she couldn't abandon you to Ceecee's care completely. It just wasn't her way. But trying to smooth the way between you and Ceecee was probably harder than dressing a flea. Ceecee can be as forceful as a hurricane when she's got it in her mind to make people happy, and your mama was always trying to pretend that she wasn't toting a broken heart. But they have always loved you something fierce. They just had different ways of showing it. And not always in a way that made sense."

I stared down into my cup, drowning the granola bits in the melting yogurt. "You can say that again." I met his eyes. "So, you knew about Mama's first husband?"

He nodded slowly. "I knew the Altons real well. Good people. My own mama was a nurse, and when Mrs. Alton got sick and was put in a wheelchair, Mama cared for her in their house. Mr. Alton was president of the bank back then, and he gave me the loan to start my own business when I got back from 'Nam. And Ellis, well, that was a shame. He was a fine young man. A fine, fine young man. We all lost something when he got killed, but your mama especially. It takes a very strong person to survive such a thing."

"She's not strong," I said softly. "I used to think so. I used to admire the way she lived her own life, even if it meant leaving me behind. I thought she was so brave, not caring what other people thought. I even wanted to be like her. Until . . ."

Gabriel's voice was gentle. "Until what?"

I shook my head. "It's complicated."

"I'm good at complicated." When I didn't say anything else, Gabriel sat back in his chair. "You remember the murals on the back wall of the shop that changed with every season? Your mama would come in after the shop was closed at night and paint them for me. It was to thank me for not hiring you." He placed a wrinkled hand over mine. "People have different ways of expressing love. It doesn't mean the love is worth any less."

Without a word, I stood and walked back into the shop and looked—really looked—at the mural on the back wall. In all the years I'd been coming to Gabriel's, the changing murals had been awarded only a passing glance from me, a background not worthy of my notice. Like so many things.

I felt Gabriel standing behind me. "Did Mama paint this one?"

"Sure did. Just recently, in fact. It had been a few years since she'd done a mural for me on account of that arthritis in her one shoulder."

I faced him. "She has arthritis?"

"Has for years. It's hard for her to raise her arm, but she said it didn't bother her too much when she was doing her furniture refinishing."

"Why didn't she tell me?"

Gabriel shrugged, his eyes meeting mine with frank directness. "Maybe because you never asked."

I cringed inside, thinking about my new life in New York, how smart and professional and fit I'd become. How different I was from the girl I had once been—and yet, still completely self-centered. I turned back around to study the mural, waiting for my vision to clear. My breath left me again in a sigh.

It was a mural of an enormous live oak, with exaggerated sweeping branches, and two martin houses dangling from twine. But when I really looked at it this time, I recognized the Tree of Dreams—its heavy green foliage, its thick broad trunk with the opening like a mouth speaking to the viewer. The river ran behind it, and there, on the bank, were the backs of three girls sitting close together, their arms linked. One had hair that was neither light brown nor quite blond enough to be called blond, and one had short, burnished red hair. But the girl in the middle had gold hair that reflected the unseen sunlight, her head tilted back as if in laughter. It was hard to determine the ages of the women, but their dresses appeared to be from another time period—fifties or sixties; I wasn't sure. There seemed to be filtered light around the central figure, making her appear to glow, the women on either side of her tilting their heads slightly toward her as if to acknowledge the golden-haired girl was the focus.

My eyes traveled up the branches of the tree, to where the limbs reached across the perimeter of the room, gourds dangling at sporadic intervals and seeming to project movement even on a static surface. I stepped closer, wondering if it was my imagination or if there seemed to be a brush of a lighter color inside the mouth of one of the gourds. A purple martin, or the fall of light from the painter's perspective. Only the painter would know for sure. Or maybe she wanted ambiguity, wanted her viewers to think it was whatever they wanted.

I stepped back, bumping into Gabriel, who'd moved to stand behind me. "I need to get to the hospital and see Mama. I'll give her your best when she wakes up."

"You do that," he said, walking me to the door.

"Thanks for the yogurt. How much do I owe you?"

"It's on the house. For all the ice cream you didn't get by not working here."

I gave Gabriel a thumbs-up, realizing that if I pushed words past the ball in my throat, I might actually cry. As I walked away, Fats Domino singing "Ain't That a Shame" from the store's stereo followed me down the steps.

There had been something about the painting of three friends beside the Tree of Dreams that made me think of Mabry. We'd known each other since we were babies, sharing everything, including chicken pox when we were eight. There was nothing we'd ever kept from each other, mostly because it was impossible since our mothers were best friends and we went to the same school. Bennett, too, but since he was a boy, there were a few things I tried to keep from him such as when Ceecee had taken me shopping for my first bra, or when I'd finally gotten my period a whole year after Mabry.

I hadn't pursued friendships with Josephine or any of my other coworkers at the ad agency. Friendship was such a complicated relationship, a perpetual give-and-take in which someone always ended up with a deficit. Growing up, I'd just never realized it, had never really thought about the nature of friendship. Until I had to.

I didn't head straight to Ceecee's house and my car to go to the hospital. Instead, my feet took me in the opposite direction toward Prince Street, where Mabry now lived with her husband and little boy. It was strange to think that the big, life-altering things had happened to her without my being a part of them. As little girls, we'd promised each other that we'd be each other's maid or matron of honor, and Mabry had made me promise that I would sing at her wedding. I told her I would as long as I could pick the music. Since she was tone deaf, she'd readily agreed.

I wondered who she'd selected to sing and who'd been her maid of honor. And who she'd called first when she'd gotten engaged. It felt silly to be hurt by childhood promises that hadn't come true. But it did hurt. Because back when we made those promises, Mabry had been my best friend.

I wasn't sure why I'd headed down her street, and I certainly hadn't expected to see her, but after I'd gone two blocks, I spotted her in the front yard of a 1920s-style Craftsman cottage with a red minivan in the driveway—something else we'd promised each other that we'd never own, much less park in our driveways, showing our shame at becoming suburban stereotypes. She was pushing a little boy in a tire swing hung from the branch of an adolescent oak.

My first instinct was to back away and pretend I hadn't seen her, but she spotted me before I could do an about-face. She straightened and looked right at me. "Larkin?"

I stood still, hoping she'd turn away and go back to pushing her son in the tire swing, but she didn't. "Nice car," I said, standing in the street with my arms crossed.

She ran over to me and gave me a giant hug just like she'd done before. "Larkin—so happy to see you!" Indicating the van, she said, "Hey, at least it's red—it's just not the sports car I always said I wanted. Does it count that my husband has a red Mustang?"

"If it makes you feel better, I don't even own a car, red or otherwise."

She laughed, then grabbed my hand and pulled me across the yard to the tree and the little boy in the swing. "I want you to meet my son."

He looked up at me and smiled, and I found myself laughing. "Oh, my gosh—you're right. He looks just like Bennett. I hope your husband doesn't mind."

"Actually, Jonathan encourages the similarity since Bennett is so tall and my husband stopped at five feet eleven." She smiled as she scooped up the little boy and set him on the ground next to her before squatting to be face level with him. "Remember that picture on the refrigerator of Mommy and Uncle Bennett dressed up as the Scarecrow, and I was the Tin Man for Halloween? And between us is Dorothy with the sparkly red shoes? That's Larkin—who's come all the way from New York to visit. Isn't that nice?"

The little boy looked up at me with Bennett's eyes and smiled. "Hello," he said, his voice light and sweet.

Mabry stood and put her hands on the boy's shoulders. "And this is Ellis," she said proudly. "He just turned four."

He reached out a hand to shake, and I almost missed it because I was still hearing the name. "Ellis?" I asked.

"E-l-l-i-s," the little boy said proudly. "I can spell it."

"He's named after my uncle. He died before I was born, but I always liked the name. Mama thought it would be a nice way to honor her brother, so it's a good thing Jonathan and I both liked it."

I looked down at the little boy, thinking of the ribbon my mother had put in the tree all those years ago. **Come home to me, Ellis. I'll love you always.**

I cleared my throat. "My mother knew an Ellis. I wonder if it's the same one."

"It most definitely is. When I was pregnant, Mama told me about Ellis marrying Ivy. Just think—we could have been cousins." Without even looking, she removed Ellis's thumb from his mouth. "She got your mama's permission because she wasn't sure if she could tell me. From what she told me, it near broke your mama in half when he died. That's why she never talked about him. It made her real happy when we told her we were going to name the baby after Ellis. She even threw the biggest baby shower for me."

I stared at her unblinking for several moments, trying to understand how I could have been so in the dark about so many things. **Because you never asked.** "I can't believe Ellis was your uncle, and married to my mother."

Mabry nodded as she stroked Ellis's fine hair across his forehead. "Yeah, weird, huh? She always planned to use the name for one of her own children, but after she got married, she had a lot of miscarriages. Her first full-term baby was a boy and she named him Ellis, but he only lived less than a week. That's why Bennett's named after her father, instead. You can imagine how thrilled she was that Jonathan and I liked the name. Not as thrilled as I was that he was a boy, or else she might have insisted I call my daughter after her favorite aunt."

"Whose name was . . . ?"

"Euphemie."

I widened my eyes in horror. "Was she serious?"

"Sadly, yes. You know how Mama gets when she makes up her mind about something. At least now you have a great name for one of your book characters."

I looked away. "Yes, well, that's not going to happen. That was just one of my many pipe dreams from when I was a kid."

"Don't say that. You're really good. Don't you already have several unfinished manuscripts under your bed or something? Can't you just go back to one of them to get your juices flowing again? Seems to me that would be easier than starting from scratch. And you can always send me chapters to read—that's the beauty of e-mail. I really miss reading your stuff."

I wrinkled my nose, trying to get rid of the sting I felt behind my eyes. "Yeah, well, I think writing is one of those things like acting and singing that I mistakenly believed I was good at. To do the world a favor, I gave them all up."

Ellis leaned against his mother's leg and put his thumb back in his mouth. "I kind of agree with you about the acting and the singing, but not about the writing. You really were good."

"Gee, thanks."

"I'm just being honest. Like I always have been. You just never listened before."

I wanted to argue, but I knew she was right. She'd never been mean-spirited, but it had always been her way to be excruciatingly honest, regardless of whether her words were what I wanted to hear. All I'd needed to do to erase any doubts about my abilities would be to ask Ceecee, and she'd always agree with me. And Bennett and Mabry would then support whatever endeavor I'd committed myself to, regardless of how ill-advised. Which meant I did a lot of things I shouldn't have. Like singing "Ave Maria" at a talent show to a tap dance I'd choreographed myself. I'd had a standing ovation, begun by Ceecee. It was only after I'd left Georgetown that I thought about the talent show, suddenly realizing that the rest of the audience had probably thought the entire performance was some kind of brilliant joke.

Mabry smiled, and I had the horrible thought that she was remembering the talent show, too. "I've been hoping you'd one day finish the book about the couple who meet at a funeral and fall in love, and it turns out that the guy was the person who killed the guy being buried, and the woman is a hit person assigned to take him out. I'm dying to find out what happens."

"Seriously? Isn't that the book where I actually used the term 'purple-headed love dart' to describe a part of the male anatomy?"

Mabry barked out a laugh that startled Ellis, who started sucking his thumb harder.

"I was fourteen. What did I know?"

She sobered. "Yeah, well, you're a good writer—

and I'm sure age has refined your vocabulary. I hope you haven't given it up entirely."

"I write ad copy now, so that's sort of the same."

"Not really." She jerked her head toward the house. "Would you like to come in and have some sweet tea? I just made a new batch last night, and it's chilling in my fridge, waiting for someone to drink it. And Ellis can show you his Matchbox car collection." Mabry ruffled the little boy's hair as a wide grin sprouted around his thumb. "I like cars," he said, his voice muffled.

I glanced around as if looking for an escape, and tried to think of an excuse not to go inside.

"I promise not to talk about anything you don't want to talk about. Like Jackson Porter."

I snapped my head to look at her and frowned. "Thanks, but I've got to go back to the hospital . . ."

"I'm sorry. I probably shouldn't have said that, but it's like the elephant in the room, you know? And he called up Bennett yesterday, trying to get a group of us out on his boat for the weekend. Said you'd already agreed to it. I have to say that surprised me."

I found I couldn't meet her eyes. "I didn't say yes. I told him that things were up in the air with my mother being in the hospital and I'd let him know."

"So technically, you didn't say no, which to someone like Jackson means yes."

Her direct gaze unnerved me, so I looked down at Ellis so I wouldn't have to meet her eyes. Mabry indicated the house again. "Come on inside. Just for a few minutes. Long enough to have a glass of sweet tea and tell me what this dream I've been having means. You're still doing that, right? Analyzing dreams, I mean."

I hesitated a moment too long and found myself being led into the house. Mabry had always been a bit on the bossy side, which was probably why we'd been friends. It was nice not having to make all the decisions. I immediately regretted it. It smelled like her mother's house, like a home is supposed to. There was a healthy clutter of primary-colored toys strewn over the small front room, where a television set was on and playing the British animated series **Peppa Pig.** I knew what it was only because a coworker of mine with a three-year-old was obsessed with the porcine cartoon figure, and she had shown me countless photos of her little girl with various Peppa Pig accessories. I tried to think of the child's name, but couldn't, leaving me to wonder if I'd never asked.

"I can't really stay . . ."

"Sure you can," Mabry said, leading us both into the kitchen at the back of the house and settling Ellis in a booster seat at the table. She set three Matchbox cars on the yellow Minions place mat in front of him.

"Snack, please," he said, opening and closing his small hands, each like a baby bird's mouth waiting for a worm.

She gave him a kiss on the cheek and a snack bag

full of Cheerios before pulling out a chair at the end for me. It looked just like her mother's kitchen, painted a soft cream with bright yellow accents, including a large clock over the sink in the shape of a daisy and a sunshine-colored blender on the counter. A pretty hand-painted border of daisies surrounded the large picture window and back doorway.

"Your mother painted those," Mabry said, indicating the borders. "You can pretty much see her work all over town. Refuses to take payment, but that's not why she's in high demand. She's really good. She always hides pictures inside her murals, and sometimes you can live with one for years before seeing it."

She pointed at a section of the daisy border to the right of the door frame. "She's painted a tiny ladybug family on most of the leaves: a grandma ladybug with white curly hair and a cane, a teacher ladybug holding a spelling book and wearing glasses and— my favorite—a little-girl ladybug wearing tap shoes. It always makes me think of you. Remember that talent show . . . ?"

I held up my hand. "Please. Don't go there. I'll have nightmares for months." I walked over to the border and peered closely at the leaves, seeing the anthropomorphic insects in various human occupations. They were beautiful, and clever, and painted by my own mother. "I had no idea . . ." I stopped, not wanting to be reminded again of how absent I'd made myself not only from my old life, but from my family that had continued on without me. It was the ultimate conceit, to believe that everything would stand still in my absence.

I returned to my seat at the table, where Mabry had set a glass of tea with a quarter of a lemon floating on top. She glanced up at the clock, and turned back to me as she sat down. "I have to leave for my shift in an hour, so that gives us a little time to catch up."

I looked at Ellis, who was happily shoveling Cheerios into his mouth with the flat of one hand while pushing a car back and forth on the table with the other, and then glanced around again at the cheery kitchen that reminded me of her mother, and I found myself nodding. "I don't think I can stay a whole hour, but long enough to catch up."

"Of course, that's assuming Jonathan gets home in time to watch Ellis so that I won't be late again. It's his day off, so he's playing golf with some of his friends from work. He's a bit addicted."

I took a sip of my tea, and studied my friend who, other than wearing her hair a little longer than she had in high school, looked exactly the same. "So, tell me about your dream."

She took a deep breath and then began strumming her fingers on the table. "Well, I was invited to a pool party by a friend—I couldn't tell you who since I didn't recognize her, just that she was a friend. There was a huge crowd, but nobody was in the pool. So, I jumped in and found that it was full of torpedoes, and it was my job to defuse them all so everybody else could swim."

I thought for a moment. "There's a lot going on there. I think I might need some time to figure that one out. Can I call you tomorrow?"

She nodded. "Sure. In my bedside table I've actually got a whole notebook of dreams I've had. I'll let you take a look."

"Sure," I said, although I wasn't really listening anymore. I was looking at the small part in her hair on the side of her head that shouldn't have been there.

She saw what I was looking at and turned her head so I could see it full on. "See? It's hardly noticeable."

I met her gaze and said the words that had needed to be said for nine long stupid years. "I'm sorry."

She sat back in her chair, shaking her head. "You saved my life, Larkin. You don't need to be sorry."

I rolled my eyes. "You wouldn't have landed in the water if I hadn't thrown the cooler at you and knocked you out of the boat."

Her face went very still. "But when everybody else was still trying to figure out what to do, you jumped in and brought me back to the surface."

I wanted to stand up and walk out of the kitchen and that house right then. Because this was the whole reason I'd been gone for so long. Why I'd left. And I thought I'd been done with it. But I wasn't. "Because of me, you had a concussion and spent the night in the hospital, and I was the one who never spoke to you again."

Her gaze drifted to her son, who was trying to Hoover up his Cheerios on the table without using his hands. "You had good reason to do what you did. I would have done the same thing if I'd been in your position."

My old anger, the self-directed anger that had made me leave when I was eighteen and never look back, poured through me. I pushed back my chair. "No, you wouldn't have. You wouldn't have had a reason to be in my position. You knew who you were. I was just the stupid chubby kid who thought I was Miss America, Albert Einstein, Liberace, and Britney Spears all rolled into one. And you and Bennett just went along for the ride, without telling me that I was making a fool of myself. That's why I've been angry with you and Bennett all these years. Because you knew and never told me."

She waited until I'd raised my eyes and met her gaze before she spoke. "You're wrong, you know. We never thought you were making a fool of yourself. Your free spirit was one of the reasons why Bennett and I loved you. The way you barged through life without caring what other people thought. It was amazing and heroic. I want Ellis to be like that. To try things whether or not he's good at them, or has the right talent. Because how do you ever know what your true calling is unless you've tried everything out?" She lifted her hands, palms out. "Despite your reasons for leaving, you packed up your stuff and moved by yourself to another state where you didn't know a soul. That, Larkin, is courageous and brave."

I snorted. "Acting like a fool is fine when you're a little kid. Then it just gets sad. Especially when your two best friends know the truth and keep you in the dark. And don't try to tell me that you didn't, because I won't believe you."

"Fine, don't. But it's the truth." She stood, her eyes studying me. "There was nothing between me and Jackson. You know that, right? Never. I would never have hurt you like that. I've always loved you like a sister. And what happened on the boat—I had no idea about any of it. I promise. You never gave me a chance to tell you that, so I'm telling you now. That's all in the past. You need to stop beating yourself up about it."

I wanted to tell her that it wasn't all in the past, that I still lived with it every day of my life. And that there was something she didn't know, that I couldn't tell her because it would make me seem even more pathetic than I was. I could never tell her about that part of me that craved attention and admiration that still flourished on the dark side of my heart, scratching to be let out, any more than I could admit that Jackson Porter could still make me forget everything I thought I'd learned.

"I've left it all behind me, Mabry. I've moved on to a new life. A new life that includes a tiny studio apartment in Brooklyn that I can barely afford, and a daily commute across a river that looks nothing like the Sampit, but it's mine. I don't lie to myself anymore. No more pretense that I was destined for greatness. I'm just . . . me."

I ruffled Ellis's hair. "Good to meet you," I said, shaking a grubby hand. Looking at his mother, I said, "Good to see you, Mabry. Maybe I'll see you again before I leave."

She lifted Ellis from his booster seat and followed me to the door. "You'd better. You need to tell me about my dream, don't forget. And you still owe me."

I stared back at her. "So much for everything being in the past and forgotten."

"Forgotten isn't the same as not remembered. I choose not to remember some things. But there are other things I'll never forget."

"Like how I almost killed you?"

She shook her head. "I'll never forget how much a part of my life you will always be."

My throat stung, and I turned away, heading down the front-porch steps.

She called, "That tap dance is something I'll never forget, though. Never."

I faced her, angry and hurt until I recognized her expression. It was the same one she and Bennett had worn the night of the talent show, standing and applauding next to Ceecee. It wasn't mocking or sarcastic. It seemed more like pride.

I almost told her then about the dream I'd had for the last two nights. A dream in which I was in

Mabry's childhood bedroom for a sleepover, but when I awoke, I discovered that she had grown up and moved away, and when I looked in the mirror, I was still a little girl. But I didn't tell her. Instead, I said, "Good-bye, Mabry."

Ellis raised his fist and waved. "Bye, Larkin."

I smiled at the sweet face that was so much like Bennett's. "Good-bye, Ellis."

"See you soon," Mabry said, closing the door before I could correct her.

fourteen

Ivy
2010

Larkin has brought me a small stereo of some sort. I'm sure it's not called a stereo anymore but something more modern and techy, but whatever it is, it's playing music from when I was younger. Larkin called it my playlist, and I heard her telling the nurses to make sure it was always playing during the day. She said she'd been doing research online and found out that music does wonderful things for people with Alzheimer's and brain injuries.

There's lots of Rolling Stones and Bob Dylan and the Beatles, and although I don't understand the science, I think Larkin's right. Because all of a sudden, my memories aren't black-and-white anymore. They're full, brilliant, rainbow-hued, and everything is real again. I see Ellis as he was at nineteen, and I'm happy because he's alive once more. I think I must be dreaming, because when he kisses me, the taste of honeyed biscuits lingers on my lips.

Larkin's heart is so big and beautiful. I wish I could take credit for it, but I can't. She's always been her own person, whether or not she sees it that way now. I guess, in a way, I can take credit for that. I spent so much of her childhood telling her to stop following me that she was forced to find her own path. Maybe everything I did wasn't a huge mistake. Larkin was forced to barrel through life with the single purpose of making herself known, but it was never done with a mean spirit. I think she wore blinders through her growing-up years, to block her from everything except what Ceecee told her was true. It's a good thing, too, or else she might have heard all the people telling her that she wasn't good enough to try things. Or maybe she did and just did it anyway. Larkin has always been the most strong-willed person I know. And I say that in a kind way.

My daughter is also brilliant. I need to thank Mack for that. I need to thank him for many things, like loving me even when I am at my most unlovable. We've both made mistakes, but never because we didn't love each other. That's another thing I've learned since lying here and trying to make sense of everything. Love and need are sometimes two completely different things.

I don't think the music's going to wake me up.

But I don't feel like I'm headed anywhere else any time soon, either. The bonds that are keeping me here are just as sticky as ever. I think I'm supposed to figure out how to let them go, but I haven't yet. Even more than I love listening to the stereo, I love that Larkin brought it to me. It makes me think that maybe we're not so very far apart after all.

Larkin takes my hand and raises it to her face, and I'm surprised to feel a wet tear dropping on my skin. I can see it from where I'm positioned up on the ceiling, but I can **feel** it. Maybe that means I'm waking up. The thought doesn't thrill me as much as it should. I'm afraid that if I do, I'll stop hearing the rumble of Ellis's car engine, idling as he waits for me at the curb like he used to all those years ago. Because then he'll be gone all over again. I nearly died from brokenness the first time, and I know I can't take it again.

"Mama?"

I'm surprised to hear a note of anger in her voice, like I'm about to get a telling-to, and if I could, I'd stand up and clap.

"I hope you can hear me. And I want you to know that I will wait until you wake up so we can finish this conversation. I just want to start now since there's so much I want to ask you. Yell at you, really. Like why you didn't want me to work at Gabriel's. You know how much I wanted to. And I could never understand why he kept saying no. It was you all along, afraid that I couldn't control myself." She places my hand gently on the bed beside me. "You're no better than Ceecee, trying to micromanage my life. I'd say that the apple doesn't fall far from the tree, but then that would mean I'm just like you both. And I'm not. Because I can tell people to their faces what I'm thinking. It didn't make me a lot of friends, but at least I'm honest. And it makes me good at what I do."

She frowns, and I want to tell her to stop, that she'll get wrinkles. But I can't.

"I really am good at my job, you know. You've never asked, so I guess you thought it was just another stupid hobby of mine or something, but I'm one of the best copywriters at Wax and Crandall. It's not the novel I always thought I'd write, but it's something I'm proud of."

Larkin stands to get a better look at me, gazing down at my face as if she imagined my eyes opening or something. They haven't.

"Advertising is a funny thing. You have to figure out what you don't want people to know so you can create something they want to hear. Maybe I should thank you and Ceecee for that. I have to have learned it somewhere."

She sits again and leans forward, her elbows on the edge of the bed and her chin resting on her hands. "I know about the fire at Carrowmore, and how Ceecee saved you. Bitty told me."

Larkin takes a deep breath. I hear it shudder like a boat's sails in strong wind, and I know she's trying to keep from crying. She's always hated to cry in front of people. I think I'm one of the only people who've ever heard her crying so hard, she has to press her face into the pillow so she can think that nobody can hear her. Even Ceecee. But I knew. Despite everything, I'm still her mama.

"You could have saved me a whole lot of trouble if you'd told me that little tidbit about your childhood. I won't even get started on the whole Ellis thing. How could you not have told me that you were married to Bennett and Mabry's uncle? Or that you threw a baby shower for Mabry and that they named the baby after your first husband?" She rubs her hands over her face with those beautiful slender hands that are just like mine. "But it's the fire that makes me angriest. Do you remember all those years when you had the nightmares about fire and you'd wake up screaming? I thought it was my job to figure out why you'd be dreaming about fires so I could help you and make them stop. What a complete waste of time. You must have thought it so funny, all the things I came up with to explain it, hoping that one of them might make you better."

Larkin stands again, her idle hands worrying themselves as she looks for something useful to do. Even as a girl, she'd always been a busy little bee, and it's not something she learned in New York. I think I'm mostly to blame.

I want to tell her that I'd never told her about the fire because I didn't remember it. Not until Mack had his affair. I'd always had a recurring nightmare about watching a house burn and knowing someone important to me was inside, burning with the walls and floors and furniture. But after I found out about Mack, the nightmares changed. It was like the pain and awareness of my own culpability in his infidelity were a key that turned a lock inside my head, waking up a part of my subconscious.

In these nightmares, instead of standing outside and watching the house burn, I suddenly was inside the house. And I could remember the heat, and the intense orange light, and the sensation of being carried. In the dream, I'd look up at the face above me, but I couldn't make out who it was, just a voice without a head telling me everything was going to be all right. Every time I had the nightmare, I'd stare into the place where the face should have been, and that was the part of the dream where I'd wake up screaming, as if I'd just seen something I shouldn't have.

So, no, Larkin, I didn't tell you about the fire. It has nothing to do with you, and everything to do with me and my past and how very much I didn't want to infect you with it. But it seems I've gone and done it anyway.

Larkin plucks a tissue from the box by my bed and scrubs at her eyes before loudly blowing her nose. How many times have I told her to be careful with the delicate area around her eyes because that's the first place that'll show wrinkles? And to try not to sound like a flock of sick geese when she blows her nose? I used to think she did it on purpose, just to annoy me. Now I think that it's just who she is, doing what needs to be done now without overthinking. How else could a person up and leave her home of eighteen years just like that, and never look back? As sad as it makes me, I'm so very proud of my baby girl.

She tosses the used tissue into the garbage can and begins pacing the room. "I feel guilty about feeling angry with you. I can't blame you for never telling me about your past, because I never bothered to ask about it. But I wish I'd known about Ellis. That would have explained so much. About you and Daddy. It doesn't excuse him, but maybe I wouldn't have been so angry with you. I'd always put you on such a pedestal—an example of a strong, independent woman that I wanted so badly to be. But then you stayed with him, even after he cheated on you. It made me mad. Or maybe I was just looking for an excuse to cut all ties when I left."

She stands and begins rearranging the flowers and plants on the deep windowsill, using a tissue to brush off the dust clinging to "get well" helium balloons. She leans down to smell the violet hydrangeas, closing her eyes for a moment and looking so beautiful silhouetted against the window that it makes my heart squeeze. Larkin looks at the card on the hydrangeas and smiles. They're from Carol Anne, my best friend. I remembered how the twins and Larkin were born in the same week, and how excited Carol Anne and I were to be raising our children together. We'd secretly planned for Bennett and Larkin to fall in love and get married, even going as far as planning what music would be played and what color the bridesmaids would wear. But the heart isn't so predictable.

For the first eighteen years of their lives, Bennett, Mabry, and Larkin were never separated longer than the time it took to be asleep. And even that rarely separated them. Though they did not happen on school nights, sleepovers at Ceecee's house and at Carol Anne's were as frequent as rainstorms in July. The children rarely came to my house, as if they knew I didn't want them there.

I would have loved the sound of running children or laughing teenagers and even the occasional slam of a door. But there was too much of Ellis in Bennett. It was there in the cowlick at the back of his head, and in the creases on his cheeks when he smiled, and the shape of his eyebrows. And, as they grew older, in the way he looked at Larkin. How when they walked, he'd stay close to her, and place his hand on the small of her back before going through a doorway. It was in the way he'd tilt his head close to hers so he wouldn't miss a word when she was talking.

But Larkin was always looking past him, or

through him, really, as if he weren't there. I probably taught her how to do that, too. Maybe Carol Anne and I shouldn't have thrown them together so much so that he'd become invisible to Larkin. Or maybe she'd spent her whole life studying me, a woman who was just about an expert in being completely oblivious to what was right in front of her face, believing something better lay just beyond.

Larkin heads toward the bathroom and fills the vase of Ceecee's roses with water and replaces it by my bedside before sitting down again, her eyes worried. The heels of her shoes are bouncing up and down beneath her chair, sounding like crabs clicking out a warning. "I found the two ribbons in the Tree of Dreams. You put them there, didn't you? I'm thinking it was you, because they both looked pretty new, and you had another one in your hand when we found you after your accident."

She stands again and starts pacing the room, rearranging chairs and restacking unread magazines on my bedside table. "I don't know what they mean, Mama. I need you to wake up and tell me. Who were you wanting to read those messages? Was it me? Or Ceecee?" She turns to face me, throwing her hands out like she used to when losing a game of Go Fish with Bennett and Mabry, like she couldn't believe she wasn't the undisputed winner.

"And why were you trying to remove Ceecee as trustee? Did you think she'd do something against my well-being? As for the insurance policy, you were the beneficiary, and it was all put in the trust. I hope you can hear this. I hope it can put your mind at rest a bit." She steps to the foot of my bed. "You know, if you'd ever called me in New York, you could have told me everything. And maybe you wouldn't be lying here in this bed, and I wouldn't be sick with worry over you. Over everything we've never said. I never knew what caring so much about a person was like, but I miss it now as if I did."

But you wouldn't have answered your phone. It was true, and it was yet another thing I couldn't blame her for, because she'd learned it from me. My decision to make her self-reliant and independent backfired, and I have no one to blame but myself.

I feel something warm trickling down my cheek, and when I look closely, I see that I'm crying. There is so much she doesn't know, so much I don't want her to know. I feel myself slipping back down into the body on the bed, a reminder that I'm still bound here, and for the first time, I feel as if I have to earn the right to leave. Only, I have no idea how I'm supposed to do that while I'm stuck here in this hospital bed.

A bell beeps somewhere, and several nurses rush in as Larkin jumps up and is forced to stand at the back of the room as they begin to fiddle with the machines that are connected to me with a hundred tubes. My chest feels like it's split apart, worse, maybe, than it did the day I got the news about Ellis. Right before the crumbling edges of the room fold in on themselves, I think of something Larkin just said. Something about finding two ribbons in the tree. My eyes flutter briefly, and I see the ugly ceiling overhead just as I remember that there should have been only one.

fifteen

Larkin
2010

I sat up in bed with a start, wondering what had awakened me. It was still dark, but pale light crept through the plantation shutters like pink spider legs scurrying across the wood floor and then crawling up the wall opposite my bed.

Tap. Tap. I heard the noise again, unsure what it was or where it was coming from. Still half-asleep, I slid from the high four-poster bed and stumbled to the door. I remembered the scare I'd had at the hospital earlier with my mother, and I felt a stiff chill invade my bones as I threw open my door, fully expecting to find Ceecee and Bitty standing there with sad faces.

Instead, I found the hallway completely empty

except for the night-light Ceecee always turned on when I visited so I could find my way to the bath-room at night without tripping on anything.

Tap. Tap. I turned around, more awake now, the sound coming from the window. I strode across the room, threw open the shutters, and peered down at the lawn. Bennett stood there with a handful of pebbles, looking up at me with a wide grin.

I shimmied the old window open, its swollen sash and wavy antique glass forcing me to go slowly. When I finally got it open high enough, I stuck the top half of my body through the opening. "What are you doing?" I asked, feigning annoyance.

I had every right to be annoyed. After tossing and turning throughout the night, constantly checking my phone to see if I'd missed a call from the hospital, I'd finally fallen asleep only an hour before. But there was Bennett, as familiar to me as the river, looking up at me with the smile that hadn't changed since he was a boy.

"I thought you might like to see the sunrise over the marsh before you leave. You once told me it was the most beautiful thing in the world."

He twisted his mouth slightly, as if waiting for me to say something. When I didn't, he reached down and picked up a Thermos from the ground next to him. "I brought coffee. And Mabry made mimosas that I have in the cooler on my johnboat. She had the early shift today, or else . . ."

I held my hand out to stop him. "You don't need to sell me anymore. You had me at coffee. Be down in ten."

I ducked back inside, closed the window, and slid the oversized T-shirt I slept in over my head. I tossed it on the floor in front of my opened and unpacked suitcase and grabbed a pair of running shorts and a running bra before heading to the bathroom to wash my face and brush my teeth. I considered for two whole seconds swiping on mascara and lipstick, but then I remembered it was only Bennett, who'd seen me looking far worse. I took a pair of old flip-flops from my closet, a pair I remembered from high school, then quietly descended the stairs while scraping my hair back into a ponytail. My feet automatically found the nonsqueaky spots on the old staircase, the movements embedded in my memory from many predawn adventures with Bennett and Mabry when we were younger. When we were still friends.

I let myself out the back door, waiting a moment for my eyes to adjust to the predawn light that transformed the wax myrtles and palmettos into spindly predators emerging from the river.

"You ready?"

Bennett's voice brought my attention to the path leading down toward our dock. I walked carefully toward him, watching my step on the uneven terrain. When I reached him, he held out his hand, and I took it without looking up. When we got to the boat, he set down the Thermos. "You remember how to get in without tipping the boat over?"

I wanted to give him some sharp remark, but when I finally looked up at him to speak, I'd completely forgotten what I was about to say. He was staring at me. Not exactly at **me,** but at the part of me below my neck that was wearing only skimpy shorts and a ratty running bra.

"I thought we were only going on the boat—if we're going someplace fancy, I can go change."

He opened his mouth, but when no words emerged, he just shook his head, then grabbed my hand tighter as I stepped into the johnboat and stood on the bottom of the boat instead of on one of the seats like a beginner would.

He set the Thermos inside the boat, before untethering it from the dock and settling into the seat behind me. I heard him clear his throat before speaking. "I, uh, it's a little chilly out on the water. You might want a T-shirt."

I turned around to see him rustling through a duffel bag and pulling out a red cotton T-shirt. "Sorry if it smells like fish—I keep it on the boat just in case I need a clean shirt, and then it sort of absorbs the smell of the boat."

I reached for it, noticing he wasn't meeting my gaze. "Yeah, you're probably right. It's been a while since I've done this." I slid the shirt over my head; it had a logo of a fish silhouette on the front, the words

I have to hold mine with both hands written be-neath it. "Nice shirt," I said, laughing.

For what was probably the first time in my life, I saw Bennett blush. He averted his head and began to dig into the bag again. "Mabry gave it to me." He pulled out a USC baseball hat and a matching visor. "Once the sun comes up, you're going to need it. I've got sunscreen, too."

"Thanks," I said, accepting the visor. "Remember how we used to get burned to a crisp when we'd go out fishing? I cringe, thinking about all that skin damage." I turned around to face him and pulled up the shirt to reveal my abdomen. "I have a tiny mole here that I get checked by a dermatologist once a year because of that horrible burn I got that time we went to North Island and I fell asleep lying on the beach."

When he didn't say anything, I looked up to see an odd expression on his face. "Are you all right?"

He nodded. "Fine. Just fine." He fiddled with the motor for a minute, and when it hummed to life, he headed out into the water without another word, looking more normal as he steered the boat away from the dock. I glanced back toward the marina and the hulking shapes of shrimp boats and sailboats and fishing boats, all bobbing sleepily on the gentle waves of the Sampit, unaware of the sun beginning its laborious rise behind them.

"Where are we going?" I asked as he headed toward the smaller creeks and waterways that couldn't be navigated by larger boats.

"I thought we'd go to one of the old flooded rice plantations. I spotted an osprey nest last time I was there. It's on a man-made platform right on the edge of the marsh, and I saw a single adult there. Probably the male, since he's the one who prepares the nest so it's all perfect for his mate when she returns from their winter retreat."

"Nice," I said. I'd never paid much attention to the shorebirds of my home, knowing I'd never be tested on my knowledge, or be expected to know anything about them except maybe for a bar trivia contest. Besides, Bennett and I had made a long-ago pact that if we ever did a trivia contest, we'd do it together so I could answer all the music questions, and he could answer all the bird trivia. Mabry would fill in on all the general stuff she knew from reading every magazine and newspaper.

Holding on to my visor, I tipped my face up toward the brightening sky, filling my lungs with the tangy salt air and feeling my ponytail tease my cheeks and the back of my neck. A large slender bird with a white chest and underwings, and a dark brown stripe at the edges, soared above us. "Look," I said, pointing at the familiar bird.

"An osprey," Bennett said. "When I saw that nest, I did a little research and came to the conclusion that Mabry should be thankful we're not ospreys."

I raised my eyebrows. "Without knowing much about ospreys, I could probably fill a page with reasons as to why she'd be thankful, but which one in particular are you thinking of?"

I could tell he was trying very hard not to smile, forcing a bored know-it-all expression to freeze his face. It was so familiar, and so "Bennett," that I could only feel enormously grateful that things weren't feeling odd between us anymore.

"Well, since you asked, osprey babies don't all hatch at the same time. There's usually about a five-day span between the oldest one hatching and the youngest. The oldest hatchling then pretty much lords it over his or her younger siblings. If there's plenty of food, it's not a problem, since there's enough to go around. But if there isn't, the oldest one will make sure that he gets the lion's share, and sometimes the younger ones will starve to death."

"Nice," I said. "Because you're what—five minutes older than Mabry?"

"Seven." He grinned at me, his familiar Bennett grin, and I relaxed. "And she'd better not forget it."

We grew silent as he made his way upriver, steering through small creeks and tributaries. I'd once known these waterways like the veins on my wrists, the curves and intersections altering only with the oncoming tide and returning when the water trickled back to the ocean. It had been so long, I wasn't sure I could navigate without losing my way, and I wondered how it had happened that I'd lost that important part of my childhood. I sat up, trying to pay attention to where Bennett was going as we passed through the black needlerush and spartina grass that rustled against the sides of the boat. We sped by tupelo trees and wide-hipped cypress draped with Spanish moss, cormorants preening on the dead branches, and it was as if I were traveling back in time to the Larkin I'd once been. A sharp twist of grief pulled at my heart. I sucked in a deep breath of marsh air, briny and moist, trying to clear my head.

I loved who I'd become. I did. Almost as much as I hated the old me. But not, I suddenly realized, all of the old me. I missed the girl who'd known these secret alleyways into the marshes and who could recognize the sounds of the different birds and open an oyster faster than anyone she knew. But I'd gotten rid of her along with the rest of me, and the grief I felt was raw and open.

"You okay?" Bennett asked as he slowed the boat, bringing it close to the edge of the creek, then turning off the engine.

"I'm fine. Just not used to this humidity, I think." I reached for the Thermos. "I'm going to have some coffee. Like some?"

"Please." He reached into his duffel and took out two Styrofoam cups. "Still drink it black?"

I nodded, pleased he remembered, and poured strong black coffee into each cup. He waited until I'd screwed on the lid before handing me mine. "See the nest?" he asked, indicating a tall platform on top of what looked a lot like a telephone pole. A pile of sticks, twigs, and grass covered the top, the panorama of the sky bleeding orange and purple into the marsh beyond it and making me wish I could paint it. To take it back with me and hang in my empty cubicle at work. It would be something of home.

"Yep, I see it. Should I go up and see if it meets with female approval?"

"You could. But if Daddy Osprey comes back while you're up there, I'm outta here."

"So much for Southern chivalry," I said, taking a sip of the hot coffee as he laughed.

"Aren't you going to start singing?" he asked. "You always used to sing that song 'Oh, What a Beautiful Morning' when we came out to watch a sunrise. It's hardly worth coming out all this way without the sound effects."

I raised my eyebrows. "There're about a million insects and tiny creatures out here right now, rubbing their wings together and doing all sorts of things with their little insect bodies to make noise. And all of them are better than me singing. I'd die if I spotted a fiddler crab using his giant claw to point and laugh."

He snorted. "Well, I think you have a great voice."

"You're also tone deaf."

"So you don't need to be shy about singing in front of me. You never used to be. I remember a talent show . . ."

"Stop," I said. "Just stop. And if you mention it again, I will pour the entire Thermos of hot coffee in your lap, and then you'll never have children."

"That would be a shame," he said, the color of his eyes shifting in the growing light.

He'd let the boat bob and drift with the incoming tide, the water moving us toward an ancient rice-field trunk, a wooden gate used to control water flow from reservoirs into the fields. The plantation was long gone, but this ancient relic clung to its spot in the marsh, facing tide after tide. I felt suddenly flustered, unsure why. I picked up the Thermos to give me something to do and poured more coffee into my half-full cup, spilling most of it into the bottom of the boat, but miraculously missing my fingers and leg.

Bennett reached over and took the Thermos from me. "Burn yourself?"

I shook my head, looking into my cup, and took a tentative sip. "Sorry about the boat."

He laughed, at least recognizing the joke. This was the same boat he'd had when we were in high school, the only cleaning it ever got the occasional hosing out, then flipping it over on a dry dock. It was like an unspoken agreement among South Carolina fishing hobbyists that to have a spanking clean boat was somehow unmanly. Beyond the scent of fish that never went away, I was pretty sure that if I looked closely in the crevices behind the planked seats, I could find remnants of my old candy bar wrappers.

We sipped our coffee in silence, listening to the insects and tiny unseen creatures that were preparing themselves for the incoming tide. A pale white periwinkle snail shared the top of a nearby long stem of spartina grass with a grasshopper, both trying to escape the incoming water-bound predators. They'd descend to the marsh again once the tide went out, but for now, they were temporary roommates. I remembered more than once seeing the marsh at high tide from a bridge and having to look twice to see that what first appeared to be a cotton field with round puffs of white sitting atop green stalks was actually those snails perched in their ancient method of self-preservation.

In silence, we faced east where the rounded edge of yellow sun began to nudge its way up into the sky, like a pat of butter spreading in a hot pan.

"Have you talked with your dad?" Bennett asked without looking at me. Experience had taught us that the sun was impatient, and if you looked away, you'd miss its grand entrance.

I thought guiltily of the unanswered texts and phone calls, of the quick avoidances in the hospital corridor as we entered and left my mother's room. "No. I need to, I know. It's just with everything going on . . ."

"Yes, you need to. I don't think this should wait much longer."

"I don't understand the rush. I think we should wait until Mama wakes up and figure out what to do then."

He glanced at me briefly before returning his gaze to the sky. "The developers are getting impatient. They've got you on their radar now and will probably contact you next."

I sat up quickly, nearly spilling coffee again. "What? But I'm hardly the expert on the best way to proceed. The property might be held in trust for me, but I don't know the first thing about it, or what's the best way to move forward."

"I know. Don't worry, though. Nothing's going to happen without Ceecee's or your mother's agreement. Or yours." He took a sip from his cup. "While we're waiting for your mother to wake up, if it's all right with you, I want to bring in someone who knows about historical structures, Dr. Sophie Wallen-Arasi. She's a professor of historic preservation at the College of Charleston and can let us know if enough of the house is salvageable. If it is, it might help you and your family better decide what to do with the property."

I shrugged, watching as the half-moon of light grew larger on the horizon, setting the water around us on fire. "I suppose. Although it's hard to believe that this has anything to do with me."

"Really? You're a Darlington, you know. And Carrowmore has been owned by the Darlingtons since before Lafayette landed in Georgetown. Not to sound overly dramatic, but that house and land are a part of not only your history, but the history of this country. Doesn't that mean anything to you?"

"No," I said quickly, not sure if I was saying that because it really didn't, or because I was angry with Bennett for sucking me into this family drama that I felt a part of no matter how much I didn't want to.

"Well, I'll let you know when she's coming, and you can decide if you want to meet with her. No pressure. I'm going to ask your dad and Ceecee, too. That way, when your mother wakes up, we'll have all the facts to put in front of her so you can all be informed before any agreement is made."

The sun chose that moment to burst fully up over the horizon, flooding the marsh with its warm light and startling a flock of egrets into flight, their graceful wings like check marks against the blue sky.

I must have made a sound, because Bennett looked at me and smiled. "It's the most beautiful place in the world."

"I've missed this." I swept my arm over the side of the boat, meaning to indicate the marsh and the sky and the whole watery world around us.

He kept his eyes on me for a long moment, as if waiting for me to say more. When I didn't, he finished his coffee and threw the cup away in a small trash can he'd attached to the side of the boat. "Mabry's mimosas are in the cooler behind you if you're interested. I think I'm good with just the coffee."

I turned to look at the cooler, the euphoria of the last few moments completely gone and replaced by an odd restlessness. "I think I'll pass, too. I have a conference call with my office at nine, and I'll need all my brain cells."

Bennett nodded, then gently guided us out of our secret corner of the marsh and headed back to Georgetown. I turned around on the seat so my back was to him, but not before I noticed how the bright light of morning filtered through his dark hair, turning the tips to gold.

When we reached my dock, he tied up the boat and helped me out, his hands strong and warm. "Thanks," I said, feeling oddly awkward with him. "For the coffee. And the sunrise." I half smiled, then felt the smile fade when he didn't return it.

"What is it?" I asked. He didn't look surprised by my question. We'd always been able to read each other, doing away with unnecessary words that would have formed the bridge between thoughts.

"Jackson said he asked you to dinner tomorrow night. On a date."

"Yes," I said slowly.

He narrowed his eyes a little. "Are you sure you want to do that?"

I bristled. "Yes, I'm sure. And I don't really think it's any of your business. Besides, I thought you two were friends."

"We are. That's why I'm telling you I don't think

it's a good idea. He's, uh, he's got a reputation with women." He looked at me closely. "He likes them a lot."

"Well, that's a relief, seeing as how I'm a woman. I'm going to dinner with him, not marrying him." I stepped back toward the house, eager to end this conversation.

"That's a relief. Because I swear I remember you telling everyone you know since you were in grade school that you were going to marry Jackson Porter."

Heat rose to my face, and I wished I hadn't left the visor on the boat, needing its shade now more than before. "I was a little girl, Bennett. I also used to tell people that I was going to be the next Leontyne Price, and I could have sworn I remember you telling anyone who would listen that you wanted to be a truck when you grew up."

He set his lips together in disapproval. "Yeah, well, just be careful. Don't forget how he wasn't so nice to you back in the day."

"That was a long time ago. We're both completely different people now."

Bennett stood there, shaking his head. "Are you? He certainly hasn't changed, and you, well, once we get past the glossy exterior, you're still the same girl craving attention from the wrong guy."

"Seriously?" I said, almost spitting with anger. "Are you saying he's only interested in me because I look better now than I did back then?"

"In a word? Yes. Jackson's not very deep. He's made a science out of skimming on life's surface and is quite happy that way. For the record, I always liked you, and I still do—although I shouldn't. I'm still a little ticked off that you left without saying good-bye and didn't keep in touch, but I'm also full of admiration for you because you did."

His words took the sting out of my anger, and I saw him once again as my lifelong friend who knew all my secrets—almost all of them—and liked me still. He knew how I loved watching the sunrise over the marsh and that I drank my coffee black. That my favorite color was yellow and that I hated green beans and watching tennis on television.

"Thank you," I said tightly, swallowing my anger. "I appreciate your concern—I do. But I'm old enough to take care of myself."

He nodded silently, realizing there was nothing else he could say to dissuade me. Among all the things he knew about me was that once I made up my mind about something, there was no turning back.

"I guess I'll see you around," I said, preparing to head up the dock toward the house.

"One more thing," he said, his hand rubbing the back of his neck. That always meant that he was thinking of the right way to present something his listener might find objectionable. "I visited Carrowmore yesterday to take some pictures and look at it more closely. I'm not going to lie to you—it looks pretty bad. Even stuff not burned in the fire has since been rotting in the wet climate. Not to mention the collapsed roof that allowed in a lot more of the elements than I'd say is healthy for an old house."

I was about to say something flippant about bringing in a bulldozer to put the house out of its misery, but the look on his face stopped me. He'd always been fascinated with old houses and old buildings, dragging Mabry and me on explorations of abandoned properties in Georgetown County and then farther afield when he'd earned his driver's license. It occurred to me that he'd found a way to corral his passion into a career that not only suited him but made him thrive. I felt an odd stirring of jealousy that both he and Mabry had succeeded where I hadn't. When we were growing up together, it had always been a foregone conclusion that I would be the one with all the boxes checked next to my goals and aspirations, yet here I was without a single check mark.

"It kind of reminds me of you."

I'd been too busy feeling sorry for myself and hadn't been listening until he said that. "What does?"

"The house. Carrowmore."

"Because it's a complete ruin?" I looked closely at Bennett to see if he was joking or just intentionally insulting me.

"No. I think because it's been waiting a long time to be rediscovered. To find its place in the world again. For people to recognize its strength and beauty."

"Like a phoenix, rising from the ashes," I said sarcastically.

He didn't laugh. "Sort of. There was something else that I noticed while I was there. The purple martin houses—someone's been tending them."

"How can you tell?"

"They're all pretty clean, and martins don't do that by themselves. It had to be a person."

I recalled the feeling of something nagging me the last time I was there, something that hadn't made sense. I realized now it was the martin houses. "Must have been Ceecee," I said.

He shook his head. "I already asked her. So I thought it might have been your mother. Except . . ."

"Except what?"

"Well, I found a ball of twine and two brand-new and cleaned gourds on the back porch today, and they definitely weren't there the last time I was there. So it couldn't have been."

"That is odd," I said. "But not earth-shattering. She must have a friend who took it upon herself—or himself—to take care of them while Mama's in the hospital."

"True. Guess I should ask my own mother."

I nodded. "Thanks again, Bennett, for the boat ride. I really enjoyed it."

He grinned broadly. "Me, too. Only thing that might have made it better would be if you'd sung that song." He shoved his hands into the pockets of his jeans. "Mama says hey, by the way. She'd love for you to come for supper sometime before you go back to New York. She's into all that healthy cooking now, so I can't promise anything tasty, but the invitation stands. I'm staying with them for a little bit, by the way. I can work remotely and avoid the trip back and forth from Columbia until we figure out what we're doing at Carrowmore. Just thought you'd want to know, in case you needed to reach me. And when you're ready to return my T-shirt."

I looked down at the red shirt I'd borrowed and took hold of the hem, getting ready to give it back.

"Don't," he said quickly, his eyes widening briefly. "I mean, it's still chilly. And I'm sure you'll want to wash it first."

"Right," I said, embarrassed. "Sorry—of course I'll want to wash it. Thanks again," I said, waving before turning around.

"Sure wish I could have heard you singing, though."

I kept walking until I reached the porch steps, and then, because we were old friends and there'd be no judging, I began belting out the words, "Oh, what a beau-ti-ful morning . . ."

I could still hear him laughing as I let the door snap shut behind me.

sixteen

Ceecee
2010

Ceecee stood at the kitchen sink, rinsing her skillet and peering out the window toward the dock. She couldn't hear anything—dang old age!— but Larkin and Bennett were apparently having a heated argument. Except when Ceecee heard the back door slam shut, Larkin was definitely singing. Not exactly in tune, but close enough.

"I hope you're hungry," she called out, bringing Larkin into the kitchen. Even without makeup and with windblown hair, and wearing a ridiculously oversized T-shirt, Larkin was stunning. She looked so much like Margaret that Ceecee had to lean against the counter until she remembered that her friend was truly gone.

"I'm starving," Bitty said from the doorway, clutching a pack of cigarettes and a lighter. "Smells like bacon and eggs."

"And cheese grits," Ceecee said as she picked up the bowl and brought it to the adjacent dining room.

"Actually, I thought I'd go for a run first before my conference call at nine," Larkin said, eyeing the platter of bacon and scrambled eggs, made with lots of cheese, just as she liked them.

"You have plenty of time to eat now and let it sit in your stomach a bit. Besides, you'll need your energy to go running, sweetheart. Sit down and I'll bring you some fresh-squeezed orange juice and coffee."

"Well, maybe if I just eat a little bit," Larkin said as she pulled out a chair next to Bitty.

Ceecee shook her head. "I don't know why you don't just exercise with Jack LaLanne on the television like I used to."

"Probably because he's retired," Bitty interjected.

Ceecee frowned in her friend's direction before turning back to Larkin. "Your daddy said he'd stop by, too."

Larkin looked at Ceecee with alarm. "Is everything all right with Mama?"

"Everything's fine," Ceecee said calmly. "The episode she had yesterday when you were with her was just an anomaly, the doctors are saying. Her brain activity spiked somehow as if she were regaining consciousness, and then returned to where it's been. But she's not worse. We have to remember that, and keep praying that she'll get better and wake up."

"So why's Daddy coming over?" Larkin asked.

"Because he wants to see you, and he thinks you've been avoiding him." Ceecee headed for the kitchen to retrieve the coffeepot. She must have missed the knock on the front door because of Bitty's coughing, but Mack tapped on the door frame of the dining room to let them know he was there. After a brief hesitation, he approached Larkin and kissed the top of her head before retreating to the chair opposite his daughter's and sitting down.

"Looks like you got some sun," he said, smiling at Larkin.

"Bennett took me out in his johnboat this morning. He remembered how much I loved the sunrises."

Mack raised his eyebrows, an unspoken question. Ignoring him, Larkin reached for the eggs and handed the platter to Bitty. "Would you like some?"

They made small talk while everyone served themselves. Ceecee watched as Larkin placed food on her plate, then poured herself a cup of coffee. Sipping it carefully, Larkin looked over the brim. "Bennett said somebody's been taking care of the martin houses at Carrowmore. It wasn't Mama, because he found some fresh twine and things after Mama went into the hospital. Considering how abandoned the whole place is, we thought it was strange."

Ceecee's expression didn't change. "It wasn't me.

And until we found Ivy there, I didn't think any-body had been there for years. Have you asked Carol Anne?"

Larkin shook her head. "No, but Bennett said he'd ask—although I sincerely doubt it's her. It's just . . . odd."

Ceecee leaned back in her chair. "Maybe not. There's a legend about the martins and Carrow-more. That as long as there are martins living on the grounds, there will always be a Carrowmore."

"Like the ravens at the Tower of London?" Mack asked, spearing a slice of bacon from the platter.

"Exactly. I'm guessing someone who knows the leg-end has been tending them. I'd like to know who—so I can thank them at least."

Bitty began another coughing fit and pushed her chair from the table. "Excuse . . . me . . . ," she man-aged, backing out of the room but not before picking up her cigarettes and lighter.

"You're going outside for a smoke?" Ceecee asked indignantly.

"You won't . . . let me smoke . . . inside," Bitty said from the doorway.

"You need to go to the doctor," Larkin said, her face full of concern.

Bitty finished with another coughing spasm, then said, "He'll just say that I should quit smoking, and I already know that. This way, I save myself the money and the aggravation." She left the room then, heading toward the back door, the sound of her coughing trailing in her wake.

They were silent for a moment while Larkin took a small bite of eggs from her plate and chewed thoughtfully. "Why do you think Mama had this sudden interest in the trust and the insurance money?"

Ceecee fought hard to keep her face calm, to lift her fork to her mouth and chew, but the food might as well have been cardboard for all she tasted. "I don't know. I didn't realize she remembered Carrowmore at all. I hadn't taken her there since she was a little girl. I thought she'd forgotten all about it until you were born and she decided to set up a trust for you."

Mack placed his hands carefully on each side of his plate, and Ceecee noticed he wore his gold wedding band, something he hadn't done in a long time. "Bennett and I were thinking it's because of the developers who are showing interest in the property, and she was trying to establish its value for Larkin's benefit."

Ceecee slowly placed her fork on her plate, trying to come up with the right words. "I spoke with the developers once but only because they approached me, and only to hear what they had to say. Ivy must have found out that I had, but she never came to talk to me about it."

"Then why?" Larkin asked. "And it wasn't spur-of-the-moment, either. Jackson told me she recently came to see him about the insurance payout."

"She did?" Ceecee asked, pouring herself a cup of coffee and spilling most of it in her saucer.

"According to Jackson."

"Did he think she seemed upset?"

"No—he didn't mention it," Larkin said. "So, you have no idea what all that was about?"

"Not at all. But you know how your mother is. Always looking for something that might distract her into thinking she's happy. For all we know, she wants Carrowmore to be turned into an artists' colony, and she thought you would be more likely to agree to it than I would."

Larkin frowned. "I doubt it. This really makes no sense. I guess it's just another thing I need to ask her about when she wakes up."

Ceecee shared a glance with Mack, then reached over and squeezed Larkin's hand. "You're right, baby. We'll just have to wait and ask."

After the breakfast dishes were cleared away, and Mack had gone to the hospital and Larkin on her run, Ceecee carried two cups of coffee out onto the porch for her and Bitty. Placing a cup on the coffee table, Ceecee moved away the cigarettes and lighter, ignoring her friend's protests.

She sat down across from Bitty, sipping her coffee. "I know you heard every word—you left the door open on purpose. What do you think was in Ivy's head?"

"You're her mother, so you know her best," Bitty

said with innocent eyes. "At least that's what you're always reminding me." She regarded her friend for a moment. "I wonder if it has anything to do with the ribbon she had in her hands when they brought her to the hospital. It said something about Margaret."

"'I know about Margaret.' That's what it said." Ceecee stared at the dark coffee in her cup. "Ivy's always known her mother died in that fire. I can't imagine what else she thinks she knows."

Bitty stared at her, unblinking. "Besides the obvious?" She started to laugh, but it came out more like a bark. "If she knows, she didn't find out from me, and if you didn't tell her, then it's impossible. We should tell her, though, when she wakes up. Not that it will make any difference, of course."

Ceecee took a gulp of her coffee, scalding her tongue. "I've only wanted the best for Ivy—you know that. To protect her from all the hurts life can throw at you. But somehow, I failed. Except for when she was with Ellis and after Larkin was born, I've never seen her truly happy."

Unexpectedly, Bitty reached over and squeezed her hand. "I don't think Margaret could have done any different, if that makes you feel better. And I think she would have approved of the choices you've made."

"But do you think she would have forgiven me?" Ceecee hadn't meant to say that, to blurt out those words she'd never spoken out loud before.

"For what?" Bitty asked, her brown eyes still as

dark and probing as they'd been when they were girls.

Ceecee looked away, wanting to ask Bitty about her coughing or anything other than her question. She lifted her chin and met her friend's gaze. "For not saving her."

Bitty squeezed her hand again, then stood, her coffee untouched. "But you saved her baby, and for that I know she'd be grateful. I hope you know that."

Ceecee nodded without looking up, something thick and unrelenting blocking her throat.

Bitty grabbed her cigarettes and lighter. "I'm headed to the hospital. I expect I'll see you there at some point."

Ceecee nodded slowly. "She's still there, you know. Our Ivy. She's lying there without moving or speaking, but I can tell she's there. And she's listening, and I know she's trying to communicate. I just don't know how I'm supposed to hear her. It's like when she was a little girl and having her nightmares, and there was nothing I could do to help her."

"She'll need your help when she wakes up. She'll need all of us. And we'll be there for her."

"But what if she doesn't?" Ceecee forced the words out, her voice barely audible so that only her oldest friend could hear her unacceptable doubt.

"She will," Bitty said with conviction. "She's a Darlington. Remember what Margaret used to tell us? Something about Darlingtons setting the sun and the moon in the sky so that light always shone upon them. There's been an eclipse for a long time, but it's about to be over. I can feel it."

Ceecee sat up and straightened her shoulders, taking in Bitty's wide gauzy pants and worn leather sandals, a hundred paint flecks giving them color. It made her realize how much of Bitty was in Ivy, too. How both Ceecee and Bitty had honored their friend by being the best mothers to Margaret's daughter that they knew how. But if Ceecee had learned anything in the intervening years since Margaret's death, it was that a thousand good intentions could never tip the scale over one unforgivable mistake.

"I hope you're right," Ceecee said. "Because I don't know how I'll survive if something happens to Ivy."

Bitty gripped her box of cigarettes tightly, the sound of crumpled cardboard overruling the whirring of a cicada in a magnolia at the edge of the garden. "You'll survive, Ceecee. All the love you keep inside your heart holds you up and forces you to go on. It's how you've always made it through, and I can't see it deserting you now."

Bitty made to leave, but Ceecee called out to her. "What about you? What makes you keep moving forward when things are so dark?"

Bitty looked down at her crumpled cigarettes as if just realizing what she was holding. "Regret," she said, her voice raspy.

"Regret? Regret for what?"

Bitty met Ceecee's gaze. "For a lot of things.

Mostly for not being strong enough to tell Margaret no when that's what she needed to hear." She turned and left without waiting for a response, her hacking cough eventually cut off by the slamming of her car door.

Ceecee picked up her coffee cup and took a sip, not caring that it had grown cool. She needed something to hold on to, something to keep her hands steady. She thought about what Bitty had said about the Darlingtons and the moon and the sun. Ceecee took another sip, then closed her eyes and remembered.

Ceecee
1951

The last notes of "Let It Roll Again" drifted out on the dance floor as the couples, sweating and laughing, collapsed onto one another and slowly made their way to the stairs leading down from the top floor of the Pavilion. After two weeks of being together every day, it was their last night in Myrtle Beach, and Ceecee found herself clinging tighter to Boyd's arm as he led her outside into the cooler air.

"I wish we didn't have to leave," she said, embarrassingly close to tears. "I don't know how I can face tomorrow without seeing you."

He lifted her chin with his finger. "We'll be together again soon," he said, sealing the deal with a gentle kiss on her lips. "We've already talked about this, Sessalee. I just need a week to go home for a bit, and see my parents, and talk to them about my plans."

"Which include moving to Georgetown." Ceecee didn't make it a question because she simply couldn't imagine it any other way.

He smiled indulgently. "I've already sent a letter to Dr. Griffith and have asked my supervising doctor who oversaw my internship to forward a letter of recommendation to him. I expect a reply to be waiting for me when I get home to Charleston."

Ceecee felt so giddy, she wanted to jump up and down, but she didn't want to appear childish. Boyd was older than she was, had been to war and graduated from medical school. She needed to give at least the outer appearance of being wiser than her years. "I know Mr. Darlington will say wonderful things about you, too. They're old family friends. All the more reason for you to hurry and come to Georgetown."

He smiled, and for a moment Ceecee thought she might be drowning on dry land, because when he smiled like that, she found it difficult to breathe. "Anything for you, darling. I hope I'll have the opportunity to meet your parents while I'm there as well."

She had to grab both of his arms so she wouldn't swoon. "I'd like that very much."

"And if you really get lonely, I think you've taken

about a thousand photographs with that camera of yours—hopefully there's one or two of me for you to look at."

He grinned, making her lean up and kiss him again. "One or two, I'm sure." Sobering, she said, "I have a huge favor to ask of you."

He pulled her close. "Anything, darling. Just ask."

"It's not for me—it's for Margaret. You're driving to Charleston with Reggie tomorrow, and I'd like to ask you to use the time to try to talk Reggie out of joining the army. I know what you said before, but I promised Margaret that I would ask you to at least try."

His beautiful eyes met hers. "I don't think I can convince him, and I'm not sure if it's even my place to try, but I'll do anything to make you happy."

"Oh, my dearest darling." She stood on her toes so her lips could meet his. "I do love you so much, you know." She bit her lip, unsure if she should have been so outspoken, to have said such a thing before he'd said it first. Margaret had taught her and Bitty never to be the first to say it.

His face became very serious, and Ceecee stood back hard on her heels. "I'm very glad to hear that," he said, his gaze locked with hers. "Because I've loved you from the first moment I saw you at the gas station. There was something about the way you walked, and the sweet smile on your face, and your gorgeous mouth with that red lipstick. I remembered thinking to myself that I'd met the woman I wanted to spend the rest of my life with. What do you think of that?"

She threw her arms around his neck, not caring who saw, and kissed him long and hard on the mouth.

"What would your mother say?" came a familiar voice behind them.

As if waking up from a long nap, Ceecee cleared her head to look at Bitty, who was offering them each a Tootsie Roll from her bag. "These will give you something else to do with your mouths that won't shock little children." Her voice was stern, but she was smiling.

"Where's Margaret?" Ceecee asked, looking around at the people still exiting the Pavilion.

"She told me to tell you two that she and Reggie would meet you at the movie theater—the movie she wants to see is playing at the Gloria right across the street from here. Margaret was hungry, so she and Reggie were grabbing a bite to eat and asked that you save them a seat."

Ceecee frowned. "I hope they're not too late—it was her idea to see the movie. I don't know anything about it."

Bitty lit a cigarette and took a long draw. "It's called **Night Train to Berlin.** I think it was directed by a friend of Margaret's uncle—a Carroll Goring. It's based on Robert Langford's latest novel." She blew out a puff of smoke before regarding Ceecee with a half smile. "Which you should read instead of the latest edition of **Vogue.**"

Bitty was in a fractious mood, most likely because, even though she'd spent the evening dancing with different partners, none of them had been "keepers," as Bitty put it. Too old, too young, too fat, too skinny. Too many freckles, not enough freckles. That sort of thing. Margaret had whispered to Ceecee that it was really because Bitty was so much smarter than the average man that it would take someone with more than a stellar ability to dance to impress her and make it worth her while to spend time with him.

"Fine." Feeling magnanimous, Ceecee slipped between Boyd and Bitty and placed a hand in the crook of their elbows. "We'll just go to the movie theater and save them seats. And if they don't show, we'll tell them how it ended and ruin it for them."

Boyd laughed, placing his hand over hers, and left it there while they walked to the theater.

Two hours later, there was still no sign of Margaret or Reggie. They waited outside the theater for another fifteen minutes, and when they still hadn't shown up, Boyd reassured her and Bitty that Margaret was in good hands and that he would drive them home.

The three of them sat in the front seat, with Ceecee in the middle. "Make sure you leave room for the Holy Ghost," Bitty said, indicating the lack of a space between Ceecee and Boyd. "Isn't that what your father would say?"

Ceecee slapped her friend lightly on the arm, then moved even closer to Boyd.

They'd expected the lights to be on in the house when they returned, but it sat dark and empty, only the moonlight guiding their way up the white brick walkway. Ceecee walked through the house, flipping on lights and calling Margaret's name, Boyd right beside her.

When they'd made the rounds of the small house, Boyd touched her elbow. "Don't worry, all right? I'm sure they've just lost track of time and she'll show up any minute. They've got a lot to talk about."

Ceecee nodded, not completely able to get rid of her uneasiness. "Will you call me if you get back and Reggie is there?"

"Of course. And you let me know when Margaret shows up. No matter how late."

He kissed her on the forehead, aware of Bitty watching, then headed toward the door. He turned around once and winked at her. "And I'll see you in Georgetown as soon as I can make it."

Unable to bear the thought of not kissing him in a proper good-bye, Ceecee raced across the room and threw herself at him, making sure he was aware of just how much she would miss him. He let her go, and she slowly backed away across the room, then mouthed, **I love you.**

Bitty rolled her eyes and looked away in time for Boyd to say it, too, before closing the door behind him.

Ceecee and Bitty got ready for bed, Ceecee taking the time to press her skirt and blouse, knowing her mother would notice if she was unkempt in any way, and then pin-rolled her hair before slipping on the sleeping cap her mother had packed for her, but which she hadn't put on once. She'd have to be careful that her mother didn't see her in a state of undress, because her suntan carried the damning evidence of the two-piece bathing suit Margaret had let her wear. It was modest for a two-piece, but her mother would probably have a heart attack if she knew that Ceecee had bared her midriff for everyone to see.

Although she had been keeping busy, a growing worry had lodged itself in the pit of Ceecee's stomach. She'd even called Boyd twice to make sure he remembered to call her if he heard anything from Reggie. She avoided looking at Bitty, afraid to see her worry mirrored in her friend's eyes. Margaret could be full of brash bravado, but she would never gamble with her reputation. That was one thing Ceecee and Bitty could agree on.

It was nearly one o'clock in the morning before she and Bitty finally decided to turn in for the night. They left the front room lights on, as well as the hall bath light, and both left their doors open so they'd hear Margaret when she came in. The only peace of mind they had was an earlier phone call from Boyd to let them know that Reggie hadn't made it home, either, leaving their friends to assume they were at least together wherever they were. Before turning off her light, Ceecee said a prayer that Margaret wouldn't be doing anything she might regret, that last word lingering in her head long after the room was plunged into darkness.

The slamming of a car door around seven o'clock the following morning awakened Ceecee. By the time she'd slid on her robe and made it to the front room, Margaret was leaning against the closed door, a serene smile on her lips. A smile that Ceecee's mother would have said looked like that of a cat that had drunk all the cream.

"Where have you been all night?" Ceecee asked as she led Margaret to the sofa. Bitty joined them, perching herself on Margaret's other side.

"Everywhere," Margaret said, her smile never fading. "We walked forever, it seems, and we talked. It was our last night together, and we had so much we wanted to say to each other."

"That's all you did? Walk and talk?" Bitty raised a cynical eyebrow.

Margaret's smile became secretive. "Maybe."

"Maybe?" Bitty nudged her with her elbow. "You've got to do better than that. What else did you do?"

Margaret's cheeks flushed a flattering shade of pink, and Ceecee noticed how unkempt her hair was, how her mascara and blush had been all but wiped off, and her skirt and blouse looked as if they'd been slept in.

"We went to a hotel." She lost her smile as she sent a surreptitious glance at each of her friends.

Ceecee's hand went to her own throat. "Oh, Margaret. A **hotel**?"

Margaret nodded. "It was a cheap, awful place, in a terrible part of town where Reggie was sure they wouldn't ask any questions. But I didn't care—I didn't. I just wanted to be with him. Mother would have been horrified that I'd ever set foot in such a place."

Bitty's lips quirked up in a lopsided smile. "There're a lot more things about this whole scenario that would upset your mother, I think." She elbowed Margaret again. "And then what did you do?"

Ceecee wanted to shout at Bitty that it was none of her business, that she was sure Margaret had acted like a lady. But she could tell by the look on Margaret's face that whatever had happened in that hotel room, acting like a lady had not been part of it.

Bitty placed both of her hands on Margaret's shoulders and turned her so that they were face-to-face. "Did you . . . ?"

Margaret kept her gaze focused on her hands, folded neatly in her lap, and nodded.

Ceecee leaped from the sofa and squatted in front of her friend. "Did he ask you to marry him at least?"

"Of course he did. He asked me twice while we were walking and once after . . ." Margaret looked up, her blue eyes blazing. "He wanted to elope last night."

"And you didn't?" Ceecee asked, horrified. "He was ready and willing to make an honest woman of you, and you said no?"

Bitty looked up at the ceiling in exasperation. "Really, Ceecee? That's all you can think about? Why can't it be about Margaret making **him** an honest man?"

Ignoring Bitty, Ceecee grabbed Margaret's hands and shook them. "Why did you say no?"

Margaret's entire face and body crumpled like a used handkerchief. "Because I can't stand the thought of him going off to fight, of him being in danger, and of me waiting every day for news. I thought I could make him change his mind if I gave him the choice. Either me or the army. I can't . . ." She burst into tears, burying her face in Bitty's shoulder. "I just can't bear it."

"And what did Reggie say?" Ceecee persisted.

Margaret spoke between sobs. "He said he loved me, but that he also loved his country, that he had big plans for our future—together. And that he thought he could do right by both of us. He said he needed some time to think, to consider his options. When he dropped me off a little while ago, I was so confident that he'd do the right thing by me, but the more I think about it, the more I think I've made a terrible mistake."

Ceecee was inclined to agree, but now wasn't the time or place to mention that to Margaret. Right now, Margaret needed their support, regardless of how they felt. Sitting back down on the couch, Ceecee picked up her friend's hand, the skin clammy and cold. "When did Reggie say he'd let you know?"

Margaret took a moment to steady her voice before answering. "He said he would go home to Charleston to see his family as planned. I do know his father's not keen on him joining the army right now, either. He'd much rather have him take his place in the family law practice. And then he'd come up to Georgetown with Boyd to see me and meet my parents. I'm hoping we can make it an engagement party."

"What about college?" Bitty said. "You've been accepted at Wellesley. Doesn't that mean anything to you?"

Margaret's eyes became cloudy, not with tears but with what Ceecee thought were dreams. "Not anymore. I'm in love, Bitty. Maybe one day you'll know what it's like and will understand how you'll do anything to be with the person you love."

"Gosh, I sure hope not," Bitty said, snatching up her package of cigarettes from a side table and thumping one out into her hand.

Ceecee sent a harsh glance at Bitty before focusing again on Margaret. "It would be nice to have Reggie and Boyd in Georgetown together. That will make the celebration even more special—to have us all together just like we've been the last two weeks."

Margaret nodded. "And I'm hoping Boyd will be able to talk some sense into Reggie."

Ceecee sat back against the sofa, unwilling to take sides. She was proud of Boyd's service, and she did believe being a veteran meant something about a man, about his sense of honor and duty. But she couldn't imagine the pain of being left behind while the love of her life marched off to war—pain that countless other women had suffered since the beginning of time. Neither could she imagine using emotional bribery to keep her love by her side.

For the first time in her life, she was thankful for her strict upbringing. It helped her put herself in someone else's shoes, to understand why Reggie felt the way he did. She'd been taught that the right choice wasn't always the choice that would make her happiest. And that was something Margaret had never learned.

Ceecee stood, then leaned over to give her friends a giant hug. "All right, then. It's out of our hands for the time being. Let's get ourselves dressed, clean up the house, and get back home."

"What will we do then?" Margaret asked.

"We'll wait," Ceecee said.

Margaret nodded. "You're right, of course. Thank you. Both of you. For being here and listening without judging. It means the world to me."

Ceecee straightened, but Margaret pulled on her hand. "Do you remember that day we put our ribbons in the tree?"

"Of course."

"Bitty wished to be a significant artist, but we both wished for a good man we could love forever. And our wishes came true. As soon as we get home, we'll have to put more ribbons in the tree."

"Saying what?"

"That the three of us will always be friends. That no matter what, we will stick together and be there for one another."

Bitty frowned. "Do we need to put that in writing and stick it in the tree? Because I thought that sort of went without saying."

Margaret sat up and took one of their hands in each of hers. "It just makes it official, that's all. No matter what happens down the road, I want to make sure you two know how much you mean to me, and how much I rely on you, and how much I want you to rely on me." She squeezed their hands. "Deal?"

"Deal," Ceecee and Bitty said in unison.

Four hours later as she watched Margaret turn the key in the front door lock for the last time, Ceecee knew they weren't leaving as the same three girls they'd been when they'd arrived. They were three women on the cusp of something grand and exciting. Yet no matter how hard she tried, she couldn't push back the dark shadow of uncertainty about life's unpredictability. Nor could she forget her mother's warnings about her friendship with Margaret, about how jealousy could be easily disguised as admiration.

She climbed into the front seat of the convertible, then tilted her head back to feel the sun on her face, uncaring of the inevitable freckles or the small seed of apprehension that had taken root the moment she'd said good-bye to Boyd.

seventeen

Larkin
2010

I stood on Front Street in the historic downtown district, admiring the tidiness of the neatly lined-up nineteenth-century buildings, the brightly striped awnings over storefronts, and the inviting chairs and tables sitting in front of several restaurants. The clock tower on top of the Old Market Building that contained the Rice Museum was like a well-known neighbor, as were the slanted parking spaces crawling up both sides of the street like a caterpillar.

So many cute and trendy boutiques and eateries had cropped up in my absence. Or maybe they'd always been there, but I'd never noticed. I had rarely eaten out, mostly because Ceecee loved to make my favorite comfort foods. That was probably one of the reasons why I hated to shop, too. Nothing had ever looked good on me, at least nothing stylish and trendy. After one attempt at shopping with Ceecee left me dissolving into tears in the dressing room, I relied on Ceecee to buy things and bring them home for me to try.

My mother, during her sewing phase, did attempt to make cute clothes for me. And she succeeded—except where fit was concerned. Her creations were always at least a size too small. More than once during this phase, she'd promised that if I'd stop eating Ceecee's brownies for one month, she was sure I could wear the new yellow skirt or the adorable navy blue tunic and matching blue-and-white capris. They'd hang in my closet, unworn, a challenge as much as a spotlight on my failure. Not that I saw it as a failure then—it took several counseling sessions after I'd moved to New York to understand that I didn't see the need to change at all, because I'd been made to believe that I was perfect.

I did a mental eenie-meenie-minie-moe and picked a shop called Miss Lizzie's with women's clothing in the window that looked like it was meant for my age group. Even though it was easier now to find clothes that fit, I was still uncomfortable with the whole process. I'd compromised on a completely black wardrobe for my New York professional life, loose and comfy long tunics and soft pants, the occasional knit dress—always worn under a baggy sweater—

and even a pair of black capris for when the weather turned hot.

Before I'd left for the hospital that morning to visit my mother, I had made the mistake of asking Ceecee which black knit ensemble would work for my date with Jackson that evening, and was given the quick and firm answer of absolutely none of them. After assuring her that her time was better spent visiting my mother in the hospital than shopping with me, she'd left, allowing me another hour to keep trying to come up with an outfit. And all for a man for whom my feelings ricocheted between adolescent hormonal urges and the stark reality of maturity telling me that I was too smart to still be infatuated with him. The man he was now still housed the boy he'd been, and whether or not he remembered him, it wasn't necessarily a good thing.

I was halfway across the broad sidewalk when I heard my name and turned to see Mabry, still wearing her scrubs from work and holding the grubby hand of a smiling and ice-cream-coated Ellis. The little boy smiled brightly at me through sticky lips.

"Hi," he said with Bennett's smile, and my heart melted a bit.

"Hello, Ellis. It's nice to see you again."

Mabry gave me a look of reproach. "We thought we'd have seen you since the last time. Guess you've been busy."

She kept her eyes innocent, but I knew she must

have heard about the sunrise trip through the marsh with Bennett.

"Pretty much." I didn't tell her that my boss had said I could work remotely for two more weeks if I needed additional time at home. If it got out that I didn't have to rush back, I'd be forced to stay longer. The thought of remaining scared me. Like I'd start shedding my new, shiny skin I'd worked so hard to achieve, revealing the scarred and ugly person beneath.

"You going shopping?" Mabry asked with excitement, her eyes widening.

"Yes, actually. I've heard it's something people do."

She slapped my shoulder as if we were still twelve. "Good one. But really, I've heard they have serious shopping in New York. Can't imagine we have something here that you can't find there."

I sighed, knowing she'd get it out of me sooner or later. "Date-night clothes. I have absolutely nothing to wear tonight for dinner with Jackson."

"May I suggest something with lots of buttons and layers? And maybe a chastity belt?" I stilled, unable to look away from her reddening face. "Oh, gosh—I didn't mean it like that, Larkin. Promise. I'm so sorry."

"Larkin!" I looked behind Mabry and saw her mother, Carol Anne, walking toward us and juggling an armful of shopping bags. "Oh, my, aren't you a sight for sore eyes!" Before I could say anything, I found myself enveloped in a cloud of Trésor perfume, Carol Anne's signature scent. She had the same hairstyle she'd had since 1988, a dark brown cap of chin-length hair, curled under neatly at her jawbone, and sideswept bangs. I found it comforting, as if this woman and her hairstyle were a reminder that the best things in life were the things that never changed.

She kissed me loudly on the cheek, then held me at arm's length to better examine me—something I was becoming used to. "I'm just heartbroken about your mama—I can't even imagine how you're feeling. I've been going to see her as often as I can and talking with her and reading **People** magazine." She frowned, her face serious. "I've been Googling comas, and I've learned that people in comas can hear everything and the best thing is to keep talking to them, and read to them. And the music-speaker-box thing you put in her room was brilliant, Larkin. But we always knew you were smart."

She beamed at me and took a couple of steps back. "You've always been a stunner, Larkin, but you've really blossomed." She faced Mabry. "Hasn't she?"

"She certainly has," Mabry said enthusiastically. "And she has a date tonight, and we're going shopping to find an outfit for her. Could you take Ellis home with you for a little while?"

"A date?" Carol Anne's eyebrows rose to perfect half circles. "With Ben . . ."

"With Jackson Porter," Mabry quickly interjected.

Carol Anne took a step back, a confused look on her face. "Jackson? Is that the same Jackson . . . ?"

"So, will you, Mama?" Mabry gave Ellis a hug and a big kiss on the cheek before steering him toward her mother.

"Of course," Carol Anne said, distracted by Ellis tugging on her hand and making the shopping bags bounce. She looked down at her grandson and smiled. "Maybe we'll make cookies. Does that sound like a good plan?"

"Cookies!" Ellis shouted, jumping up and down as if on a pogo stick.

"Because he sure needs more sugar," I said wryly, glad to have everyone's attention diverted.

Carol Anne squeezed my hand. "It's so good seeing you, Larkin. I'm guessing Bennett forgot to extend my invitation to supper, because we haven't seen you, but please know you have an open invitation to stop by anytime. I'd love to talk about your new life in New York, and I can show you all the articles I've printed out about comas."

"Thank you, Mrs. Lynch. I don't know if I'll be able to—I'm at the hospital a lot—but I promise to try."

"You be sure and do that. It'll be just like old times with you at our kitchen table." She tugged on Ellis's hand and waved it like he was a string puppet, causing him to giggle.

They began to walk away, but I called them back.

"One quick question, if you don't mind. Did Mama ever mention Carrowmore to you?"

Carol Anne shook her head. "No, dear. We never talked about it. Not even as girls. I remember stories about how it was haunted. But I knew Ivy's mama died there in a fire, so I never brought it up. And Ivy, well, you can imagine why she wouldn't want to talk about it." She leaned toward me. "We've always been the best of friends, but I suppose there are some things we keep to ourselves. Maybe we believe deep down that sharing the darkest parts of ourselves makes them more real. Kept to ourselves, well, then we can just pretend they were a bad dream."

I nodded, then said good-bye again, and I stared after them, deep in thought over what she'd said.

"You ready?" Mabry asked, jerking her head in the direction of the boutique.

"As ready as I'll ever be. I hope they have what I need, because I'm not in the mood to go to multiple stores to find a single outfit."

"This is a great store," Mabry said, holding the door open for me. "They have terrific belts, too."

I glanced at her and she winked, and I knew everything was okay between us again.

Despite my attempts to gravitate toward every black article of clothing in the store, Mabry sent me to the dressing room with an armful of brightly hued outfits. I had to agree they were lovely, but I did notice a conservative trend—nothing too low-cut, or too short, or too revealing. It went along with my own clothing sensibilities, but I did draw the line when she selected several cotton sweaters to wear over the sleeveless dresses. She frowned when I handed the sweaters back to her, still on their hangers.

"This really isn't necessary, Mabry. I'm not the same stupid eighteen-year-old with an infatuation, okay?"

She was thoughtful for a moment before speaking. "I know that. But sometimes it's hard to see a person from our past with new eyes. Like they've become a statue to their previously perceived old wonderfulness, and that's all we see—not the real person they are."

I felt a flash of anger—not because I thought she was wrong, but because I was afraid there might be a glimmer of truth in what she was saying. I turned my back on her and picked out the dress I'd liked the best and walked toward the register. "It's just dinner, Mabry. Not forever."

"You're right. Sorry. It's always been my role to be bossy, you know? It makes me a great nurse." She gave me a small smile. "So, where did you say you were going to dinner tonight?"

"The River Room Restaurant. They don't take reservations, but Jackson said he's taken care of it so that the nicest table outside facing the water is ours at seven o'clock. I guess he knows people because of his business."

Mabry rolled her eyes. "Or he just steamrolled

someone into making them do something he wanted them to. That's more his style."

I thanked the saleswoman, then took the bag containing a new dress, new shoes, and new earrings. I'd declined the matching necklace because I never took off the gold chain with the three charms Bitty had given me.

I pressed my lips together as I headed toward the door. "I thought you and Jackson used to have a 'thing.' Is that what this is all about?"

Mabry followed me out of the store and waited until we were on the sidewalk before facing me and pointing a finger at my chest. "Like I already told you, Jackson Porter and I never had a 'thing' then or now despite what he might have said. You were my best friend, and I knew how you felt about him, so I would **never** have had a 'thing' with him, even if I'd wanted to. And I didn't." She dropped her finger. "I'm just concerned about you because I think you're too good for him—both before and now. I just wish you could see it."

I bristled under her scrutiny. There was so much I wanted to ask her, but there was so much more I didn't want to tell her, so I let my questions die in the back of my throat, where they belonged. "Yes, well, I'm an adult now, and I can take care of myself." I softened. "But thank you. I'll take your caution under advisement."

Her frown gradually turned into a smile as she glanced over at one of the nearby restaurants where music played from an outside speaker. It was my turn to roll my eyes. "'Your Love' by the Outfield."

She hugged me tightly. "So glad you haven't lost your touch."

I smiled back. "Thanks for helping me shop today."

"You're welcome. And don't be a stranger while you're here. I'd love to do more catching up. You still haven't told me what my dream means."

"Oh, yeah—I meant to call you. It means you're overwhelmed and need a vacation. And that your little boy needs a puppy."

"Really?"

"The first part, anyway. The second part is just my suggestion. Every little boy needs a dog. You and Bennett always had one."

"Seems if I'm overwhelmed, the last thing I need is something else to take care of."

I shrugged. "Just saying." I waved before turning around and walking down the sidewalk toward Ceecee's house. I recalled what I'd almost said to Mabry, all the loose words that wanted to form into questions jumbling around my head like the golden seeds of spartina grass in a fall wind.

When I came down the stairs later that evening wearing my new ensemble, Ceecee fussed over me before telling me to head back up to my room so that it wouldn't look like I was too eager. Bitty simply yanked on my hand and pulled me into the foyer before leaning into my ear and asking me if I had a can of Mace in my purse.

"Why would you say that? You don't even know him."

"I know he broke your heart once, so he will always be on my hit list."

"People change, Bitty. Just look at me."

She brushed my cheek with the backs of her fingers. "But you're the same beautiful Larkin on the inside. It's the outside of a person that we can get creative with, but that won't change what's on the inside. You can put lipstick on a pig, but it's still a pig."

The doorbell rang, and I rushed to answer it before Ceecee could invite Jackson inside, where I'd be forced to listen to her and Bitty bombarding us with questions and looking for opposite outcomes. My heart lurched in a double take as I took in the white button-down shirt and navy blue blazer, his broad football-player shoulders filling it out nicely. When he leaned in to kiss my cheek, I smelled his cologne again, and all the old feelings sifted over me like confetti.

"You look gorgeous," he said, his lips close to my ear.

"Thanks. You look pretty good yourself."

He stepped back and greeted Ceecee and Bitty, but before they could say anything beyond an initial salutation, I was pulling on his hand and leading him down the porch steps. A red BMW convertible was parked at the curb, and he opened the passenger door for me, then closed it behind me as soon as I'd buckled my seat belt.

As the engine purred to life, he said, "I hope the River Room is okay. There's a new Italian place that I've been dying to try, but I didn't know if you'd be all right with that—you know, with all those pasta carbs and things. Not to mention cheese." He gave me a self-deprecating smile, and I was too confused to come up with a response.

Taking my silence for appreciation, he said, "There are lots of veggies and grilled stuff on the menu, so I'm hoping there are enough choices for both of us."

He started the car, put it in gear, and pulled away from the curb with a squeal of tires. Once I'd found my voice, I said, "Thanks, Jackson, but I eat pretty much everything—even dessert. Just not two helpings of everything." I smiled to set him at ease.

"Sorry," he said. "I didn't mean . . ."

I put my hand over his on the stick shift. "I know. It was sweet of you to think of me. I appreciate it. I really do." And I did, although I now had an uncomfortable hollowness at the back of my throat.

It was a short drive down Front Street to the restaurant, but I was thankful for the ride because my high heels weren't conducive to walking more than a block. The hostess greeted us with warm familiarity and immediately took us past the large reef aquarium and to the perfect corner table, with two windows offering a panoramic view of the harbor. Boats of various sizes bobbed at the dock, and gulls perched on masts and shiny deck railings, occasionally swooping down low over the water in acrobatic and picturesque contortions that made me wonder, just for a moment, if they were deliberately placed to add to the ambience.

I smiled at Jackson as he pulled back my chair. "Great table."

He pulled his chair next to mine, sliding his place setting closer, too, then sat down, his thigh close enough to touch mine. I'd been fairly confident that if there'd been anybody at the restaurant who'd known me, they wouldn't have recognized me as we'd walked through the dining room. But for one irrational moment, I wanted the entire varsity cheerleading squad from my senior year to be there. I found myself glancing into the dining room just to be sure they weren't, then flushed with embarrassment when I realized what I was doing.

"You okay?"

I nodded. "Yeah. Just trying to remember the last time I was here."

"Probably senior banquet. Were you here for that?"

I blinked at him for a moment, remembering. "Yes. I was." I wanted to remind him that he'd asked me to sit at his table along with Mabry and some of the players and cheerleaders. I'd sat next to him, and he'd smiled directly at me. Twice.

"It was a fun night," he said.

I nodded, happy for the distraction of the waitress approaching the table.

We lingered over our dinner, eventually splitting a dessert and two bottles of wine. He'd made a toast over our first glass to "old friends," and I hadn't questioned it, still pinching myself that I was having a romantic dinner with Jackson Porter. We spent most of the time talking about people we'd known—what they were doing, where they were living. He spent a lot of time talking about his best football plays, and when he was done, he asked me about my own high school extracurriculars.

For the second time that evening, I found myself blinking stupidly at him. Finally, I said, "I was the editor for the school paper. You know, the one everybody got on their desk in homeroom each Friday." I could tell that he was probably one of the many who'd made paper airplanes with it and then used them as weapons against their classmates.

"Right," he said. "That's cool."

"And I was in charge of the pep rallies before the games. Made sure there were posters and stuff, and led the chants."

"That was you, huh?" he said, nodding his head as if he actually remembered. I didn't bother telling him about my walk-on parts in every school play or how I'd won sophomore class president by promising a Coke machine in the lunchroom if my fellow students voted for me. After I'd won, Ceecee had made sure that the machine was installed, insisting that I'd really won because everyone liked me and I was capable of doing a great job.

He poured more wine in my glass, then upended the rest of the bottle into his own. Raising his glass in a toast, he said, "To new memories."

I hesitated a moment, studying his eyes. I wondered whether he was hoping for new memories because he couldn't remember the old ones, or because he did. Too fuzzy-headed to decide for sure, I raised my glass and clinked the edge of it against his. "To new memories."

We smiled giddily at each other, and I felt that I'd been here before, Jackson and me, sharing a bottle of wine. But of course I had, in the dreams of a young girl who'd never doubted that dreams were meant to come true.

"Jackson . . . ," I started, unsure of why I'd spoken. Wondering if the new Larkin was lurking under the surface of the old me, interrupting my dream with a cold splash of reality.

He looked at me, his smile slowly fading as if he recognized the serious note in my voice. "Yes?"

"You do remember, don't you? That time on your dad's boat. When it was just you and me."

He looked uncomfortable, like a child scolded in class, and I expected him to squirm in his seat. To deny it, say that it was too long ago to remember. I didn't want him to, because then I'd have to be my adult self and leave. Tell Mabry that she was right about him. Except Jackson didn't deny it. Instead, he took both of my hands in his. "Of course I do. It's not something a guy could forget." Softly, he added, "It was your first time, which made it special for me, too."

I sat very still, barely able to breathe.

Glancing down at our clasped hands, he said, "I was a bit of a jerk back then, wasn't I?"

I didn't hesitate. "Yes. You were," I said, wanting to cheer the new, mature Larkin almost as much as I wanted to tell her to go away, not to ruin this long-held fantasy.

He looked apologetic and maybe even a little ashamed. "I didn't call you afterward. I remember that, too. And I've always regretted that. See—I did think of you while you were gone." He squeezed my hands as if to add sincerity to his words.

"And at the party . . . what you said . . ." I trailed off, my memory having long ago exorcised the exact words as a form of self-preservation.

Jackson shook his head. "I was just blowing smoke in front of my friends. And Melissa. She was there, too, and we hadn't broken up yet because I was too much of a coward back then. I'd heard some rumors, and I thought it made me look tough in front of my friends, so I didn't deny anything. Didn't even think how much you'd be hurt by everything."

I bit my lip, not sure if I should be laughing or cry-

ing. If I'd ever scripted this scene the way I wanted
it to play out, he was speaking the exact dialogue I'd
have given him.

Jackson cleared his throat. "I think I got caught
up in all the end-of-senior-year stuff, but that's no
excuse. My behavior was inexcusable, and I've been
waiting all this time for you to come back so I could
tell you I'm sorry. To ask for your forgiveness. And
to tell you I'm not that same jerk anymore."

I smiled, my shoulders relaxing. "I needed to hear
that. Thank you. And I accept your apology."

His thumbs caressed the tops of my hands for a
moment before he pulled away. "What do you say we
get out of here?"

I sipped my wine and watched as Jackson paid the
bill; I admired the move of muscles under his jacket,
and how the sunset sky shone like a halo behind his
head. He leaned forward and took my hand. "What
would you like to do now?"

I forcibly held back the words that threatened to
come out of my mouth, my brain knowing and somehow managing to communicate that I needed a bit
of time to sober up before I could responsibly answer
that question. Forgetting that my shoes were what
Ceecee always referred to as "sitting-down shoes," I
said, "Let's go for a walk. It's such a beautiful night."

"Good plan," he said, taking my hand, then leading me through the restaurant to the front door.

Before we'd reached it, I became aware of someone

saying my name and a table of people pushing back chairs and moving toward us. It took me a moment to register Mabry and a tall young man—presumably her husband—her parents, and Bennett.

"What a coincidence," Mabry said a little too loudly, and reached over to hug me. "I had no idea you'd be here. Are you leaving? We are, too!"

My brain was foggy, but not too foggy to remember I'd told her when and where Jackson and I were planning to eat tonight. I started to laugh, but it came out as a half burp that thankfully nobody but Mabry seemed to hear.

"Have you met my husband, Jonathan?" The tall man, with wavy dark brown hair and glasses, reached for my hand, then said, "What am I doing? Mabry's told me so much about you that I already feel like we're kin." He hugged me tightly, and behind his shoulder I saw Bennett smiling with the same intensity with which Jackson was frowning.

We left the restaurant in a large group while Mabry introduced Jackson to everyone, and I got another hug from Mr. Lynch, who'd been like my second dad while I was growing up. Except for a little less hair, he looked exactly the same as I remembered.

"Where are y'all headed?" Bennett asked.

"Home," Jackson said at the same time I said, "For a walk."

Ignoring Jackson, Mabry said, "We were all planning on going for a walk, too—it's such a gorgeous evening. Why don't you join us?" She tucked her hand into the crook of my arm and began leading me down Front Street.

"Larkin's with me," Jackson said loudly, and I noticed he was slurring his words. "Come on, Larkin—let's go somewhere . . ." He took a step forward and missed the edge of the curb, which left him sprawled in the street. When he didn't immediately get up, Mr. Lynch and Bennett went over to help him. They pulled him to his feet, his face scraped and bleeding, gravel sticking to the wound.

"I hope you're not planning on driving anywhere, young man," Mr. Lynch said, brushing dirt off Jackson's jacket. "You can barely walk. Why don't you let me drive you home, and I'll catch up with the group later."

Mrs. Lynch stepped forward with a tissue. "And you might want to put this on your chin. I recommend giving that cut a thorough wash when you get home."

Jackson stared at the tissue, as if trying to figure out what he was supposed to do with it. For a moment it looked as if he might protest; then he took it, pressed it to his chin, spotted the blood, and frowned. "Fine, whatever," he slurred. Looking at me with glassy eyes, he said, "I'll call you tomorrow."

"Okay." Remembering my manners, I said, "Thanks for dinner."

"Any time."

"That's his car," I said helpfully, pointing to the space right in front of the restaurant. After getting the keys from Jackson, Mr. Lynch opened the passenger-side door of the BMW, and Jackson got inside, Mr. Lynch placing his hand on top of Jackson's head so he wouldn't hit it on the door frame like cops do when apprehending criminals.

We all waved as Mr. Lynch drove past us, popping the clutch only once, while trying to get it into second gear.

We'd made it only a few blocks to Cannon Street before I stopped. "My feet hurt."

"Of course they do—look at those heels!" Mrs. Lynch leaned down to get a better look at my feet. "I don't know how you young people walk in those things."

"Bennett should drive her home," Mabry announced.

"Good idea," her mother said with a finality that brooked no argument.

"That's okay," I said, noticing with horror that my words were bumping into one another. "I'll just walk." I bent down to unbuckle my shoes, and Bennett's arm going around me saved me from toppling over.

"Why don't you go with her, Bennett? Jonathan can drive Mama and me back home, and it's not too far for you to walk. Sound good?"

I looked up to see Bennett nodding, his arm still holding me up as Mabry bent down, unbuckled my shoes, and helped me slide them off my feet before handing them to Bennett like she wasn't sure I could keep track of them. I stood on the sidewalk, spreading my toes and flexing my ankles as if I'd just been given a new set of feet. "My feet feel like they've died and gone to heaven."

Bennett began leading me away, and I waved to Mabry, Jonathan, and Mrs. Lynch, trying to make a mental note to tell Mabry that I thought she'd made a good choice of husband.

We walked without talking for an entire block, me hanging on to his arm to keep going in a straight line. As soon as we got past the historic district and the street became more residential, we moved to the grassy yards of the homes we passed to give my feet a break.

I stopped in the middle of one of the yards, enjoying the damp coolness of the grass. I looked up at Bennett as if I'd just invented something important. "I haven't gone barefoot in years—not a good idea in the city, you know? But there's something nice about it—feeling the ground beneath your feet. Reminds me of the old me, I guess."

"Good," he said, his voice so quiet, I wasn't completely sure he'd spoken.

We walked in silence until we reached Ceecee's house. I had to lean on Bennett's arm to climb the steps. The porch lights were on, and Ceecee had kept the front door open, with just the screened door closed to keep out the bugs.

Bennett handed me my shoes. "Do you want me to make sure you can climb the stairs all right?"

I shook my head. "I'm sure Ceecee is lurking inside, so I'll be okay." Then I remembered my manners again and added, "But thanks."

"I'm pretty sure you won't remember this in the morning, so I'll call to remind you, but I wanted to let you know that Dr. Wallen-Arasi wants to come out on Friday morning to see Carrowmore and give us her professional opinion." He looked at me closely as if deciding whether to say anything more. "Also, my mother was getting ready for a garage sale and found a couple boxes of old files and newspapers that had belonged to my granddaddy. There're a few things in there you might want to see."

I hadn't really been listening, just enjoying the cool river breeze and the sound of his voice. It didn't appear that Bennett was expecting an answer, so I didn't say anything. The walk had cleared my head to a certain degree; instead of swimming, the world rocked gently, like a docked boat in a safe harbor. I looked up at Bennett, enjoying the calming sensation of being rocked, and felt his arms around me again.

"You're going to fall over if you keep leaning backward." His smile belied the sternness of his voice.

I decided I liked the feel of his hands on my waist, so I kept leaning backward, studying his face. "You're not too hard on the eyes, Bennett Lynch. And in the morning I'll probably regret having said this, but I think you're funny and smart and fun to be with. How come some girl hasn't laid claim to you yet?" I pulled back as another thought crossed my mind. "You're not gay, are you?"

His mouth twitched, and I noticed how nice his lips were, how full and well formed and probably great to kiss. "No, Larkin. I'm not gay."

"Not that there's anything wrong with that," I said earnestly.

"No," he said. "But I'm not." He was definitely smiling now, but when I peered at him in the dim glow of the porch lights, his eyes seemed sad.

"So, there's no one special in your life right now?"

He sighed, his breath warm on my face. "There is, but I don't think she knows I'm the perfect man for her."

"Well, maybe you should introduce us so I can talk some sense into her."

"Yeah. Maybe I will."

We were standing very close, with his arms around me. My gaze drifted to his mouth again, to those lips of his.

"You should go inside now," he said.

"Hmm," I murmured.

He leaned toward me and I closed my eyes, surprised to feel the soft brush of his lips on my forehead before he stepped back, moving his hands to my shoulders. "Here, let me help you."

He opened the screened door and with a gentle

pressure on my back, pushed me inside, then placed my shoes neatly on the floor. "Good night, Larkin. I'll call you tomorrow."

As he walked away I watched through the screen, listening to his footsteps cross the porch and move down the steps, and wondered why I suddenly felt so bereft.

eighteen

Ivy
2010

"Mama?"

Larkin waits, as if expecting me to answer. And I try; I really do. I focus on the big toe of my right foot, putting all my effort into just making one movement. According to one of the articles Ceecee found on the Internet, that's where all coma patients have to start—with moving their big toe. I think. I wasn't really listening; I was paying attention instead to Ceecee's face, and to how much I associate it with love. It was her face that calmed me when things were bad after Ellis left.

And I keep thinking about my memory—or was it a dream?—of being carried out of the fire, and looking up into the face of the person who'd saved me.

The smoke blocks my vision, but the arms holding me hug me close and I feel safe.

As with all mothers and daughters, we had our struggles. But after the accident and my being in this room, the hard edges of my resentment have softened like butter left on the counter. The softer I feel, the fuzzier the ceiling of my room becomes, like I've found a part of the combination to spring me loose. I just need to figure out the rest of it.

"Please wake up, Mama. There's so much we need to talk about."

Larkin seems so near tears, and my heart breaks a little more. She's pulled out that gold necklace Bitty gave her, and she's playing with it. I didn't want Bitty to give it to her. I thought she was trying to tell Larkin she could choose where she belonged. As if she could call anywhere else home. I understand the pull of this place, how you can't leave no matter how hard you want to. When your blood runs with salt water, you might as well drop anchor and get comfortable.

"We're having a consultant meet with us at Carrowmore on Friday to see if it's salvageable. It's Daddy's idea, and he says he's working for our best interests." She reaches for a tissue and blows her nose, the sound like a flock of geese flying across the room. "It would be so much easier if you'd just wake up and tell us what you think. I know it will all belong to me, but only because you gave it to me, and I'd like your thoughts on what I should do. I really would like to know why you went to Carrowmore that day of your accident. I think the ribbons you put in the tree are some kind of clue, but I can't figure it out."

I want to answer her, but I can't because I no longer remember why. I struggle to recall, but my memory keeps taking me down the same path, to me refinishing a desk in Ceecee's detached garage, then parking my car at Carrowmore before walking toward the Tree of Dreams with a ribbon in my hand. One ribbon. Not two. A shock of light flits through my body, and I'm transported upward again, and I'm looking down at my bed and at Larkin, who's taken my hand in hers.

She's talking, and I'm listening carefully because I know this is important. "I think I understand what the first ribbon is about—the one that said 'I miss you. I wish I'd been given the chance to know you.' That's about Margaret, my grandmother, isn't it? You never got to know your mother because she died when you were so young. I get that. I also believe that's the same reason why you never wanted to own Carrowmore, and gave it to me instead." Larkin lets go of my hand and leans back in her chair.

She tilts her head to look up at the ceiling, and for a moment I wonder whether she can hear the crackling, see the light creeping through the openings. But then I see she's doing it so that she can cry without the telltale tears running down her face.

"I wish I'd known about Ellis. Then maybe I would have seen your need to always try new things as a desperate need to be happy. We might have been able to figure out how to be happy together. And I wouldn't have made myself so miserable trying to be someone I wasn't.

"I don't blame Ceecee, you know. I was so angry with her when I left—yet another reason why I stayed away. But my therapist helped me see that Ceecee had made lots of mistakes trying to cover for your absence and to make me feel special. It's hard to find fault in someone who just has love in their heart for you, you know?"

The crackling noise continues, and behind it I hear the rumble of a car engine. For once I want to tell it to go away, that I need to hear what Larkin is saying.

"I don't understand the other ribbon, Mama. The one that said 'Forgive me.' Who are you asking? And why?"

Silence again, and I know she's really holding out for me to answer her. I see the flash of a yellow dress somewhere over in the corner by the window, and I know it's my mama because Ceecee said that yellow was Mama's favorite color. It's why when I made clothes for Larkin, I used a lot of yellow. Sort of as a nod to us Darlington women. I always felt that despite everything, we had that bond.

Larkin's question lingers in the room, the machines keeping me alive pumping and moaning like floundering fish. And I'm remembering something, too—something in one of Ceecee's stories she's been telling me, something important about Mama. I couldn't answer Larkin's question even if I could speak. Because I didn't put two ribbons in the tree, just one. And the one I stuck in the tree's opening didn't say **Forgive me.**

Ceecee
1951

Ceecee struggled to fit back into her old life once they returned from Myrtle Beach, but it was as if she'd returned from summer camp and found that all of her school clothes no longer fit. She wondered if her mother noticed how her feet no longer seemed to touch the ground when she walked, or how she daydreamed through most of her days while going through the motions of her chores. She barely even protested when Will Harris stopped by for supper and Ceecee's mother had her sit next to him, and even suggested they sit out on the front porch while she brought them lemonade. She did protest, however, when Will leaned over to kiss her, turning her head just in time for his wet lips to glide across her cheek.

Ceecee wasn't allowed to use the telephone in their house—it was solely for church business, just in case a parishioner needed her daddy—so she had to walk over to Bitty's house or wait for Bitty or Margaret to pick her up and take her to Carrowmore to make a quick call to Boyd. They'd say hello and then hang up; then Boyd would call right back so he'd take care of the long-distance phone charges.

The calls would be short with only quickly whispered **I love you**s and, before they hung up, a reminder of how many days they had to wait until they'd see each other again. Ceecee couldn't remember two weeks dragging by so slowly, and kept a calendar under her mattress where she could painstakingly mark an X through each day as it ended.

At the very least, it told her how many days she had to tell her parents about Boyd. That he was kind, and smart, and a gentleman. A doctor. And that she'd met him in Myrtle Beach and he was planning on coming to Georgetown to meet them, and to speak with Dr. Griffith about taking over his practice when it was time for the older doctor to retire. She knew they'd love Boyd once they met him, but they would be highly suspicious of him until then since they hadn't known him since birth, and didn't know who his people were. Which was why she was waiting until the very last moment to tell them, giving them less of a chance to interrogate her.

She didn't mention that Margaret's new beau was Boyd's brother and that she was already dreaming about being real sisters with Margaret if they should marry brothers. Ceecee knew that any connection with the Darlingtons wouldn't endear Boyd to her parents, so she kept silent. She also had no doubt that if they did discover they'd been to Myrtle Beach unchaperoned for two weeks, they'd put her in a convent, Catholic or not, and never allow her to see Margaret or Bitty or Boyd ever again.

Reggie called Margaret every day, but not from Charleston. He'd decided to visit a law school buddy in Charlotte to give himself some thinking time. Even though Margaret pressed him for decision, he told her to wait. She'd told her parents that she'd met a nice young man, and when Mr. and Mrs. Darlington said they knew of his family and were suitably impressed with Reggie's lofty ambitions, they approved him as a worthy beau for their daughter and allowed the phone calls. Margaret hadn't mentioned Reggie's proposal, or her plans to forgo college, but as with everything else in her life, everything would go her way. It always did.

The three young women were at Carrowmore in the middle of the second week following their return, Boyd and Reggie not due for their visit until the following Monday. Margaret met them on the front steps, and Ceecee could see right away that something was wrong. Her eyes were swollen, her nose pink—neither of which detracted from her beauty— and when Ceecee and Bitty approached her, she started to cry.

They moved to either side of her, led her up to the porch, and sat her down in the middle of the porch swing before joining her. "What's wrong, Margaret?" Ceecee had never seen Margaret cry, at least not as if what she was crying for really mattered.

"Reggie didn't call today when he said he would."

Ceecee felt enormous relief. "Well, that could be for any number of reasons. Maybe he's sick, or had an unexpected family obligation. Did you try phoning him?"

Bitty lit a cigarette, after making sure Mrs. Darlington was still safely inside the house. "Why, goodness, Ceecee, every properly brought up young woman knows it is simply tacky and ill-bred to call a gentleman." She rolled her eyes, then blew out a mouthful of smoke.

Ceecee frowned at her over Margaret's bowed head. "Of course you shouldn't call—you don't want your future in-laws to think you're fast." She put her arm around Margaret. "I'm sure there's a reason and he'll call tomorrow, and next week when he's here with Boyd, we can all laugh about how worried you were."

Margaret lifted her head, her damp eyes like a blue crystal vase Ceecee had once seen at Berlin's department store in Charleston. "Do you really think so?"

"Absolutely," Bitty said. "And if for some reason he doesn't, I will get on the phone myself and call and pretend I'm the housekeeper at his dormitory back at school and say he left a watch or something behind and I'm trying to get it to him. Seeing as how I don't mind lying to strangers to get an answer or calling a man's house, I'll be happy to do it."

Margaret giggled, and Ceecee relaxed. Throwing her arms around her two friends, Margaret said, "You gals are the best friends I could ever have hoped for. What would I do without you?"

"Grow into a reclusive old maid, I'm sure," Bitty

said, hiding her smile by taking a drag from her cigarette.

Ceecee leaned into Margaret. "Don't listen to her. We all know that you're destined to be the queen of the universe with or without us."

Her mood restored, Margaret gave them a quick squeeze before sliding off the swing. "Come on, then. It's time to put our new ribbons in the tree."

"What new ribbons?" Ceecee asked.

"The ones we talked about in Myrtle Beach— about being friends forever, that no matter what, we will stick together," Bitty said. "Although I still don't know why we have to put it in writing. It's like she doesn't trust us or something."

"Silly," Margaret said. She reached into the large pockets on the skirt of her yellow dress. "I've already made them, and they all say the same thing." She gave each of us a wide sunshine-colored hair ribbon, her neat penmanship inked down the length of each one in blue. **Friends forever, come what may.**

"Come on. Let's make it official." Margaret ran down the porch steps, her mood changed as quickly as the weather, as if she truly believed things were bound to go her way. Because, of course, they always had. Ceecee felt a moment of resentment, but quickly pushed the feeling away as she and Bitty followed her to the back of the house, under the dangling martin gourds, to the old tree at the edge of the river. One by one they stuck their ribbons into the opening, then stood grinning at one another. Distant thunder rolled over the marsh, dark and heavy clouds billowing sleepily across the sky.

Ceecee shivered, remembering how it had rained the last time they'd done this and how so many of their dreams had come true. She looked back at the house and at the retreating forms of her two friends, and she had the sudden desire to freeze that moment in a photograph, a memory of three friends before everything changed.

Shaking off her dark mood, she shouted for them to wait for her, then quickly ran to catch up.

On the day Boyd and Reggie were expected to arrive, Ceecee was back again at Carrowmore, pacing the front porch while Bitty sat with Margaret on the swing. Despite multiple attempts to reach Reggie—including Bitty following through on her threats to call incognito—Margaret hadn't heard a single word from him. Even Boyd was having trouble reaching him, but promised he'd go out of his way to stop in Summerville on his way to Georgetown to find out what was going on with his brother.

Boyd was due any minute now, with still no word from Reggie. Ceecee refused to dwell on what might have happened, fearing the worst. As her mother always told her, she'd cross that bridge when she came to it. Although, from what she could tell, the bridge was just around the bend.

A small part of her hoped that Reggie wasn't with Boyd. She didn't want him to see Margaret like this. She glanced at her friend, alarmed at the change in her. The golden hair lay dull and lifeless against rounded shoulders, her face lacked its usual glow, and even the light in her eyes seemed to have dimmed. The only color in her skin was the purple of the half-moons under her eyes, a testament to her inability to sleep and to her incessant worry. But this would be the measure of true love, she reasoned. To see a person at her worst and love her anyway.

Ceecee watched as Bitty offered Margaret a Tootsie Roll, and Margaret turned away, shaking her head. Mrs. Darlington had given up trying to entice Margaret with the usually forbidden sweets she craved, and was threatening to call the doctor. That was the only thing that had evoked a strong reaction from Margaret, who told her mother that no doctor could mend a broken heart.

Mrs. Darlington's expression had suggested that Margaret was being overly dramatic, but there was worry there, too. She'd promised that if they hadn't heard from or seen Reggie by the end of the day, she'd have Mr. Darlington make a phone call. Not to appear eager on their daughter's account. After all, Margaret Darlington was not desperate or the kind of girl without other options. They just wanted to show their concern over Reggie's welfare.

By the time they saw the cloud of dust announcing an approaching vehicle, Ceecee had chewed off all of her fingernails, and Margaret had collapsed against Bitty's shoulder on the swing. Ceecee ran to the screen and threw good manners aside to shout inside the house, "Someone's here!"

The uniformed housekeeper who'd been dusting the foyer stared back at Ceecee through the screen. "Yes, miss. I'll let Mr. and Mrs. Darlington know."

Ceecee ran back to the top of the steps, pausing long enough to watch Bitty helping Margaret stand, their hands clutched together. Her heart gave a leap of relief when the car was close enough for her to recognize it as Boyd's. She strained to see whether someone was in the passenger seat, but the dust obscured her vision. Impatient, she ran to the bottom of the steps but forced herself to stop at the drive upon hearing the arrival of Margaret's parents behind her. Their regal bearing and strict adherence to social niceties had always intimidated Ceecee, and she knew she had to be on her best behavior for Boyd's sake.

When the car pulled up and the engine stopped, she heard the cry of despair from Margaret before her own brain registered that Boyd was alone. But Boyd was here. **Her** Boyd. It took every ounce of restraint not to throw herself into his arms and kiss him. Instead, she walked around the car to greet him sedately as he shut his door, and when he smiled at her, it was with the same mix of emotions she was feeling.

"Hello, Sessalee. I've missed you," he said quietly.

"Me, too," she whispered back, and then, because she couldn't not touch him, she took his arm and slid her hand into the crook of his elbow. "Let me introduce you to Margaret's parents. We're hoping you've brought us good news."

He looked down at her and gave a quick shake of his head. Ceecee's heart sank as he guided her up the steps toward the gathering group. She couldn't look at Margaret, couldn't bear to see her friend's agony any more than she could bear the guilt of her happiness because she had Boyd by her side.

Margaret surprised them all by moving to stand between her parents to make the introductions. She appeared cut from glass, her skin bloodless, her movements sharp and deliberate as if someone else had moved into her body and left only a shell.

The housekeeper appeared and pulled the door wide open, and Mrs. Darlington ushered them all inside. Margaret even managed to walk on her own, following her mother's lead by asking about Boyd's trip and how his family was doing in Anderson. But her voice didn't sound like hers; it reminded Ceecee of a talking doll.

They were led through the gracious paneled entryway lined with antiques and family heirlooms, Dresden figurines and French crystal, and to the white parlor on the right. Ceecee had always thought of this room as the wedding room, and not just because generations of Darlingtons had been married within its four walls but because of the layers of filigreed moldings and heavy chandelier medallions that resembled the white spun sugar of a wedding cake. It was the room where she was sure Margaret had already dreamed of her wedding with Reggie taking place.

Ceecee made sure her back was straight and her ankles crossed as ancient Darlingtons looked down their perfect noses at the visitors from framed portraits on the walls. The housekeeper and another maid brought in a silver tea service and small cakes, along with the treasured Darlington Chinese porcelain that had been in the family for two centuries.

They made small talk as cups and plates were passed. A cup and saucer were placed on a table next to Margaret, and she accepted a plate of cakes, which sat perched on her lap untouched. Boyd sat next to Ceecee on the sofa, and she had to keep remembering not to stare at him, to keep her focus on Margaret, who appeared to be shattering beneath her skin.

Bitty, who sat in a chair to Ceecee's left, kept shooting her glances, her eyes widened with worry. Mr. Darlington was in the middle of telling Boyd that he would be more than happy to formally introduce him to the retiring Dr. Griffith, when the sound of shattering china quieted the room immediately.

Margaret had stood, her plate and teacup crashing together onto the Aubusson rug. Her fists were clenched by her sides, her eyes wild as she regarded Boyd. She opened her mouth to speak, and Ceecee held her breath.

"Where is Reggie? He's supposed to be here today."

She was shaking as if with fever, and Ceecee admired Mrs. Darlington's poise as she gracefully stood and put her arm around her daughter's shoulder. "Margaret, I think you might be ill. Let Delphine draw you a bath . . ."

Margaret pulled away. "No, Mama. I need to know. I cannot go on pretending that this is just another day and that everything is all right."

Boyd placed his cup and saucer on the coffee table and walked to stand in front of Margaret. Taking a sealed envelope from his pocket, he said, "Neither I nor my parents have been able to reach him for several days. When I went to his friends' house today to see him, they gave me this note addressed to you from Reggie."

She took the note, but didn't open it. She stared at it for a long moment before raising her eyes to meet his. "He enlisted?"

Boyd nodded. "Yes."

The sound that came from Margaret's slim frame seemed filled with all the grief and sorrow of a hundred wounded souls, from a heart pierced by as many arrows. Her knees buckled, and it was Boyd who held her up and allowed her to press her sobbing face into his chest to be comforted. And when the wailing didn't stop, Mr. Darlington went to call Dr. Griffith, and it was Boyd who lifted her and carried her upstairs to her bed, the letter still clutched in her hand.

Bitty and Ceecee clung to each other, unsure of what they should do or how they could give comfort, staring after Boyd's departing back. And Ceecee, who loved Margaret like a sister, felt the sharp stab of jealousy wedge its way like a blade into her own heart.

nineteen

Larkin
2010

On Friday morning, I waited on Ceecee's front-porch steps for Bennett to pick me up and take me to our meeting at Carrowmore, his cleaned and folded red T-shirt in my lap. Even my father conspired against me, saying he and Ceecee would drive together, leaving directly from the hospital after visiting my mother. I'd tried desperately to convince Bennett that I was happy driving myself, fairly confident that I couldn't take the awkwardness of sitting alone in his truck for the drive to Carrowmore following my disastrous date night with Jackson.

Flashes of my conversation with Bennett kept up a constant rotation in my brain, making me cringe each time I remembered how drunk I'd allowed myself to become, and some of the things I'd said to Bennett. I still had no idea how Jackson and I had gotten separated or how it was Bennett who'd walked me home. Mostly, I remembered his lips and how appealing I thought they'd seemed, and how I might actually have closed my eyes in anticipation of a kiss. Which hadn't happened, I was pretty sure. Because he was Bennett, who wouldn't have been thinking about kissing me unless we'd both happened to lose our minds on the same night.

Jackson had called twice—once to apologize for not being the one to see me home safely, and once to extend another invitation to go out on the boat with him. I'd put him off, saying I'd let him know, since it was hard to make plans now, considering my mother's situation. He said he had to go out of town on business for a few days, but would call me to set up another date when he got back. I was excited by the thought of seeing him again, but was just as excited that I had a few days' reprieve. I was like a child leaving a gift unwrapped, the anticipation more exciting than the reality.

Bitty, sitting next to me on the steps and smoking her morning cigarette, elbowed me. "Why are you puckering?"

I stopped as soon as I realized she was right—I was puckering. "Just thinking. I usually pucker when I'm thinking."

She snorted and sucked on her cigarette. "You still wearing that necklace I gave you?"

I reached under the neck of my shirt and fished it out. "I never take it off. Still not sure what it means, but I like it."

She nodded. "Have you thought much about what you're going to do with Carrowmore?"

"Not really. I'm still surprised to know it even exists, much less belongs to me. I guess we'll have to see what the preservationist has to say and go from there."

A bee landed on her arm, and she didn't move, allowing it to crawl to her wrist and turn in a circle as if it might find pollen. "All the bees you see out of the hive are female—they're the worker bees. And you should never kill one."

"Because it's bad luck?"

She frowned. "No, because it's a living creature. And they're endangered. If bees go away completely, it's been said that they'll take the human race with them. They're responsible for so many of our food sources."

"Ceecee always told me it's bad luck to kill a bee."

Bitty took another drag from her cigarette. "Ceecee would know about bad luck, I suppose."

"What do you mean?"

She didn't answer right away. "The Darlingtons were so lucky for so very long. It's as if they always knew ahead of time how to protect their interests. Rumor had it that one Darlington was a blockade runner during the Civil War, and he had managed to not only squirrel away his earnings, but he had also asked to be paid in gold and not Confederate dollars. That's how they survived the war still prosperous when many if not most of their neighbors didn't."

"What's that got to do with Ceecee?"

Bitty waited for coughing fit to pass before speaking, the bee keeping its ground. "She and I were allowed in the Darlington inner circle, so we could experience their good fortune firsthand."

"And then my grandmother died, and the house was ruined. Sort of the beginning of the end."

Bitty watched the bee fly away, tracing its path before it landed on Ceecee's tea roses. "Not really. It had started a bit before that. Before your grandmother married your grandfather. Sort of the rumblings before an earthquake."

My eyebrows knit together. "What happened?"

Bitty flicked ash from the end of her cigarette, then looked at me. "It's a long story. But it seemed as if a single incident split a fault line. The one good thing about it all was that it made me stop believing in luck and making wishes." She settled her gaze on me. "We all have to find our own way in life, Larkin. There's no such thing as luck."

She reached over and lifted the arrow charm hanging from my neck, the smell of nicotine thick on her fingers. "I think we're all born with an internal compass that leads us to where we're meant to be. And whether it's a good place or a bad place, there's nothing you can do about it. I think our best friends are the people whose compasses are pointed in the same direction. That's how we find one another."

"Like you and Margaret and Ceecee," I said.

She didn't answer right away, taking her time pulling a last puff on her cigarette before stabbing it out in the ashtray by her feet. "That's the thing," she finally said. "Sometimes it takes an earthquake to find out that your compasses are set in opposite directions."

I wanted to ask her more, but Bennett's truck pulled into the driveway. I stood and looked down at Bitty, tempted to ask her to come along just so I wouldn't have to be alone with him.

"Don't even think about it," she said, standing and brushing off the seat of her long skirt.

I was clutching Bennett's red shirt. "How did you know what I was thinking?" I asked, surprised and horrified to know I was so easily read.

"You're so much like Ceecee. Always worried that people might think less of you if they knew what was really in your heart." She waved at Bennett, then picked up her ashtray. "That boy there is a keeper. I think when you scrape away all those old thoughts and misconceptions about who you used to be, you'll start seeing people in a whole new way."

Without waiting for me to answer, she went inside, leaving me to fend for myself.

By the time we rumbled over the bumps and ridges of the road into Carrowmore, my nerves were on edge. Our conversation had stuck strictly around neutral topics like the weather, how the fish were biting, and how many tourists Georgetown could expect for the upcoming summer season. But the whole time Bennett wore a slight grin, the kind of grin that told the world that he knew a secret and wasn't going to tell. It irritated me, and I could tell he knew it.

My father's car was parked next to an olive green Jeep Cherokee in front of the house. A young woman stood several yards away from it, pointing a camera up at the crumbling façade and then taking notes on a notepad. After we parked and approached on foot, I could see that she was close to my age, with medium brown hair with bangs. Her eyes were hidden behind designer sunglasses, but her eager expression and enthusiasm were evident when she introduced herself.

"Hi," she said, extending a hand for a shake. "I'm Meghan Black. I'm sorry Dr. Wallen-Arasi couldn't make it today—her baby is sick, so she asked me to cover for her. I'm her research assistant." She smiled broadly, as if to reassure us that she knew what she was talking about. "I've done tons of research on this house and others like it in the area, so I'm probably the best person to speak with anyway. I got here about an hour ago, and I've had a lot of time to look around and take pictures." She indicated the camera hanging from a pink strap around her neck.

While she was talking, I noticed the string of pearls she wore, the polished fingernails, and that, although she wore boots, she was dressed in a cute cotton knit tunic with jean leggings that screamed J.Crew. Either a research assistant made more money than I would have thought, or her mother bought her clothes.

"Great," I said, watching as my father and Ceecee came from around the corner of the house to join us.

"So, what can you tell us?" Bennett asked.

"Unfortunately, more bad stuff than good. As you indicated on the phone when you spoke with Dr. Wallen-Arasi, the house has been in the Darlington family since it was built."

She looked around for corroboration, and we all nodded, the movement mimicking that of two martin gourds strung in the branches of the enormous live oak above us.

Meghan continued. "This is usually a good thing, because when a house is considered a family heirloom, it's usually cared for consistently. According to my research, the original house was built in the mid-eighteenth century, but that was torn down for a larger house built in 1803—thankfully with a brick foundation that has given it stability over the years." She grinned, then immediately became serious again. "But the rest of it is wood—not so good. There have been updates and changes—some made mid-nineteenth century to change it from a Federal façade to Greek Revival, and there was extensive roof repair done after Hugo in 'eighty-nine along with some shoring up of the front columns, porches, and chimneys."

She began walking to the corner of the house so we could see where long boards had been nailed in a crisscross pattern across the chimney, bracing it against what appeared to be imminent collapse. "It really is remarkable that any of this is still here. Pure luck, really."

We were all staring at the peeling paint, the places where bricks were missing in the chimney, and the sagging front porch as she spoke. I noticed for the first time a partially rotted wooden swing collapsed onto the remaining floorboards, a reminder of when the house had been a home. When people had lived their lives here, had sat out on that swing looking out at the alley of oaks. Had probably rocked babies and welcomed guests. This was the house where my grandmother had died, and where my own mother had been pulled from the flames. This house was a part of who I was, and yet I knew nothing about it or the family who'd lived here for generations.

Ceecee cleared her throat. "My husband thought to restore it in the nineteen eighties, and he hired a contractor. I think they got as far as the roof and supports before they stopped."

"Why did they stop?" Meghan asked.

Ceecee looked at the young woman, but I could

tell she wasn't really seeing her. "My husband got sick. He fought cancer for about three years and didn't have the strength to deal with this, too."

"I'm sorry," Meghan said. "But doing what he did certainly helped—I doubt any of the house would be left otherwise. There's so much wood rot and mold, and you have a very large pigeon infestation. Probably more critters, too, but I'm not going inside to see for myself on this visit—I'd need to take some safety precautions first. Although I will admit to having peered in where I could. There are still some incredible dentil moldings and cornices that look salvageable. I even saw a few strips of wallpaper clinging to the plaster."

She faced us, like a doctor ready to divulge bad news. "Believe me, it really hurts me to say this, because I'm an old-house hugger, but I'm afraid, in the preservation world, we'd call this structure in danger of sudden catastrophic failure."

I watched as my dad put his arm around Ceecee. "Meaning . . . ?"

"It's on the verge of collapse. One strong storm could be the end of it. If you're planning on salvaging any part of it, you'd have to do it soon. Everything would need to be replaced—walls, ceilings, floors, supports. Roof. Everything. To restore would mean a complete gut and rebuild. Meaning it would be more of a replica than a restoration." Meghan shook her head sadly. "And it wouldn't be cheap to do it the right way." Her voice held a warning tone to it when she said "the right way."

Ceecee pressed her forehead into my father's shoulder, and he continued to hold on to her.

Meghan smiled hopefully. "It's a beautiful piece of land and a great site for a house if you want to rebuild it. You may or may not be aware that the Library of Congress has drawings, plans, and other records for many old houses in South Carolina and the rest of the country. I know they have an architectural rendering and a landscape survey prepared after 1933 that you might find helpful if you decide to go that route."

Bennett moved to stand closer to me. "Are there any other options? Besides selling to developers?"

Meghan made a face as if he'd just asked her to saw off her leg with a dull penknife. "That should be your last resort. The National Forest Service might be interested in acquiring the land without the house to protect the area from development. They did that with Tibwin Plantation in McClellanville back in the nineties. Sadly, with all the forest fires out west, the Forest Service is a little strapped for cash right now. And, of course, Tibwin had a house that was preservable, which made it more valuable to the NFS, although between you and me, I think they'd prefer the house to just collapse and go away. It's an expense and responsibility they're not really prepared to deal with. So they wouldn't want the ruins of Carrowmore. They'd just want the land it stands on to protect it from development." She looked genuinely disappointed. "I'm sorry I don't have better news."

We all thanked her and said good-bye, watching her slip out of her boots into cute kitten heels before she got into her Jeep and drove away.

"So, what do we do next?" I asked.

Everyone looked at the house, with its blackened roof and sagging porch, as if it held all the answers. Ceecee said, "We wait for your mother to wake up, and we let her know the options. And then we'll collectively make a decision on how to move forward."

I nodded, and then we all said good-bye before piling into our respective vehicles for the ride back into town.

"Well, that's not exactly what we wanted to hear," Bennett said.

I liked his use of the word "we," yet it couldn't rouse me enough from my despondency to respond.

"I'm guessing the developers already knew all that before they even approached Ceecee. Still, I'm glad we looked into it."

I managed a nod before turning to look out the window.

"At least we have the information now to present to your mother when she wakes up so we can make an informed decision as to what we should do. Not that we have to do anything, really. We can do nothing, and wait for Carrowmore to collapse. And then hold on to the land forever, rebuild, or sell. Whatever it is, we certainly don't have to decide today."

I figured his continued use of "we" had to be on purpose, so I faced him, unable to suppress a smile. "'We,' huh?"

He shrugged. "Yeah, well, I kind of feel involved. Our families have been connected for a long time."

I continued to look at him as his gaze remained fixed on the road.

"And, you know. Us."

"Us?"

"Yeah. We've been friends forever."

"True," I said, recalling something from the night he'd walked me home. I sat up. "You said something about finding some newspapers or pictures in your mother's attic. Something to do with Carrowmore."

"You're remembering our conversation from that night?" His cheek creased in a grin.

I crossed my arms but resisted the impulse to jut out my chin. "Not all of it. But I do remember that part."

He glanced at me, his expression making it clear that he didn't completely believe me. "It was a few things that belonged to my grandfather. Wasn't really sure you'd be interested."

I thought of the broken porch swing at Carrowmore, the sense of loss and disconnect I'd felt. I didn't want to move forward without questioning the past, which was how, up until now, I'd lived my life. "I'd like to see what's in those boxes, if that's all right."

Keeping his eyes on the road, he said, "Well, that can be negotiated."

"Negotiated? You already told me I could see them."

"Yeah, but I didn't expect you'd take me up on my offer." His lips quirked upward.

"You want me to pay you?"

"In a manner of speaking. The Shag Festival is coming up on May first. Go with me."

"But . . ."

"I know, you might not be here, but if you are, you should go with me. You're the best shag dancer in Georgetown."

I glared at him.

"No, really—I'm being serious. You were always the best dancer. Ask Mabry. Or my mother. Anyone, really."

I remembered the backyard barbecues at the Lynches', the Tams or the Drifters playing loudly from the stereo, and myself, Mabry, Bennett, their parents, and whoever else was there dancing the shag on the patio. Sometimes even my parents would join us, and that would be the best part of all. Until that moment in Bennett's truck, I'd forgotten about our impromptu dance contests, the smell of a Lowcountry boil, the taste of my first beer behind the house with Mabry and Bennett. Those evenings had been some of the happiest moments of my childhood.

Slightly mollified, I let out a slow sigh. "Fine. If I'm here, I'll go with you. Can I see the boxes now?"

He grinned, greatly pleased with himself. "Actually, how about Sunday? I know my mother is planning on asking you to supper. And then you can tell me what else you remember from our conversation the other night."

I picked up the red shirt that had fallen to the floor and threw it at him, then turned to look out the window so he couldn't see me smile.

twenty

Ceecee
2010

Ceecee knelt in front of the bed full of alyssum and zinnias, ruthlessly yanking out weeds and occasionally a flower stem, her vision watery from what she was telling herself was perspiration. She kept going over the scene earlier in the day at Carrowmore, of hearing what was, essentially, a death sentence. But not just for the house. A death sentence for so much more.

She heard Bitty behind her before she smelled the ever-present scent of cigarette smoke. When Bitty drew in a raspy breath to speak, Ceecee cut her off. "You really need to stop smoking. Your breathing sounds like an old mule that's pulled a hay wagon uphill for a mile."

"And you would know what that sounds like," Bitty barked out.

Sitting back on her heels, Ceecee snorted. "I've been on more farms in my life than you have." She tried to stand but realized that she couldn't quite get her knees to agree with her. Glaring up at her friend, she said, "No human being should sound that way unless they've already got one foot in the grave and the other on a banana peel."

"You can't get up, can you?"

Without a word, Ceecee held out her hand and allowed Bitty to pull her up, wheezing and coughing as she did.

They stood looking at each other, both breathing heavily, until Ceecee walked a few feet toward the wrought-iron bench under the branches of an elderly magnolia tree that faced the river and sat down, indicating the seat next to her for Bitty. Bitty hesitated briefly, then sat. She opened her mouth to speak but was overcome with a coughing fit.

Ceecee studied her old friend closely in the tree's shade, really seeing her for the first time in years and noticing the sunspots and deep lines embedded in Bitty's cheeks, the thin lips and even thinner eyebrows, and the pale spots showing through the bright red hair. It was easy to avoid one's own reflection, or not to wear glasses when applying makeup so that the illusion of still looking youthful could be maintained. As she'd grown older, Ceecee had learned one unyielding fact: Lying to yourself was always so much easier than facing the truth. But as she stared close up into Bitty's face in the unadulterated light, there could be no denying it. They were old.

"Please tell me you've been to a doctor about that cough."

"Of course I have. I'm not an idiot. I had a nasty bout of acute bronchitis, but it's much better now. I'm on antibiotics and he gave me an inhaler and I'm using both, if that makes you happy. You should have heard me before."

"Did he tell you to stop smoking?"

"Is the sky blue?" Bitty countered, her gaze challenging.

Ceecee knew it would be pointless to continue the conversation, so she sat silently, staring at the river. This place here in her garden overlooking the Sampit River had always been her refuge, the place where she could hide from the world. But after this morning, she wasn't sure there was any place left to hide.

"So, what's going to happen with Carrowmore?"

Ceecee shrugged. "I don't know—although it doesn't seem we have as much of a choice as we thought." She was silent, watching as a sailboat slowly made its way toward the harbor, a young woman in an orange bikini lowering a sail. It reminded Ceecee of the yellow two-piece bathing suit Margaret had let her wear on their trip to Myrtle Beach when they were eighteen, and how scandalous she had thought it was.

"Is that why you're so angry?" Bitty asked. "Because you can't just forget it's there like you have been doing for more than thirty years?"

Ceecee continued staring at the river. "You've always been so good at reading my mind. I wish you'd just quit."

Bitty started to laugh, but the laugh ended in a cough. "I wish I could. Old habit."

They sat in silence, watching the river flow in the same direction it always had, a ribbon connecting the past with the present, and a reminder that time moved on regardless of whether you wanted it to.

"I've wanted to forget," Ceecee said. "That horrible night. It's why I never go back. I don't want to see the ruins. In my memory, Carrowmore is still whole and freshly painted, with a swing and rocking chairs on the wide porch."

"And Margaret is still with us," Bitty said quietly.

Ceecee nodded. "Yes. To me, sometimes the house **is** Margaret, and if I tell myself that she's fine and well and at Carrowmore, I don't have to remember the night of the fire."

Bitty faced her, her eyes unreadable. "You were asleep for most of it." Bitty's gaze didn't leave Ceecee's face.

Ceecee nodded slowly, recalling herself saying that more than she recalled the actual event. But that made sense, her doctors told her. They said her brain had blocked out most of her memories of that night, and they wouldn't return until she was ready to remember everything. And she still wasn't. She'd been found with her body thrown over Ivy's on the front lawn while the fire burned behind them. They told her she'd saved Ivy's life. She glanced away from Bitty's probing stare. "I dream about that night sometimes. I hear Ivy crying, and I smell burning wood and feel the heat of the flames. And then . . . nothing."

"But you still feel the guilt."

Ceecee jerked her gaze from the river to stare at her friend. "Guilt? For what happened to Margaret?"

Bitty slowly shook her head. "No. For what happened after she died."

Ceecee's head hurt. "That's the thing that scares me, Bitty. I never did. But I still miss her. Every single day."

"I know. And I'm glad you don't feel any guilt. Because I think I have enough of that for both of us."

"What are you talking about? You weren't there."

Bitty stood, bracing herself on the arm of the bench. "You say you don't like to go to Carrowmore because you like to think of it as still whole, with Margaret still there. You know what I see in my head when I think about it? I see the ruin exactly as it is and as it should be. It's a burned-out shell. A perfect reminder of ill-advised dreams and wishes and broken promises. The only reason I don't go and set a match to the rest of it is because of Larkin. In my dreams, I like to think of her as the salvation not just for the house, but for all of us."

Ceecee remained seated, Bitty's bitter words like dull arrows pricking her skin before ricocheting to the ground. "You never told me you felt that way. All these years, and you've never told me."

"Because you never want to see the ugly parts of people, so you pretend they're not there. You insist on seeing everyone, with very few exceptions, as perfect with good intentions. Frankly, it's been exhausting protecting you from a lot of ugliness, and I'm simply not going to be around forever to keep doing it, so it's time you start figuring it out yourself."

Ceecee stood so fast that her head swam for a moment. "I'm going to forgive you for saying that because you're old and sick and feeling crotchety. But none of that tells me why you feel guilty about Margaret's death."

Bitty pressed the palm of her hand against her chest as if it might help her breathe. She took a deep breath through rattling lungs and said, "Because on that day at Carrowmore when we heard about Reggie enlisting, I put another ribbon in the tree."

The chirping of the insects and a cicada's whirring in the magnolia tree suddenly seemed to stop. All Ceecee could hear was the blood rushing in her head and Bitty's breath wheezing in and out of her chest. "What did it say?"

Bitty closed her eyes for a moment. "It's funny, the things we remember, isn't it? I remember each and every word, so much that I sometimes dream about it." She took two rattling breaths. "I wrote, 'I wish to be there on the day that Margaret Darlington's bill for the price of a promise broken comes due.'"

"What broken promise?" Ceecee asked, although she already knew. She'd called it so many other things so she'd never have to call it that. Which meant, of course, that Bitty was right.

She reached for Bitty's hand, and they sat down on the bench again, their fingers entwined, their hands papery and veined, yet still strong and capable. They sat for a long while, watching the sun dip in the sky, and the river skimming past them as it always had, finding its inevitable end in the deep waters of the Atlantic.

Ceecee
1951

It had been a month since they'd learned of Reggie's enlisting. The days had grown longer and hotter, the mosquitoes more plentiful. Ceecee would normally have been miserable, as all bloodsucking insects had always loved her, and the humidity made her hair frizz. But she barely noticed. Even her mother had commented on her bright mood. As long as she didn't slack on her chores, her mother left her alone to daydream about Boyd and their future together. Ceecee's parents had both met Boyd during his earlier visit and, given that they had invited him to supper twice during his stay, had apparently approved of him.

Although there was nothing official yet, old Dr. Griffith had invited Boyd to work in his practice to meet the existing patients and to take over gradually. It helped that Boyd was a veteran, since the doctor had lost his only son in Guadalcanal. Boyd was staying temporarily with the doctor and his wife in the carriage house on their property, and they had offered it to him as a permanent place to live should he be interested in staying long-term.

All of this meant that Ceecee had started thinking about her wedding gown, and what flowers she'd have at the service, and how her father could walk her down the aisle and perform the ceremony. Surely that had been done before? The only part she couldn't decide on was who would be her maid of honor; she switched between Bitty and Margaret with almost the same frequency as the turning of the tides. She had time to decide, she knew—she didn't even have a ring yet. But every single night she dreamed of her wedding day, and even the shadow of Margaret's misery couldn't dim her happiness. It was odd to have their positions inverted, and even if she wasn't given any satisfaction over the reversal in fortune, she'd be lying if she didn't admit it was exhilarating to be the lucky one for a change. Still, she remembered the promise to be friends, come what may, and she'd been raised to believe that a promise made was a promise kept, so she tried. She really tried, no matter how hard Margaret made it.

Margaret had finally shared the contents of Reggie's letter. Although it had been filled with vows of his undying love for her, he was enlisting to do his duty, to build a better future not only for him and Margaret but also for the country. If she would still have him when the war was over, he would come back to her and they would be married.

By the time she'd read the letter, he'd already been shipped out for basic training at Fort Sill in Oklahoma. He'd given her an address to write to and promised he'd wait for her letter before writing again to her. He didn't want to bother her if she didn't wish to hear from him. As far as Bitty and Ceecee knew, Margaret had not written.

On a sunny Tuesday afternoon, Bitty and Ceecee walked slowly down the sidewalk on Front Street with Margaret tucked protectively between them. She wore sunglasses and a hat to protect her skin from the sun, but neither hid the fatigue under her eyes or the sallowness of her skin. Even her arm where it was linked with Ceecee's felt like thin flesh against bone.

Mrs. Darlington had tried tempting her daughter with a trip to Paris and London, or even a short shopping trip to Charleston, but Margaret showed no interest. As a last resort, Mrs. Darlington had asked Bitty and Ceecee to take her to downtown Georgetown—anything to get Margaret out of the house and into the sunshine.

The lure of a shopping trip had done nothing to perk her up, nor had the Darlington cook's best efforts enticed Margaret to eat. Ceecee had always thought the term "pining away" was something found only in fairy tales and the gothic romance novels Bitty would pull out of the donation bins at the school's library. But here was Margaret, fading right in front of them, to the point where Ceecee was reminded of the shadows of the A-bomb victims in Hiroshima and Nagasaki that were forever embedded on the pavements. She was afraid that would be Margaret's fate, one day just slipping away from them and leaving behind only a pale shadow.

"You should write to him," Bitty said, chewing on a Tootsie Roll. "It's time to swallow your Darlington pride. Tell him you love him, and that you will wait for him. Tell him you'd like to set a wedding date. Because if you keep going this way, there will be nothing left to fit into your mother's antique lace wedding dress."

Margaret shook her head. "I can't. If he truly loves me, he'll come home and admit he's made a big mistake. By not writing, I'm hoping he'll figure that out on his own."

Bitty rolled her eyes. "I don't know much about

men, Margaret, but I do know that they're about as good at mind reading as women are. Just give me the word, and I will write to him for you."

When Margaret didn't give her a response, Bitty looked at Ceecee. "I give up."

Ceecee could only nod, having already tried over and over again to talk sense into Margaret. It was wearying and sad, not to mention hopeless. Bitty was right—without a letter from Margaret, Reggie would think she'd forgotten about him. But apart from writing the letter themselves, as Bitty had threatened, there wasn't anything they could do about it.

"I'm starving," Ceecee said. "Anybody up for the Whistling Pig? I don't think I've been there since graduation."

"Best hot dog in the world," Bitty said. "I'm game."

Margaret didn't answer but stopped to stare listlessly into the window at Nancy's Dress Shop, watching the reflection of the sky behind them instead of the pretty dresses on mannequins. "I like that one on the left, Margaret," Ceecee said in her most cheerful voice. "It would look just beautiful with your coloring and would show off your tiny waist. That sweet girl Marilyn Tompkins works there and has the best taste. Let's go inside."

Margaret frowned and turned her head, as if just becoming aware that she wasn't alone. "I'm sorry?"

Ceecee dug into her purse, pulled out the tube of Certainly Red lipstick that Margaret had given to her on the day they'd left for Myrtle Beach, and handed it to her along with her mirror. "I think you forgot to put your lipstick on. Here, use this. Everybody says that just putting on a bright lipstick will make a girl feel like a million dollars without having to spend a million dollars." She wasn't sure if that was really what "everybody" said, or where she'd heard it, but she was desperate to get Margaret to smile again.

Margaret took the lipstick and mirror and stared at them as if she had no idea what they were for. Bitty grabbed them out of her hand and gave them back to Ceecee. "For pity's sake, Margaret. He's just a man. And if he can leave you without a by-your-leave, then he's not worth mooning over."

Seeing Margaret's face begin to pucker, Ceecee prepared herself for another torrent of tears and began to hunt for the nearest bench. Suddenly, she saw a cab pull up in front of the jewelry store and the back window roll down just as the store owner hurried out to the car.

"Who's that?" Ceecee asked.

Bitty wore a sly smirk. "One of Hazel Weiss's working girls from the Sunset Lodge. I hear they make as much as a thousand dollars a month. In cash."

Ceecee glanced over at Margaret, who was watching with a strange expression, but at least she wasn't crying. They continued to watch as the store owner went back inside and then reemerged a short time later with a flat black display box. They couldn't see what was inside, but the sun glinted off something bright and sparkling as he opened the car door for the woman inside to see.

"Why don't they shut them down?" Ceecee asked Bitty. Bitty was always the person to ask about sensitive topics since she talked openly with her parents about everything.

Bitty snorted. "Because the politicians who make the laws are their best customers." She took out a pack of cigarettes from her purse, but Ceecee's glare made her put it back. Ladies simply did **not** smoke on the sidewalk. But it was apparently appropriate for a prostitute to shop on one.

Through the open door, Ceecee could make out a pair of long, elegant, stockinged legs leading down to high-heeled black shoes. A wide-brimmed hat with netting covered the face, giving the unidentified woman a secret allure.

"Come on," Bitty said, grabbing Ceecee's hand and not waiting for Margaret to follow. "Let's go look at the engagement rings."

Aware of how Margaret might feel about it, Ceecee tried to pull away, but Bitty wouldn't let her. "She should be happy for you," Bitty said, not letting go. "A real friend would be."

They were almost at the jewelry store when Ceecee glanced back and saw Margaret slowly following them, her gaze focused on the parked car at the curb.

Bitty stopped at the store window, pointing out diamond engagement rings, her eyes occasionally turning to the reflection of the car and the woman seated inside. There was a high trill of laughter, and Ceecee turned in time to see a small gloved hand accept a small black velvet bag from the jeweler, but no offer of payment. The woman said good-bye, and the door shut before the car pulled away and disappeared down the street.

"Did she steal the jewelry?" Ceecee asked, shocked that a shopkeeper would openly be doing business with a prostitute.

"No," Bitty said with a condescending air. "Apparently, most of the women have accounts at the businesses downtown. During the Depression, the owners liked to see Hazel and her girls walk through their doors. Can't imagine them turning them away now."

Ceecee shook her head. "I can't believe that just happened in front of me," she said, making room at the window for Margaret. "I wonder if my parents know about it."

"Oh, they know," Bitty said. "The Sunset Lodge has been there since the thirties. When your daddy preaches against fornication, that's most likely what he's referring to."

At first, Ceecee thought she was listening to a mewling kitten, but when she didn't see one, she looked up at Margaret, who was crying again, but it was different this time. Her sobs were so quiet, it was as if her hurt had turned in on itself, unable to find a way out.

Margaret pressed her gloved hands against the glass window, holding herself up as her body shook with silent sobs. Bitty met Ceecee's eyes, and a worried glance passed between them. It was Bitty who took Margaret's arm this time, led her to a bench, and sat next to her as Ceecee remained standing and did her best to hide her from passersby.

"Margaret, please. Speak to us. Tell us how we can help you." Bitty was holding Margaret's hands in hers.

In between hiccups, Margaret finally spoke. "That . . . woman. I wanted to speak . . . with her."

"Why on earth would you want to speak with a **prostitute**?" Ceecee whispered the last word.

"Because she . . . might be able to help me. To tell me . . . what to do." She paused to take a deep gulp of air. "Aren't they supposed to be experienced with these kinds of things?"

Bitty sat up straight, looking at Margaret with an expression that said she couldn't quite believe what she'd heard.

"What do you mean?" Ceecee asked. "What on earth could a **prostitute** tell you?"

Ignoring Ceecee, Bitty hissed, "You don't want that, Margaret. You know you don't. You could **die.** That's a whole lot worse than any shame you think you need to hide from the world. You and Reggie love each other. There's no shame in that."

"Shame in what?" Ceecee nearly screamed, unable to understand what they were talking about.

Bitty reached into her pocketbook, pulled out her cigarettes, and lit one, regardless of what Ceecee or anyone else might think. "We need to reach Reggie. Let him know."

Margaret squeezed Bitty's arm, her nails unkempt and chewed down to the quick. "He'll come back for me then, won't he?"

"I don't know," Bitty said softly. "But we have to at least try. For everyone's sake." She looked at Ceecee when she said that, and it made her shiver.

"Would someone please tell me what's going on?" Ceecee said, loudly enough that a man and woman walking nearby looked up.

Bitty smiled at them and waited for them to pass before taking another deep drag from her cigarette. "She's pregnant, Ceecee. Margaret's going to have a baby."

Ceecee sat down heavily next to Margaret, sick to her stomach as all sorts of thoughts ran through her head, the most shameful one being that Margaret couldn't be her bridesmaid now since she would certainly be showing by the time Ceecee walked down the aisle.

"Have you told your parents?" she asked.

Margaret shook her head. "How can I? They'd be so ashamed. They'd disown me."

Ceecee put her arm around Margaret's shoulders. "I know this is hard. But you love Reggie and he loves you, and you're going to have a baby. A baby! Reggie's baby. I know this isn't what you planned, but it's not the end of the world. You know that, right?"

It took a moment, but Margaret finally nodded.

Ceecee continued. "If we put our heads together, we can come up with a plan. We'll help you figure out what to do. You're not alone. Bitty and I are here. We're friends forever, remember?"

She looked over Margaret's head at Bitty for confirmation. But Bitty simply stared at her, then blew out a mouthful of smoke, obscuring her face.

twenty-one

Larkin
2010

I parked my rental car at the curb in front of the Lynches' house and picked up the macaroni casserole Ceecee had given me to take to Sunday dinner. I paused before heading down the familiar front walk, staring up at the white Victorian with its deep wraparound porch. Weeds still grew between the pavers, and Mrs. Lynch's vinca and ageratum shouted and waved from various pots on the porch and beds in the yard. I knew if I looked closely at the corner of the third paver from the end, I'd see my initials carved next to those of Mabry and Bennett. Immortalized together in concrete.

"They're still there," Mabry called from the porch where she sat in a metal rocker with Ellis in her lap.

I stopped to look down, and saw she was right. The space next to our initials, reserved at the time for the initials of our future children, was filled only with green lichen.

"Sure are." I continued walking, listening to the strains of music sifting through the screened door. "'What Kind of Fool (Do You Think I Am)' by Bill Deal and the Rhondels."

"Dang, you're good," Mabry said as she stood, placing Ellis on his feet. "I'm going to assume you're right, because I have no idea. You could be making stuff up for all I know."

"Maybe I am."

"Ha. You couldn't lie if you wanted to. I think that's why all the kids in school were scared of you— because they knew you'd tell them stuff they didn't want to hear. Of all the things Ceecee taught you, that one's a keeper for sure."

"Seriously? It was a good thing for my peers to avoid me?"

"Sure. If they didn't want to hear the truth, then they wouldn't have been worthy of being your friend." She sniffed deeply. "Let me guess—Ceecee's macaroni casserole."

"Of course. Some things never change."

"Thank goodness," Mabry said, lifting Ellis to get a better look.

A memory hit me, and my mouth actually salivated. "Did your mother make her special cake?"

"Of course. She knew you were coming."

"Some things never change," I repeated, laughing this time.

But Mabry didn't laugh. Instead, she peered closely at me, her green eyes just like her brother's. "Learning who you are and changing aren't always the same thing, you know. Sometimes we think we've changed, but all we've done is grow into the person we were always meant to be."

While I was still mulling over her words, she took the casserole from my hands. "Bennett's in the garage, sorting through those boxes of papers that belonged to our grandfather. Said to send you back when you got here."

Anticipating my next question, she said, "And no, Mama and I don't need your help in the kitchen. We've got it covered."

I smiled at her departing back, wondering how I'd learned to survive without a friend who knew me better than I knew myself.

I walked down the driveway—two dirt tracks with a grassy strip down the middle—toward the detached garage at the back of the house. As long as I'd known the Lynches, they'd never used it to park cars. It had always been filled with what Mabry, Bennett, and I had thought of as treasure. Old, discarded toys and clothing from different eras, ancient tools and holiday decorations, and an entire assortment of forgotten detritus of past lives. It was heaven to us as children, and as I approached it, I felt a thrum of nostalgia.

Inside, Bennett sat on a steamer trunk in front of an ancient card table shoved against the far wall. Several stacks of papers were piled in front of him, and he was slowly flipping through the pages when I greeted him and he looked up.

"Hey, Larkin," he said, and the sound of my name did something twisty to my insides. He stood and shoved the steamer trunk over to make room for a chair with a vinyl cushion that wore most of its stuffing on the outside. "Your pick," he said, indicating the seats.

"I think there's room for both of us on the trunk. I can't see you sitting on crumbling foam." I sat down on the trunk and slid over, absently patting the space next to me while glancing down at the papers. There were several nearly transparent official-looking forms with smeared black type as if they'd come from an ancient mimeograph machine, and a small pile of yellowed newspaper clippings.

"What am I looking at?" I asked, painfully aware of Bennett sliding onto the trunk next to me, and trying not to notice how close he was, or how I felt a jolt each time his forearm brushed mine.

"These were all in a single folder. It was with a bunch of other files that had probably been in my grandfather's desk drawer when he was fire chief—nothing original or confidential. This was the only file that seemed to contain information about a single case."

"The fire at Carrowmore?"

Bennett nodded, then began rifling through a stack, pulling something out from near the top. "I thought you might want to see this." He slid one of the clippings in front of me, and I found myself holding my breath. "It's a photo of Margaret, your grandmother, but it looks just like you, doesn't it?"

I nodded, staring at the strange yet familiar face in black-and-white of my grandmother in her wedding dress. She wore a lace veil that framed her oval face and looked to be light blond like me, her eyes and nose and lips shaped exactly as my own. Her jaw was softer, her cheekbones not as pronounced, but there could be no denying that we were closely related.

A longing to have known her, to remember what her voice sounded like or what it felt like to have my hair stroked by her hand consumed me, constricting my throat as if filling it with ashes. I studied her face, desperately wanting to understand why her memory had been erased from my past. In that photo she seemed to be looking at me, begging me to hear her story, as if in hearing hers, I would finally understand my own.

"It's her obituary," Bennett said softly.

I nodded, taking note of the day she died. October 16, 1954. "The day after Hurricane Hazel, right?"

"Yes. And the day of the fire. What's really interesting is that my grandfather kept all of the nonrecords and records in a file together in his office. And he chose to bring them home when he retired."

"Were our families close, then?"

He shook his head. "Not according to my mother. She says her family first met Ceecee and Ivy when they moved into the house on River Street after the fire. Ivy and my mama started school together and became best friends."

"Maybe because it was such a tragic story, he wanted to save a reminder of it," I offered.

"We're talking about my grandfather here, remember. I don't think he had a sentimental bone in his body. When he moved out to the fishing cabin after my grandmother died, he got rid of everything except for a few essentials. And this box."

He pulled out the official-looking form I'd glanced at before and moved it in front of me. Even though **Georgetown County Fire Department** was written at the top of the page, it took me a few moments to realize what I was looking at.

Bennett tapped his index finger to lines at the top. "Your grandmother's name."

I followed to where he pointed, and I realized I was looking at a box on the form labeled **Deceased.** Next to it, **Cause of death: smoke inhalation.**

I let out a sigh of relief. I'd been imagining my grandmother burning to death, one of those horrible ways to die that always made the hypothetical "Which would you prefer?" lists. But she'd died instead of smoke inhalation, which was, although still awful, maybe not as agonizing as being burned alive.

My gaze slowly slid to the box below it, the one labeled **Cause of fire.** And there, in plain black ink on yellowed paper, the single word **undetermined.** Beneath it, in pale blue pen, someone had handwritten the word **suspicious** and underscored it twice.

I sat back, trying to place a distance between the paper and me. "What does that mean?" I knew what it meant, of course. I just needed someone else to say it out loud before I could believe it, and I was suddenly glad that Bennett was right there, sitting so close to me that I could lean on him if I needed to.

He shrugged. "I'm guessing it means that someone—I'm thinking my grandfather—didn't believe the fire that caused your grandmother's death was accidental. Remember, this was almost sixty years ago. They didn't have the forensic capabilities we have now. So maybe 'suspicious' just means there was a lack of evidence to rule on one side or the other."

"Is there any more of the official record in here?" I asked.

"No. Just a few clippings about hurricane damage and flooding in the area, and a couple of articles about your mother, who was a toddler at the time." He riffled through the small pile of newspaper articles, and slid one toward me. "This talks about how Ceecee was found unconscious on the front lawn, her body thrown over Ivy's to protect her. Ceecee was called a hero, but apparently she couldn't remember what happened or how she managed to escape."

I looked down at the photo of my mother, about age two, her fine hair pulled back with an enormous bow. She sat on someone's lap—I imagined it was my grandmother's—smiling into the camera. There was something pure and untouched in her expression, and I realized I'd never seen my mother without haunted, burdened eyes that always seemed to be looking beyond what was in front of her.

My first instinct was to put all the papers back in the folder, out of sight. To move on to something new, to forget. Because that was what I'd always done. The whole reason why I'd left was to start over and pretend I didn't have a past.

"What are you going to do now?" Bennett asked, his tone expectant instead of chiding.

"I don't know," I said without meeting his eyes. "It all happened so long ago." I looked down at my grandmother's photo. She was younger when she died than I was now. "I wonder if Mama might have found something—maybe that's why she went to ask Jackson about the insurance on Carrowmore. I'll just wait for her to wake up, I guess."

"Larkin." Bennett's voice was gentle.

"I know." I paused, taking a deep breath. "She might not." It was the first time I had allowed myself to truly consider it, to press on that particular bruise.

"You know you've got people here. You don't

have to go it alone. And you've got your daddy. He's dying to be a part of your life again."

I looked away. I'd been avoiding that whole situation, hoping I could put it off till I left again. "He left a message on my phone this morning. Wants me to come over later."

Bennett just looked at me, which was worse than him scolding. Uncomfortable, I looked at the obituary and fire record again, and the handwritten, double-underscored word **suspicious.** I thought of my quiet studio apartment in Brooklyn, the bare walls of my cubicle. The gym where I worked out every evening but knew no one's name. That was my life now, and if I wasn't exactly happy, I was content. The past was done; there could be no changing it or reliving it.

"Just a thought," Bennett said, reminding me of when he tutored me in high school algebra and he was about to point out a big flaw in my calculations. "Wasn't Bitty good friends with your grandmother and Ceecee? She might know more."

"Does it really matter now? I don't see the point in raising the dead."

"Don't you?" he asked. "Because the way I see it, what happened to your grandmother affected not only your mother, but Ceecee, too. It dictated the way you were raised. Aren't you the least bit curious?"

"Not really," I said, although his scrutiny was making me squirm. "It's all tragic and sad, but even if we rebuild Carrowmore, there's nothing we can change. Thank you for showing me all this, though. I had no idea how much I looked like her."

He avoided my gaze by stacking folders and papers on top of the card table. "I have to go back to Columbia tomorrow. There are some work projects I need to deal with that can't be done from here. But I'll be back Friday—just in time for the Shag Festival."

I was surprised by the disappointment I felt knowing he wouldn't be just a few blocks away. Which was silly, really, because we'd been in different states for the last nine years and I'd barely thought about him. "You're not serious about taking me to the festival, are you? Because I doubt I even remember the steps."

He smiled, and my insides did that warm, twisty thing again. "Like I said before, it's like riding a bike. Your body will remember what to do."

Before I could argue, he'd stood and pulled me up with him. "I'll do the eight-count while you hum 'Never Make a Move Too Soon' by B.B. King. And don't tell me you don't know how it goes, because you know every song ever written."

Taking my right hand firmly in his left, he stepped backward with his left foot, making me move forward with my right. "One-and-two, three-and-four, five-six," he said as I hummed.

And he was right. I did remember, my feet easily moving with the familiar steps, my hand held tightly in his as if he was afraid to let me go. I remembered parties in his parents' backyard and how I used to wish Jackson Porter would stop by and ask me to dance. How I used to pretend sometimes that Bennett was him. Looking at Bennett now, I couldn't remember why.

I kept humming until I realized he'd stopped counting, and then I stopped, too. We stood absolutely still, facing each other with our hands clasped. The space was quiet enough that I could hear the cicadas in the trees outside, and our heavy breathing that matched the rhythm of my thumping heart.

"Dinner's ready," Mabry shouted from the doorway. Bennett and I quickly moved apart.

"Perfect timing," I said, hoping my voice didn't sound as high-pitched as it did to me. "I'm starving."

Without looking at Bennett, I followed Mabry to the house, trying to reconcile all I'd just learned with the unsettling knowledge that the past wouldn't let me go no matter how much I wanted it to.

twenty-two

Ivy
2010

"I saw the mural you painted at the ice-cream store."

Bitty is sitting close to my bed, her hands clasped together like she's praying. Her hair is bright red, the spikes beginning to wilt as the hair grows longer. I guess it's because she's been here since my accident and hasn't been home to get it cut. She speaks quietly so no one else can hear her.

"I knew you'd painted it even before I asked Gabriel. I recognized your style. Your creativity with the little details. It's what sets you apart, that attention to detail. I don't think you learned that from me, so I won't try to take credit. Although maybe I should.

I bought you your first easel-and-brush set, remember? You're a fine artist, Ivy. A very fine artist."

She looks down at her nails. They're starting to grow out, too, but they're still ragged and stained at the beds with dark paint, and I can tell she bites them. This must be a new habit, because I don't remember her biting her nails before. Must be since my accident.

We've all changed since then. Besides being unable to communicate, I don't dream anymore, either. I'm convinced this means I'm in a dream already. Larkin always told me that dreams are meant to teach us something. So, I'm waiting to learn whatever it is and move on. I have my suspicions. Whatever it is that I'm supposed to learn has something to do with Ceecee and Larkin. And me. Because each time they come talk to me and tell me something new, I feel myself get lighter.

"I saw what you painted in the corner, that little detail you have to know to look for. Being artists means we're different from others. We see so much, don't we? Things others are blissfully unaware of. It's a burden, isn't it?"

Bitty sits up straighter and begins to cough, and thin black clouds like crows form around her head. I don't think they're real. I think they exist in my dream, so only I can see them. But they're there, and she's coughing out all that toxic air, cigarette smoke, and secrets trapped inside her. And each time she coughs, I feel a slackening of my tethers, a slight release in the tension, and I think I'm onto something here. The ceiling crackles above me, and I know that I am right.

She runs her hand through the droopy red spikes on top of her head. "I wondered why you'd been asking about the insurance, and about removing Ceecee as trustee. And then when I saw the mural, I understood. You must have remembered something from the night of the fire." She's silent for a moment, thinking. "And whatever happened to make you remember wasn't recent, was it? Mack and Bennett seem to think it's connected to the developers' interest, but I disagree. I believe it's something else entirely. Because I happen to know that you've always been one to chew on a hurt, taking your time before deciding what to do. You didn't tell anyone what you remembered because you needed to think about it first. And the way you think through your problems is by being creative. Like sewing new curtains for your dining room. Or painting a mural."

She sits back in her chair. "I've figured that whatever it was that made you remember that night of the fire happened somewhere around the time you went to see the lawyer. I just can't decipher what that could have been."

She coughs again, and the crows lift from around her head like a cyclone, circling the ceiling and attempting to flit through the widening cracks, but their wings are too big, and they fall down to the floor in a sooty heap.

Bitty takes a bottle of water from her large purse and drinks about half of it before putting it down. "There's so much you don't know. Things that happened before you were born." She leans forward. "We only kept secrets because we wanted to protect you. And Larkin. Please know that. Our choices were made out of love."

She sits back in her chair, exhausted. I know what it means to make choices out of love. Just ask Larkin. Love, I have found, is a treacherous companion. When you do something out of love, it usually backfires. People need to know that. They need to know that they should do something because it's the right thing to do and not because they feel they have to because of love. It's the best way to destroy it.

"Open your eyes and talk to me, Ivy." Bitty's voice is pleading, and that scares me a little, even more than the black crows coming from her mouth. She's always been so bossy and take-charge. To hear her plead breaks my heart.

"I want to tell you the whole story. What Ceecee and I should have told you long ago. Before you discovered something by accident, and perhaps misunderstood. I wanted to, but Ceecee didn't want to upset you. Because she loves you. So do I, but I've found that keeping secrets is never the way to show love."

There's fluttering up by the ceiling, and I see the crows again, perched upside down with their claws in the cracks, their beady black eyes staring down at

Bitty. What did she say about me asking about the insurance, the trusteeship? As if someone has suddenly turned on a fan, the burning smell of paint thinner wafts across my nose, erasing the hospital smell of disinfectant and latex.

And that's when I remember where I was and what I had been doing when I discovered a truth about the night my mother died. Remember how the world seemed to crash in on me as I tried to put the pieces together, and understand how so many lies could have been told in the name of love.

I feel the anger that's anchored me to my bed begin to slide away like unlocked handcuffs. I remember why I was at Carrowmore. Why I put my ribbon in the tree. And I at last know why there were two ribbons stuck in the tree after I fell through the rotting wood floor and the world crashed in on me for real.

Ceecee
1951

A week after finding out about Margaret's pregnancy, Ceecee and Boyd were sitting on the front-porch swing at her parents' house. Boyd had moved in to the Griffiths' carriage house two days earlier and had already started meeting Dr. Griffith's patients. Despite appearances that all her wishes were coming true, Ceecee couldn't overlook the heavy stone in the pit of her stomach. It was as if she were sitting in a boat in strong wind with her eyes closed, wondering from which side the waves would strike and how high they'd be.

She'd told Boyd about Margaret's baby, even though Bitty had pleaded with her not to. But Margaret had asked her to tell him, believing that Boyd might be able to reach Reggie. It also had allowed Boyd, as a doctor, to ask her about her condition and give her advice on the pregnancy without giving her a full exam. She needed one, but Boyd also understood that since Dr. Griffith was good friends with Mr. Darlington, that would be out of the question.

Ceecee was torn between her love for and devotion to her friend, and her all-consuming love for Boyd. She'd once believed that loving more than one person—a friend, a child, a husband—just meant your heart was supposed to get bigger to accommodate all of that love. Yet she found herself resenting Margaret for her demands on Ceecee's and Boyd's attention and affection, Ceecee's heart seeming to shrink as it sought to exclude her friend.

The more Ceecee felt guilty over her unsettled feelings about the time Boyd spent with Margaret, the more she overcompensated, showering Margaret with affection and impromptu gifts of flowers from her garden and pretty ribbons for her hair to brighten the limp strands and the paleness of her skin. Bitty simply stood by in silence, smoking her cigarettes, her eyes silent as if she were watching an epic movie unfolding on the big screen.

Boyd had informed them that Reggie had already been sent to a training camp in Japan. Margaret's only hope was that he'd come home in time to marry her before she started showing. Except for Margaret, none of them saw that as a feasible option. Boyd suggested that Margaret tell her parents as soon as possible so that her mother could orchestrate a visit to her fictional old maiden aunt in Columbia until the baby was born, and then the Darlingtons could pretend to adopt the child of an impoverished relation and raise it as their own. It had been done enough times for them to think it could work. All Margaret had to do was find the courage to tell her parents. Something she was struggling to do.

"Have you spoken with Margaret today?" Boyd asked.

Ceecee shook her head. "No, but Bitty and I are planning to visit her tomorrow. I'm not sure if she realizes that she's running out of time. I'm worried about her. She's so thin, it just can't be good for her or the baby."

"No, it's not," he agreed. He put his arm around her. "I feel partially responsible for all this. Reggie's my younger brother. I know we're both adults, but I've felt responsible for him my whole life. I hope Margaret knows that she can turn to me for guidance in Reggie's absence."

"I'm sure she does," Ceecee said stiffly.

"You're a good friend to her, Sessalee. I hope she knows it."

"You think so?" She paused a moment before blurting out, "Because I find myself feeling so much anger toward her. Anger for getting herself in this situation. And anger because she's doing nothing to help herself."

"Maybe she doesn't know how," Boyd suggested gently. It's one of the things she loved most about him. His compassion for others even when they didn't seem to deserve it.

He continued. "She's been raised with others taking care of her every need. Being born beautiful doesn't help, either. She's never had to work very hard to get people's attention, so she's never had to wait for something she's wanted or needed. She expects it all as her due."

Everything Boyd said was immediately forgotten as soon as he said the word "beautiful." "You think Margaret's beautiful?" Ceecee asked, trying to keep her voice light and playful, and was afraid she'd failed completely. It was a stupid question that did nothing to hide her insecurities. A person would have to be blind not to notice that Margaret Darlington had a rare kind of beauty.

"Yes. But in the way a marble statue in a museum is beautiful. So lovely to look at, but you're a little afraid to touch it in case it might break."

Mollified, Ceecee curled her legs up on the swing and rested her head on Boyd's shoulder. She knew he was getting close to proposing, felt it in her bones.

She'd been working very hard to ensure they had enough time alone. Which was difficult, considering she had two younger brothers and a mother with eyes like a hawk. Even now, before dusk, the front-porch lights were on, and the front room draperies were pulled wide open to allow ample viewing of the porch from inside the house.

Boyd looked down at her, his eyes twinkling. "Have I told you lately that I think you're the most incredible woman I've ever met?"

"I don't remember. But I don't mind you repeating yourself."

He smiled, his gaze traveling down to her lips, and something that felt like fire raced from her heart to her toes and back again. "Have I told you how much I love you?"

"Yes," she whispered, stretching her neck so that their lips were almost touching. "But you can say that as many times as you want, too."

His lips brushed hers just as the front door slammed open and her brother Lloyd ran out onto the porch, stopping in front of the swing. "Mama wants to know if you want some sweet tea."

Ceecee could tell Boyd was trying very hard not to laugh. "Thanks, Lloyd. I wouldn't mind a glass, and I'm sure your sister would like one, too. Please thank your mama for being so thoughtful."

Lloyd stood staring at them, as if he hadn't anticipated Boyd's answer, and for a horrible moment,

Ceecee wondered if her mother had any sweet tea at all or was just playing her chaperone role a little too thoroughly.

"All right," he said, dragging his feet as he moved closer to the door and opened it, the sound of the phone ringing inside.

The door banged behind her brother as Boyd turned back to her. "Where were we?" he asked softly, his lips brushing hers.

"Sadly, here on my parents' porch instead of somewhere with a little more privacy." She pressed her lips against his, hoping his head blocked her mother's view from inside.

Boyd pulled back, his eyes searching hers. "I haven't spoken with your father, yet, and I haven't even begun my medical career, but I believe my prospects are good."

He pressed his forehead against hers as Ceecee prepared to say the word "yes" without shouting it.

The front door opened again, and Ceecee started to tell Lloyd to go away, but she paused with the words still on her lips. It was her mother, her face ashen. Ceecee stood, Boyd following and standing next to her. "What is it, Mama? What's wrong?"

"That was Dr. Griffith. On the phone." Her gaze drifted to Boyd. "He's looking for you. There's . . . there's been an accident."

Ceecee rushed to her mother and grabbed her arms. "Is it Daddy? Is Daddy all right?"

Ceecee's mother shook her head. "Your father is

fine. It's the Darlingtons. Margaret's parents. They were in their car on the South Santee River Bridge, and a truck swerved . . ." She stopped, regained her composure. "Their car went over the side."

Boyd was already struggling into his jacket and putting on his hat. "Where are they?"

She reached for Ceecee's hand and squeezed. "Dr. Griffith needs you to bring Margaret." She paused again, taking a deep breath. "He's at the morgue. Both of her parents are gone."

"Come with me, Sessalee," Boyd said, already stepping quickly from the porch. "Margaret's going to need you."

Ceecee met her mother's eyes, seeing beyond the grief and sadness the same kind of resignation she'd seen in Bitty's eyes, a recognition of an inevitability that everyone except for her seemed to have anticipated.

twenty-three

Larkin
2010

As I walked up to my parents' front porch, my phone beeped again. Glancing down, I saw it was another text from Jackson, letting me know he was back in town and asking if I wanted to go out on his boat. While half of my brain was already planning what sort of bathing suit to buy, the other half was shouting at me to tell him no, reminding me that I'd received the apology I'd been waiting for and should move on. I had no problem identifying which message was being conveyed by the old Larkin and which by the new.

I put my phone on "silent," then threw it in my purse before ringing the doorbell. I felt odd not walking right in, but it had been years since I'd lived there, and even more since I'd believed the house was my home.

My dad opened the door, and his face softened in relief. "I was afraid you wouldn't come." He stepped back, and I walked past him into the foyer, staying beyond arm's reach. Not that I expected him to hug me, but just in case.

He shut the door and turned to me. "Did you have trouble finding the place?"

It took me a moment to realize he was making a joke. I gave him a reluctant grin. "No. I'm familiar with the neighborhood. Had dinner a couple of nights ago just a few blocks away."

"I know. Carol Anne invited me, but I told her you'd be happier if I didn't go. Did you dance?"

"No. It started to rain after dinner, so we all went inside."

"That's a shame. Those were good times, weren't they? Dancing in their backyard on summer evenings, watching the fireflies . . . Your mama never wanted to leave, so they always played us one more song until our feet hurt too much to dance anymore."

Then why did you ruin it? I wanted to ask, but I didn't. That was an argument that had lasted almost a decade, and I didn't have the time or energy to revisit old wounds.

"So, what is it that you wanted to show me?"

He nodded in understanding, matching my businesslike tone. "It's upstairs. Follow me." He led the way through the small entranceway, to the steps. As

I made my way after him, I noticed a painted trellis climbing up the stairwell, bunches of bright yellow flowers hanging from it. The petals looked real enough that I paused to touch one, just to see what it would feel like.

"Your mama started it right after you left. She works on it every year, adding a little each time. It's reached your bedroom now."

"It's beautiful," I said, moving up the stairs. Then I stopped on the next step, staring at the wall. Painted in a yellow sundress, so that the figure blended into the flowers, was a tiny blond girl climbing the trellis beside the blossoms.

"Is that supposed to be me?" I asked, pointing toward the beginning of the trellis at the figure, which was wearing a mortarboard and standing in front of a tiny sketched skyline of New York City.

Daddy squinted, leaning in closely as if he'd never noticed it before. "Well, don't that beat all," he said, straightening, then moving up a step. "I guess it is—from when you graduated from college."

"You didn't know?" I asked.

He shook his head, his eyes troubled. "Your mother always did her own thing. I just came home from work one day, and she'd taken off the wallpaper and painted all these yellow flowers on the wall. I didn't mind them, so I didn't say anything."

"And you never thought to ask her why she was painting the stairwell?"

He didn't answer right away. "Do you think it would have made any difference?"

I continued to walk up the stairs, watching milestones in my adult life depicted in miniature: the Brooklyn Bridge, the prewar building on Madison Avenue where I worked, a tube of lipstick for a large ad campaign I'd worked on. Even the small figure of me wore bright red lipstick as a nod to the product.

It was as charming as it was humbling. How had Ivy known all these details about my life? The few times we spoke, it was always in generalities like the weather or popular songs on the radio, nothing too personal. I'd kept my simmering anger at her near the surface, not allowing her to get too close. She'd disappointed me once, and I clung to that, knowing it was one more reason why I could never go home again.

I stood back, blinking away the pinpricks of tears. A wave of emotion engulfed me, and I found myself again fervently hoping she'd wake up so I could ask her why, during all those years of my growing up, she had allowed me to believe she never noticed.

My dad had reached the top of the stairs, and I followed him across the short hallway into my childhood bedroom. It contained the same type of four-poster bed and dressing table I had at Ceecee's, the same yellow ceramic lamps, except here I'd been allowed to express my various interests. There were all sorts of art projects hung on the walls, and my karaoke machine still stood in its place of honor in the corner along with my elaborate costume collection, including a fringed jumpsuit that would have made an ABBA fan drool.

Science projects hung on fishing line from the ceiling, and on the bookshelf between the windows, shoved between dog-eared copies of **Gone with the Wind,** the Harry Potter series, and the entire collection of Lurlene McDaniel and Sarah Dessen books, were the leather-covered notebooks I'd asked my mother to buy for me to contain my epic manuscripts.

It was so different from my bedroom at Ceecee's, where, despite her encouragement, she always tucked my artwork in boxes to be stored under the bed, and claimed the karaoke machine gave her migraines. Staring at my participation trophies lined up on my dresser, I blinked hard, feeling as if I might cry. Despite all the verbal encouragement Ceecee had given me, it seemed to me now, looking at the detritus of my childhood, that it had been my mother who had allowed me the freedom to explore whatever passion struck me.

"I keep telling your mother that we can make this room into an art studio for her, but she won't hear of it. She says you'll need a place to come back to whenever you're ready."

I wiped at my eyes so he couldn't see my tears. I was about to correct him, to remind him that I had a beautiful room always ready and waiting for me at Ceecee's house, but I stopped. That was a room to sleep in, a comfortable guest room neatly curated for the casual visitor. This room was a slice of my childhood, an integral part of my growing up. Of beginning my journey to who I really was. How had I been so blind to the world around me that I had never recognized this? My equilibrium shifted, like I was staring in a fun-house mirror, seeing my past being turned on its head.

"Look over here." My father was leaning against my childhood desk—white wood with yellow gingham-patterned knobs—pointing at an Apple desktop computer on the top. "I bought this computer for your mother a few birthdays ago, and put it in here so she could have a bit of office space." He shrugged apologetically. "It's the only desk we have. Anyway, she was just starting up her furniture-refinishing business, and I thought she could use this to make flyers, create a mailing list, prepare invoices—that kind of thing, or even design a Web site. To be honest, I don't know if she ever did any of that."

He looked away, embarrassed, and I wanted to reach out and tell him I understood what it was like to live with blinders on because that's just the way you've always seen things.

"I helped her create a screen name on an e-mail program, and then I put your e-mail address and a few others in her address book to get her started. But that's the last time I saw her using it." He wiggled the mouse, and the computer came to life, showing an e-mail screen. "Until this. Your mama was sending you an e-mail the day she had the accident. She either forgot to hit Send, or intentionally didn't send it. I thought you might want to read it."

"I . . ." I looked at the computer, the thought of my mother owning a computer and even having an e-mail address hard to comprehend. She'd always hated technology and been slow to give up her VCR and her cassettes. As far as I knew, she still used a first-generation flip phone. "She's never sent an e-mail to me."

"She wrote letters to you plenty of times. Just most of them never got mailed. She'd fill a wastebasket with them. She knew you were angry with her. I think she was just waiting for you to tell her why."

I sat down in the desk chair, my heart hurting. I hadn't written to my mother at all, except for a once-a-year birthday card where all I wrote was **Happy Birthday.** "I was angry because she stayed with you," I said softly. "I felt as if I'd been lied to my whole life, believing her to be strong and independent. It was like the whole world had been lying to me about everything, not only Mama, but Ceecee and my friends."

"And I made it worse," he said.

"Yes, you did." He met my eyes and didn't flinch. I turned back to the computer. "Can I read it?" I asked.

"Of course. I guess it belongs to you anyway." He put his hand on my shoulder, and I didn't want to shake it off, instead appreciating the warmth and the gesture of being in this together.

My Dearest Daughter,

You're probably wondering why I'm writing to you out of the blue like this. That reads funny, doesn't it? Because you're my baby girl, and we should be telling each other everything. That's not your fault. It's nobody's fault. Everything I've ever learned has brought me to this one conclusion—we are all thrown into this world without a road map, and it's up to us to muddle through. We are free to make a mess of it or to make a success out of our lives. Most of us choose something in between.

I need to talk to you about something important. About something I found out about Carrowmore and the night it burned. I can't talk about it with Ceecee or Bitty. Just you. You're the only person who can help me make sense of this. Nothing is as it seems, Larkin. I thought I knew what it was like to make sacrifices for love, but I didn't. Not really.

I thought about picking up the phone and calling you, but I know you're so busy with your life in New York, and I didn't want to bother you. Maybe you can call me tonight? After work? It's really important.

Love,
Mama

PS: I found an envelope full of old photographs while I was refurbishing my daddy's desk. There's one of you and me when you were a little girl, and you're wearing a ballet tutu, a tiara, and those **Wizard of Oz** red Dorothy shoes. It's my precious daughter the way I remember you—so clever and so courageous in your choices. So confident. I always wished I could be more like you. I guess that's why I mothered you from behind. I didn't want who I was to rub off on you too much, like a weak spirit was contagious. I'd like to send the photo to you. You can let me know tonight when we talk if you'd like me to mail it.

I read the e-mail twice, then looked at my dad, who was sitting on the edge of my bed. "Did you read this?"

"Yeah. I thought it might be important."

I looked back at the screen, trying to picture my mother sitting there at the desk and typing it, and I realized I couldn't remember the exact shade of her hair. "Do you know what she's referring to?"

He shook his head. "I don't have a clue. And I can't find the envelope of photos, either. I've torn this house apart looking for them."

I thought for a moment. "She mentioned something about her daddy's desk. Is that here?"

"No. She used Ceecee's garage to refurbish furniture. That's where you'll find it."

I nodded absently, my gaze traveling around the room again, taking in the artwork and the costumes, the shadow box containing every single issue of the school newspaper that I had edited. I noticed a small frame by my dresser that I didn't remember having seen before and saw it contained my SAT and ACT scores. They were better than average, but by no means stellar. I remembered asking Ceecee to have them framed, her telling me later she'd misplaced them, and then finding them in the kitchen garbage can. I'd thrown them into my desk drawer and forgotten them.

After a year of therapy in New York, I'd realized that Ceecee had always been good at telling me how wonderful I was as long as the assessment was subjective, but she'd not been a big supporter of hard evidence to the contrary. I stared at the scores now, wondering why my mother had thought to have them framed.

I stood, my knees shaky. "Thanks, Daddy, for showing me."

"Of course." He smiled, but his face was tired and worn, his eyes sad.

"You still love her," I said, the truth of it settling in my bones with a jolt.

"I never stopped."

I didn't drop my gaze. "Are you still seeing that woman?"

He didn't look away. "I haven't since you left, Larkin. It was a mistake, and I knew it at the time, and I've regretted ever since that I hurt your mother that way. And you. I don't think I can ever forgive myself, and I can only dream that you and your mother will find it in your hearts to forgive me." He rubbed his hands over his face, his palms raspy over his unshaven jaw. "You have no idea how hard it is to love a person with all your heart and know that they only have a piece of their own heart to give back. It's a pathetic excuse for what I did, but there you have it. For what it's worth, I'm sorry."

"Oh, Daddy." I closed my eyes, remembering the ribbon I'd pulled from the tree all those years ago. **Come home to me, Ellis. I'll love you always.** I couldn't condone what my father had done, but I couldn't blame him, either. "Oh, Daddy," I said again, taking a step forward and embracing him. I couldn't remember the last time we'd touched, but the feel of his chest under my head and the scent of him brought me back to when I was a little girl who knew her father could do no wrong.

We stayed that way for a long time, until my phone vibrated with a text and we broke apart. It was Jackson again, telling me he'd pick me up at five o'clock and that he was bringing a picnic supper, even though I'd never responded to his invitation. I glanced at the time on my phone. "I've got to go buy a bathing suit. I didn't pack one, and Jackson's taking me out on his boat for dinner."

"Jackson Porter?"

I slid the strap of my purse over my shoulder, not eager to rehash the same conversation I'd had with Bennett. "Yes, Jackson Porter. We've reconnected since I've been back."

"Isn't he the one who started all that ruckus your senior year?"

I took a deep breath. "That was a long time ago, Daddy. Stupid high school stuff, you know? We're not kids anymore."

He frowned. "Is Bennett going, too?"

I moved to the doorway. "I doubt he was invited."

I could sense his disapproval. "One more thing," he said. "While looking for the photographs, I found this in your dresser drawer. Not sure if you want it."

He picked up a bottle from the top of my dresser and handed it to me. I recognized the bottle of Jackson's cologne I'd bought in high school and felt myself coloring. "Thanks," I said, throwing it into my purse as I avoided his gaze. "I'd forgotten all about this."

When I turned around to leave, I noticed the painted trellis from the stairwell had crept around the corner from the hallway and into my bedroom, the small figure standing on a pale yellow wall, the trellis beneath her as yet unfinished. I stepped closer to get a better look, seeing that behind the girl were the columned ruins of Carrowmore, flames shooting out from the rooftop while four purple martins soared overhead, a ribbon clutched in each beak.

I looked closely at the painting, trying to pick out any details that would tell me what I was looking at. I felt my father come up behind me, and I said softly, "I wonder if this has anything to do with what Mama was wanting to talk to me about."

"Could be," my father agreed, his eyes sad again.

My fingers lightly brushed the painting, and it was as if I were a little girl holding my mother's hand again. My phone vibrated with another text, and I headed into the hallway and down the stairs.

My father called after me. "I've got about a dozen casseroles from neighbors in the freezer on account of your mother being in the hospital. You should join me for supper sometime so they won't go to waste."

I smiled. "I will," I said, surprised that I meant it.

twenty-four

Ceecee
2010

Ceecee stepped into the house from the back porch after working in her garden, the smells of moist earth and perspiration clinging to her. Whenever she was troubled, she found solace in weeding her flower beds and deadheading spent blooms. If only all of life's problems could be eradicated as cleanly and swiftly.

She heard a thump from upstairs and quickly slid out of her Keds and pulled off her gardening gloves. "Bitty?" She said it while she was still on the landing, not wanting to get to the top and find her friend collapsed on the floor, her last cigarette still clenched between her lips.

"We're in here," Bitty called from Larkin's bedroom.

Ceecee paused in the doorway, noticing how every single dresser drawer had been pulled out, an assortment of brightly colored clothing strewn on the bed and floor.

Larkin gave her a worried smile. "Don't worry—I'll clean this all up. I was just hoping to find an old bathing suit that might work to go out on Jackson's boat. Everything at the stores was so . . . revealing."

Bitty, sitting on the bed, held up a bright yellow one-piece that Ceecee remembered Larkin wearing when she was about fifteen. "I told her I could use shoestrings to hold this one together in the back." She didn't laugh, which meant that she might actually be serious.

"But it's at least four sizes too big for her now." Ceecee glanced around the piles on the bed, then moved to the ones on the floor. "All of these are."

"Exactly," Bitty said, leaning back against the pillows.

Larkin rolled her eyes and turned to the suitcase on the floor. She still hadn't unpacked, as if she continued to believe that her mother would wake up any day now and she could leave.

"Or," she said, rummaging through a stack of clean and previously folded clothes Ceecee had placed on her dresser the day before, "I could wear this." She held up a long black cotton dress as shapeless as a curtain panel. "It's a maxi, so it goes down to my ankles, but it's sleeveless, so I won't get too hot."

"Perfect," Bitty said at the same time Ceecee said, "No."

Larkin looked apologetic. "Sorry, Ceecee, but I think I'm going to go with Bitty on this one. It's quick and easy, and I don't have to go to another store."

"It's just so . . . plain. Maybe you can take off that ridiculous necklace and wear something bigger and more eye-catching."

Bitty sat up, ready to argue, but Larkin held out her hands like a cop trying to stop traffic. "I'll figure it out when I get dressed—it's no big deal." She glanced down at her watch. "I've got almost an hour, so since the two of you are together, I have some questions I was hoping you might be able to answer for me."

Bitty stayed on the bed but didn't lean back on the pillows. Ceecee sat carefully on the tufted ottoman she'd bought when Larkin was little because Larkin had seen one just like it in an old black-and-white Hollywood glamour film and wanted one.

Larkin began folding the scattered clothes as she spoke. "Mrs. Lynch was cleaning out her garage and found a bunch of papers that had belonged to her father when he was the fire chief."

Ceecee felt a frisson of alarm begin at the base of her spine, but she didn't look up at Bitty. She couldn't.

"Anyway, he hadn't kept much, but he did keep a folder about my grandmother and the fire. It included her obituary. There was a picture of her in her wedding dress." She stopped moving for a moment and looked directly at Ceecee. "I don't think I'd ever seen a picture of her before. I didn't realize how much I look like her."

"You do," Ceecee agreed. "Sometimes, when you walk into the room, I can almost think it's her."

"Do I act like her?"

"No," Bitty said quickly. She met Ceecee's eyes for a moment. "Margaret wasn't like anyone else. She was beautiful, and kind, and giving until . . ."

"Until her parents were killed," Ceecee said, cutting her off. "She'd lived the perfect life before that, you see. And she wasn't prepared to deal with her new . . . imperfect life."

Bitty coughed, turning away with her hand over her mouth. "I guess that's a nice way to say it."

Larkin turned to Bitty. "Are you saying she changed after her parents died?"

"No. More like . . ."

"I have photo albums in the attic, Larkin," Ceecee said, cutting Bitty off. "You might want to look at them. There're photos of your grandmother when she was younger. But you're going to have to go up to find them. I don't think I can manage those stairs anymore."

"Thank you," Larkin said, closing a dresser drawer

with her hip. "I will." She turned around to face them, leaning against the dresser. "There was something else in the file, too, that I was hoping one of you might be able to explain."

Ceecee schooled her expression into bland interest. "And that was . . . ?"

"The official report of the fire that showed one person deceased—Margaret. The cause of the fire was marked as 'undetermined.'"

Ceecee nodded. "Yes, that's how I remember it. Don't you, Bitty?"

It took Bitty a split second to nod her head in agreement.

"But that's not all. Someone—Bennett and I were thinking it was probably his grandfather, since he was the fire chief back then—had handwritten the word 'suspicious.'"

Ceecee found herself wondering if the blood could freeze inside your veins on a warm day. Or if she would be the first. She wasn't sure where she found her voice to ask, "Was there anything else? Any further explanation?"

Larkin shook her head. "No. But there were a lot of papers, and Bennett said he'd go through them and let me know if he found anything new."

"Maybe when the cause of a fire can't be determined, they consider it suspicious," Ceecee said, avoiding Bitty's gaze.

"Maybe," Bitty said.

"So, you never heard anything about a formal investigation, no rumors of anything suspicious?"

Ceecee shook her head. "No. I was interviewed, of course, because I was there. But I have no memories of the night. All I remember is falling asleep, and then waking up outside with Ivy."

"Why were you there—at Carrowmore? That was the day after the hurricane."

Ceecee imagined she could hear the wind and the rain, the distant sirens. Taste the salt in the air. Hear, somewhere in the house, glass splintering as debris smashed a window. She'd been upstairs, in one of the guest rooms. She remembered that, remembered that there was no electricity and she'd left the drapes open so she could watch the fading daylight as the hurricane blew itself back to the sea. She remembered, too, that she hadn't been afraid.

She met Larkin's questioning gaze. "I came to Carrowmore looking for Margaret and Ivy. I wanted to make sure they were safe."

"But where was everyone else? Where was Margaret's husband?"

"He'd been called away," Ceecee said. "And Margaret . . . wasn't well. She had what we called the 'baby blues'—of course, now it's postpartum depression. And I'm sure that wasn't all of it—she missed her parents something awful, to start. There were other disappointments she'd faced in a short period of time. But she loved her baby; there was never any doubt about that. She was just . . . sad all the time. So, when we heard there was a hurricane coming, we were worried when we couldn't find her."

"And you, Bitty? Where were you?" Larkin asked.

Ceecee imagined she could hear the room hold its breath in anticipation.

"I went looking for her, too. I even called the police, but they were too busy with keeping an eye on the storm to help me look for a woman we weren't even sure was lost." Bitty shrugged. "We're not really sure of the timing of events, but at some point, Margaret found her way to Carrowmore to ride out the storm. Or she could have been there all along—we'll never know."

"So, it could have been a lightning strike, or a candle Margaret lit for light." Larkin's voice sounded far away, as if she'd placed herself on that dark night in the old house as it faced a hurricane. She turned to Ceecee. "Where did they find her . . . afterward?"

"Does any of this matter now?" Ceecee asked, trying not to remember what the house looked like when the fire trucks arrived. How she pictured the beautiful wedding room covered in soot. Everything the Darlingtons had ever cherished reduced to ashes.

"Probably not," Larkin agreed. "It's just that Mama wrote me an e-mail the day she disappeared. She said she'd found out something about Carrowmore and the fire. About us. So, no, none of this matters now, I guess. But it might explain why Mama was at Carrowmore. Maybe even explain what she found out about Margaret, and why she thought it important enough to write on a ribbon."

"We'll ask her when she wakes up," Ceecee said. But even she was getting tired of it, of forcing an optimism she no longer felt. She stood, brushing her palms against her gardening pants. "I'd best see about supper." Facing Larkin, she said, "You know, Larkin, if you take all of those old clothes out of the drawers, I'll take them to the charity shop, and you'll have room for the clothes you brought so you can finally unpack."

"I know—I just keep thinking that Mama will wake up any minute now and I can go back to New York. I can't put my job on hold forever."

"Of course not. I just want you to feel more at home. Not like a visitor."

"But that's what I am," Larkin protested.

Bitty stood, her knees cracking, and laughed. "You tell yourself that over and over again, sweetie, but it'll never drain the salt water running through your veins. The outgoing tide might suck all the water from the creeks and marshes here, but eventually the ocean pushes it all back where it belongs."

Larkin turned back to the dresser and shoved another pile of old clothes inside. "Yeah, well, being here reminds me of that stupid girl I used to be. And I never want to find her again."

Bitty put her arm around Larkin's shoulders

and said fiercely, "You were never stupid. You were smarter than everyone else, because you didn't let others tell you what you should think or say or do. Ceecee might have been over-the-top in her encouragement, but that's what your staunchest supporters are supposed to do. You were brave, Larkin. That's what your mama said, you know. After you left. And she was right."

Larkin kept her head down, her hands gently touching the items that had been on top of her dresser since her childhood. A **Little Mermaid** hairbrush, a participation trophy for a talent show in the shape of a quarter note. A framed photo of Larkin, Bennett, and Mabry in **Wizard of Oz** Halloween costumes. A dried piece of sweetgrass stuck between the glass and frame of the mirror.

The clock chimed downstairs, and Larkin's head jerked up. "It's four thirty—I'd better hurry. Jackson will be here in half an hour."

Bitty squeezed her shoulders, then reached up to kiss her cheek. "Let me know if you want that can of Mace. I never leave home without it."

Ceecee kissed Larkin's other cheek, then used her thumb to rub off the lipstick print. "I'll go wrap a plate of my brownies for you to take with you."

Ceecee followed Bitty out of the room, glancing back as she closed the door to see Larkin looking at her reflection in the mirror as if she didn't recognize the person staring back.

Larkin
2010

I held the plate of brownies while I waited on Ceecee's dock for Jackson, neatly avoiding the necessity of Jackson coming inside.

My conversation with Bitty and Ceecee had unsettled me more than I wanted to admit. I wasn't brave. I wasn't. Misguided, yes. Brave, no. The memory of the worst day of my life came back to me with horrifying clarity. After almost killing my best friend, I'd proceeded to walk away without any explanation, clarification, or excuses. I was a coward, too afraid to face the truth of what I was. Of what I'd done. And that girl was still there, inside me. I knew the longer I stayed, the better the chance would be that she would reemerge.

Yet here I was, on the dock, waiting for Jackson Porter to come pick me up like in some sick form of déjà vu. Maybe I hadn't shoved the old me far enough down into my psyche. And maybe I was waiting for the chance to relive that day, to hope for a more positive outcome. I almost laughed. Larkin Lanier—always the eternal optimist. That was one thing, at least, that I hadn't buried completely.

I heard the low rumble of a boat engine and turned to see Jackson approaching on a twenty-two-foot MasterCraft. Even in high school, he'd always had the nicest boat, even if it actually belonged to his father.

But this boat was brand-new, the red paint of the manufacturer's name vivid and bright. My first thought was that he was showing off, something the old me had once dreamed of. My second thought was one of relief that he hadn't brought his father's cabin cruiser. I remembered the small bunk with messy sheets in the cabin belowdecks, and shivered.

Jackson slowed as he approached, his smile white in his tanned face, his eyes hidden behind Ray-Bans. His brown hair curled up over his USC baseball cap, and he looked so much like the boy I'd thought I'd been in love with for so long that I imagined I could feel the reel of years unspooling beneath my feet. I felt unsteady, unable to find a foothold, and it had nothing to do with the boat's wake rocking the dock.

"Whoa," Jackson said, shutting off the engine and slowly drifting toward me. He took the plate first and set it down with his free hand, then helped me into the boat, but didn't immediately let go of my hand. "You look beautiful, Larkin."

I couldn't see his eyes, but I imagined they were on my mouth. I licked my lips. Even though I was twenty-seven years old, my high school daydreams hadn't lost their luster.

"Thank you." I licked my lips again, my mouth dry. I breathed him in, smelling the familiar cologne and the male scent of sweat and sunscreen. I wished he'd take off his glasses so I could read his eyes, to confirm the sincerity of his apology in the bright light of day.

He let go of my hand, eyeing my maxi dress with a frown. "I sure hope there's a bathing suit under all those clothes. I brought the skis."

"I was hoping you'd remember that I don't ski. When you had that party when we were juniors and everybody was skiing, I stayed on the boat and kept an eye out for anybody who fell."

"No, sorry, I don't remember." His forehead wrinkled in thought, but he shook his head. "Lots of people on the boat that day."

I didn't mention that he'd asked me once before if I skied, and I'd told him that I didn't. He said he'd teach me, but that's not what happened.

I sat down in the front of the boat while he pushed us away from the dock and started the engine again. As it idled, Jackson said, "I thought we'd go out into the bay and see if we can spot the smokestack from the **Harvest Moon,**" referring to the Union side-wheeled steam gunboat sunk in Winyah Bay by a Confederate mine. "I thought I'd drop anchor and we'd have a nice picnic dinner. I brought a bottle of champagne to celebrate."

"To celebrate?"

"A reunion of old friends," he said. "And our blank slate."

"I didn't think we were friends, Jackson." Why did I say those words? Maybe because I'd just been

with Bitty, who knew the truth of everything without ever needing to be told. Or maybe it was because I was remembering dancing with Bennett in
his parents' garage and trying to recall why I'd once
wished my dance partner was Jackson instead of
him.

"Weren't we?" he asked, his smile intact, and I had
the sudden realization that he actually thought we
had been.

For self-preservation and the need to know the
truth, I pressed on. "I used to hang around the periphery of your group, but I don't think you ever said
more than ten words to me. Until that time on your
daddy's boat."

"Really?" he said, still smiling, the boat idling and
the thrum of the motor reminding me why I didn't
want to let this go.

He held out his hand to me, and I stood to take it.
Pulling me close, so I could smell the scent of him
again, he said, "Larkin, as I said the other night,
I remember you. And not just because we share a
special memory. I remember that you were always
the loudest fan in the stands at the football games,
holding up those great banners." His grin widened.
"You helped some of the guys on the team with
their English essays, too, because you were such
a good writer. And I remember everyone standing to clap after your performance at the talent
show . . ."

I put my free hand over his mouth. "That's enough."

He kissed my fingers, and I thought the heat would make my hand melt. Reluctantly, I dropped my hand.

"See?" he said. "I remember."

I reached up to take off his sunglasses so I could see his eyes. They were bright green today, I noticed, reflecting the color of his T-shirt that molded nicely to his chest and football-player biceps. He leaned toward me, and I tilted my head back and closed my eyes, waiting for his kiss. **A clean slate.**

"Hi, Larkin!"

I jerked my head back at the child's voice calling my name and turned toward the dock behind Ceecee's house. Ellis ran toward us, wearing swimming trunks and a life jacket. He was running in front of Bennett, who was strolling casually behind him.

I waved to Ellis but directed my annoyed gaze at Bennett. "What are you doing here? I thought you had to go back to Columbia."

Bennett stopped at the edge of the dock, his hand on Ellis's shoulder. "Mabry and Jonathan are working the same shift today at the hospital. I decided to delay my departure so I could spend time with my favorite nephew."

"And Mama said I gets to go on the boat!"

I frowned at the two of them, wondering what they were doing there, and how Ellis knew there'd be a boat. My gaze traveled to the screened porch at the rear of the house. A shock of unnatural red hair stood out against the house's white paint. I heard a cough and smelled the acrid scent of a cigarette, and I knew who must have called to let Bennett know where I was going. And with whom.

"Sorry, sport," Jackson said as he put his arm around me. "You're too late. Good seeing you, Bennett." He moved his other hand toward the throttle, but I held it back.

"Wait a minute," I said, unable to take the look of complete abandonment and desolation on Ellis's little face. "Can't we give him just a quick ride down the river and bring him right back?"

Jackson shrugged and let out a big sigh. "I guess." He maneuvered the boat up to the dock again, Bennett helping to pull the boat closer so he could hand Ellis inside. As I was getting Ellis settled, I felt the thud of someone landing on the boat and turned to see Bennett standing next to me, grinning.

"Hate to miss an opportunity to be seen in this boat, Jackson," he said. "Can't let Ellis have all the fun, can we?" He gave a friendly punch to Jackson's shoulder.

Jackson had replaced his sunglasses so I could no longer see his eyes, but his smile was definitely dimmer. "Of course not." He waited for everyone to sit down, then pushed the throttle forward, making the boat jump.

Bennett sat down on Ellis's other side, and put his

arm around the boy, his hand resting on my shoulder. "You might want to slow it down, Jackson," Bennett shouted so Jackson could hear. "Mabry said Ellis loves to ride on boats, but he gets seasick pretty easily. We're hoping he'll outgrow it. No boy living this close to the water should be allowed to get seasick."

Jackson sent a worried look over at Ellis, who'd propped himself up on his knees and was staring backward at the spray of water from the motor splashing behind us. He slowed the boat so that we were barely going faster than I could swim, and I was a slow swimmer.

"You serious, man?"

"As a heart attack," Bennett said with a wide smile, leaning back and crossing a tanned leg over his knee.

Jackson continued to steer the boat at a low speed, looking back often to check on Ellis while I glared at Bennett.

"What are you doing here?" I hissed.

"What?" Bennett shouted, cupping his ear as if he hadn't heard. Despite the sound from the motor, I knew he'd either heard or read my lips, because he kept grinning like the village idiot. He leaned forward and flipped on the sound system, then looked at me expectantly.

"'Bad Man.' Pitbull." I rolled my eyes.

"You never disappoint," he said before turning to Jackson. "Does she?"

"What?" Jackson shouted. He pointed to his ear. "I can't hear."

I shook my head, then looked away from Bennett to watch the water spray up from the sides of the boat. I wasn't sure what made me look back a few minutes later. Maybe it was the sense of Ellis turning around in his seat, or the feeling of Bennett hopping up very quickly, but by the time I realized what was happening, Ellis had thrown up all over the seat, the floor, and me.

"Aw, man," Jackson shouted, carefully turning the boat around and heading back to the dock.

Ellis didn't seem to hear and was now beaming happily, despite his uncle wiping him down with paper towels from a roll he'd found inside an armrest. "I feel good now."

I smiled at the little boy, glad he was no worse for wear, although I couldn't say the same for myself. I sat in stony silence, listening to more Pitbull on the stereo until Jackson brought the boat up to the dock again. I ignored Bennett's offer of the paper towel roll.

Bennett got out first and reached for Ellis, then me. I was about to protest when I realized that there was nothing salvageable about my outfit and that the smell was beginning to make me feel sick, too.

"I'm sorry, Jackson. Can we try this again?"

He managed a smile. "Of course. Just give me time to clean and deodorize the boat. I'll call you, okay?"

I nodded and almost leaned in for a kiss before I remembered I was covered in vomit. Bennett's hand was outstretched for me to take and I wanted so badly to ignore it, but I couldn't get out of the boat in my maxi dress without help, so I grudgingly took it and allowed him to pull me up onto the dock.

"See you later, Jackson. Sorry about the boat," Bennett called as Jackson pulled away, waving a hand in either good-bye or resignation—I couldn't tell which.

I knelt in front of Ellis, trying to ignore the odor emanating from both of us. "You sure you're feeling better?"

He smiled and nodded.

"Great," I said, rubbing the top of his head and standing. "Your uncle Bennett is going to hose you off in the outdoor shower at the side of the house. I'll bring you a towel, and then you can come inside and have one of Ceecee's brownies if you're still feeling better, all right?"

"What about me? Don't I get a brownie?" Bennett asked, his eyes wide and innocent.

"No," I said, unable to hide the anger in my voice even though Ellis was there. "What is your game here, Bennett?"

His face became suddenly serious. "It's no game. I just don't want to see you hurt again."

I stepped closer to him. "What I do and with whom is none of your business. Stay out of it."

"And allow you to revert to your adolescence?"

My hand lifted involuntarily, and I would have slapped him if Ellis hadn't been there watching with wide eyes that were just like his uncle's.

Without a word, I turned on my heel and marched back to the house, smelling cigarette smoke wafting from the screened porch.

twenty-five

Ceecee
1951

The night before the funeral for Margaret's parents, Ceecee dreamed of a burial, but she was the one in the coffin lowered into the dark earth. She'd awakened, still smelling the pungent aroma of freshly dug dirt. Despite the predawn hour, she'd been unable to go back to sleep, the lingering sense of helplessness crowding her bones and making them press against her skin. Even fully awake, she'd gasped for air, searching desperately for a way out of the dark hole in which she'd been buried. The dream's meaning tapped at her brain, its message hidden from her as she struggled to breathe, the sense of something terrible about to happen as real as looking up from the grave and seeing a shovelful of dirt slowly sliding its way into the hole.

Now Ceecee stood in the churchyard at Prince George Winyah Episcopal Cemetery and lifted the black netting on her hat in an attempt to get it to stop making her nose itch. At the Darlington plot, the two freshly dug graves stood out like dark scars on the patchy grass and dried earth of the ancient cemetery, where generations of Darlingtons had been laid to rest for nearly three hundred years.

Ceecee pressed her handkerchief against her cheeks to dab away the perspiration, giving the appearance of wiping her tears. It was a funeral, after all, and they wouldn't have been out of place. And she'd known Mr. and Mrs. Darlington practically her whole life. The way they'd died had been a tragedy, everyone in Georgetown kept whispering, as if Margaret might shatter should they say it loudly enough.

But Ceecee couldn't cry. She was too hot and miserable in her black wool dress that already seemed as heavy as armor in the humid air of late May. And her emotions were frayed to a point that seemed beyond tears.

Bitty, standing next to her, took Ceecee's gloved hand and squeezed it. The Darlington luck had been legendary, so why had it stopped? What did it mean? Ceecee's minister father said there was no such thing as luck. Or fate. It was God's will and nothing more.

But if God was good and merciful, why were Margaret's parents both gone?

Her thoughts turned darker, remembering what her mother had told her long ago about her friendship with Margaret. How jealousy was one of the seven deadly sins, and whether you disguised the green-eyed monster with admiration or friendship, it would always be a sharp-toothed beast, waiting to pounce. She watched Margaret lean into Boyd, pressing her face into his shoulder as the reverend said the graveside prayers, and she watched as Boyd placed his arm around Margaret to keep her from slipping to the ground. And as Ceecee watched, she felt her heart grow heavier and heavier, a rock tied to her ankle that dragged her to the silty bottom of despair.

The reverend said his final amen, and the mourners began to drift away. Bitty squeezed her hand again, jerking her chin in the direction of the Hardings, who'd flown in from London, where Margaret's uncle Milton had been assigned a diplomatic role at the American embassy. Aunt Dorothy gently took hold of Margaret's arm and led her away from Boyd to the backseat of a black sedan driven by a uniformed driver. Uncle Milton turned around and asked Boyd to join them, and Boyd nodded, sending an apologetic glance in Ceecee's direction.

They were headed back to Carrowmore, where Margaret's aunt had orchestrated a tasteful wake. Her firm and unyielding will would have made her late sister proud. She had no time for dawdling or grieving.

In the corner of her heart where charitable thoughts were allowed, Ceecee was glad Aunt Dorothy was there; she imagined her to be a great comfort to Margaret. And then, not as charitably, she wished Margaret would turn to Aunt Dorothy for guidance and consolation instead of clinging to Boyd as she had since that awful day at the morgue.

Because of Uncle Milton's pressing duties, the Hardings were due to fly back to London the following week. They'd wanted Margaret to come to London and live with them, but Margaret had turned them down, saying she wanted to stay at Carrowmore. Only after reassurances by both Ceecee and Bitty and their families that Margaret would be well attended, her emotional and physical needs cared for, had they reluctantly agreed.

Bitty, knowing how progressive Aunt Dottie was, tried to convince Margaret to tell her about the pregnancy. Maybe this would be the perfect opportunity for Margaret to have a baby without anyone back at home ever knowing.

But Margaret had insisted she wanted to stay at Carrowmore. She was convinced that Reggie would show up any day now. It was the one thing that she clung to, the one thought that seemed to be keeping her sane. Bitty and Ceecee were unwilling to threaten the well-being of the baby growing inside her, or sever the one remaining tie that connected her to a sound mind.

The family's attorney would make sure that Margaret lacked for nothing financially and would handle all estate matters, with Uncle Milton acting as executor and trustee. Margaret would land on her feet, as she always had, the thought darkening Ceecee's mood even further. Grief and love for her friend battled with the little green-eyed monster that kept prodding her in the sensitive spot between her shoulder blades.

Ceecee took one last look at the gaping holes in the ground, and shuddered as she recalled her dream. She made to join her own family, but Bitty pulled her back. "Come with me. I need a cigarette first."

Ceecee called out to her parents that she'd join them at Carrowmore, ignoring her mother's look of worry. Ever since the day Dr. Griffith had called with the news of Margaret's parents, Ceecee's mother had been hovering near her daughter, just like she probably had when Ceecee was learning to walk. It was as if her mother were anticipating a sharp corner or an uneven surface that would rise up and hurt her little girl.

Bitty took off her gloves to light her cigarette, shoving them into her purse. They'd be impossibly wrinkled. Not that Bitty cared about wrinkles or uneven hems or poker-straight hair that wouldn't curl. She kept threatening to cut it off and wear it like a boy's.

Now Bitty took a deep drag, closing her eyes as she held the smoke in her lungs. She blew it out in widening rings, which she and Ceecee watched float through the thick limbs of an oak tree whose roots were nudging at some of the older Darlington gravestones.

"So, what are you going to do?"

Ceecee looked at her, not understanding. It wasn't as if she had control of anything right now. "About what?"

"About Margaret's leaning on Boyd for everything. I don't like it, and you shouldn't, either."

"Of course I don't." Ceecee looked away so Bitty couldn't see her eyes. "But Margaret has just lost her parents. Not to mention she's pregnant and unmarried, and the father of her baby is halfway around the world training for war. Boyd is Reggie's brother, so I suppose it's logical that Margaret would lean on him in Reggie's absence."

"Are you listening to yourself, Ceecee? Because the one thing you forgot to mention is that Margaret is one of **your** dearest friends. 'Friends forever,' remember? Yes, she's in a twisted mess right now—most of which is of her own doing—but she's either blissfully unaware or, worse, aware but ignoring the fact that you are her close friend and Boyd is yours."

Ceecee stepped back, feigning surprise. "Really, Bitty. How can you say that? I'm sure if the tables were turned, Margaret would understand if it were Reggie comforting me."

"No, she wouldn't. She has no idea how to put another person first. It's not her fault, of course. She was never taught that. It's easy to be generous with your friends when your needs are met, and hers always were—tenfold. But that doesn't mean she's a generous person."

Ceecee began to walk away, too afraid to listen. To acknowledge that what Bitty was saying was not only the truth, but echoed her own shameful thoughts. "She's our friend . . ."

Bitty pulled on Ceecee's arm, jerking her around so they were face-to-face. "To a point. Remember that. I love her, too. We've always considered ourselves sisters, haven't we? And I will do what I can to help her get through this." She put her lower lip between her teeth, as if deciding whether to say more. Eventually, she said, "I told Mrs. Harding about the baby."

"You what?" Ceecee was torn between abject horror at the breach of confidence, and relief that—with this revelation—Margaret might end up an ocean away. "What did she say?"

"Not what I expected. She told me in no uncertain terms that any hint of scandal would destroy her husband's career. He'd like to be ambassador to the Court of St. James's one day, and one doesn't get there with scandal riding one's coattails. Those were her exact words." Bitty took another drag from her cigarette. "Her best offer was to ask her husband to solicit his friends in high office to find Reggie and get a message to him. But that's all."

"That's horrible. And so unfeeling. Have you told Margaret?"

"Of course not." Bitty stepped closer, her breath heavy with the smell of nicotine. "It's our job as friends to stand by her. But never forget that Margaret's made her own bed, and now she has to lie in it. Don't let her mistakes become yours."

~ ∂

It had been almost three weeks since the Darlingtons' funeral. Ceecee was yanking weeds from her mother's flower bed when she saw Boyd's car pull up to the house and park. Her mother stood, a worried look on her face.

Ceecee stood, too, wondering why it was taking Boyd so long to get out of the car. When he did, his movements were slow. His face, under the brim of his hat, couldn't hide the grim set of his jaw. Ceecee moved to greet him, but her mother held her back.

"You go on inside and get some sweet tea and let me talk with him for a moment. I don't like the sound of your father's cough, and I want to get Boyd's opinion."

Ceecee almost argued, but the look in her mother's eyes made her realize she shouldn't. With a quick glance behind her, she went into the house, leaving her mother and Boyd to talk. Were they discussing the marriage proposal, which had yet to materialize? Or, she thought as she walked into the kitchen, was it Margaret's mental health?

Although Ceecee and Bitty had been to see Margaret every day, their friend seemed to slip further and further away from them. Mrs. Purnell had offered to fix up the spare room for Margaret and have her move in with Ceecee's family for as long as she needed. But Margaret had turned her down, saying she felt closer to her parents at Carrowmore. Ceecee was secretly glad. Her friend had already taken up so much of her life; she didn't want to give up her house and family, too.

In the kitchen, Ceecee took her time pouring sweet tea into tall glasses, her hand shaking so badly that she had to stop and clean up the mess twice. Finally, her mother came in.

"What has gotten into you, Sessalee?" she asked, taking the pitcher out of her hands.

"It's nothing. It's everything," she said, closing her eyes so she wouldn't cry. "Is he here to tell me that he doesn't want to marry me? Because I know he was planning on asking me that day Dr. Griffith called with the news about Mr. and Mrs. Darlington. But he hasn't mentioned it since, and I'm sick with worry that he's changed his mind."

Her mother regarded her with pinched eyes. So much gray had appeared in her dark hair, Ceecee noticed, and deep wrinkles had formed between her brows.

"My sweet girl," she said gently, "true love doesn't change its mind. It might get waylaid or sidetracked, but if it's real, it stays true. Don't forget that, you hear?"

"But I know how I feel about him, and I know how he feels about me. I just don't understand, Mama."

Her mother pulled her into her arms, and Ceecee placed her head on her chest just like she had when she was a little girl. "Boyd is a good man. With a strong sense of responsibility. He understands, as I know you do, too, that one of your dearest friends just suffered a terrible loss and any celebration now would be not only inconsiderate but cruel."

She pulled Ceecee away from her to look in her face. "You are so young, Sessalee. With all of life's joys and disappointments ahead of you. Be patient. Your life will unfold the way it's supposed to, but not necessarily the way you plan or expect. Your father would tell you it's God's will, and he'd be right. But I'd also like to think that if you follow your heart, it will lead you to where you're supposed to be."

This was the first time Ceecee's mother had ever mentioned matters of the heart, and it warmed her as much as it scared her. "Why are you telling me this, Mama?"

"Because you're my daughter and I love you. I know you're a woman now, but that doesn't mean I'm going to stop worrying about you." She pursed her lips, considering her next words. "Remember how I used to caution you about a friendship with Margaret?"

Ceecee nodded, feeling suddenly light-headed.

"It's easy to be kind and giving and loyal when you have everything. But the mark of a true friend is when everything is taken away and you're still kind, giving, and loyal."

"Margaret's going through a difficult time, Mama. We need to be forgiving."

Her mother took a step back, her eyes darkening. "I'm afraid Boyd's come with bad news. I could tell from the look on his face when he arrived, and I sent you in here because I thought it was about Margaret."

"Is she all right?" Ceecee tried to keep her voice calm as she picked up the three glasses.

Her mother lifted the pitcher of tea. "Yes, thank goodness." She stopped in the doorway. "But I'm afraid Boyd has bad news about his brother."

Boyd rose from one of the porch chairs and opened the screened door for them. His eyes met Ceecee's, the intensity of his gaze making her stumble. He caught her with a hand on each shoulder, the tea from the glasses splashing up onto his sleeve.

"You have news of Reggie?" she asked, hardly recognizing her own voice.

He nodded, his expression one of pure misery. "He's gone, Ceecee. Reggie was killed during a training mission in Japan."

Ceecee was aware of the sound of the glasses hitting the wooden porch floor and almost obliterating the sound of screaming that kept reverberating in her ears. She only realized they were her own screams when Boyd put his arms around her and held her close, telling her everything would be all right.

But even then, she knew that things could never be all right again.

twenty-six

Ivy
2010

The ceiling above my hospital bed is an azure blue now, the same color as the sky after a hurricane has come and gone. People always find it surprising that the sky could be so clear after so much turmoil, but they shouldn't. As Gabriel once told me, hurricanes scrub the skies clean to give us something to distract us from the debris left in their wake.

Life's like that, I've found. If you can find the one good and pure thing to focus on in your life, the rest won't matter. I didn't realize the truth of that until the day I fell through the floor at Carrowmore.

Ceecee is humming along to the music as she waters the various flowers and plants that have begun to accumulate in my hospital room. I recognize the song but can't name it, and I find myself hoping that Larkin will walk in and tell us what it is. It's such a peculiar habit, her reciting the titles of songs, but I know why she does it. When Mack and I fought, music was her pure blue sky. It's what she focused on to take her mind away to something good.

I'm pressed against the ceiling again, and I keep seeing flashes of the yellow dress that I know is Mama's, and Ellis's car engine just keeps revving and revving, like he's impatient to go.

"I asked Mack to bring down my old photo album and pictures to show Larkin," Ceecee's saying. She puts the watering can on the floor by the window and comes to sit in the chair by my bed. "I always promised you that we'd look at them together, so I'll leave them downstairs so we can when you wake up."

I wonder if she believes what she's telling herself, or if she's just saying it to make me feel better. She clasps her hands between her knees like a schoolgirl, and I wish I could laugh, because it's funny to see her like that. Ceecee has always been so serious, the job of motherhood too important for her to act like she was anything but. Of course, it all makes sense now. Maybe if I'd known earlier, I could have made it easier for both of us.

"Larkin saw the records from the fire. The fire chief marked your mother's death as 'suspicious.'" She waits a moment as if expecting me to answer. "I'm thinking you must have known that, but I can't figure out how. You were just a baby at the time."

Ceecee looks out the window, although there's nothing to see except the side of another building. "'I know about Margaret.' When you wrote that on the ribbon, that's what you were talking about, wasn't it? About what happened during the fire."

Again she pauses, and I strain and push and tug against the weight that's pressing me into this world. I want to tell her what I know. And how I found out. Not from the official reports at all. But a place she'd never think to look. A place hidden in plain sight.

"I remember being interviewed by the police, and by the fire chief," she says. "I told them that I was there looking for you and Margaret, and that's true. But there was something I didn't tell them. I thought it would look bad. That they wouldn't let me have you if they knew. Nothing else mattered, you see. Because you should have always been mine to begin with."

The ceiling light shifts and twinkles as if it's made of water, and my bonds feel looser somehow. I'm listening carefully to Ceecee, knowing that whatever she needs to tell me is part of why I'm still here.

"I was so exhausted that night. Worried about you and your mother. We thought you were both wandering somewhere outside, and we were all so scared. For both of you, but especially you. You were an innocent baby—just two years old. Margaret was the one who'd put you in danger. She was supposed to have evacuated to Augusta.

"I remember being so angry. I didn't know where

you were, if you were in trouble, even. Bitty and I went out in the storm, searching for you and your mother. Of course, the first place I thought of was Carrowmore. I remember driving my car through the rain, my nerves making my hands slip off the steering wheel. I thought for sure I'd drive off a bridge. I honestly have no idea how I made it, but I did."

She swallows, her eyes distant, as if seeing something beyond the four walls of the hospital room.

"I didn't see your mama's car when I got to Carrowmore," she continues, "so I thought you weren't there. I figured out later that Margaret must have parked at the back of the house, but the storm was so bad, it never occurred to me to look there."

She reaches over to the bedside table and picks up the bottle of hand lotion she brought me when I first got here. She'd been upset at the condition of my hands and nails, as if it were the hospital's fault. I wanted to remind her that I'd been refinishing furniture.

She picks up my hand and begins massaging lotion into the dried skin and cracked cuticles. I can barely feel it, like when your arm falls asleep and you pinch it. I'm like a cicada, fooling everyone into believing that I'm in the bed, even though my spirit has flown away and is trapped against the ceiling.

But I want to feel Ceecee's touch, to know that I am loved and to recall just how much. And I want her to remember the reason why my hands and nails are in such bad shape.

She stops, lifts her elbow to wipe her eyes on her sleeve. "I thought you were lost out there in the storm. If something had happened to you, it would have been Margaret's fault, and I would never have been able to forgive her. Or myself."

Ceecee is quiet, but I hear her sniffing and see a tear drop onto my hand. "I found you, though. You and Margaret, safe and sound. At first, anyway.

"I told the police and the fire chief that I must have been sleeping when the fire started. And that's true. They asked me why I was upstairs in one of the bedrooms instead of in the wine cellar or someplace safe from the storm, and I told them I didn't know. That's the only lie I told that night. Because I do remember, and the truth was too shameful."

She moves with the lotion to the other side of the bed and picks up my right hand. She moves slowly, like an old woman, and it saddens me. I've done this to her. I know that. I want to tell her that I love her. And I want to tell her good-bye. But I can't seem to figure out how.

"I need you to tell me what you know about Margaret. I'm so afraid that I did something when I was asleep, or thought I was asleep. I need to know the truth of what happened."

She stops rubbing lotion into my hand and looks down at the shell of my body, as if I'm still there. "When I was being interviewed, the police and fire chief asked if maybe I'd dropped a candle, or left one lit too near a curtain. Or if I was smoking cigarettes. Which was nonsense.

"I've never smoked a day in my life." She bristles. "They said they found cigarette butts in a charred ashtray that managed to survive the fire. But of course they did. Bitty smoked, and she and I were at Carrowmore almost every day."

There is something in her voice that makes the cracking sound in the ceiling stop, magnifying the sound of the lotion and the pump on the bottle. It's like Ceecee's just been forced to take a bitter medicine, and she can't quite get the taste off her tongue.

"Almost every day," she says again, and I can tell she's crying, using the sleeve of her shirt to wipe her eyes. "And each time I went, it was like walking on broken glass. But I did it gladly, because it meant I could spend time with you."

The nurse appears in the doorway to say it's time for my bath, and Ceecee stands and smiles. She puts the lotion away and kisses me on the forehead. "Good-bye, sweet Ivy. I'll be back tomorrow." She walks to the doorway, but turns back, her eyes troubled. "Please wake up, darling. Please."

I hear her footsteps in the hallway, and I smell the lotion she's put on my hands. I say a prayer that she smells it, too, and that it makes her wonder why my nails and the skin on my hands are as frail as the filament that seems to be keeping me from pressing through the ceiling.

I'm in a thin place, I think, where this world is so close to the next. I just wish I knew what I'm supposed to do about it.

Larkin
2010

I sat down at the dining room table where Ceecee had left a thick photo album and a shoebox stuffed with photographs. She'd apologized for their being so disorganized, but it had been too painful for her to sort through them, which was why they'd ended up in the attic. I thought I'd go through them, and if it looked like I'd be here for another week, put them in some kind of order. Maybe place them in new albums, those archival ones. Although if they'd survived this long in a South Carolina attic, perhaps they didn't need anything so technically advanced.

Before I had opened the album's cover, the doorbell rang and the front door opened. I froze. Only a few people I knew would walk into Ceecee's house without waiting for the door to be answered, and one of them was someone I really didn't want to see ever again.

"Larkin? Are you here?"

It was Mabry, not Bennett, and I let out a sigh of relief. "I'm in the dining room."

She appeared in the doorway, holding two lidded cups with the name **Gabriel's Heavenly Ice Cream**

& Soda and the logo printed on the side, two pink plastic spoons and napkins clenched in her other hand. "I've come to apologize."

"For Bennett?" I asked.

She looked surprised. "No—although from your expression, it looks like maybe he owes you one, too. We'll talk about that later." She held up the ice cream. "This is an apology for Ellis. He would have come himself, but Grandpa said he needed Ellis's help painting the shed out back."

"An apology? For what?"

"For throwing up on you. He did say it was an ugly black dress, so it didn't matter, but I think he could have just been repeating something Bennett said."

Mabry sat down at the table and placed a cup, spoon, and napkin in front of me. "It's sea salt caramel and pecan—your favorite. But only one scoop and in a cup, instead of a giant waffle cone like we used to eat." She made a face. "The older I get, the less my stomach can handle that kind of sugar overload." Leaning over, she popped open the lids on both cups. "It got kind of soft on the walk over here, but I remember that you like it almost like pudding."

"Thanks," I said, grinning. Slipping back into our friendship was like finding a favorite pair of sweatpants that had been shoved into the back of a drawer and forgotten. If only it were possible to eradicate some memories and past experiences that hovered over us like a storm cloud.

I took a big spoonful and put it in my mouth, letting it slide over my tongue and drip down my throat. "Oh. My. Gosh. Just as amazing as I remember. Not that Ellis is the one who should be apologizing, but thank you. Perfect timing, too."

She sat in the chair next to mine. "What's all this?"

"Old photographs. Of Ceecee, Bitty, and my grandmother Margaret when they were younger. And a bunch of Mama when she was growing up. They've been in the attic this whole time. I guess it's not entirely my fault that I never asked about my grandmother. No one ever mentioned her. I barely knew she existed."

Mabry raised both eyebrows but didn't say anything. I pulled the album in front of me, the dark brown leather dry and cracked around the edges, the spine flap stretched almost to capacity. Seeing my hesitation, Mabry reached over and flipped open the front cover.

"It's Carrowmore," I said. Not the ruined Carrowmore that I knew, but the way it once was. The photograph was black-and-white, but the columns gleamed in the sunlight, the trees and grass trimmed and manicured. Glass-paned windows reflected sky and tree limbs, and intact brick steps led invitingly up to the front porch and massive front door.

"Look," Mabry said, pointing a finger at something on the porch.

I followed her finger to the porch swing, the collapsed and rotten one I'd noticed before on what was left of the porch. Except in the photo, the swing still hung, and the figures of three young girls, not much older than seven or eight, sat on it, the frilly crinolines of their dresses smashed together. It must have been a birthday party, because there were balloons tied to the back of the swing, and the girls all wore ribbons in their hair, and black patent leather Mary Janes with ankle socks on their feet.

"I bet that's Margaret," Mabry said, pointing to the girl in the middle. It was impossible to see her features clearly from where the photographer would have been standing, but the girl's hair shone like spun gold. She eclipsed the two girls sitting on either side so that at first glance, it appeared there was only her.

"And Ceecee," I said, pointing to a girl with light hair that was clearly blond but not as bright as Margaret's. Her hands were folded demurely in her lap, whereas Margaret's were held tightly together and pressed against her chest as if she were full of love and joy and everything good in the world.

"And Bitty," Mabry said, indicating the other girl. She was putting something in her mouth, and her gaze was facing the photographer. Her hair, though longer than it was now, was shorter than that of her two friends, the bow hanging haphazardly over her ear as if getting ready to abandon ship.

"I bet that's a Tootsie Roll she's eating," I said. "But only because she's a little too young to be smoking."

I turned the page. More pictures of apparently the same party, including several other children all wearing party hats and holding balloons, but in the photos of Margaret, she always had the other two girls at her side. Even in the posed photos of Margaret with her parents—my great-grandparents, whose names I didn't even know—Ceecee and Bitty stood at the edge of the picture, waiting to return to their rightful places at Margaret's side.

I flipped slowly, eating my ice cream as it melted, as Mabry and I pointed and commented on pictures of the three friends growing up together from elementary school to high school graduation and beyond. There were more pictures at Carrowmore, with a large number centered on a white room that looked like a wedding cake. It was for more formal gatherings, such as one where Margaret was dressed as a debutante, the brilliant white of her dress almost blending into the exquisite trim and moldings of the wall behind her.

There were photos from the grounds, too, of the three girls sunbathing on a dock of which there was no trace now, and sitting on the back-porch steps, painting their toenails. There were photos of them by the Tree of Dreams, too, a look of conspiracy gracing the face of each girl.

My favorite photo was of the three of them piled into the front bench seat of an old-fashioned convertible, with Margaret at the wheel, wearing a nearly sheer scarf over her hair and enormous dark sunglasses. She was breathtaking in her elegance and style, her poise and sophistication in direct contrast to her two friends.

"Want me to go get more?" Mabry asked, indicating my empty ice-cream cup. "You've been scraping the paper bottom for a while now."

I glanced down at my empty cup with surprise. "Thanks, but no. I'm good."

"Look at this one," Mabry said, stacking our cups in the middle of the table. "If I didn't know better, I could swear this was you."

It was a photograph of Margaret in the driver's seat of the convertible. She was looking out over the door at the camera, her sunglasses off and her hair uncovered. Mabry was right. It could have been me. But I had never in my life worn such an expression. It told the world this was a woman who knew she was beautiful. And knew how to use that beauty to get what she wanted. I sat back in my chair as if I'd been stung.

"I know what you mean," Mabry said, even though I hadn't said anything. "Kind of full of herself, you know?"

"Exactly," I said, looking at the nose, the brow, the cheeks. All of which could have been mine.

Mabry reached over and flipped the page. "Oooh—the beach!"

The first photo was of the three girls posed in front of the convertible next to a large sign that read WEL-COME TO MYRTLE BEACH. I looked up at Mabry. "Ceecee told me about this trip—it was a high school graduation gift from my great-grandparents. They would have been . . ."

"About seventeen or eighteen. Which makes this . . ." Mabry squinted one eye as she did the mental calculations.

"Don't hurt yourself. I'm happy to get a calculator."

"Nineteen fifty-one!" she shouted triumphantly.

I would have guessed early fifties, judging by the clothing and cars. But I wasn't sure I would have recognized Myrtle Beach. There weren't any high-rises or tacky tourist shops or packs of motorcycles. Just peaceful neighborhood streets with small, unassuming cottages and inns lined up on both sides, colorful names like THE JUANITA and THE PERISCOPE on signs in the yards.

"Wow—doesn't even look like the same place, does it?" Mabry said, echoing my thoughts.

I flipped a page and saw a photo of an open black iron gate topped with the words MYRTLE BEACH PAVILION. A palmetto tree motif was emblazoned at the top, on either side, and behind that, I could see the Ferris wheel and carousel, which were only legend now.

"I can't believe they tore all this down," I said. "When was that—four years ago? I remember reading about it in New York and crying. A piece of history wiped out so they could build more condos."

I shook my head, then bent close to the pages, looking at the faces of the tourists waiting in line at the various concessions. "I remember going there with you and Bennett and getting sick from eating junk food and going on the rides." I smiled. "Those were good times."

"You, me, and Bennett went there once with Ceecee, remember?" Mabry asked. "She was feeling nostalgic and said she'd look silly all by herself, so she brought us kids. We were about ten years old, I think."

I nodded, remembering riding the carousel and eating popcorn and cotton candy for dinner. I had an odd memory, too, of Ceecee. How we three kids were hollering and laughing and having the best time of our lives, but she seemed close to tears. I thought at the time it was because she wasn't a kid anymore, and that was making her sad. But now, seeing these pictures of her with Margaret and Bitty, I thought I understood why.

I sat back in my chair. "Remember that long, circular drive she showed us on North Ocean Boulevard? It didn't lead to anything, but she said that's where the grand Ocean Forest Hotel used to be. She cried, but I didn't say anything because she hardly seemed aware we were there."

Mabry was impatiently pulling at the corner of the page. "Look, Larkin—boys!"

"Seriously, Mabry?" I said, annoying her by turning the page very slowly. "I've seen boys before."

She yanked the page from my hand and laid it flat. "Yeah, but I think one of these guys might be your grandfather."

She had my attention now. The two facing pages were filled with photo-booth pictures with cardboard cutouts with holes where the faces should be. The first two were of Bitty and Ceecee as a fat and skinny swimmer, respectively, wearing old-fashioned bathing suits. The next was of a mermaid-type figure with **Miss Myrtle Beach** written across her scales, and Margaret's beautiful face peering innocently from the opening.

But it was the next photo that captured my attention. The sign painted at the top read MYRTLE BEACH JAIL, and behind cardboard bars were two young men trying to look miserable. I looked closer at the young men in the black-and-white photo, trying to remember my grandfather from my girlhood. He'd died when I was about eight, so I didn't have many memories of him. "My mother has that same hairline, doesn't she? And definitely his nose."

"No, silly—not him. The other guy. I just thought because he looked so nice, he'd be your grandfather. Although, to be honest, they actually resemble each other. They must be related."

I shook my head, pointing to the first man, and then the second. "I think it's that one—definitely."

Mabry nodded. "You might be right. We can ask Ceecee later." She reached over and flipped to the next page. "That's odd." She turned the album to face me. "It's blank."

I took the album from her and thumbed through the remaining pages, all empty. "That is odd. I wonder why. There had to be my grandparents' wedding pretty soon after, right?"

"What year were they married?" Mabry asked.

"I don't have a clue. Except . . ." I thought for a moment. "My mother was born in 1952, so Margaret must have been married in 'fifty-one or 'fifty-two."

"And Hurricane Hazel happened in 1954. I can understand why Ceecee wouldn't have any photos after 'fifty-four, but why not before? I'm sure she and Bitty would have been bridesmaids or co–maids of honor or something at Margaret's wedding."

"You'd think, wouldn't you?" My eyes fell on the envelope full of loose photos. "Unless they're in here."

I took out the photos and gave half of them to Mabry. We were silent for a while as we flipped through them. I paused at a photo of my mother, about age five, standing in between Ceecee and a man I assumed was my grandfather, their faces cut off by the camera as they swung a laughing little Ivy in the air.

"It's nice to know Mama had a happy childhood," I said, indicating the stack of photos that all included my mother during different holidays or school events or vacations, most showing Ceecee touching her or standing nearby. "But I don't see any photos beyond her growing-up years."

"I have a few of her with my uncle Ellis." Mabry slid three Polaroid photos toward me. "Looks like a prom or something. They're both wearing corsages."

The photographs were all taken in the backyard of

Ceecee's house, their backs to the river. Mama looked beautiful with long, straight blond hair parted in the middle, wearing a long prairie-style dress, a large magnolia blossom fastened to her wrist as a corsage. I couldn't tell if her bare toes meant she was wearing sandals or was barefoot. Probably barefoot, I decided. Because that was the way she would dress for a formal event.

In all three photos she was gazing up at Ellis, tall and handsome despite the powder blue velour tuxedo, mustache, and sideburns that Elvis Presley would have envied. He was glancing at Mama sideways, as if he knew he should be looking at the camera but couldn't take his eyes off her.

Mabry stood and put her arm around my shoulder and squeezed, making me realize that I'd started to cry. "I'm sorry. I shouldn't have shown that to you."

I shook my head. "No. I'm glad you did. I don't think I've ever seen her look so completely happy. She loved him, didn't she? Really loved him."

Mabry nodded. "That's what Mama said. But she also said that your mama never regretted marrying your daddy. She loved him, too. He always thought her heart was secondhand by the time he got it, but Mama said that secondhand doesn't mean used or worn-out. It means it's become wise and seasoned. Of course, your mama also said that the most love she'd ever known was the love she had for you."

I met my friend's eyes, knowing she wouldn't judge the tears freely flowing down my cheeks. I cleared my throat and used one of the ice-cream napkins to wipe my face. "Did you see any photos of Mama and me? Any of me wearing a tiara, a tutu, and my sparkly red shoes? She said in an e-mail she'd found it in an envelope and was going to send it to me. But that was the day she disappeared."

"Nothing," Mabry said. "Maybe she put it in your bedroom?"

"No. Daddy already checked." I sat back, recalling my conversation with my father. "He mentioned she'd been refurbishing my grandfather's desk. Maybe it's in the detached garage."

Mabry was already standing. "Come on, then—let's go look." She was out the back door before I stood to follow.

By the time I caught up to her, she'd flipped on the overhead light, illuminating a nearly empty garage that smelled of dust, paint thinner, and time. Standing in the center of the space, directly beneath a large light fixture with a bare bulb, was an ancient partners desk. The finish had been sanded from the surface, and bared wood made the desk look like a naked chicken. Bottles of different liquids and paint, along with brushes, rags, and newspaper, littered the floor. The drawers had been pulled out and stacked against one wall, but after a cursory glance, I could tell that they were empty.

We both examined the desk but found nothing. "I'll keep looking," I said. "And I'll ask my coworker Josephine to check my mail and see if Mama mailed it. I probably have an avalanche in my foyer by now, anyway. I wasn't planning on being here this long."

"Me, neither," said Mabry, smiling softly. "And I'm sorry it took your mama's accident to bring you back. But I'm glad you're here. I've missed you."

I was already backing out of the shed, knowing her well enough to anticipate what her next words would be.

"We need to talk about that day on the boat. We need to talk about what happened."

I was shaking my head, moving forward without looking back. I was so good at it now, I didn't even need to think about it. "We really don't," I said.

"Larkin, please."

Something in the tone of her voice made me stop and turn around.

"This is your home. I don't want misunderstandings to keep you away. Don't you miss us? Don't you miss the smell of the marsh early in the morning? Or the sounds of the creeks when you sit really still in a paddleboat? I would. I think my heart and soul would shrink if I had to spend months without seeing the sun rise over the sea oats. Don't you feel that way, too?"

I kept walking toward the door of Ceecee's house, my stride purposeful so Mabry wouldn't suspect that I wanted to stop and run to her and tell her yes to all of the above. That I sometimes woke up with wet cheeks because I dreamed of the creeks and rivers of my childhood, missing them like the tides would miss the moon.

But I didn't. Nine years spent telling myself that I couldn't go home again made my separation permanent and official. I was nothing if not decisive.

I paused at the back door and faced her again. "Thanks for the ice cream—and tell Ellis that I'm glad he's feeling better. I'll see you around."

Mabry stood there, watching me, the same expression on her face that I remembered from the last time I'd seen her, before I left nine years ago, right before I threw a cooler at her head that pushed her into the dark water of the Sampit River.

twenty-seven

Ceecee
1951

Ceecee and Bitty sat in the white parlor, staring at the tea tray with its untouched sandwiches and sweating glasses of iced tea. Summer had appeared with a vengeance, as if it wanted to match Ceecee's internal misery.

An antique French porcelain carriage clock ticked incessantly on the desk, reminding Ceecee of flies battering their hard black bodies against a closed window until Bitty forcibly made it stop. In other circumstances, Ceecee would have told her to be careful not to damage the fragile antique, but she could no longer find it in herself to care about such trivial things.

Unable to sit still any longer, Ceecee jumped to

her feet. "I've got to find out what's going on. I can't stand not knowing for one more moment."

Bitty stood, too, but her eyes were wary. "Sometimes it's best to wait, even if it just means postponing the knowing."

Ceecee turned on her with an unexpected fury. "Knowing what? I don't know anything except Margaret is near death with grief, and her baby's life is hanging in the balance. And the man I love is the only person she will talk to. The only person who can help her." She faced the door and took a step toward it before stopping. "If I go upstairs, if I force her to see me . . ."

"It won't accomplish anything," Bitty said calmly, taking out her pack of cigarettes from her pocketbook and pulling one out. "Damn," she said under her breath, crumpling the now-empty pack and tossing it across the room.

Ceecee turned to look at her friend, her anger and frustration—her grief—momentarily defused. "I have a stash of Tootsie Rolls in my pocketbook if you need them. I save the ones you give me because I don't like them." She wasn't sure why she was being honest about that now. Maybe because she was so raw and bare, and felt the need to shed what skin still clung to her aching bones.

"If I had another cigarette, I'd offer you one," Bitty said, only half joking.

The sound of slow footsteps coming down the grand staircase caught their attention. Bitty waited while Ceecee ran out into the foyer, feeling all the past Darlingtons looking down their aristocratic noses at her in their portraits. Her gaze skimmed over them to the tall figure carefully making his way down the stairs, his hand tightly gripping the banister.

"Boyd." She'd meant to say it in a normal tone of voice, but his name came out as if her mouth were coated with feathers.

He looked awful. His face was pale and drawn, his hair uncombed as if he'd been repeatedly running his fingers through it. His collar was unbuttoned, his tie askew, his jacket discarded somewhere, and his sleeves rolled up to his forearms as if he was prepared to do battle.

"Sessalee."

It didn't sound like her name or his voice. It was a cry of defeat and longing, of frustration and grief, and it scared her enough that she turned toward the front door. She was grasping the handle before she felt his hands on her arms, his warmth behind her.

"I need to tell you something," he said, his voice tight, his mouth stingy with the words.

"Don't." She wasn't even sure what he needed to tell her, but she knew whatever it was would break her heart.

The grip on her arms tightened as he pulled her against him, resting his chin on the top of her head. "I love you, Sessalee. From that first moment I saw you, remember?"

She turned in his arms, stood on her tiptoes, and

kissed the underside of his jaw before laying her head on his shoulder. "Then let's run away. Far from here. We'll get married and have children together and live happily ever after."

"Oh, my darling Sessalee. You have no idea how much I wish we could."

A thin crackling sound came from inside her chest, like that of stepping on a frozen puddle in the middle of winter and shattering its surface. She felt suspended in time, somehow, as if this all weren't happening, or had already happened to someone else.

They both turned at the sound of running feet moving up the staircase and saw Bitty pausing at the curve of the landing. She leaned over the railing. "I'm going to see if I can talk some sense into her." She angrily brushed at the tears streaming down her cheeks. "This . . . It cannot be allowed." Without another word, she disappeared around the graceful curve of the staircase, her feet heavy and quick.

Ceecee had seen Bitty cry only once, when her favorite dog had died when they were twelve. And seeing her cry now, more than anything, chilled her heart. Ceecee could lie to herself and pretend that her darkest fear didn't exist, could pretend that because she and Boyd loved each other they would be married and live the life they both dreamed of. But Bitty's tears were nails in the coffin of Ceecee's dream. There could be no more denying or pretending. No more dreaming. No more thinking that the Darlington luck would pull through one more time.

But then again, she thought, it had. Just not for her.

She tried to pull away from Boyd, but he held her tightly. Taking her hand, he led her through the front door and then around to the back of the house. She struggled again to make him let go when she realized where he was taking her.

"Sessalee—please. Please. I need to show you something."

She allowed him to lead her to the giant oak tree near the bank of the river, resentful of the bright sun that glinted off the water and through the shiny leaves of the oak. "Let's sit," he said, pulling her down onto one of the thick roots protruding from the earth like an arthritic knuckle.

Boyd took a deep breath before reaching into his shirt pocket and retrieving a white envelope. "Before Reggie left to enlist, he wrote two letters. One was for Margaret." He pressed the letter into Ceecee's cold and stiff fingers. Despite the heat of the day, she shivered.

"This one was for me. It was sealed, and he left instructions for me not to open it unless something happened to him."

She looked at the torn flap of the envelope, and her breath caught in the back of her throat.

"Read it," Boyd said gently.

She shook her head. "I can't."

He waited for a long moment, and she felt his gaze

on her, heard his breathing. Finally, he took the envelope from her and opened the letter inside before he began to read aloud.

Dear Boyd,

I've been doing a lot of thinking recently, and it occurred to me for the first time that I have never lived a day of my life without knowing you were in it, and knowing I was better off for it. You've always been the best big brother and role model a man could ever want. Even with our age difference, it never seemed that you and I were very far apart in the way we viewed the world and our place in it. I'm prouder than I could ever say to call you my brother.

Ever since that summer on Folly Beach when I saved your life, I've always known that I was meant to be there. To maybe save you for better things. You've always said that you owed me your life, that you would go to the ends of the earth to repay the favor, but I never once viewed it that way at all. Yet perhaps you've been right all along. Maybe we both have.

I love Margaret Darlington and wish to spend the rest of my life with her. I know she feels the same, despite our difference in opin-

ion about whether I should enlist. I love my country, and I am compelled to serve it in any capacity and do my duty as you did and our ancestors have done. Enlisting was the toughest choice of my life, and that decision does not lessen how I feel for Margaret. Please make sure she knows that.

I think we are all born with just half a heart, and we are meant to spend our lives looking for the other half. Margaret is mine, and I am hers. I haven't doubted that from the moment she took my hand on the dance floor at the Ocean Forest. That's how I remember her—gold hair shining under the moonlight as she danced in my arms.

All the plans and hopes in the world can't make our dreams come true, which is why I'm calling in the debt. I behaved dishonorably, and even though I asked Margaret to marry me, she said no—but only until I'd changed my mind about enlisting. I don't blame her. This isn't what she planned for. But we can't always plan for everything, can we? Life has its own plans sometimes, and we've no choice but to follow.

I need you to promise me, Boyd, that if something should happen to me, you will repay the debt you owe me and take care of my Margaret. And if there is any result from my transgression, I'm counting on you to do the honorable thing by me. You know that I would do the same thing if our positions were reversed. But of course they're not. You've always known how to turn away from temptation and do the admirable thing. I'm not nearly as strong.

Be well, Boyd. I hope you never have to read this letter. And if you do, then I thank you with all of my heart. Knowing you are there for Margaret brings me the greatest comfort.

Your brother,
Reggie

Ceecee tilted her head back, looking up at the sun to reassure herself that it was still there. She was lightheaded and feverish and thought she might throw up. She wanted to dive into the cool water of the river, deeper and deeper until she'd run out of breath and simply let go of this world. "Are you going to marry Margaret, then?"

He let out a long breath. "Yes." He closed his eyes for a moment. "I've gone over and over all the options with Margaret, and she's turned them all down for one reason or another. She won't give up the baby because it's the only thing left of Reggie. I mentioned that you and I could raise the baby as ours, but she won't hear of it. She's adamant that the baby remain with her. She is the child's mother." He drew a long, shuddering breath. "Reggie is not only my brother, and the baby my niece or nephew, but I owe Reggie my life. I can't ignore that. I don't have a choice."

"Of course you do," Ceecee said, not caring about the desperation in her voice. "Reggie wouldn't ask you to do this if he knew how we felt about each other."

He was already shaking his head before she finished speaking. "It's not Margaret or Reggie I'm thinking about. It's the baby. The only hope for a future for that child is if I marry Margaret now and let the world believe that it's mine. A healthy child is the one good thing that can come of all this. You see that, don't you?"

Ceecee shook her head. "I want to. I do. But all I can see right now is a lifetime of emptiness, and Margaret walks away with everything. Just like she always has." There. She'd said it. The words she'd thought for years. The truth of what her mother had been trying to tell her since they were children. "I'm sorry, Boyd. I know you think you're doing the right thing, but you're wrong. We belong together. You and me." She didn't care that her face was streaked with tears and mascara. Nothing mattered anymore. Nothing.

He took her hands in his and kissed them. "We do, Sessalee. We do belong together. But doing the easy thing is rarely the right thing. Think of the baby. Of that innocent life whose future depends on us." He pressed his forehead against hers. "We can pretend the baby is ours—yours and mine. It will be the thing that we can share."

She wrenched her hands away and shook her head. "It's not enough, Boyd. You know it's not enough."

He put his hands behind her head and brought her face close to his. "It has to be, Sessalee. We'll just have to make it be enough."

Boyd reached up and tugged at her ponytail, setting loose the ribbon she'd put in it that morning that now felt like a million years ago. "What are you doing?" It didn't sound like her voice any more than she felt like the same Sessalee Purnell she'd been when she'd put that ribbon in her hair.

"I'm putting a ribbon in the Tree of Dreams," he said, drawing out a pen from his shirt pocket.

She stared at him uncomprehendingly.

He flattened the ribbon on his leg and began scribbling something on the fabric. Her gaze traveling to the black opening, she remembered the first ribbon she'd put in there, about her finding the perfect man. And how Margaret had written the same thing.

"Don't." Ceecee scrambled to her feet.

But Boyd had already stood and was stuffing the ribbon deep into the tree's trunk. When he turned to look at her, beads of sweat covered his forehead. Ceecee grabbed his wrist and pulled him away from the tree. "What did it say?"

He looked at her as if he didn't understand her question.

She tugged on his arm. "What did you write? On the ribbon?"

His eyes, dark and brooding, bored into hers. "'I will love Sessalee Purnell until I die, and will hope every day that we will find a way to spend our lives together.'"

"Don't, Boyd. Don't say it if you don't mean it. You can't marry her and love me. You can't have it both ways. We will both die inside trying."

"I have to try, Sessalee. Because this is breaking my heart, too. I don't believe in this stupid tree any more than you do, but I can't imagine it will make our situation any worse."

"No!" she shouted, straining forward toward the tree, desperate to pull out the ribbon. But Boyd held fast, wrapping his arms around her before pressing his lips against hers. She was lost for a moment, in his kiss and in the love she had for him, until the sound of the returning martins made her open her eyes to see the darkening sky filled with the rattle of birds coming home to roost.

~

When Ceecee returned to the house alone, Bitty was waiting for her on the porch swing, an ashtray full of cigarette butts at her feet. "I found more in Mr. Darlington's study. Want one?"

Ceecee shook her head, listening as Boyd's car disappeared down the drive, and tried to think about what she was supposed to do next but couldn't. So she stood on the bottom step and looked up at Bitty. She opened her mouth to say something, to scream, or cry, but there was nothing left. She was an abandoned shell on the beach, whole and unscathed on the outside, but hollowed out and empty inside.

Bitty stood and took a step forward, her arms outstretched, but Ceecee shook her head, knowing that if she received one ounce of compassion, she'd start to cry and never be able to stop.

"They're getting married," Ceecee said with the same tone she'd have used to compliment her on her shoes or hairstyle.

"I know." Bitty's face was pinched, as if she'd just been forced to taste a bitter medicine. "I tried to talk Margaret out of it, to look for other solutions, but her mind is set. For her, it's perfect. She gets a husband and a baby, all without shame. Her biggest worry is that the baby will be big when it's born so no one will believe it's premature."

Bitty's voice warbled, and Ceecee had to look away, knowing that if Bitty started crying again, there'd be no hope for either one of them.

"Friends forever, right?" Ceecee said, and tried to laugh, but it came out wrong.

"Don't let her do this, Ceecee. Please don't."

Ceecee shook her head. "Boyd says he's doing it for the baby's sake."

Bitty's face was hard. "And Margaret is doing it for her own selfish reasons. If she loved you like she says she does, she wouldn't do this."

Ceecee could only stare at her friend, knowing everything she wanted to say had already been said. Every possible solution and outcome had already been dissected and discarded.

"She wants to see you," Bitty said.

"Now?"

Bitty nodded. "It has to happen sooner or later, so you might as well get it over with. Do you want me to come with you?"

Ceecee shook her head. "No. I'd best do this alone."

"I'll be here when you get back. I'll go ahead and pour some of Mr. Darlington's scotch and have it waiting for you. You're probably going to need it."

Ceecee made her way up the elegant staircase, leaning on the banister because she wasn't sure her legs could bear the weight of her grief. She made it to the wide upper hall, the tall doors on either end opened to create a cross-breeze that did almost nothing to alleviate the stifling heat. A maid came out of Margaret's bedroom, carrying an untouched food tray. Her face was apologetic—either because of the untouched food or because she knew what was happening.

Ceecee stepped inside and stood in front of the door, blinking at the sudden darkness. The curtains had been drawn, and even though a ceiling fan and a floor fan were turned on high, they only shifted the stifling air around the room. Margaret sat in the middle of the bed, a pile of white lace-covered pillows behind her that matched the virginal white nightgown buttoned up to her neck. Her pale face almost blended into the bedding, and all Ceecee could think was, **Good.**

"You're not dying," Ceecee said, marching over to the large French doors that faced the river and throwing them open. A welcome breeze cooled her forehead, calming her. She spotted the Tree of Dreams across the yard and quickly turned her back on it.

"I'm so sorry, Ceecee. I didn't mean for any of this to happen." The voice coming from the woman on the bed wasn't recognizable as Margaret's. It was timid and hesitant, so unlike the forceful, confident tones of the friend she'd known and loved. It made Ceecee pause, feeling a moment of sympathy for the woman on the bed who'd lost so much.

But then she thought of Boyd, and what Margaret had done, and she continued her march around the room, throwing open curtains and turning on all the lamps. Because she still couldn't get her nerves under control, she refilled the water glass on the bedside table, her hands shaking so badly, she thought she might drop it.

"Thank you," Margaret said softly.

Ceecee didn't respond but stood looking down at Margaret, her emotions ricocheting between pity, anger, and grief. "For what?" She knew, of course. She just wanted to hear Margaret say it.

But what Margaret said next wasn't what she'd expected to hear at all. "For your loving and generous heart. For your sacrifice. For your friendship."

Ceecee could only stare at her.

Margaret pressed a handkerchief to eyes that were bloodshot and sunken, a fact that Ceecee didn't castigate herself for feeling good about. "I've done a terrible thing. To you. To Boyd. And I'm more sorry than I can ever say. But I can't figure out another way out of this."

Ceecee remembered the look on Boyd's face as they'd sat under the Tree of Dreams, the dreams and plans she'd made for their life together. "So you've made up your mind, then. You've decided there is no alternative to ruining my life."

A fresh torrent of tears cascaded down Margaret's sallow cheeks. "I know there is no way I can ever make this up to you. If only it were just me. But it's not. There's another, innocent life to protect. It's Reggie's baby, and I owe it to his memory to do whatever I can to make sure his child is loved and cherished and taken care of for the rest of his or her life."

Ceecee allowed her gaze to move down the bedclothes. Margaret's slim frame showed no sign yet of the baby growing inside her. She felt the edges of her heart soften, curling like a rose petal. But not for Margaret. For the baby. She remembered what Boyd had said, and she felt a small stab of light filtering through her dark thoughts.

"I want to be godmother."

Margaret looked up at her with a surprised and tear-stained face. "You do?"

"Yes. I do. I want to be an important part in this child's life. You at least owe me that."

Margaret nodded. "All right." She attempted a smile, but it looked like a grimace on a skeleton hung out at Halloween. "I never imagined my life without you or Bitty. No matter what, I want you both in my life. And in my child's life."

Ceecee thought for a moment, frowning down at Margaret. "If it's a girl, I want you to name her Ivy."

"But that's the name you always said you would give your daughter if you ever had one."

"Yes, it is. But it doesn't look like I'll be getting married and having my own children now, does it?"

Fresh tears oozed from Margaret's blue eyes. "I'm sorry, Ceecee. I'm so very sorry. I know how inadequate the word is, but I hope in time that you will find it in your heart to forgive me."

Ceecee pulled her chin up. "It's not me you have to wait to forgive you."

"What do you mean?"

"Boyd's the one who will have to live with you for the rest of your lives. You'd better hope he finds it in his heart to forgive you. And himself."

Margaret straightened her shoulders. "I can make him happy. I can be a good wife to him."

Ceecee took a step forward, pointing her finger at Margaret's chest. "Don't you ever say that to me again. Do you understand? I will be a part of your life because of the child, but I will never, ever think of you and Boyd as husband and wife. I will never see you that way. Because he was never meant to be yours."

Margaret pressed her back against the headboard to create distance between them, but she didn't lower her gaze. It was as if for the first time they saw something new in each other, something that equalized their standing. Something unexpected and just as terrifying.

Ceecee stepped back. "I'm going downstairs to tell the maid to bring the food back, and I will stay to watch you eat every last bite. This baby **will** be born healthy and strong, and I will come here every single day to make sure of it."

She began walking toward the bedroom door, stopping when Margaret spoke again.

"I didn't mean for this to happen, Ceecee. I loved Reggie with all my heart. If it weren't for his baby, I'd happily die. If I could bring him back, you know I would."

Ceecee turned to look at Margaret. Softly, she said, "So would I." Then she left the room, the door closing behind her with a soft click.

twenty-eight

Larkin
2010

I sat at the nearly empty counter at Gabriel's ice-cream shop, slowly sipping at my Brown Cow. Music played from the speakers, and I gave Gabriel a questioning look. "'Runnin' Down a Dream' by Tom Petty. Definitely eighties. What's up with that?"

He shrugged. "It's Tom Petty. One of the few who are allowed to share a playlist with the classics."

I laughed, looking around the store. Being here was a welcome break; I continued to do my job remotely, with almost daily reassurances to my boss that I would be back soon. As Gabriel finished with a few customers, my gaze settled on the mural. Recalling what Mabry had told me about my mother always hiding a small image, I climbed off the stool and moved closer. But all I saw was what I'd seen before, the tree and the river, and the three girls with their backs to the artist. It was a beautiful, peaceful scene, yet there was something about the colors used for the background, and the visible strokes of the artist's brush, that agitated the image. Like shaking a snow globe distorts the picture inside.

I stepped back to get a different perspective, seeing for the first time a nearly hidden edge, tucked into the back corner of the room. I put my glass on the counter and moved away a table and two chairs to see it better. There, in the crease where one wall ended and another began, was Carrowmore, painted as it must have once been, with its graceful columns and still-intact roof. This hidden picture was larger than the other ones I'd seen, making it easier to make out the details. I leaned forward. In a first-floor window, a fork of orange-yellow flames shot out from the shattered frame. Behind the flame, a shadowy figure was barely visible—the shape of a woman with red hair.

I jerked back, as if I'd just seen something obscene.

"Are you all right?" Gabriel put his hands on my shoulders, steadying me.

"I'm not sure," I said. "Look." I pointed to the corner.

Gabriel whistled softly. "Never saw that. Your mama came in not too long ago, said she needed to add a few details. I got busy with customers and didn't see what she was doing, and she left before I could ask what she'd added."

"Do you remember when that was?" I asked.

He thought for a moment. "Yeah—either the day before or maybe the morning of her accident."

I stepped closer again, trying to see if I might have missed any other details. There was another blurry image in an upstairs window, and I squinted to see it better. There were flames in the background here, too, but pressed against the window frame were the blurred faces of two women, both blond.

"I can't believe this was here all this time and I never noticed." Gabriel shook his head. "One thing she did tell me while she was painting it the first time was that she was trying to paint her nightmare so that it would be stuck on the wall and out of her head. She didn't want to answer any of my questions, so I didn't press her to explain. I wish I had."

"Me, too."

"Hey," he said, squeezing my arm. "I have something to show you. Something your mama gave to me."

My interest piqued, I followed him behind the counter and into the back room that he used as his office. Tall, metal shelves covered the walls, stacked with a mishmash of boxes, all of them labeled with neat, bold lettering. I pointed to the one that read **Napkins.** "I'm assuming your wife does your organizing?"

He looked genuinely surprised. "How'd you know that?"

"Lucky guess." I smiled. "So, what do you have to show me?"

From a bottom shelf, he pulled a rectangular wood box the size of an ankle-boot shoebox with brass corners and a matching brass lock and key in the middle. The dark cherrywood had been polished to a gleam, and a brightly colored image had been painted on top and around the sides. He cleared a bit of space on his cluttered desk and placed the box on top.

I stood in front of it, gently brushing my fingers over the paint. "Did Mama paint this?"

Gabriel nodded. "She did. It's an old cigar humidor that used to belong to Ellis's daddy. When my mama worked for the Altons, she'd always admired it, so when Mrs. Alton died, Mr. Alton gave it to her. Before my mama died, she gave it to me. I was starting my business, and she thought I'd need a safe place to hide extra cash. She'd lived through the Depression and didn't believe in banks. Can't say I blame her."

I studied the small painting on the lid, noticing how it swooped and dipped along the sides and front as if it had been painted on a flat canvas. In the middle on the top was a painting of the store and Harborwalk, showing the river behind it with boats and gulls and even a tourist taking a photograph. An intricate time line that showed events in the business's history and Gabriel's story—his wedding, the birth of his children—were included, along with the introduction of new ice-cream flavors, complete with tiny ice-cream cones depicting each one.

"It's a history of Gabriel's Heavenly Ice Cream and Soda shop," he said proudly. "I hadn't used the box in a while, and Ivy found it here in the storeroom when she was working on that last mural and asked if I'd like her to make it pretty."

He turned the brass key and opened the lid. Although it had been stripped of whatever mechanism there might have been inside to keep cigars moist, it still smelled of fresh wood and tobacco.

"It's empty," I said, strangely disappointed. As if inside I'd find out what my mother had been trying to tell me the day she fell.

"Sort of," he said. "Look what she found while she was working on it."

He reached inside the box and touched a spot on the bottom near the rear edge. We heard a small click. Pressing his thumbs against the sides, Gabriel lifted the bottom out of the box, displaying an extra inch beneath.

"It's a false bottom," he said, grinning like a kid. "Probably used to hide money or valuables. I've seen a few antique desks like it. It was empty when I got it, and I'm not sure if Mama even knew this was here." He replaced the bottom, then closed the lid and locked it with the key. Then he picked up the box and handed it to me. "I want you to have it."

"Oh, I couldn't, Gabriel. She made it for you. It's your store painted on the top."

"I know. But I'm here every day, so I don't need something to remember it by. I thought this would be a nice memento for you to bring back to your office in New York. Sort of a daily reminder of your mama and where you come from." He grinned again. "And of your favorite ice-cream store."

I thought of my deliberately empty cubicle at Wax & Crandall, how stark and devoid of anything personal it was, and I couldn't remember why I kept it that way. I took the box and smiled at Gabriel. "Thank you. I promise to put it in a place of honor."

He led me out to the front of the store, and I found myself staring at the mural again, at the corner where the bright orange flames licked at the white house. I turned to Gabriel. "Did Mama ever talk to you about the fire?"

"No, not that I remember. It was more local legend than anything else."

"Local legend?" I straightened. "What did people say?"

He thought for a moment, his eyes not leaving my face. "Just stupid stuff."

"I'd like to know, Gabriel. Anything, really."

"You want to know what gossip said, or do you want to know the truth? Because nobody knows the truth except for Ceecee. She was the only one there old enough to remember. The gossip's just a bunch of lies."

"I want to hear all of it. Because for twenty-seven years I've heard absolutely nothing. Don't you think I'm smart enough to separate the gossip from the truth?"

The bell rang over the front door as a young couple walked in, a baby with a pink sunbonnet strapped to the chest of the man. "I'll be right with you," Gabriel called out to them, then turned back to me.

"So, what does local legend say?" I pressed.

"Really, Larkin, I don't think . . ."

"Tell me, Gabriel. Or I'll ask someone else who will. But I'd rather it come from you."

The man with the baby looked impatiently over at us, making Gabriel raise his finger. "One second."

"Gabriel . . ."

"Some people said at the time that the fire was intentional." He pressed his lips together as if he didn't want to say more, then spoke again as if he knew I'd keep at him until he told me everything. "They said your grandmother was murdered. That's all I remember, and that's the truth. It's all a bunch of garbage, you hear? Just something for people to wag their jaws about. Except for the Sunset Lodge, there's never really been a lot of news here in Georgetown. People had to make stuff up to give them something to do."

He squeezed my arm, then turned to his customers.

I looked back at the mural, at the three young women sitting with their backs to me, then slowly allowed my gaze to slide to the right, where the tableau of a house on fire with people trapped inside played itself out.

What were you trying to say, Mama? What do you want me to see?

I waved good-bye and left the shop, hugging the box against my chest, then stood on the sidewalk, remembering the photos Mabry and I had seen of the three friends growing up together. Of their trip to Myrtle Beach. And how there weren't any pictures from after that.

"Larkin!"

I startled at the sound of my name and turned to see Mabry approaching me, carrying a clear dry-cleaning bag with something yellow inside. She stopped next to me and tilted her head. "You all right?"

I showed her the cigar box. "Gabriel gave me this."

"Nice," she said, her tone questioning.

"Mama painted it."

Mabry nodded. "It's beautiful," she said. "But that doesn't explain why you look like they've just discontinued your favorite flavor."

I considered not telling her, not wanting to give voice to the dark thoughts running around my brain. "Do you remember ever hearing a local legend about the fire at Carrowmore?"

She shook her head. "No. It happened thirty years before we were born, so probably not much of a topic of conversation on the playground, you know? Why do you ask?"

"Gabriel just told me that some people thought the fire had been set intentionally. That it might have been murder."

"But that's just legend, right? Like the old rhyme 'Lizzie Borden took an ax.'" Mabry stopped. "Well, that probably isn't the best example, but you know what I'm saying. People love stories—the more sala-cious, the better. That doesn't make them true."

"Yes, except Bennett found the official report about the fire in your grandfather's papers, and someone had written the word 'suspicious' under the cause of fire. So . . ."

"So?" Mabry asked, her eyes looking steadily into mine.

"So, I'm wondering if there's a glimmer of truth to it. Isn't that what they say? That every legend, or ghost story, has a crumb of truth at its heart?"

"I don't know—is that what they say? What about Ceecee and Bitty? I'm assuming you've asked them?"

"Of course. But Ceecee said she was sleeping and doesn't remember anything, and Bitty wasn't there."

"Sure, but maybe they'll know why people would say something so awful about what happened. Let's go ask. I was on the way to Ceecee's house anyway."

I nodded, took a step, then stopped. "There's one more thing. Something in the mural inside Gabriel's store—the one my mama painted. There's a hidden picture in the back corner that shows Carrowmore on fire. In one of the windows, two women are star-ing out, and in another window, there's a figure of another woman—with red hair."

"Bitty?"

"Who else could it be?" I asked. "Except Bitty wasn't there."

I was afraid for a moment that Mabry was going to tell me to wait until my mother woke up and we could ask her about it then. But she didn't, and I was glad. Mama had been in a coma for more than three weeks, without any change or good news from her doctors. Even I had stopped lying to myself.

"Let's definitely go ask Ceecee, then. She's bound to have heard **something.** And then I can show you the dress." Mabry smiled secretively and threw her bundle over her other arm.

"The dress?"

She nodded. "When your daddy went up to the attic to get the album and photos, Ceecee asked him to bring this dress down, too. It needed a hem fixed and the zipper mended, so she brought it to Mama, who is just about a genius with a needle. It looks practically brand-new."

I kept trying to steal a glance at the dress under the plastic, but she continued moving it out of my sight. "Why aren't you letting me see it?"

"Because it's supposed to be a surprise."

"A surprise? For what?"

Mabry rolled her eyes. "You're the worst at surprises, Larkin. I don't think I ever gave you a birthday or Christmas gift without you hounding me to death until I told you what it was. Can't you just wait until I give this to Ceecee and let her tell you?"

"Or you could just tell me now so I don't have to hound you to death. It's your fault—you shouldn't have said anything." I reached for the dress, but she twisted away from me.

"Really, Larkin? How old are you, anyway?"

"Old enough to know that I can keep badgering you, or you can just tell me. Either way, you're going to spill the beans before we get to Ceecee's house." She stopped and I smiled. "I promise to be surprised when Ceecee tells me."

"Fine." She held up the dress so I could see it better. "Ceecee said she thought it would be the perfect dress for you to wear to the Shag Festival."

My eyes widened. "What? I'm not going to the Shag Festival."

"Well, Bennett sure thinks you are. He's already bought tickets—and Jonathan and I are going, too. You can't back out now."

"I said I'd go—but only because he'd bribed me into it, and then he pulled that stunt with Ellis on the boat. I can't believe he thinks I'd want to see him again after that."

"But I'll be there, Larkin! You can ignore Bennett and hang with Jonathan and me. You know you love to dance—how could you even think about missing it? And Mama and Ceecee have gone to so much trouble with your dress."

I lifted the plastic to see the dress better. I couldn't identify the fabric, but it looked like a heavy, high-sheen cotton. It had wide straps and a square neckline, a tight bodice and a flared skirt. I lifted the bottom to look underneath. "Crinoline?"

Mabry nodded with excitement. "Isn't it gorgeous? Considering how old it is, it's hard to believe that it's still such a bright sunshine yellow."

I frowned. "How old **is** it?"

"It belonged to your grandmother—Margaret. I think Ceecee said she only wore it once—but that it was the happiest night of Margaret's life. You can ask her about it. Mama wanted you to try it on today so that she can take care of any tweaks if you need them."

I dropped the plastic. "I'm not going. And I'm certainly not wearing that dress. It has a crinoline."

"You are. I don't think I could stand Bennett's disappointment if you didn't show up. Just come. I promise you won't have to say a single word to him— you can just talk to Jonathan and me. And what's wrong with a crinoline, anyway?"

"Besides its being really scratchy and old-fashioned, you mean?"

"Fine—I'll have Mama take it out. Problem solved."

"Mabry . . ." I stopped. We'd reached Ceecee's house and started to climb the porch steps when I spotted Bitty. Her attention was focused on the dress Mabry carried. She stood, walked over to us, and pulled up the plastic.

"It's Margaret's, isn't it?" she said, her fingers brushing the fabric as if it were the face of a long-lost friend.

"It sure is," Mabry said. "And Larkin's going to wear it to the Shag Festival tomorrow."

"I'm not . . ." Ceecee's appearance at the front door interrupted me.

"You brought the dress!" she exclaimed, taking it from Mabry before thrusting it at me. "Go try it on—I'm dying to see what it looks like. Although it was supposed to be a surprise." She sent Mabry a disapproving glance.

I looked around at the three expectant faces and knew there would be no arguing. It would be faster to try it on and then tell them no. "Fine," I said. "But first, I wanted to ask you both another question. About the fire."

It seemed as if Ceecee and Bitty were studiously avoiding looking at each other.

"Was either one of you aware of the rumors and speculation at the time?"

"Rumors?" asked Ceecee, her tightly clenched fingers belying her indifference.

"Yes, rumors. About the fire maybe being intentionally set, which would make my grandmother's death a murder. But why would anyone want to kill my grandmother?"

"Why, indeed?" Bitty said.

Ceecee's face remained impassive. "Like you said, they were just rumors. Now, go on up and try on that dress. We can't wait to see you in it!"

I looked at the two older women, then moved past

Ceecee and into the house. I ran upstairs to my room, dropped the cigar box on the dresser, and pulled off my clothes, leaving them on the floor next to my suitcase. Impatiently, I removed the plastic cover and slid the dress over my head, fumbling with the zipper as I walked back across the room to the door, eager to have this over with.

As I walked in front of the cheval mirror in the corner, I stopped, my hand involuntarily moving to my mouth. The woman reflected in the glass was the woman in the photographs, the woman smiling and laughing with her friends on a trip to Myrtle Beach. I stepped closer, studying the stranger staring back at me. Except she wasn't a stranger. I recognized the eyes and the hair, the silver hoop earrings I'd put on this morning, and the pale pink lipstick.

Yet I didn't recognize **her.** That woman was beautiful. Intelligent and self-assured. The kind of woman I'd always wanted to be and for a long time had pretended I was. She couldn't be me. But, somehow, she was.

"Hurry up," Ceecee called from downstairs. "We're dying to see you in the dress!"

I reluctantly backed away from the mirror, as if afraid the woman would escape and I'd never find her again. "Coming," I called, then headed toward the stairs.

The three women stood in the foyer, watching me walk down the graceful stairs, the stained-glass window in the stairwell shining a prism of rainbow-hued light around me.

"Oh." The sound came from Ceecee, and I wasn't sure whether it was a sigh of happiness or distress. Bitty reached for her hand and held it tight.

"You are stunning," Bitty said, smiling widely. "Simply stunning."

"I couldn't have said it better myself," Mabry said. She moved behind me and began tugging on the dress in various places to see if it gaped or might be too tight. "It's a perfect fit," she announced. "I wouldn't change a thing. I wouldn't even get rid of the crinoline. It accentuates your tiny waist, and it'll look gorgeous when you dance."

I wanted to roll my eyes, but the memory of what I'd looked like in the upstairs mirror stopped me. This would be my first and only chance to live my girlhood fantasy, to play Cinderella before the clock struck twelve and I had to rush back to the life I'd salvaged from the wreckage of ill-advised fantasies.

"You look so much like her," Ceecee was saying, her voice wobbling. "Just like she looked that night at the Ocean Forest, remember, Bitty?"

"Of course," Bitty said. "How could I ever forget? Margaret always said that was the happiest night of her life."

"Why is that?" Mabry asked.

Bitty and Ceecee exchanged a glance. Then Bitty said, "Because that was the night she met the love of her life."

"My grandfather?" I asked.

The doorbell rang, and we all turned toward the

front door. Mabry crossed the foyer and peeked out of the glass sidelight. She faced us and in a loud whisper said, "It's Jackson Porter."

"I hope he brought back the brownie plate," Bitty grumbled as Mabry opened the door.

"Hello, Jackson," Mabry said, standing in the doorway and blocking his view inside. "Can I help you?"

I couldn't see his face, but I could imagine his confusion at seeing Mabry and having her interrogate him. "I'm right here, Jackson," I said, winding my way around the two older women. "Were you looking for me?"

He didn't say anything right away, his gaze taking in the dress, traveling down to my bare feet, then to my neck, settling a little too long on my chest before quickly moving back up to my face.

"If I knew how to whistle, and thought you'd appreciate it, I would," he said, making me laugh. "You look beautiful. What's the occasion?"

"She's going to the Shag Festival tomorrow with Bennett," Mabry said.

He looked genuinely disappointed. "That's why I stopped by. I was driving home and thought I'd say hello, invite you to the festival tomorrow."

"Sorry, she's already got a date." Mabry actually made to close the door. I shot her an angry glance as I stopped the door with my hand.

"But if you're there, too," I said, "I'm sure Bennett won't mind if I dance with you."

I felt Mabry's gaze boring into the side of my head.

"Terrific," Jackson said, sending me his quarter-back smile. I felt a small ripple roll through my veins. "I'll see you there."

"Not if I see you first," I said, and want to slap myself for saying something so stupid and incomprehensibly immature—something the sixteen-year-old me would have said—but I didn't get the chance, because Mabry had already closed the door in his face.

twenty-nine

Ceecee
2010

Ceecee hummed to the music on the stereo as she swept the dusting rag across the dark wood of the dining room table, carefully lifting one silver candelabra and then the next so as not to scratch the table's varnished surface.

The pair had been a wedding gift from Bitty's parents, and now Ceecee considered them a cherished heirloom that she'd one day pass down to Larkin. She didn't think Larkin had a dining table, much less a dining room, in her Brooklyn apartment, but that didn't worry Ceecee. She had no doubt that by the time she departed this earth, Larkin would have come to her senses and moved back home.

She moved to the sideboard, spotting the album Mack had brought down from the attic, open to a page near the back. She pulled the album closer to look at the photograph stuck in the middle, then carefully lifted the plastic cover and removed it. Her heart ached as she looked at it, her memories thick with grief and longing. It was the photograph of Reggie and Boyd on the day they'd all gone to the Pavilion and posed behind the cardboard cutouts.

In the years since, Ceecee had often wished she could turn back time to that exact day. That moment. So much pain could have been avoided. And Margaret might still be alive.

She turned at the sound of feet clattering on the stairs, and spotted Larkin wearing a too-large bathing suit held together in the back with shoestrings and carrying a frayed **Little Mermaid** beach towel that had probably been in the linen closet since Larkin was a little girl.

Larkin poked her head into the room. "'Moon River.' Andy Williams." Grinning, she said, "Am I right?"

"Have you ever been wrong?"

"No, ma'am," Larkin said, still grinning. She eyed the album. "I've been meaning to ask you about something."

Ceecee felt a prickle of heat trickle down her spine.

"When Mabry and I were looking through these photographs, we found one of two young men, one of whom I assumed was my grandfather. It was black-and-white, so I wasn't sure, but I couldn't figure out which one was him."

"That's because you take after your grandmother. And that's not a bad thing." Ceecee pressed the photograph she'd been looking at against her housecoat, hoping Larkin didn't notice.

"Yes, but I could swear Mama resembled one of them more than the other. Although Mabry and I thought the men looked related."

Ceecee forced a laugh and continued dusting. "Yes, well, as you said, it's an old photo."

"Let me show you what I mean." Larkin flipped through the album, the crease between her brows deepening. "That's funny. I'm sure we didn't take it out." She glanced over at the gleaming dining table. "I wonder where it could be."

"It can't have gone far," Ceecee said reassuringly. She scrubbed at an imaginary smudge on the sideboard as she carefully slid the photograph into the pocket of her housecoat. "Where are you off to this morning?"

"Thought I'd lay out on the dock and try to get some color. I'm as pale as the underside of a fish. I think a tan would complement the yellow dress, don't you agree?"

Ceecee nodded, remembering Margaret's golden

skin against the yellow of the dress. That was in the days before people knew what UV rays or skin damage were. It was almost unfair that Margaret would never have to regret her days of sun worship, remaining young and unwrinkled for eternity.

But even as the thought passed through her mind, Ceecee cringed. "Yes, it would. But you need to protect your skin, too. You don't want to look like shoe leather before you're thirty."

"Don't worry—I already put on my sunscreen. And I've got a conference call at eleven thirty, so I can't stay out too long. I'll visit Mama at the hospital when I'm done."

There was a hitch in her voice, and Ceecee reached over to stroke Larkin's cheek. "It's hard on all of us, sweetheart. But I know how extra hard it's been on you."

"I'm finding out so much about her now. I just wish . . ." She stopped.

"Don't. Wishing won't change anything. Your mama raised you the way she did because that's what she thought was best. Heaven knows I did my best to fill in, but I think we can both agree that there were big faults in my methods. The one thing you should never have to wonder is whether you were loved. If every child was given the amount of love you were, the world would be a much better place."

There were tears in Larkin's beautiful eyes as she regarded Ceecee. "Then why am I such a mess?"

Ceecee leaned forward and kissed her forehead. "Oh, sweetheart, don't you know? It's because everything that's beautiful and worthwhile on this earth starts out as a pile of mess. Think of butterflies. It's the struggle to get past the messy part that makes us who we are."

"But what if I can't get past it? Does that mean I'm a failure?"

"Never," Ceecee said. "You are so strong and brave. You always have been, with or without my interference."

She studied Larkin for a long moment, remembering her as a young girl, how she'd tried to smooth over any bumps in Larkin's life, and wondered how much she should say. "I probably shouldn't have interfered so much in your life. You would have been just fine figuring it out on your own. I was trying to fulfill an obligation I owed. I couldn't have been all bad, because you've never stopped kicking and screaming. Some people give up the first time they fall down. For others, failure makes them stronger. It makes them keep trying until they figure out their purpose in this world."

Larkin looked at her skeptically. "Really? So my purpose was to be a copywriter for an advertising agency?"

Ceecee hugged her, smelling the coconut scent of sunscreen. "If that makes you happy, then yes. But if something's still missing, then you're not done fighting."

"I was afraid you were going to say that." She handed the album to Ceecee. "I'll be on the dock if you need me." She walked to the foyer, then retraced her steps. "What did you mean about fulfilling an obligation?"

The tightness in Ceecee's heart came back again, the weight of the years pressing hard against her chest. "To Margaret. Because she died so young. Before she could see her daughter or granddaughter grow up."

"But it wasn't your fault." Larkin's eyes were sad as they regarded Ceecee, her expression so much like Margaret's that Ceecee thought her heart might break all over again. "Whether or not you needed to be, I'm glad you were always there for me."

Larkin gave her a small smile, then disappeared around the corner. Ceecee didn't move until she heard the slamming of the back door. Then she sat down, took the photograph from her pocket, and began to cry, only vaguely aware of it slipping from her fingers and onto the floor.

Ceecee
1952

Ivy Darlington Madsen arrived on an early-February evening. Her birth was almost as quiet an affair as Margaret and Boyd's wedding with the justice of the peace. Bitty and the court clerk were the witnesses. Ceecee remained at her mother's house, tending roses, pricking her fingers repeatedly until her mother told her to weed the vegetable patch instead.

As promised, Ceecee visited Margaret every day of her pregnancy, making sure she ate and taking her for walks in the Carrowmore gardens. She made sure they stayed far from the Tree of Dreams, focusing instead on Mrs. Darlington's beloved cutting garden, planted with boxwood and southern yew hedges and decorated with silver germander, sage, and dainty flowering serissa. She and Bitty drove Margaret into Charleston several times to buy supplies for the baby and the nursery. Despite the baby's untimely existence, it would want for nothing.

Boyd was busy with his growing medical practice. Gradually, he took over more and more of the work from Dr. Griffith; his hours were long, which made it easy for Ceecee to avoid him. She could almost pretend that he was back home in Charleston, that Margaret's husband was someone else entirely. It was easier that way.

The week of Margaret's wedding, she'd begun to dream of drowning. The cool water of the river would sweep over her head, and she'd be looking up through the surface to see the Tree of Dreams and Carrowmore. She would drift farther and farther from shore, reaching out her hand for someone to grasp, but no one did. She'd jerk awake just as her feet touched the riverbed, gasping to fill her lungs with air.

Bitty said it was because she wouldn't confront the reality of her life and that as soon as she did, she could sleep again. But Ceecee couldn't let it go. The pain was all she had to hold on to. The only thing keeping her afloat.

So, each day Ceecee visited a demure version of Margaret she hadn't quite gotten used to yet, checked on the progress of the pregnancy and Margaret's health, and then crossed off the day on the calendar, as if she were a prisoner marking time until release.

She and Bitty were with Margaret when her water broke. Before Boyd or an ambulance could be called, Margaret announced that the baby was coming; true to the impulsive and impatient Darlington nature, the baby was born in the foyer at Carrowmore on Mrs. Darlington's Aubusson rug. Boyd and Dr. Griffith were both on house calls, so it was Ceecee's mother who cut the umbilical cord and delivered the afterbirth, declaring the rug already ruined.

When she made to hand the squalling baby to Margaret, Margaret looked at it for a moment, her face a mask of pain and grief, then turned her head. So Ceecee's mother gave the baby to Ceecee.

"What are you going to name her?" Mrs. Purnell asked gently, her gaze on Margaret.

"Ivy," Ceecee said, looking down at the bundle in her arms. Their eyes met. When people talked about love at first sight, Ceecee would always remember that moment. Because that's what it was between her and Margaret's daughter. As soon as she was placed in Ceecee's arms, Ivy quieted and began suckling on her fist, her warm round body pressing against Ceecee's chest as soothing to her heart as honey.

"Ivy," Margaret repeated, her voice dry. "Her name is Ivy Darlington Madsen." Her eyes were glazed with pain, and darkened with sorrow and despair. Despite everything, Ceecee felt pity for her. Margaret had made a mistake, a permanent one. Overwhelmed by grief at the loss of her parents and the man she loved, she had snatched at the closest solution. But as Ceecee's mother had told her more than once, making a decision in haste was like building a house on a swamp.

"Ivy," Ceecee repeated, looking into the baby's perfect face, pink and rounded because little Ivy had decided not to go through the trauma of a long childbirth. "She's beautiful," Ceecee said, surprised to find herself close to tears. "Just like her mama."

"Don't say that," Margaret said, turning her face away again. "Make sure she knows she's smart and strong. Those qualities will help her through life a lot more than just beauty."

"Go fill a basin with warm water so we can properly wash mother and baby," Mrs. Purnell said to Bitty.

Turning to Margaret, she said, "I don't want to move you until Boyd gets here, but do you think if we prop you up on some pillows, you would be able to nurse the baby?"

Margaret's dead eyes fell on Ivy, as if she finally comprehended what had just happened, that she had brought another human being into the world and had absolutely no idea what she was supposed to do next.

"We bought powdered formula and bottles," Bitty said. Ceecee could tell by her shaking hand that she was dying for a cigarette.

Ceecee's mother gave a curt nod. "That's probably best." She put a gentle hand on Ceecee's arm. "Are you okay with feeding the baby?"

Ceecee lifted her chin and met her mother's sympathetic eyes. She'd not told her mother everything, but somehow her mother knew. Knew of her heartbreak, and her resolution to survive it. Maybe that's what being a mother was—not so much the act of giving birth, but the sense of understanding and love born from the need to protect. "Yes," Ceecee said, looking down into Ivy's face as the baby began to cry a pitiful chirp that sounded like a tiny bird.

After the baby had been washed and a diaper placed on her small bottom—after only three tries—Ceecee settled into a rocking chair in the nursery upstairs. She held the bottle to Ivy's rosebud lips. When Boyd said they could pretend the child was theirs, she hadn't believed him. How could someone without blood ties ever love a child the way a real mother would?

But sitting in the chair and feeding Ivy, feeling the warm body relax against her own and the tiny hand encircle her finger, Ceecee knew that she could.

The door opened and Boyd was there, filling the doorway, his eyes on hers. For a brief moment she allowed herself to believe that Ivy really was theirs, that Margaret and Reggie didn't exist, and that they were a family of three.

"Hello, Sessalee," he said hesitantly, hanging back.

The sound of her name on his lips brought her back to harsh reality, the bottle slipping from Ivy's mouth and making her cry. Ceecee quickly replaced it, glad for the distraction.

"Bitty said you were very brave."

Ceecee shook her head, reluctantly meeting his eyes. "The baby came so fast that we didn't have time to think about it. Besides, we've both seen **Gone with the Wind,** so we knew what to do."

His mouth quirked, making her pulse quicken no matter how much she told it not to. "Bitty said you did all the work, and she just did what you told her to. I'm proud of you."

She wanted to tell him that she wasn't his to be proud of, but she didn't. It felt too good to be the object of his pride and attention, no matter how wrong she knew it to be. "How's Margaret?"

His expression sobered. "She doesn't want to go to the hospital. I've examined her and I agree, so she'll stay here at Carrowmore. I've just brought her upstairs to her bed. Bitty and your mother are dressing her in a fresh nightgown. I've asked the cook to bring her something to eat."

Boyd approached and knelt next to the chair, placing his large hand over Ivy's mostly bald head, a patch of strawberry blond hair sprouting in small swirls at the top. "She's beautiful, isn't she?"

"She is. But not very patient." Ceecee tried to smile but found she couldn't. It had been a while since she'd offered a real smile, as if the weight of her sorrow tugged too hard on the sides of her mouth.

Boyd used his thumb to gently brush Ivy's peach fuzz. They watched as Ivy's eyes drifted closed, the nipple slipping from her lips. "I was hoping she'd have Reggie's red hair. He always hated it, but every generation in our family has always had at least one redhead." He took the bottle as Ceecee shifted the baby to her shoulder and began to pat the tiny back.

"So, what do we do now, Sessalee?"

She made the mistake of meeting his gaze, remembering how much she loved him, no matter how hard she'd tried to stop. But she couldn't forget the platinum band on Margaret's left hand, or the baby in her arms. Or the vows and promises she and others had made that she would not break.

She closed her eyes, gently rocking the baby, the motion keeping her calm. "I go home to my parents' house and assist my father in his parish, arrange for all the flowers at weddings and funerals. I'm quite good at it, you know. I will teach Ivy to call me Aunt Ceecee because that's what I will be to her even though I will always love her like a daughter. And you will remain at Carrowmore with your wife and child and become a respectable doctor just like you planned."

"This isn't what I planned, Sessalee." His voice sounded broken, and she had to keep her eyes closed so she couldn't see him and want to go to him.

"It's not what I planned, either. But it is what it is, Boyd. There's no changing any of it. And the sooner we both realize that, the sooner we can both find new happiness."

"Run away with me," he said impulsively. "You, me, and the baby. We can start a new life somewhere. A place where no one knows us. I can always find work. And you know that Margaret would be happier, too. She would thrive, playing the wronged and deserted wife."

Ceecee felt sick. If only she could pretend that she hadn't thought the same thing; if only she knew that they wouldn't be tormented for the rest of their lives by what they'd done. "You know we can't," she said. "We both know you could never do such a thing."

She'd stopped rocking, and the baby began to squirm. Standing, she began pacing, patting the baby's back until she settled again.

"I love you, Sessalee. I don't expect I'll ever quit."

Ceecee stood still at the window overlooking the rear yard and the river, the Tree of Dreams a solid frame to the left side of the view. She recalled the ribbons that had been placed in the tree, dreams and wishes made with innocence and naïveté, or careless vanity and false bravado. **I will love Sessalee Purnell until I die, and will hope every day that we will find a way to spend our lives together.**

Gooseflesh pricked her spine, as if an unseen breath had been blown against the back of her neck.

Without turning around, she said, "Don't ever say that again, Boyd. Not ever. For Ivy's sake, if nothing else. Wishes and dreams aren't real, no matter how much we'd like them to be. I made the mistake of once believing they were. I won't make that mistake again."

He moved to stand behind her, his hands on her shoulders, and she felt his lips on the top of her head. "Just tell me one more time that you love me, and it will be enough for the rest of my life. I'll be able to face it if I only know you love me."

A strong breeze pushed at the martin houses strung from the old oak tree below. Watching them, Ceecee remembered the story Margaret had told her long ago, about how the small birds relied on others to make their homes for them. It made sense to her now, knowing that so much of life was reliant on things outside of oneself, how the whims of others dictated people's hearts and lives. How dreams and wishes were just so much dust when held against the will of another human being.

Ivy whimpered, and Ceecee realized she'd been holding her too tightly, using the small body to anchor her where she stood. Ceecee cupped her hand around the tiny head, transferring all the love she possessed with a promise to protect her always and forgetting, for a brief moment, that promises weren't meant to last.

Looking out the window, she said, "I don't love you, Boyd. You are my friend's husband, and the father of a baby I will always love as if she were my own. But I don't love you." She'd said it twice, as if that might somehow give credence to the lie.

A cough came from the doorway. Boyd's hands dropped from her shoulders as she turned and saw Bitty. From her expression, Ceecee knew that she'd heard most if not all of her conversation with Boyd. "If the baby's finished eating, your mama thinks Margaret should spend some time holding her."

She looked at Bitty with alarm. "But she's settled now, and sleeping."

"I know," Bitty said gently. "But she's Margaret's baby. They'll need to get to know each other."

Her body felt empty and cold as Bitty lifted the baby from her arms, and she shivered. Bitty turned to Boyd, her face expressionless. "Mrs. Purnell also suggested you go visit with mother and baby. For the same reason."

Boyd gave her one last glance as he followed Bitty and Ivy from the room, leaving Ceecee as desolate as a debris-strewn beach following a hurricane.

thirty

Ivy
2010

My Ellis has been sitting on the side of my bed now for two days. I knew something was different when his Mustang went from revving the engine to just idling, like it was waiting.

And then Ellis walked through the wall of my hospital room and sat down. He doesn't say anything, just smiles, and it's like no time has passed. The love I feel hasn't changed. I want him to take my hand, or kiss me, but it's clear that I'm here and he's there and the distance might as well be as wide as Winyah Bay because Ellis is unreachable to me.

Mack comes in carrying flowers that I'm pretty sure came from Carol Anne's garden, and I hope he asked her permission first. Mack is probably one of the most thoughtful and considerate people I've ever known, but he usually acts first and then thinks. I'd like to say Larkin gets her impulsive nature from him, but I think we all know that's a Darlington trait that I have suffered from myself for most of my life.

He moves a vase of flowers from Bitty on the table by my bed, replacing it with his bouquet and setting Bitty's vase on the floor right by my bed. If he paces like he usually does when he visits, he's going to knock the vase right over. Like I said, he's really good at acting before he thinks.

He starts pacing, and I'm glad, because it would be awkward if he and Ellis were sitting on the bed together. I know Ellis sees him because he's watching him with kind eyes, his expression appreciative. Like he's thanking Mack for taking care of me all these years. He's right. Despite that one big lapse in judgment, Mack has always put me on a pedestal, making sure I wanted for nothing. Well, except for the one thing I couldn't have.

But now Ellis is here, and it seems like Mack has brought him to me. I feel whole now, as if the two halves of my heart have come together. I wonder if that's a sign of some kind.

"I miss you, Ivy. I miss you so much." Mack stops at the side of my bed and looks down at me, touches my cheek. "I can't remember the last time I told you I love you. I guess I gave up waiting for you to say it back. I just want you to know that I'm okay with that. I know you loved me in your way, and that really was enough for a long time. But then that thing with Larkin her senior year. When something bad happened but she wouldn't talk about it." He stops and shakes his head. "I didn't know what to do. I needed a partner then, someone to talk with about it. And you were off painting murals in other people's houses. I saw the one you did in Carol Anne's laundry room, you know. I saw the highway with the 1960s cars, and the red Mustang convertible with you and Ellis in the front seat, your hair streaming behind you. Hard to miss that hair. I think I told you once it's the color of sea oats with a slice of fire in it. Not sure where that red came from, but it matches your personality. It's just one of the many things I love about you."

He starts pacing again. "I liked feeling needed, too. By someone I could talk to who wasn't wishing I was someone else." He stops by the window. "I'm sorry for what I did. I know I've said that a million times, but it's true. You didn't deserve it. I would have ended the affair even if Larkin hadn't seen me with Donna at the movie theater. I promise. I just wish Larkin hadn't seen that. Everything was going wrong in her world, and then that happened. And when you refused to leave me, that was the last straw, it seemed. Like everyone in her life had disappointed her, and she couldn't stay. I just wish I could go back and change all that."

Mack shakes his head. "I've been having strange dreams lately. About Ellis, of all people. I know what he looks like from all the photos at Carol Anne's. It's always the same thing. He's sitting in his Mustang outside Ceecee's house, looking at the front door like he's expecting you to come out. I feel the anticipation like it's me waiting in the car. That's the whole dream, and the door never opens. Maybe because I'm waiting for you to wake up—who knows? I guess I should ask Larkin about it, since she's the expert."

He comes back to the bed, thrumming his hands against the footboard. He approaches like he's about to say good-bye, but stops. "Did Ceecee or Bitty tell you that Larkin and Bennett are going to the Shag Festival together? I've always liked that boy. Didn't you and Carol Anne used to plot for them to get married? Anyway, she's going to wear one of Margaret's dresses—a pretty yellow one that Ceecee's had in her attic all these years. Bitty says she's the spitting image of your mother."

He smiles, and it's the smile of the young and earnest man that I remember, the man I thought could save me. "I have no idea how I could possibly have fathered such a gorgeous child, but apparently I did. Not a surprise, since you're her mother. How lucky for her that she got the Darlington genes."

Not all of them, I want to tell him. Larkin somehow managed to get the worthwhile genes from all the branches of her family tree, leaving the bad ones on the ground like overly ripened fruit.

"By the way, when Larkin stopped by the house, she saw the mural you'd made of her accomplishments. I could tell it made her happy." He frowns. "Although we're both confused about the painting of Carrowmore on fire. And the four martins. Not sure what you meant by that. And I sure as heck hope you wake up soon so you can explain it to us."

I wish I could wave my hands, make him backtrack. I think hard, remembering painting the mural. Remembering why. And all of a sudden, light like confetti begins falling from the ceiling, and I feel myself lift a little higher off the mattress.

Mack steps to the side of the bed and leans over to kiss me on the forehead. "Good-bye, Ivy. I'll come back tomorrow. Hopefully we won't have another one-sided conversation. It's like I'm talking to myself, and I've never been a great conversationalist."

He steps back and just like I knew he would, he tips over Bitty's vase of flowers, the sound of breaking glass bringing a nurse rushing in as water spreads over the floor. It's Donna, the other woman. She must be new here, because I haven't seen her before. Neither has Mack, judging by the look of surprise they give each other.

I look over at Ellis, but he's already gone. I can still hear the Mustang, its engine idling as if waiting for something to happen.

Larkin
2010

Mabry knocked on my bedroom door and opened it. I sat on the stool in front of my vanity table, painting my nails with a color that matched the Certainly Red lipstick Ceecee had let me borrow. I probably should have been embarrassed to admit to anyone that I was borrowing makeup from a seventy-seven-year-old, but it was such a luscious red color that I didn't care. Plus, it had matching polish. No matter my years in New York City, my Southern roots showed every time I matched my shoes with my purse, or my nail color to my lipstick.

Mabry pulled a full-sized suitcase on wheels behind her and carried a garment bag over her arm, a bag of shoes tied around the handle. "I thought we were getting dressed for a party, not planning a three-month getaway," I said.

"Ha-ha. I think you've been living outside the South too long, sugar," she said, deepening her already thick accent. She rolled the suitcase to a stop and eyed me critically. "It's really disgusting to the rest of us, you know."

"What is?" I asked, feeling suddenly self-conscious.

"That you look so good without makeup. Don't tell anyone I said this out loud, but you don't need any. Still, I'm going to try." She bent down to look at me more closely, her grin widening as she spotted something she could fix. "Your eyelashes are pretty pale and so are your brows." Straightening, she said, "This will be fun," then began unzipping her suitcase, pulling out makeup bags, hair-styling tools, and a bottle of wine.

"Just like old times." I grinned, remembering school dances from our not-too-distant past. We'd get dressed and do each other's makeup and sneak up a bottle of wine with Bennett's help, using a grocery bag attached to a string dangled outside my window.

"Yep. And we can either be civilized and borrow glasses from Ceecee's china cabinet, or we could really be retro and take turns drinking it straight from the bottle."

In answer, I reached over and unscrewed the cap and took a long swig before handing it back to her to do the same. "I hope this is the only part that reminds me of the old school dances," I said, remembering how I would mostly stand against the wall, pretending I was busy watching the colorful lights on the ceiling or head out on the dance floor and act like I enjoyed dancing by myself. All the while I'd be keeping an eye on Jackson Porter, waiting for him to finally notice me, to see what a great dancer I was and ask me to be his partner. He never did.

Bennett would usually save me from myself and dance with me, or Mabry would pull me to the dance floor to dance with her partner as she feigned the need to use the restroom. Either way, those dances were miserable experiences for me, and yet I always looked forward to them, hopeful each time that it would be different.

Mabry snorted. "Hardly. I might need to bring a stopwatch to time your dance partners since I'm sure there will be so many. I can be your handler tonight."

I rolled my eyes. "I sincerely doubt that will be necessary, but I appreciate your enthusiasm."

Mabry began pulling out makeup, lining up the bottles, tubes, and brushes like soldiers preparing for battle. "Well, I know for sure that Bennett will be at the front of the line."

I took another swig from the wine bottle. "I wasn't planning on speaking to him tonight."

She rolled two eyeliner pencils in her palm. "You don't have to. Just dance."

"Have you ever danced without talking? Actually, I don't think you've ever slept without talking. You're pretty vocal, you know."

"I've been told that a few times," Mabry said, shoving one of the eye pencils back in the bag, then picking up three blushers and popping open the lids to compare. Or blend. I had no idea. I'd always loved makeup, but despite Ceecee's tutelage, I'd ended up looking more like Ronald McDonald with my efforts and had mostly given up. But Mabry knew what she was doing, and had always been in charge of making me look less like a clown and more like a girl someone might want to dance with. Not that it had helped, unless I counted Bennett, but at least I'd felt good.

"How long do you think this will take?" I asked, eyeing her arsenal.

She looked over at my bedside clock. "It's five o'clock now, and the boys aren't expected until six thirty, so we can pace ourselves." She looked at my straight hair, oversized jeans shorts, and faded extra-large T-shirt from a Backstreet Boys concert I'd gone to with Mabry. "I've got a lot of work ahead of me."

"Gee, thanks."

She peered at me over an open bottle of liquid foundation she was swatching on the underside of my forearm. "The band doesn't start until seven, but they're having a little refresher course at six. Although from what I recall, Bennett was doing a pretty good job of reminding you of the steps when I saw y'all in Mama's garage."

I hid my blush by bending close to my arm and pretending to study the various shades. "I expect I'll only have two dance partners, and I'm sure they'll both be forgiving."

Mabry met my eyes and frowned. "Are you including Jackson in that number?"

"Of course. He texted me, saying he's so looking forward to it. He's already bought a ticket."

Mabry snorted. "That's because he's cheap. Tickets are only twenty dollars if you buy them ahead of time, but twenty-five at the door."

"You don't think he's excited about seeing me?" I

surprised myself at how eager I sounded. How hopeful and insecure.

She put down a handful of lip glosses and faced me. "Larkin, have you analyzed your feelings for Jackson? I mean, have you considered that your infatuation with him is for the idol you knew and worshipped when you were sixteen? Has the adult Larkin, the one who's learned a thing or two in the last nine years, actually looked at the adult Jackson?"

Before I could think of a way to respond, she leaned closer, lowering her voice. "Let's not forget the senior party on his dad's boat. There were some awful things said. A lot of accusations, a lot of denials, and I ended up with a concussion."

She held up her hand to stop me when I opened my mouth to speak. "We're not having that talk now, but we will. Before you leave Georgetown. Even if I have to follow you onto your plane and ride with you back to New York so there won't be an escape. What matters, what I've always wanted you to know, is that I feel no ill-will over what happened, and that I understand, with every fiber of my being, that Jackson was responsible for all of it, and that you were an innocent victim. You thought you were in love with him, and you got caught up in his nastiness and swollen ego."

"Stop," I said. She handed me a tissue, and I wiped my eyes, surprised to find that I was crying. "You don't know what it was like to be me, to be the loser kid who never got picked for teams in PE or to be someone's lab partner. Jackson Porter was out of my league, and I knew it. All I'm asking is that you humor me while I live the fantasy of finally being in his league, to be worthy of consideration."

"Worthy of consideration?" She rolled her eyes. "Are you listening to yourself?" Mabry asked. "Because you were never out of his league. You've always been far above him in all ways. I want to slap you for even saying that. Especially after what he said . . ."

I held up my hand. "He apologized. Deeply and sincerely, and I believe him. He said he was a jerk, and that he was sorry. He wants to start fresh. I respect a man who can apologize. Besides, we're older and smarter now. Both of us."

She sighed heavily. "Being older doesn't mean a person has changed. There are a lot of old jerks still around as proof. Jackson's the same pompous jerk he's always been. You just happen to have blinders on where he's concerned. You haven't realized it yet, but you left Jackson Porter in the dust years ago."

We were interrupted by a knock on the door. Ceecee pushed it open. "I brought you ladies glasses for your bottle of wine. Don't think I wasn't aware of what was going on in my house back in the day. Why do you think I never called the police when I spotted a tall man loitering in my backyard?"

Mabry took the glasses; I pretended to study the

assortment of makeup in front of me so Ceecee couldn't tell I'd been crying. "Thanks, Ceecee. Now we can feel more civilized."

"Can I get you anything else? Maybe some cheese and crackers to absorb the alcohol?"

"Good idea," Mabry and I said together, and we both laughed, dispelling the sour mood.

To save Ceecee another trip up and down the stairs, Mabry and I retrieved the cheese and crackers, then returned to my room to begin the transformation— her words, not mine. But as my face and hair began to take shape, my thoughts kept returning to our conversation about Jackson. Was I wrong in believing him? To think him changed? And did it really matter? Just one night to live out my fantasy, and then, like Cinderella, I'd be gone.

"You ready to put on your dress?" Mabry stood in front of me, wearing her fluffy pink robe, her hair pinned and sprayed within an inch of its life to create the illusion of carelessly tossed beach waves.

"As ready as I'll ever be," I said, unable to mask the small sensation of excitement I felt at transforming into someone new, even if it was just for a night.

She took the yellow dress from the hanger on my closet door and unzipped it. "Mama aired it out real good when she finished with the alterations to get that mothball smell out of the fabric. And then I sprayed it with Febreze just to make sure. It smells brand-new now."

I dropped my robe onto my bed and stepped into the dress, then turned around to let her zip me. She stopped me before I could look at myself in the cheval mirror. "Don't forget the shoes. We've been the same shoe size since seventh grade, so I hope these will fit." Mabry buckled a pair of strappy metallic silver high-heeled sandals on my feet, and then stepped back to admire her handiwork. "You sure you don't want another necklace?"

I reached up and touched the chain Bitty had given me all those years ago, feeling the sharp point of the arrow charm. "I'm sure."

With a wide smile, she said, "You may look now."

I turned and stared at my reflection. When I'd tried the dress on for the first time and seen myself, I'd been amazed. But that was before hair and makeup and strappy sandals—not to mention a soft tan that made my skin glow. "You're a miracle worker, Mabry."

"Not really—at least not when I have such a great canvas to work with." She came to stand behind me, admiring my reflection. "Bennett won't be able to resist you, that's for sure."

I met her gaze in the mirror. "Bennett? He's like a brother to me."

"Uh-huh. And the sky is pink."

We heard the sound of car doors closing outside. Mabry rushed to the closet door where she'd left her own dress hanging. "I'd better hurry and throw this on. Can't wait to see Bennett's expression."

My phone buzzed as I zipped up her dark green dress. I picked it up and looked at the screen. It was an 843 number I didn't recognize, so I hit "ignore" and threw the phone into my evening bag next to Ceecee's lipstick.

"You ready?" she asked.

I followed her out the door and down the stairs, leaving behind a bedroom that looked like a hurricane had passed through it. Jonathan and Bennett were waiting in the foyer, talking with Ceecee and Bitty, who immediately turned toward us and started making a fuss over Mabry and me and our dresses. I saw Jonathan and greeted him, then watched as he approached Mabry and kissed her.

"Hello, Larkin." I turned and saw Bennett leaning on the newel post, his smile like that of a boy who'd just learned a secret. He wore a white button-down shirt with the sleeves rolled up and khakis, which somehow managed to make him devastating. "You aren't planning on dancing?"

I smiled back at him, forgetting that I didn't want to speak to him, and wondering if his eyes had always been that shade of green, if that was a new cologne he was wearing, or if maybe I'd never noticed it before. "Of course I am. Mabry's carrying our flats in her bag. She said something about making a grand entrance."

His gaze traveled from my feet up to my eyes, yet it felt different from when Jackson's had done the same. As if Bennett was admiring me without claiming ownership.

Which made sense, of course. I'd never been his. But then I'd never really been Jackson's, either.

"I think you'd do that with or without the shoes." Bennett's voice sounded different, like he'd just swallowed peanut butter and it was stuck in his throat. "You . . ." He stopped. "You look as if you're wearing moonlight."

I wasn't sure if that's what he'd meant to say, but the way he said it, and the way he looked at me while saying it, made it sound like something wonderful and extraordinary. "Thank you," I said, suddenly shy.

"Shall we?" He formally extended his arm, and I placed my hand gently in the crook of his, feeling a small shock as my fingers touched his warm skin. "We're driving to a friend's house on Orange Street. He said we could park in his driveway, so you won't have to worry about walking too far in those shoes."

"Good," I said. "I'd hate to have to make you carry me."

"I don't think I'd mind," he said softly, stepping back to allow Mabry and me to pass through the front door.

We said our good-byes to Ceecee and Bitty, whose eyes were strangely bright, then piled into Jonathan's Mustang with Bennett and me in the backseat. Mabry made Jonathan put the top up to protect our hair, then flipped on the car stereo. I leaned back against the headrest and said, "'Save the Last Dance for Me,' Michael Bublé."

Mabry turned around and stuck her hand through the front bucket seats for a high five. "You're amazing."

"That you are," Bennett said, close to my ear, but I pretended I hadn't heard.

thirty-one

Ceecee
1954

Ceecee huddled under her umbrella, feeling the strap of her plastic rain hat rub the tender skin under her chin. Although it was close to the middle of October, the temperature was nearly eighty degrees, the cloying humidity doing nothing to help her hair, which she'd washed the day before and then carefully rolled.

Not that she'd been able to sleep, anyway. She had a sore throat that sucking on Sucrets did nothing to help, but she'd not been able to get a full night's sleep in the two years since Ivy was born. Despite still living in her parents' house, she arose at regular intervals throughout the night, imagining she heard a baby crying. Except there was no baby for her to go to.

For the first two weeks of Ivy's life, Ceecee had slept on a cot in the nursery at Carrowmore, arising at every move and whimper the baby made, feeding her, changing her. When the baby was asleep, she'd leaned over the crib she and Bitty had selected and would rest her hand on Ivy's back to make sure she was breathing.

Then Margaret hired a nanny and Ceecee went back to her childhood home as if nothing had changed. Except everything had. At least she no longer had to avoid Will Harris. He'd finally given up on her and married Emily Perkins, who was already expecting, judging by the loose dresses she wore to church each Sunday.

The only surprising thing about Ceecee's life was that nobody could tell that she was an empty shell, a building that had imploded on the inside while the exterior had been left miraculously intact. She was able to smile and hold a conversation, clip flowers and put them together in beautiful arrangements. She could toss a baseball with her brothers, and sing in the church choir. But it was as if someone else were doing all these things. Though she was moving, she felt nothing. It was as if she were at the bottom of the ocean, trying to run underwater, her limbs slow and heavy while the world around her wavered through milky light.

Her mother would occasionally ask her how she was doing, would touch her arm and smile sympathetically. Although Ceecee had always known that her mother loved her, she had never been the demonstrative type. This was new to both of them, and it made Ceecee wonder if her mother, before she'd married Ceecee's father, had known heartache and loss, feelings she'd long since buried, but remembered enough to offer solace to her only daughter.

Even Bitty had abandoned her. She was in her second year of college, studying art and education. She came home often to visit with Ceecee, although it wasn't a hidden secret that her main goal was to see little Ivy. Margaret's daughter had become the bright, shining light in all of their lives. Bitty and Ceecee had brought her into the world, which made them both feel protective if not a bit proprietary. But Ivy's sunny nature, creative imagination, and inquisitive mind made her easy to love—and had made it equally difficult to understand Margaret's apathy.

Bitty's mother called it the baby blues, and that could have been most of it. Margaret said she loved her baby, just didn't know how. Mrs. Purnell said that her loss of her parents had left Margaret hollowed out with grief. But Ceecee knew it was the opposite. The grief for Reggie had filled her, taking up all the empty spaces she might have used to love her baby girl. Grief was like that, Ceecee had learned. It either opened your heart or closed it.

At least for Ceecee, Ivy's presence in her life was the thing that saved her. She hoped, for Margaret's sake, that she would find something soon. Something to grasp and hold on to, something permanent and worthwhile like the love for her child. Ceecee refused to think of Margaret turning to Boyd for comfort. It was this thought that kept her awake most nights, leaving her to wallow in abject misery and self-pity.

Ceecee stopped in front of the doctor's office and closed her umbrella. Despite leaden skies, the drizzle had stopped. She took off her rain cap and folded it neatly into her purse, surreptitiously finger-combing her hair so it wouldn't look too flat. Clearing her throat, she approached the front door of the office and walked inside.

Since Boyd and Margaret's wedding, she'd been seeing a doctor in Murrells Inlet for her frequent headaches and general fatigue, unwilling to risk the chance of running into Boyd. But today her father had taken the family sedan to visit a parishioner who lived out in the country, and Ceecee wasn't sure she could wait another day to see a doctor about her sore throat and throbbing head.

She opened the frosted-glass front door in the old downtown building. The interior of dark wood and thick rugs hadn't changed since the last time she'd been in to see Dr. Griffith, nor had the large mahogany reception desk in the corner or the framed diploma on the wall. She saw that there were two now—one with Boyd's name on it, but she gave it only a cursory glance.

A middle-aged woman in a nurse's cap whom she'd never seen before sat behind the desk and smiled brightly. "May I help you?"

"I have an appointment with Dr. Griffith," Ceecee said, her raw throat hurting when she spoke.

The nurse smiled sympathetically. "I'm sorry. The doctor had an emergency house call. But Dr. Madsen is in and can see you now."

Ceecee started thinking of excuses, already retracing her steps, when a door that led to the back hallway and examining rooms opened and Boyd stepped into the reception area.

"Sessalee," he said, his face registering surprise. "I didn't know you had an appointment."

"I don't. I mean . . . I have an appointment with Dr. Griffith."

"Dr. Griffith was called away, but you have half an hour before your next appointment, Dr. Madsen," the nurse helpfully pointed out. "So you have time to see Miss Purnell now."

"It's just a sore throat. And a headache. It's probably the weather. I'll come back," she said, half wanting him to agree.

"Of course not," Boyd said, his eyes giving nothing away. "Let's bring you back to the examining room and take a look at that throat. The headache could be the change in air pressure from Hurricane

Hazel. Apparently, it's caused quite a lot of damage in Haiti. It's expected to stay out at sea, but we'll definitely feel the effects here." He glanced at his watch. "Actually, I'm closing the office early as a precautionary measure. I'll be headed to the hospital to ride out the storm, but Margaret and Ivy are driving to Augusta to my mother's sister's just to be safe." He considered her for a moment. "Why don't you go with them? I know Margaret would love the company, and of course Ivy would love to have you along, too."

It seemed so odd to be having this normal conversation with him about his wife and child when the entire time all Ceecee could think about was how she felt in Boyd's arms, and how his presence in the same room seemed to take all the air from her lungs.

"Thank you, but no," Ceecee managed, her voice cracking, and she was glad for the excuse of a sore throat. "I doubt the storm will amount to much."

He nodded. "Why don't you follow me, and we'll get a look at your throat?"

"Will you be needing my assistance?" the nurse asked.

"No, that won't be necessary. Miss Purnell and I are old friends."

The woman frowned slightly, then went back to whatever paperwork she'd been busying herself with when Ceecee had entered.

Boyd led the way to the door, then indicated for her to proceed ahead of him down a short hallway. Instead of taking her to an examining room, he took her to Dr. Griffith's office, and sat her down in the same chair she'd sat in when she'd been diagnosed with chicken pox as a little girl and the old doctor had given her a lollipop. Boyd closed the door behind him and sat in the chair next to Ceecee's instead of behind the desk.

For a moment she thought he would reach for her hand, and she found herself relieved yet disappointed when he didn't. Everything was half-measure with Boyd, her heart and head waging a never-ending battle over what she wanted and what she couldn't have.

"How are you?" he asked, his eyes warm. "It's been so long since we've talked—just you and me and not in a room full of people."

When she didn't respond, he pressed on. "I miss you, you know. I miss knowing how you're doing."

"I'm fine," she lied, trying not to notice the way his hair fell over his forehead, not to remember the way it felt under her fingers.

He held her gaze, and she knew she hadn't fooled him just as surely as she knew she hadn't wanted to. "You look tired. Are you sleeping?"

She shook her head. "Not really."

"I'm sorry," he said gently. "Maybe if you tell me why, I might be able to help you."

"You can't help me, Boyd. No one can."

His voice held a hint of desperation. "Won't you let me try? I know I've caused you so much unhappiness. Please, let me try to help you."

Through her pain and exhaustion, she wanted to strike out at him, to make him feel just one fraction of the pain she felt every day. She held his gaze. "I keep hearing a baby crying at all hours of the night. And I've been having the same recurring dream. A nightmare. I can't go back to sleep afterward."

His eyes remained steady, but his jaw throbbed. "What's the dream about?"

"You. And Margaret." She closed her eyes, recalling the stream of images. "We're at Carrowmore in the white room. The room is filled with candles—candles everywhere. On the furniture, in the windows. On the floor. We're all in the room together, but we can't reach each other because of the candles. That's when I realize that it's not candles. The room is on fire. The heat is insufferable, and my skin is blistering with it, and I can't breathe. And somewhere, the baby is crying. That's when I wake up."

He watched her for a long moment. "I don't know what to say. I could refer you to another kind of doctor, someone who might be able to help you figure out what your dream means."

"I don't need another doctor," Ceecee said, not bothering to hide her anger. "I know what I need to make me better, and I can't have it. No doctor can fix that."

He looked stricken, and Ceecee felt a dull satisfaction. Her words had hit their mark.

It wasn't that she blamed him fully for what had happened. They were all willing contributors to the train wreck they found themselves in. Margaret had been the conductor, and Boyd and Ceecee passengers with no idea how to jump the tracks. Not one of them had any idea how to extricate themselves from the wreckage. But Ceecee couldn't direct the anger she felt toward her friend, because Margaret was suffering, too, unwilling to see the joy her child could offer, or the wonderful life she'd been given a second chance to live.

Boyd cleared his throat. "I don't sleep well, either. I volunteer for a lot of the on-call shifts since I know I won't be sleeping anyway." He took a deep breath. "I want you to know that Margaret and I have separate bedrooms."

Ceecee shook her head. "Please don't say anything more. Your life with Margaret has nothing to do with me."

"Doesn't it?"

Ceecee blinked, feeling tears prick at her eyes. "Of course not. How could it? She's your wife, and I am her friend." She closed her eyes and took two calming breaths. "Could you please give me something for my throat? And my head? I'm in so much pain right now."

Placing his elbows on his legs, Boyd leaned closer. "Of course. I think the headache could be due to your lack of sleep. I can give you something to help, if you like. You might find yourself feeling much better in the morning if you could get a decent night's sleep."

Even though Ceecee was confident that no pill could make her feel better, she was desperate enough to nod. "Yes. I could try it."

Boyd stepped behind the desk, pulled out a prescription pad, and began to write. "You have to make sure you follow the dosage exactly. Take one, and wait half an hour. If you're still awake, take one more, but no more than that. These are strong, and you could find yourself in trouble if you take more than your prescribed dose. Do you understand?"

"Yes," she said. Her smile failed, ending in what probably looked more like a smirk.

He returned to her side of the desk and handed her the prescription. "Let me look at your throat." He pulled a small instrument from his pocket and asked her to open her mouth. She tried to pretend he was Dr. Griffith, so that the nearness of him or the touch of his fingers on her face didn't erase all the resolve she'd built up over the last two years. But it did, and she pulled away as soon as he finished his examination.

"It's very red, but most likely due to drainage from your cold. Throat lozenges should help, but I'd also recommend taking two aspirin if those don't work."

Ceecee stood, eager to leave, to resume the life she was trying so desperately to live without him in it. "Thank you, Boyd. For seeing me without an appointment."

He stood, too, and stepped closer to her. She could smell his aftershave, and she suddenly wanted to close the distance between them and press her nose into his neck, to ask him if he remembered what it was like to kiss her.

"You still wear the red lipstick you wore when we first met," he said quietly.

It was her only nod to the girl she'd been for those short months when Boyd was hers. The girl who let the wind blow through her hair and wore a two-piece bathing suit. The kind of girl who wore bright red lipstick. Without flinching, she met his gaze. "Do I? I don't recall."

"That's too bad. Because I do." His voice carried with it defeat, and before she could stop herself, Ceecee lifted her hand to touch his cheek.

There was a knock on the door, and she dropped her hand, her eyes meeting Boyd's.

"I'm sorry to bother you, Doctor," the nurse said, opening the door. "But your wife just called. She didn't want to wait, but she asked that I pass on a message." Her gaze shifted to Ceecee, then returned to Boyd. "She and Ivy are leaving now for Augusta. She's closed up the house and let the nanny and maids go home to their families to prepare for the storm. There's no need for you to go home first before heading to the hospital." She clasped her hands primly in front of her. "I thought you should know, just in case you wanted to catch her before she left."

"Thank you. I'll call her from this phone."

The nurse nodded. "If it's all right with you, Doctor, I think I'm going to go home myself. I want to secure the shutters and bring in my flowerpots. My sister said the National Weather Bureau expects the hurricane to remain offshore, but I'd rather be safe than sorry." She looked again at Ceecee. "Unless you'd like me to stay a little longer."

"That won't be necessary. I'll see Miss Purnell out and lock up the office. Remember that I'm at the hospital for the next two nights, maybe longer if the storm gets bad. I'll call in for any messages."

The nurse nodded, then exited, leaving the door open behind her. Boyd picked up the phone on the desk and tried calling Margaret, but there was no answer. He hung up slowly. "I wanted you to go with her and Ivy. She could use your company."

Ceecee looked at him, alarmed. "Is Ivy all right with Margaret?"

He shook his head. "She loves Ivy. She'd never do anything to compromise her daughter's safety. It's just that Margaret's so sad all the time. It can affect her judgment." He shrugged. "I'd feel better knowing you were with them."

Ceecee almost sighed with relief. She couldn't

imagine being forced to spend time with Margaret for the car trip and however many days the visit stretched out.

Except she'd be with Ivy. The one good and beautiful thing to come out of this untenable situation. "It's too late—she's already gone. And I'd hate to get anyone else sick, especially the baby." She forced a smile. "Bitty is supposed to be coming home today for a short visit. Imagine how annoyed she'd be to find out that both Margaret and I had deserted her."

Ceecee turned and headed back to the lobby, babbling now in her effort to keep her emotions intact. They were suspended from a weblike strand, susceptible to breaking from one more look from Boyd.

The nurse had already gone, the desk empty, a cloth pulled over the typewriter. Ceecee reached the door and put her hand on the knob. She'd almost made it outside when Boyd spoke.

"Margaret thinks we're having an affair."

She stopped, keeping her gaze trained on the frosted glass of the door. "What did you tell her?"

"The truth. That I would never dishonor her. Or you." He paused, and she could feel his warm breath on her hair. "But I'd be lying if I said that I didn't still love you. I've tried to stop, but I can't."

She didn't turn around, knowing if she did, all would be lost. "Good-bye, Boyd. Stay safe." She twisted the knob and yanked the door open, then fought the wind to slam it shut behind her. Bullets of rain stung her face, reminding her that she'd left her umbrella in the office. She didn't bother with her rain hat, and kept walking without any direction until her hair was plastered to her face, her skirt clinging to her legs.

Eventually she stopped, out of breath, looked up at the darkening sky with its layers of billowing gray clouds, and felt her heart echoing the atmospheric turmoil of the hurricane brewing out in the Atlantic.

thirty-two

Larkin
2010

We stepped from the air-conditioned car and were slapped in the face with what felt like a wet towel. It was just after seven o'clock in the evening, but the temperature still hovered close to eighty, and the air dripped with moisture. A heavy cloud cover blanketed the sky, obliterating any possible stars and the moon and hugging the humidity close to the ground.

We began to walk the block to King Street, which had been closed off for the festival, and where a large dance tent had been set up. I stuck by Mabry's side, leaving Bennett to walk with Jonathan.

You look as if you're wearing moonlight. I

couldn't erase the words from my head, or the way he'd looked when he said them. Or the way they'd made me feel. He was Bennett, and he shouldn't be saying things like that to me. It was as if we were in the second half of a football game and all of a sudden the rules had changed.

"Don't worry about your hair, Larkin," Mabry said, interrupting my thoughts. "I used about a can of humidity-defying hair spray. It won't budge, no matter how much you dance."

"Seriously? Because I already feel as if I've been swimming." I placed my palm against the side of my head.

"No worries," she said, pulling a black elastic hair tie from her wrist and handing it to me. "I always have a plan B."

I slid it on my own wrist with a laugh and stopped, looking down at my heels. "And when did you say we could switch to our dancing shoes?"

"After we make our grand entrance, remember?"

"Do you really think it's going to matter, Mabry?" Jonathan asked with a grin. "We're probably going to be the youngest people there. I'm thinking you could walk in barefoot and wearing sackcloth and not many would be able to tell unless they got close enough to see better."

Mabry smacked him playfully on the arm. "Don't be rude. Just because it's organized by the Rotary Club and benefits Alzheimer's doesn't mean it excludes those under thirty. Besides, they say you have twenty-twenty vision after cataract surgery, so don't you be challenging anyone to a duel."

"Have you been before?" I asked. The Shag Festival was new—at least to me. It didn't exist when I lived in Georgetown. If it had, I'd have attended every year and danced until my feet bled, spurred by Ceecee's confidence and my love of dancing. I would have danced with whoever asked me or by myself. I'd have worn an outrageous outfit and bad makeup, and I wouldn't have thought to think I was making a spectacle of myself.

"We've been a couple of times," Mabry said. "This is the fifth Shag Festival, and it seems to get bigger every year. My parents usually come, but tonight they're our designated babysitters." She slipped her arm through Jonathan's and squeezed it against her side. "There are advantages to living near your parents."

With Mabry and Jonathan walking together, Bennett fell into step beside me. Neither of us spoke.

"Hey, Larkin," Mabry called. "Did your coworker ever check your mail for those pictures your mama might have mailed to you?"

"She did," I said, remembering my half-hour conversation with Josephine. She'd told me in excruciating detail about a date she'd been on, and the dream she had the same night in which her date—same guy but with a different face—doused her with water.

"She didn't see anything that wasn't a bill or junk mail."

"What were you looking for?" It was the first thing Bennett had said to me since we'd left the house.

"The day she disappeared, Mama wrote me an e-mail," I said briefly. "She never sent it, but Daddy found it on her computer. It mentioned some old photos she wanted me to have."

"And you haven't found them?"

I shook my head. "No. That's why I was thinking she might have mailed them before she . . . before the accident. But apparently not."

Eager to change the subject, I asked, "What band is playing tonight?"

"It's the Band of Oz. They're real good," Mabry said. "I think they know every song ever written in four-four time. Maybe even more songs than you do."

"Ha," I said, accepting the challenge. As we approached the tent, we could hear the music playing inside, the sound carrying enough that more than a few people standing in line at the various food and drink vendors were tapping their toes.

I turned to see all three faces looking at me expectantly. "'What Kind of Fool (Do You Think I Am).'"

They continued to stare at me.

"Originally sung by the Tams." I looked through the open sides of the tent, to where the band members, dressed in matching cream-colored tunics and black pants, were playing. Large paper lanterns were strung along the top of the tent like miniature moons against a canvas night sky.

Bennett reached into his wallet for the tickets and handed them to a white-haired woman wearing capris, large red-framed glasses, and a wide smile. "Y'all have fun now."

"Yes, ma'am," Bennett said, sounding determined enough to mean it.

"You want to get something to eat and drink, or dance first?" Mabry asked.

"Give me my dancing shoes," I said, eager to step out onto the red-tiled floor in front of the stage.

We changed quickly, and I began heading for the dance floor, but a hand on my arm pulled me back.

"Where are you going?" Bennett's expression was stuck somewhere between amused and annoyed.

"I want to dance." I followed his glance over my shoulder to the packed dance floor filled with dancing couples.

"I think it would be more fun if you had a partner," he said, extending his hand.

I stared at it, remembering the spark I'd felt when we'd touched at Ceecee's house. Then, not entirely reluctantly, I accepted it, anticipating the jolt of electricity that seemed to flow between us. **You look as if you're wearing moonlight.**

Trying to find familiar ground, I said, "Sorry—old habits die hard."

Mabry stashed our shoe bag under a folding chair along the periphery; then Bennett and I followed her and Jonathan out onto the dance floor just as the opening notes to "Sixty Second Man" began.

We faced each other on the dance floor, my right hand in his, our opposite hands loose by our sides. **Stay relaxed. Let the lower body do all the work. Don't sway with the upper body.** I knew all of that, of course, but I needed something to distract me from the feel of my hand in Bennett's. We'd danced together too many times to count, but somehow, tonight was different. As if the stars that remained hidden behind the clouds had aligned in a new pattern, shining their light in unexpected places.

He stepped forward, and I moved with him in the familiar pattern, our bodies perfectly in sync. "One and two, three and four, five-six," I said aloud as we moved into the first song.

"It's like riding a bicycle, remember?" Bennett said. "You don't need to do that."

"Do what?" I said, feeling the music in my feet and the warmth of Bennett's hand.

"Count out loud," he said, a smile behind his eyes. "Although I'm sure I could think of a fun way to make you stop."

His gaze settled on my lips, and I stumbled. He didn't miss a beat but kept dancing, dragging me through a couple of steps until I caught up. "I'm sorry," he said. "Let's go back to pretending we're at a school dance. Just do me the favor of not looking over my shoulder for Jackson like you used to."

I startled at the mention of Jackson. I'd forgotten all about him. And after what Bennett had said, I refused to look around, not only because I didn't want to justify his conviction that I couldn't resist, but also because I didn't think that Jackson would actually show up. I'd spent most of my adolescent years with the bitter taste of disappointment in my mouth. It was one of the reasons why I'd found it so easy to settle into a life of low expectations. Writing ad copy was a lot less risky than attempting a novel. And loneliness was a lot easier than handling the vagaries and eventual disappointments of friendship.

"Sure," I said. "Let's pretend we're fifteen. I'll get a hot dog and get ketchup all over my dress and not realize it's there until I get home and look in a mirror, and you can roll up your pants so that they're too short, because you're growing so fast your mother can't keep you in clothes that fit."

He threw back his head and laughed, not missing a step, and we were teenagers again, two friends who loved to dance, who knew each other better than they knew themselves. Everything was the same—except for the way it felt where our hands were clasped together, skin to skin.

We stopped when we got hungry and had a couple of beers and hot dogs—mine without any condiments. I danced twice with Jonathan, who was almost as good a dancer as Bennett, and true to Mabry's prediction, with several other men who cut in. Despite being gray-haired and moving slightly more stiffly than Bennett, they were wonderful dancers and fun partners, and I found myself laughing freely and enjoying myself thoroughly.

The sun had long set behind the clouds, the light beginning to fade from the sky, when a familiar voice came from behind us. "May I cut in?"

I smelled his cologne before I turned, the scent reminding me of Jackson Porter the football star I'd cheered from the stands, and whom I'd loved from afar for too many years to count. I pushed back Mabry's words about him still being a pompous jerk and me having blinders on. It was easy when I looked at him, with his broad shoulders and cleft chin, his casual confidence as he faced Bennett, not expecting him to argue.

Instead of letting go of my hand when I moved to pull away, Bennett held tight. Ignoring Jackson, he turned to me. "Are you sure, Larkin?"

I stared back at him, wrestling with his meaning, and with what I really wanted now as an adult and not a teenaged girl.

"Dude, come on—we're all friends here," Jackson protested.

"Are we, though?" Bennett asked, still gripping my hand.

I pulled my hand away, keeping my eyes on Bennett. "I'm really hot. I think some fresh air and a cold beer are what I need." I turned to Jackson and smiled. "Is that all right with you?"

His return grin hit all the familiar notes in my insides. "Absolutely." He put his hand on the small of my back and began leading me away. "See you around, Bennett. And don't worry. I'll take good care of her."

I didn't turn to look, but I felt Bennett's eyes on us until Jackson and I had left the tent.

I was so thirsty, I drank my first beer too fast. Jackson had a second plastic cup in my hand before I could ask for another. We hadn't brought chairs from home, so we walked slowly down the street, people watching and breathing in the cool night air.

"Are you enjoying your visit back home?" he asked.

"Except for my mother being in the hospital, yes. It's been good seeing old friends. And family." I laughed. "Even the humidity's okay." I handed him my beer. "Here—hold this for a sec." I pulled the hair tie off my wrist and made a ponytail, trying not to notice how his gaze moved to my chest when I put my arms up. I quickly lowered them and took my beer back.

"You look real sexy in that dress."

I almost choked on my beer. "Excuse me?"

"Sorry—I meant it as a compliment. I guess it didn't come out the right way. I meant that you look really gorgeous tonight. You should be real proud of yourself."

I didn't say anything, waiting for him to mention my job in New York, and how I'd started a new life from scratch.

"Losing all that weight . . . man. I can't stand being

hungry. I can't imagine what it must have been like to starve yourself for so long."

I took another sip of my beer, appreciating the dulling effect it had on what might otherwise have been interpreted as an insult. "I didn't starve myself. I just started eating better and exercising. My therapist called it 'being mindful.'"

"Well, however you did it, congratulations. You did good." He raised his cup to mine, and we knocked them together gently, managing not to spill a single drop.

"Yes, well, thank you." **I always thought you were beautiful.** Bennett's words came back to me, and I suddenly wished he were there so I could tell him thanks for saying that. Thanks for believing it, and meaning it, because I had no doubt that he really had.

A cold, fat raindrop landed on my shoulder; more drops began dotting the street in front of us. I glanced back at the tent, trying to judge whether we could make it before the deluge.

As if reading my mind, Jackson said, "My car is right around the corner. Come on." He grabbed my hand, and we began running just as a rumble of thunder vibrated in the sky and the clouds opened up, drenching the world beneath. Jackson closed the passenger door behind me before racing to the driver's side and jumping in. We looked at each other in the dim light of a streetlamp and laughed at our dripping hair and soaked clothing. I turned to peer out through the windshield.

"I hope it doesn't last long. I wasn't done dancing."

Jackson reached over and pushed a damp strand of hair behind my ear. "I'm sure we could come up with a few things to keep us busy while we wait for it to stop." His hand slipped behind my head and cupped it gently as he brought my face to his.

He was an expert kisser, his lips surprisingly soft. Yet for all the years I'd spent fantasizing about this very moment, there was no spark between us. No bright flash of light behind my eyelids. No moment of surrender, and no part in the proceedings where I melted into him and the world disappeared. Instead, I was aware of the pressure of his lips against mine, and the taste of beer on his tongue, and the sound of rain pattering against the car's roof. I opened my eyes, my memory shining a spotlight on the truth. This was the first time he'd kissed me, but it wasn't the first time he'd touched me.

I stopped moving my lips, aware of the lingering scent in the car of a woman's perfume that wasn't mine. I remembered how late Jackson had shown up at the dance, and pulled abruptly back, surprising him.

"What's wrong?" he asked.

Before I could prioritize what I wanted to say, he was kissing me again, one hand pressed against the back of my head, the other one sliding up my rib cage until it was cupping my breast.

I pushed him away. "Please stop," I said, my voice

shaky, the collision of my fantasy world with this reality shattering something inside me.

"You don't mean that," he said, a half grin gracing his face, his white teeth in the streetlamp's glow giving him a feral appearance.

"I do," I said, my voice nearly lost in a rush of air from my lungs as I saw everything with a glaring clarity. Knew without a doubt that everything Mabry had said about Jackson was right.

Memories were flooding back. The day during senior year, right before finals, when he'd invited me out on his dad's boat, just the two of us, because, he said, he wanted to get to know me better. How he'd brought me down to the cabin with the double bed and the messy sheets, and I'd gone willingly because I thought I was in love with him.

I held him back with the heels of my hands pressed against his broad shoulders. "That time on the boat— you said it was special for you, too. Do you say that to every girl?"

His grin dipped, either because he felt shame or thought that's what I wanted to see. "Maybe not **every** one, but when I say it, I sincerely want the girl to feel special."

Spots danced before my eyes, either from anger or from forgetting to breathe. He must have taken my silence for something else entirely, because he leaned forward for another kiss, his hand snaking around the back of my dress and tugging at the top of the zipper.

"Stop!" I shouted, trying to pull away, beating on his shoulder with one hand while the other searched for the door handle.

"You don't mean that. You weren't such a tease before, if I remember correctly." I felt the zipper slide lower down my back as he tried to pull me over the console toward him. I was mad at my own naïveté and stupidity almost as much as I was angry at him.

"Stop!" I screamed, hitting out as hard as I could with both fists. I opened my mouth to scream again, but the sound died in my throat as the driver's side door was yanked open. A pair of hands reached inside and grabbed hold of Jackson's shirt, hauling him out of the car.

I jerked upright as my door was opened as well, and almost cried with relief when I recognized Mabry. She helped me stand, and pulled up my zipper. "Are you all right?"

I started to nod, but was distracted by the sound of a scuffle coming from the other side of the car. Mabry and I both ran over to find Bennett holding Jackson by the collar of his shirt. "What do you think you're doing?" Bennett was yelling, shaking Jackson so hard, his head was moving back and forth like that of a bobblehead.

Jackson pushed on Bennett's chest with both hands, dislodging his grasp. "It's none of your business. Just me and a girl in my car."

Bennett stepped forward, jabbing an index finger in Jackson's chest. "That's not 'just a girl.' That's Larkin."

The feral grin was back on Jackson's face. "You think I don't know who she is? I know her a lot better than you do, that's for sure."

"What are you talking about?" Bennett asked, his voice low with warning.

"Don't say anything, Jackson." Mabry had moved to stand in front of the two men. "Just get in your car and go. We're done here."

"What are you talking about?" Bennett asked again as he took hold of Jackson's collar and gave him a hard shake. They were the same height. Bennett was lean and muscled, but Jackson was built like a bulldog. I didn't see how any fight between them would end well.

"Oh, come on, Bennett. Didn't you pay into the betting pool senior year? All the guys on the team did. I made a lot of money, but it was a tough job. Larkin wasn't so good-looking back then. I had to keep my eyes closed." He jerked his chin in my direction. "I just thought she owed me a second round."

"Stop it!" Mabry said through gritted teeth.

Jackson feigned surprise. "Oh, that's right, Mabry. You made me give back the money that I'd earned fair and square. Then you gave me all your baby-sitting money and went out with me so I wouldn't tell that I got Larkin's virginity on a bet. You still owe me, by the way. I didn't even get past your bra."

I had started backing away, the sound of the rain hitting the pavement and the car like bullets. Bennett was looking at me now. "Is this true?" he asked. "Is what Jackson's saying true?"

I shook my head. **A bet?** No. That wasn't true. It couldn't be. But then I looked at Mabry's face and knew that it was. And she'd tried to protect me, and all she got for her troubles was a concussion.

"Tell him, Larkin," Jackson said. He was still grinning like this was all some big joke. "Tell him how you begged me. How you told me you loved me and wanted me to be your first."

Bennett lunged for him, but Mabry threw herself forward, blocking him again.

"Go!" she screamed at Jackson. "Get out of here before someone gets hurt."

He didn't even look at me. Just got back in his car and peeled off, the tires slipping and spraying on the wet pavement.

The rain had petered out to a thin drizzle, coating everything with a fine mist. Bennett looked at me, his eyes widening with realization. "That day of the senior party, when we were all on the boat. That's what that fight was about."

I closed my eyes, remembering the worst day of my life.

Jackson's voice rang out loudly. "Do you really think I'd sleep with her? You're kidding, right? I'm only letting her on my boat because Mabry and Bennett like her. Maybe if she weren't such a

dork and looked more like Mabry and less like a whale, I'd be interested."

Jackson hadn't seen me approaching his boat. I stood on the dock, holding a small cooler full of Ceecee's lemon bars and homemade lemonade ice pops, my fingers numb from grabbing the handle so tightly. Bennett was still unloading beach chairs from the car, but a bunch of our classmates and Mabry were already on the boat. Mabry was wearing a pink string bikini that showed off her tan. She placed a slim hand on Jackson's arm to get his attention, and that's when he saw me.

But in my stupid adolescent mind, I hadn't been angry at him. I'd been angry at Mabry. For that arm on his. For being thin and beautiful. For being all the things I thought I was until that moment when Jackson held up a mirror and I saw the truth. Mabry had known, but she'd let me deceive myself. Bennett, too. He was guilty by association. I imagined him laughing with Mabry and Jackson behind my back.

"Stop, Jackson," Mabry had said, and all the hurt and anger and mortification bubbled up inside me. I was barely aware of lifting the cooler and throwing it as hard as I could in her direction. She hardly made a splash when she fell over the side, hitting her head on the dock with a sick thud.

Jackson and the others already on the boat just stared in surprise, and Bennett was too far away.

So I dove in and pulled her out of the water, but I never believed I'd saved her. I was the one who'd put her there in the first place.

"So it's true?" Bennett said, the rain plastering his hair to his forehead and making him look like a little boy.

I met his gaze, unable or unwilling to hide my shame and embarrassment. That I had allowed it to happen to me. Then, and now. Because there was no sense in concealing so many years of being stupid and naive and listening to no one brave enough to tell me differently. It was humbling to admit to myself that I hadn't changed at all.

"Yes," I said. "All of it."

His eyes were serious as they regarded me, the distant sound of the band mixing with the closer sound of tires on wet pavement and a dog barking in a nearby yard. Then, without a word, he turned on his heel and stalked off.

thirty-three

Ceecee
1954

On Thursday morning, Ceecee woke to the sound of the television in the living room. A soft wind blew a mist at her window as she slid from her bed and threw on her bathrobe. In the living room, her mother stood in front of the set, wiping her hands on her apron, the smell of bacon and coffee emanating from the kitchen.

"Good morning, Sessalee," she said, and returned her gaze to the screen. "The National Weather Bureau has issued a warning for the Carolinas. Hazel made a sharp northwest turn and is headed toward land, with possible landfall sometime tomorrow morning." She wiped her hands on her apron again, a sign of agitation. "I'm going to keep the boys home from school and have them help me with shuttering the windows."

"What does Daddy say we should do?"

"He went to the church early this morning, but he left the car so we can run to Poston's and stock up on food. I called to see if I could get a delivery, but they've already got a waiting list for that. Your daddy's been having one of his headaches, which always means there's a bad storm coming."

Ceecee rubbed her temple, feeling the throb of her own oncoming headache. She'd taken the two aspirin Boyd had suggested, which had helped her sleep for a little bit, but she hadn't taken any of the pills from the prescription. She hadn't even intended to fill it, much less take one. There'd been something in his warning to her, about not taking more than she needed. Because she needed more than sleep. She needed oblivion. And when she poured the little white pills into the palm of her hand, she'd been afraid that she'd take more than she should. So she'd closed the bottle and thrown it into her pocketbook.

Her mother flipped off the television. "Go ahead and get dressed. I'll go wake the boys, and we'll get to work preparing the house."

Ceecee returned to her bedroom, already dreading the shuttering of the windows, of closing out the light. It would make her headache worse, she knew, and deepen her sadness.

Later that afternoon, she was on the front porch with Lloyd, fastening the shutters, when a car pulled up in the driveway. She had to look twice before she recognized Bitty in the driver's seat. The petite, red-haired woman climbing out of the car hardly resembled the friend Ceecee had last seen during Bitty's summer break. Her hair had been cut very short, almost as short as Lloyd's, and she was wearing denim capris with loafers, a bright scarf tied around her neck for Parisian flair. The ubiquitous cigarette was held in her right hand, impervious to the misty weather.

Ceecee looked behind her to see if her mother was there to disapprove and ruin her reunion, then gave silent thanks that she wasn't. "Bitty!" she shouted.

True to form, Bitty strolled toward her, sucking on her cigarette as she walked. They embraced when she reached the porch. "I'm surprised you came up from school," Ceecee said. "Haven't you heard there's a hurricane in the Atlantic?"

Bitty took another drag. "It's not the first, and it won't be the last. Besides, I thought my parents would feel better if I was with them."

"Well, I'm glad you're here. I've missed you." She touched Bitty's head, the strands soft under her fingers. "And I love what you've done to your hair."

Bitty laughed. "No, you don't, but thank you." She looked behind Ceecee to where her brother was struggling to nail down one of the shutter latches. "Hey, Lloyd. Want a Tootsie Roll?" She reached into the large front pocket of her jeans and pulled one out.

He grinned, his freckles stark on his face. "Thanks,

Bitty." He lifted a hand to catch the Tootsie Roll as she lobbed it across the porch.

"I'll give you another if you go inside and see what else you can do to help your mama. Your sister and I would like to chat."

He didn't wait to be asked twice, letting the door slam shut behind him. Ceecee brought over the ashtray her daddy used for his pipe, then sat down in the swing, Bitty joining her with a jolt as she jumped up on the seat, causing it to rock wildly.

Bitty flicked ash into the ashtray. "Have you seen Margaret lately? I've been trying to call her for the last three days, but she won't return my calls. Yesterday, no one was even there to pick up the phone. I'm starting to worry."

Ceecee hesitated before speaking. Finding sympathy for Margaret and her moroseness had gotten harder and harder. If they lined up her losses and wins against Ceecee's, Margaret would come out far ahead. Ceecee was still waiting for her to acknowledge, just once, that Ceecee had lost something precious, too.

"She's . . . She's not happy," Ceecee said. "I try to visit almost every day, but really, I go to see Ivy. It's a miracle she's such a happy child. Boyd dotes on her, but he works most of the time. I spoil her something fierce, but really, we're just trying to make up for Margaret. She treats that child like a pet. Stroking her, letting her sit on her lap when it's convenient, but otherwise she's forgotten. I give Ivy double the affection and attention to make up for it."

Ceecee pushed against the floorboards of the porch, then added, "I saw Boyd yesterday, and he said he'd sent Margaret and Ivy to Augusta to stay with relatives until the storm blows over. That's probably why you couldn't reach her." Keeping her hands palm down on her lap, she said, "Margaret thinks I'm having an affair with Boyd."

"It would serve her right if you were, but that's not who you are. She should know that."

"I'm sure she does. She's just looking for an excuse for why her life isn't the way she always thought it should be," Ceecee said.

"And you? What are your excuses for not leading a fulfilling life?"

Ceecee stared back at her friend. "What do you mean? My life is very fulfilling. I have my flowers, and my father's church. My mother says she can't imagine running the household without my help."

Bitty rolled her eyes. "Very fulfilling. But what are you doing for **you**?"

Ceecee thought for a moment. "I take care of Ivy. She's the only thing that matters right now."

"I hope you don't mean that. I love her, too, but you have to give her enough space to maneuver on her own. Look what happened to Margaret."

"I do give her space," said Ceecee, shrugging. "But I can't help spoiling her. It's what gets me out of bed in the morning."

Bitty reached for her hand and squeezed, no words needed between them.

The front door opened, and Lloyd burst out onto the porch. "Mama wants to know if Bitty will be here for supper. Daddy's staying at the church to help anyone looking for shelter, so we have an extra place."

Bitty smiled at him. "Please tell your mama thanks, but my parents will be expecting me home."

Instead of running back in, he said, "Mama wanted me to tell you that the man on the radio said the storm is expected to make landfall in the Carolinas sometime tomorrow morning."

"Did he mention where exactly?" Bitty asked.

Lloyd wrinkled his forehead. "I think she said north of here—maybe Myrtle Beach?"

"Thank you, Lloyd," Bitty said, throwing him another Tootsie Roll. He caught it and grinned, then retreated back into the house. "I guess I should be getting home." She faced Ceecee. "Are you scared?"

Ceecee shrugged. "I should be. I've always hated hurricanes. But after all that's happened in the last couple of years, I can't find much of anything to be scared about anymore."

Bitty stood, frowning down at her. "I'm sorry. If I could think of something that would make all of this better for you, I would."

Ceecee met her gaze. "I know you would. But unless we can figure out how to turn back time, I can't think of anything either one of us can do to change the way things are now."

They were silent for a long moment as they regarded each other. The sound of the phone ringing from inside the house startled them both.

"That's probably my mother, wondering where I am," said Bitty. "At least we know the phone lines are still up."

"For now," Ceecee said, trying to feel nervous or grateful or scared. Anything but numb.

Ceecee's mother opened the door, a deep furrow between her brows. After a brief greeting for Bitty, she said, "Boyd's on the phone, Sessalee. He says it's urgent."

Ceecee looked at Bitty. "I'll wait," Bitty said, following Ceecee inside to the kitchen.

Ceecee closed her eyes at the sound of Boyd's voice, and faced the wall so no one could see. "Hello?"

"Sessalee. Thank goodness you're there. I'm sorry to be so abrupt, but I'm at the hospital and I don't know where Margaret is." His voice was clipped, devoid of warmth, and she was glad; it helped her focus on what he was saying. "She and Ivy never made it to my aunt's house. I've called the highway patrol, and there haven't been any accident reports on any of the roads she might have taken. I was hoping you'd heard from her."

"No, I haven't. Bitty's here, and she hasn't heard from her, either. Do you think she might still be at Carrowmore?"

"It's possible, but I've called and called, and no one answers."

"And Ivy's with her, wherever she is," Ceecee said, the first prongs of fear nudging her out of her inertia.

"Presumably, yes. I've called the police to see if they can send someone over to check, but they're busy with the storm preparations. And I'm needed here at the hospital . . ."

"I'll go."

"No," he said, his voice adamant. "The thought of you out on the roads right now . . ." He stopped and drew in a breath. "I'm sick enough with worry as it is. I just . . . If she calls, would you please have her call me at the hospital to let me know she and Ivy are all right?"

"Of course," Ceecee said. "And before it gets dark, I'll drive around town to see if anybody has heard from her or seen her. Maybe she decided to stay a little longer, get supplies. I'm sure they're fine." She wasn't sure at all, but it sounded like the kind of thing she should say.

"Thank you, Sessalee. You're a good friend."

Ceecee flinched. He'd said that to her before, after they'd found out about Margaret's pregnancy. Before her life had caved in. Before Margaret had pulled out the first rock that had started the avalanche.

"We'll find them," she said with more conviction than she felt. "You go back to work and don't worry."

She heard a muffled male voice speaking to Boyd. He returned and said, "I've got to go. Please let me know as soon as you hear anything."

"I will. Boyd . . ." She wanted to tell him what

she'd almost told him the day before at his office. When he'd told her that he still loved her. But he'd already hung up.

Carefully, Ceecee replaced the receiver and turned to Bitty. "Margaret never arrived in Augusta. Boyd's called the police to get them to check at Carrowmore, but they can't go right now." She felt again the frisson of fear for Ivy and embraced it. Fear was a good enough motivator to hang on to when there was nothing else left. Nothing but her love for a golden-haired little girl.

Bitty was already shaking her head. "You are not going to Carrowmore. Not with a hurricane coming. And it will be dark soon."

"If I leave now, I'll still have daylight. It's hardly even raining yet."

"Ceecee . . ."

Ceecee cut her off. "I'm thinking of Ivy. What if she's hurt? What if Margaret is hurt and Ivy is left to fend for herself? She's just a baby!"

"You could get trapped there if the bridges go out."

"I know—but Carrowmore has weathered more than two hundred years of storms and turbulent weather. It can withstand one more hurricane."

"Then I'm going with you." Bitty jutted out her chin.

"No." Ceecee shook her head. "You need to stay here and go looking for them. Ask neighbors and friends. Drive around and see if you can spot her car. Anything."

"And if I find her?"

"Call Boyd at the hospital first, and then call me at Carrowmore."

"But what if the phones go down? They always do during a storm."

Ceecee forced a smile. "Then we pray that we're all fine, and that we'll meet up again when the storm passes."

Bitty stared at Ceecee for a long moment before giving a reluctant nod. "All right. But the minute the storm passes, I'm coming to find you." She started walking to the door. "I'll go looking now. Are you going to tell your mother where you're going?"

"No. I don't want her to worry—there's enough of that going around. I'll tell her that I'm borrowing the car to go looking for Margaret. I just won't tell her where."

"And if she calls our house wondering where you are? What should I tell her?"

"Tell her that I've gone to help a friend." Ceecee's lips twisted. "Friends forever, right?"

Bitty rolled her eyes. "Right. Maybe if we're lucky, the river will rise enough to take out that damned tree."

After Bitty left, Ceecee retrieved her purse and her father's car keys from the hook by the front door. As an afterthought, she threw a couple of apples and a box of animal crackers in her purse. She thought about telling her mother she was leaving and taking the car but didn't want to waste any more time trying to avoid telling her the truth.

On the front porch, she found Lloyd chewing on another Tootsie Roll that Bitty must have just given him. "Tell Mama I've taken the car to go look for Margaret, all right? I expect to be back by nightfall, and I'll stop and get groceries on my way home. Tell her not to worry. I'll be fine."

"She's gonna be mad."

"I know. But she won't be mad at you—just me." She ruffled his hair, even though he was too old for her to be doing that. "If I'm not home by dark and she's worried, tell her I'm with Bitty and I'll call her as soon as I can."

He started to say something else, but Ceecee ran down the porch steps, eager to leave before she lost her nerve.

Errant raindrops splattered on the windshield, and the wind blew hard, saturated wisps of air. For a moment it felt as if Ceecee had forgotten how to drive, how to shift the car into reverse and which pedal to use to accelerate. She focused on the mechanics, forcing herself to get them right if only to give her brain the distraction it needed from worrying about Margaret and Ivy.

Daylight clung to the sky with the kind of desperation Ceecee felt, a lost hope facing the inevitable. She flipped on the car radio, then shut if off again when news of Hazel heading toward the Carolinas filled the car.

No cars were headed north on Highway 17, though heavy traffic flowed south, away from Myrtle Beach.

Ceecee gripped the steering wheel tightly and thought of the Pavilion and the Ferris wheel, imagined the force of the wind shattering them into a million pieces and scattering them to the four corners of the earth along with her memories.

She turned on her headlights to make sure she didn't miss the turnoff from the highway, carefully navigating her father's car over the unpaved road and through the massive iron gates that announced to any visitor that they were on Darlington property.

The large white house shone against the darkening sky, the tall white columns seeming too sturdy to capitulate to a strong wind. At first glance, it appeared the house was empty, each window dark, no sign of a car. But as Ceecee stared at the front of the house, she thought she saw a shadow pass in front of one of the floor-to-ceiling windows in the white room.

She didn't want to go in, and had almost convinced herself that it had been a trick of the fading light, but then she saw it again, the light from a candle, moving slowly across the width of the window before disappearing from sight.

Ceecee reluctantly put the car in park, then grabbed her pocketbook from the front seat. With hesitant steps, she climbed to the porch and stood for a moment in front of the door before pushing the doorbell. She listened as the sound echoed off the marble tiles of the foyer. She waited for a few minutes, straining to hear footsteps, then pressed the bell again.

After two more tries, she turned to leave, then stopped at the sight of the porch swing. She remembered sitting there with Margaret and Bitty hundreds of times during their girlhood. All the secrets and confidences they'd shared while swinging on it, Margaret always in the middle, Bitty and Ceecee on either side, willing conspirators. All the happiness. All the good memories.

She thought she heard something and turned to face the door again. What if Ivy was in there? What if she needed her?

This time, Ceecee didn't bother ringing the doorbell. She turned the handle and was surprised to find it unlocked. She remembered the nurse telling Boyd that Margaret had already locked up the house in preparation for leaving. For the first time, Ceecee felt a fear that had nothing to do with her worry over Margaret and Ivy.

She pushed on the door, letting it swing open into the empty foyer, the faint light from outside casting a gray glow on the polished wood of the banister, dulling the crystal pendants of the chandelier.

She glanced to her right, to the entrance to the white parlor, and recognized the glow of candlelight bouncing off the walls. She took a step forward. "Margaret? Is that you? It's Ceecee."

She took a few slow steps more, then stopped, her breath trapped in her throat.

"Margaret," she finally managed.

In the silence, Ceecee drew a deep breath and

walked into the room, holding her pocketbook in front of her like a shield. She paused at the threshold, trying to process what she was seeing.

Margaret wore a long, white nightgown Ceecee remembered selecting with her at Berlin's in Charleston for her wedding night with Reggie. She held a candle in her hand and was lighting one of the three-pronged candelabras Ceecee remembered from the Darlington dining table. The second was already lit and sitting on the fireplace mantel, creating a halo of light against the white wall.

As if this were any visit and any day, Margaret didn't turn around as she continued to light the candles. "We lose power during storms, and Ivy's afraid of the dark. Mama always lit these candelabras during a storm. They give the most light for the longest time."

At the mention of Ivy, Ceecee's eyes darted around the room, settling on a small white bundle on the settee. Ivy's eyes were closed, her head resting on a pillow, a white blanket spread on top of her, her stuffed bunny, a gift from Ceecee when she was born, tucked into the crook of her arm. Her chest rose and fell in sleep, her little rosebud mouth settled into a small smile.

Ceecee knelt on the floor beside the settee, almost groaning with relief. Gently, she pulled the blanket up over Ivy's shoulders, then quietly walked toward Margaret. Whispering loudly, she said, "Why aren't you in Augusta? Boyd is so worried."

Margaret gave her a sharp glance. "Is he?"

"Of course he is. That's why he called me."

"He wanted us to go—I didn't. I don't know his aunt, and I really think we'll be safer here. So I just pretended to agree. Carrowmore is built on a high bluff and has weathered more than its fair share of storms and floods. I know it can weather one more." Her lips turned up in a small smile. "You don't need to whisper, you know. Ivy won't wake up."

Ceecee looked back at the bundle, lying so peacefully. "What do you mean?"

"I gave her a pill—just half of one, actually. Boyd gave them to me to help me sleep. Ivy gets really scared during storms, so I thought it would help."

"You gave it to a child?"

"Don't be such an alarmist, Ceecee. You're always expecting the worst. I've done this more than once. She'll sleep for a long time and wake when the storm is over."

"Why didn't you just call me? I would have taken her."

"Yes, well. But she's not yours, is she? I'm her mother, and I choose how to take care of her."

Ceecee walked back to where Ivy slept and placed her hand on her chest to make sure she could feel her breathing. Then she turned toward Margaret, watching as she placed the final candle back in its place, the long sleeves of her nightgown dipping perilously close to the flame.

"Careful," Ceecee said, straightening.

"Are you afraid I might get hurt?" Margaret quirked an elegant eyebrow.

"Of course I am. Why wouldn't I be?"

Margaret's expression became serious, her tone less mocking. "Because if something happened to me, Boyd would be free."

"Don't say that, Margaret. You know you don't mean it."

"Don't I, though? I sometimes think that if I went away, everyone would be better off. You, Boyd, even Ivy. I love her so much, but it's like my heart is wrapped in cotton. I just can't feel anything. I just . . . I just don't see the point anymore."

"Oh, Margaret," Ceecee said, understanding her grief with the same depth as with which she felt her own anger. "Please don't say that. Because then everything will be for nothing."

Margaret's beautiful blue eyes followed her as Ceecee walked to the elegant white-and-gold telephone on a side table. "Let me call Boyd and Bitty. Let them know that you and Ivy are here and unharmed. The hurricane is supposed to hit well north of here, so we should be safe from the worst of it. We'll figure this out in the morning. Everything always looks brighter in the morning."

"Yes," Margaret said, her voice oddly monotone. "Everything will be better in the morning."

Ceecee held the phone receiver to her ear. She heard only empty air and the sound of the storm picking up outside, the wind tossing dead leaves and debris onto the window glass. After two more tries, she hung up in defeat.

"The phone lines always go out first," Margaret said. "It's the wind."

They were silent, the popping noises from the candle wax mixing with the sound of the wind and the smattering of rain as it slammed against the side of the house. As they stood listening, the single electric light, a small lamp by the phone, went dark. Ceecee moved to the switch on the wall and flipped it, but the room remained dark except for the flickering candlelight.

Ceecee went to one of the windows and peered outside. Daylight had finally given in to the clouds and setting sun. The wind had picked up, the rain now blowing almost horizontally. "I should probably stay. I don't know how safe the roads are. I'll just have to hope that Bitty remembers to tell my parents where I am." She turned to Margaret. "Have you eaten? I've got two apples and some cookies if you're hungry. Although I think I'll save the cookies for Ivy for when she wakes up."

"We already ate," Margaret said, her words spoken slowly, distractedly, almost as if she'd already forgotten what she was saying by the time she finished her sentence. "I suppose the only thing to do now is go to bed and wait for morning." She looked around at the candles. "I'll stay here with Ivy. So she doesn't wake up in the dark."

"It's still early," Ceecee said. "I could stay down here, and we could talk for a while."

Margaret smiled, her face cast in shadow. "I have a book. Why don't you go to sleep? You can have the bedroom you used to stay in. The blue one at the top of the stairs."

"Shouldn't I stay down here with you and Ivy?"

"I doubt that I'll sleep. If the storm gets bad, I'll come and get you. We can all hide in the wine cellar." She smiled again, her lips thin. "Everything will look better in the morning."

Another gust of wind and rain hit the house. Something in Margaret's voice, something lost and desolate, made Ceecee cross the room and embrace her friend. "It will. And remember that you still have Bitty and me."

"Friends forever," Margaret said, pulling away. Her eyes searched Ceecee's. "If there was anything I could do to change the way things are, you know I would."

Ceecee felt a chill race down her spine, recalling Bitty saying the same thing just hours before. A spark of anger chased the chill, making her straighten. "What would you change, Margaret? Meeting Reggie?"

Margaret stared back at her with dull eyes. "No," she said eventually. "I should probably say yes, but I can't."

"Well, then," Ceecee said. She moved to the settee and kissed Ivy on the forehead, feeling again the rise and fall of the small chest.

"Good night. I'll see you in the morning, if not sooner."

"All right," Margaret said, settling herself into a stuffed armchair and placing her feet on an ottoman. "Good night, Ceecee."

Ceecee took a tapered candle in an old-fashioned candlestick and lit it using one of the candelabras, then went upstairs to the familiar bedroom. Everything was the same—the wallpaper, the navy blue bedding, the rug. The only thing different was her reflection in the dressing table mirror, the candle in her hands casting dark holes where her eyes should be.

She didn't bother to close the drapes, wanting whatever morning light there was to awaken her. Weather allowing, she had to get back home, reassure her parents that she was all right, and call Boyd.

Mostly, she wanted to get Ivy away from this place. She'd ask Margaret to come, too, but she wasn't going to ask her permission to take Ivy.

Ceecee placed the candle on the bedside table and pulled back the covers, taking off only her shoes before lying down. She closed her eyes, but sleep was as elusive as ever. Her head hurt and her heart hurt; she went back and forth from feeling pity for Margaret to anger. And pity for herself, too, for a life she found almost unbearable.

The wind outside pushed at the trees, the loud rustling of the branches like a bristled brush being pulled through hair. Twice she got out of bed and headed toward the stairs. Twice she headed back to her bed without going farther than the top step. She tripped over her pocketbook the third time she rose from the bed, and she heard the bottle of pills hit the wood floor.

Ceecee sat on the edge of her bed, listening to the storm raging outside, and placed one pill on her palm. She saw Boyd's face in his office as he'd asked her how she was, and heard him telling her that he loved her still. And she heard Margaret's voice, saying she'd never give up meeting Reggie.

Desperation for an escape from heartache and the oblivion that only sleep could offer raged inside Ceecee. She wasn't afraid of the storm—she was at Carrowmore, and if the storm got bad, Margaret would come get her. She stared at the pill in her hand for a long time, then placed it on the back of her tongue and swallowed it dry. When sleep still didn't come, she took one more. After waiting another half hour, restless and wide-awake, the storm tossing itself against the windows and walls of the old house, she thought about taking half a pill. Maybe the original dosage hadn't been right. Maybe she was more resistant than most. Either way, she needed to sleep.

Sighing, Ceecee shook out one more pill into her hand. She tried biting it in half, then considered going to the kitchen for a knife to cut it. Finally, in tired desperation, she put the whole pill in her mouth, lay back on the pillow, and closed her eyes, waiting for the blessed relief of sleep. It was only as she was finally drifting off that she thought of the candle on her bedside table, a single light in the interminable darkness, and was unable to remember whether she had doused the flickering flame.

thirty-four

Larkin
2010

Sitting at the dressing table in my bedroom and staring at my reflection in the mirror, I absently played with the small cigar box Gabriel had given me, releasing the hidden bottom again and again. I'd already torn two nails, and a third was getting ready to break off.

The yellow dress lay like a puddle of spent moon-light on the floor, its presence a glaring accusation of my stubborn inability to see things as they were. The gold charms on my necklace winked back at their reflection, seeming to mock my inability to figure out who I really was.

My growing-up years had been spent seeing only

what I wanted. I'd believed everything Ceecee told me. With Bennett and Mabry in the cheering section, I never had any doubt that what I was seeing was real. Until that day on the boat when I saw everything unfiltered for the first time.

I'd run away because I didn't see any other options. Besides being unwilling to relive my mortification every time I saw someone I knew from school, I'd lost my two best friends. I needed to start someplace new, to find my own way without effusive praise and blind encouragement. And I had. I'd graduated with honors and found a career I was good at. I'd become healthier in mind and body. I thought I'd forgotten the past, my need for applause. My craving for approval and admiration from the one person who didn't deserve either one. I thought I'd changed.

Sometimes we think we've changed when really all we've done is grow into the person we were always meant to be. Mabry had said that. I needed to tell her she was wrong. That some people are too stupid and pathetic to change or grow. That some of us are simply destined to continue repeating the same mistakes until we die. Maybe the fantasy world I'd lived in for the first eighteen years of my life had robbed me of the ability to face reality.

I looked at my reflection again, and saw Margaret as she'd been on her trip with her two best friends to Myrtle Beach. She was an enigma to me, her story untold. Or hidden—I wasn't sure which. Her daughter, my mother, lay in a coma from which there appeared to be no awakening. How disappointed they must be with me, their only living legacy.

I'd thought I'd be returning to Georgetown in glory, a newer and better version of myself. Out to prove something, to fulfill a perverse desire to show the likes of Jackson Porter that I was a woman to be admired, not mocked. That he was no longer out of my league. Of course, if I were really a new and improved version of myself, I would have realized long ago that Jackson was the unworthy one. But that's the thing with self-denial. Nobody can tell you what an idiot you're being except yourself.

I closed my eyes, once again feeling the shame and humiliation of the night. The feel of Jackson's lips on mine. My fists pushing him away. Bennett pulling him from the car, and Mabry zipping up my dress and putting her arm around me as if I were a little child who needed protecting.

My gaze slipped across the floor to my suitcase. I'd decided it was time to go. I'd visit my mother in the hospital one more time, then drive to the airport and take the first flight to New York. I'd come back if there was any change in Mama's condition, but I couldn't stay. I couldn't face Mabry and Bennett after what Jackson had said tonight, and with what they must think about me, knowing I'd willingly gone out with him despite their warnings. I knew I was running away again. At least everyone could agree that was the one thing I was very good at.

My phone buzzed, and I flipped it over to look at the screen. There were eight missed calls from Bennett, and he was in the process of leaving me a voice mail. I didn't pick up. Every time I saw his name on my screen, all I could think of was the look on his face when I'd told him that everything Jackson had said was true.

I started to place the phone facedown but hesitated when I saw the missed 843 number under Bennett's. The call had come in while Mabry and I had been getting dressed, which seemed like a million hours before, and whoever it was had left a voice mail.

Already realizing that sleep wouldn't be an option tonight, I clicked on the icon and listened.

Hi, Larkin. This is Gabriel. I was rearranging the tables and chairs in the shop, and I pulled out the ones in front of your mama's mural. I was able to get a real good look at all those tiny details she likes to add, and I think we missed one of them the last time you were here—something she painted in a bottom-floor window of the house. It's another person—a man—staring out the window, and there's fire behind him. The thing is, he's carrying something. Looks like a child. So, thought you might want to know, maybe even come by to see. There's a free cup of frozen yogurt in it for you.

I listened to the message once more, then replaced the phone on top of the dressing table, trying to recall the mural. I remembered the two women in one of the upstairs windows, and another downstairs. Now, according to Gabriel, there was another face inside the burning house. A man. And he was carrying a child. I recalled the mural my mother had painted in my bedroom at my parents' house, the four martins flying overhead in the painted sky, each carrying a ribbon in its mouth, as if each were transporting a separate message to the thin place.

I stood to head toward the bathroom to shower and dress, but caught sight of the alarm clock by my bed. It was just past midnight. I felt as if I'd lived a lifetime since I'd headed out for the dance at six thirty. I sat down on the bed, accepting that Gabriel's shop would be closed and it was too early to visit the hospital. I was about to lie down, when I heard a familiar clattering on my window.

Bennett. I wanted to ignore it, to pretend I was asleep. But my lamp was on, and he'd already seen it. He was the last person—or second to last—I wanted to see, and I couldn't imagine why he'd want to talk to me. The look on his face as he'd left had spoken volumes.

The sound came again, harder this time, as if he was using larger stones. Afraid he'd break the window, I reluctantly slid it open, then leaned out into the humid night air. Ceecee had left on the back-porch light, so even though his face was shadowed,

I could make out Bennett's tall form standing on the ground beneath my window.

"Did I wake you?" he asked.

Even though he couldn't see, I rolled my eyes. After all that had happened, that was not what I'd expected to hear. "No, you didn't. I had to get up to open my window anyway."

"Funny," he said. "I wanted to see if you were okay."

Something wasn't right about the way he sounded. It was almost like he had a sock in his mouth. "Have you been drinking?"

He stepped back into the light and looked up. "No. Although I'd like to start. Alcohol might sting my lip, though."

I pressed my elbows into the sill and leaned over for a better look. His face was blotchy and shiny in parts, his mouth swollen. One of his eyes was completely shut. I jerked back, hitting my head on the bottom of the raised window. "Oh, my gosh—what happened to you?" Although I was pretty sure I already knew.

"You should see the other guy."

"Hang on," I said. "I'll bring ice." I bumped my head again in my haste to get back inside; then, leaving the window sash open, I rushed downstairs to the kitchen, grabbed one of Ceecee's dishrags, and filled a bowl with ice from the freezer. I tripped over the rug runner in the hallway as I rushed to the back door and threw it open.

Bennett was sitting on the back steps. I sat down

next to him and wrapped a handful of ice in the dishrag. I held it in front of his face, unsure where to start.

"My eye," he suggested.

Gently, I pressed it against his swollen eye, making him wince. "Easy," he said. He took the ice from me and held it to his eye while I surveyed the rest of his face.

"You look like you've been in a wreck," I said.

"Yeah, well, if it's any consolation, Jackson looks a whole lot worse."

"Is he in the hospital?"

"He would be if someone hadn't stopped me."

"Who else was there?" I asked.

He managed to look sheepish even with the swollen mouth and dishrag held to his eye.

"Tell me," I insisted, pretty sure I knew what he was going to say.

"Some girl who works in his office. She was at his house when I rang the doorbell."

"Oh," I said, sitting back. "What a jerk."

"Yeah, that's what I said, although I'll admit to using stronger language. That's why I gave him one last punch. I think I may have broken his nose."

"Good." I looked at him in the light of the porch. The bruises on his face somehow added to his appeal. "But why, Bennett? When you left, you were so angry with me. And disgusted. I didn't think you'd ever want to see me again."

His one good eye widened in disbelief. "I was

angry. And disgusted. But not with you. Never with you, Larkin. You've always been this fearless, free spirit. So brave and original. Remember that talent show . . . ?"

I put my hand on his arm. "Please stop."

He started to smile, then winced as his lip cracked. "Yeah, well, listening to Jackson tonight made me angry at myself. Everybody knew what happened nine years ago, I guess, except me. Either I was really oblivious, or the guys knew I'd never have let it happen, so they didn't tell me. Jackson needed to have the crap beaten out of him back then. Maybe I could have protected you from what happened tonight. Maybe I'd have protected you back then if I'd just been paying attention. I'm sorry. I know that's pitiful and way too late, but I am really, really sorry."

My chest got warm as if my heart were expanding, pressing against my ribs and making it hard for me to breathe. I took his free hand in mine, careful not to touch his scraped knuckles, then gently lifted it to my mouth and kissed it. "Thank you," I whispered. "I know that's pitifully lacking, but thank you."

His one good eye regarded me in the dim light, and my stomach did a little flip. I had to remind myself that this was Bennett, the boy I'd grown up with. The young man who'd given me a standing ovation at every performance and clapped like he meant it. He'd called me fearless, brave, and original. And for the first time in my life, I thought I could begin to believe it. I leaned forward and pressed my forehead into his neck, breathing in his scent, as familiar as it was enticing. "I want you to know that I didn't know about the bet, either. If I had, I wouldn't have gone out with him again. Even my stupidity has its limits."

I felt him smile. "Larkin?"

"Hmm?"

"I know you don't like talking about that talent show, but I thought I should mention something about it that might change your mind."

I sat up, our faces close. "What?"

"That was the night I realized I was hopelessly and pathetically in love with you. I still am."

I opened my mouth to speak or breathe or do both because I needed to, but only a single sound came out. "Oh."

The door behind us opened, and Ceecee poked her head out. She wore old-fashioned bristle curlers held in place with bobby pins—insistent they were better than curling irons or anything invented in the last forty years—and my grandfather's plaid robe, belted tightly around her slight frame. "I thought I heard people talking." She caught sight of Bennett. "Oh, my. You'd better come in and let me take a look at your face."

Bitty appeared behind Ceecee, and the two older women clucked and fussed over Bennett as they brought him into the kitchen. Ceecee went to the sink and began filling another bowl with warm water as Bitty got close to Bennett.

"Your beautiful face," she said with a wink. "I like this rugged addition." She leaned in closer. "Jackson, I presume?"

Bennett nodded.

"Good. I hope he looks worse than you. If not, I'll go hit him with my pocketbook until he does."

Ceecee sat down at the kitchen table with the bowl of water and dipped a dishrag in it with a little soap. "I'm guessing that Jackson wasn't the nice boy I thought he was."

Bitty's laugh became a cough as she gave a gentle fist bump to Bennett's bruised hand.

"No, Ceecee. Jackson is definitely not a nice boy," I said.

She nodded, her lips pressed tightly together. "Glad you had this nice boy to help you figure that out."

I glanced at Bennett. His good eye was on me, his lips lifting in a half smile. I blushed, recalling what he'd said outside on the porch. **That was the night I realized I was hopelessly and pathetically in love with you. I still am.** I quickly looked away, pretending to mix the soap into the water. How had I not known how he felt? I had a strong suspicion that Jackson had something to do with it. Not to mention the pervasive cluelessness I'd clung to like a life raft since I was old enough to talk.

Eager to change the conversation, I said, "I just picked up a voice mail from Gabriel. He found something interesting in the mural Mama painted in his shop."

Bitty sat up straighter, and Ceecee seemed to be very focused on looking for Band-Aids in her kitchen drawer.

"You know how Mama liked to hide pictures in her murals? She did in Gabriel's, too. I saw it before—it's a beautiful scene of you two with my grandmother at Carrowmore, sitting near the Tree of Dreams. I think it's somehow tied to the mural in my bedroom at Mama's, where she painted four martins flying in front of Carrowmore, each with a ribbon in its mouth."

"Four, huh?" Bitty said, her hand twitching as if searching for a cigarette. "I wonder what Ivy meant."

"Gabriel said he found something else while he was moving tables in the shop. He saw two more people inside the house. One was a man, and it looked like he was carrying a child."

Bitty and Ceecee glanced at each other, but didn't say anything.

"Well," Bennett said, his gaze focused on the pink water in the bowl, "she painted five people inside the house when it was on fire—three women, a man, and a little girl. We know that Margaret and Ceecee were in the house, so my guess would be that they're two of the women."

"One of them had red hair," I said, looking at Bitty, whose fingers continued to twitch as she tried to appear uninterested.

"The man could have been a firefighter," Bitty said helpfully.

I shook my head. "No—Mama was found with Ceecee outside the house when the firemen arrived. Could it have been Granddaddy?"

"He was at the hospital," Ceecee said without hesitation. "He'd called me earlier and said that's where he'd be for the duration of the storm. He was looking for Margaret and Ivy. Margaret was supposed to have taken Ivy to Augusta, you see . . ."

"And she didn't?"

"No." Ceecee dropped the washcloth in the bowl, then took the ice Bennett had been holding up to his eye and stood to empty it in the sink. "She said she felt safer at Carrowmore. It had been standing for more than two hundred years and had withstood so many storms already."

"Just not fire," Bitty said softly.

"Assuming the other two figures are Bitty and Granddaddy, why would Mama paint them in the house if they weren't there?" I picked absently at my chipped nail, worrying it with my thumb.

"When she wakes up, we can ask her," Ceecee said, letting the faucet run. But even her optimism had waned, her words as empty as our hope that my mother would wake up.

I continued to flick my cracked nail, faster now as if trying to keep up with my racing thoughts.

"Remember when I was at Carrowmore, and I found two ribbons in the tree? They were both new, so I assumed Mama put them there. One said, 'I miss you. I wish I'd been given the chance to know you.'

I'm pretty sure that **was** Mama, and she must have been talking about Margaret. She was only two when her mother died."

No one said anything until Bennett asked, "And the other one?"

"It said, 'Forgive me.' The words were painted, instead of written with a marker, so it was hard to tell if the handwriting came from the same person. Hang on. I've got them upstairs—I'll go get them."

I made to stand, but Ceecee touched my arm. "Let's talk about this in the morning, after we've all had some rest. I'm so exhausted, I can barely hold my eyes open. Bennett, you are welcome to sleep on the couch. Let me get you some fresh ice for your eye . . ."

"No." The word came out as a shout. My emotions were raw, my patience having already run its course. I didn't want to wait. I'd been a passive bystander to my own life for too long. "I'll be right back." I ran upstairs and joggled the vanity drawer to get it to open, the cigar box on top sliding toward me from the movement. I shoved it back, snagging my nail again, then grabbed the ribbons and ran back downstairs.

Three sets of eyes were watching me as I placed the ribbons on the table. "See?" I flipped on more lights to get a better look. I studied the words more closely, this time noticing how different they were, how the shapes of the letters were completely separate.

Bennett smoothed down a fold in one of the ribbons, the scrapes on his knuckles making my heart squeeze again. I pressed my fist against my chest, as if that could somehow cure my reaction, not yet wanting to be distracted.

"Definitely written by two different people," Bennett said, sliding back against his chair.

My gaze traveled between Bitty and Ceecee. "So if Mama wrote the first one, who wrote the other? Who would need forgiveness?"

"Could be the same person who's been tending the martin houses," Bennett suggested.

"I don't think so." I shook my head. "I think that was Mama. She must have known the legend about Carrowmore and the martins—that it would only be there as long as there were martins on the grounds." I frowned, trying to think not of the frail woman in the hospital bed, but of the little girl who'd lived at Carrowmore for the first two years of her life, and lost her mother so young. The house was her only connection to the woman she barely remembered.

The silence in the kitchen was almost deafening as the two older women avoided looking at each other and Bitty's fingers continued to twitch. I was exhausted, as I'm sure we all were, and I knew we all needed to sleep, but my mind wouldn't shut down. The self-examination I'd been forced into earlier in the evening wouldn't allow it. I had twenty-seven years of obliviousness to make up for.

I felt a hand on my forearm and looked up to see Bitty watching me closely. "Stop," she said, indicating the nail I'd been flicking back and forth. "Please."

"I'm sorry." I withdrew my hand to my lap. "I broke it on the cigar box . . ." I stopped, recalling something else Gabriel had said. How my mother had painted the cigar box and shown him the secret compartment. And how she'd just recently made additions to the mural in his shop. I recalled what she'd written in the e-mail to me, the one she'd never sent. **I need to talk to you about something important. About something I found out about Carrowmore and the night it burned. I can't talk about it with Ceecee or Bitty. Just you.**

I stood suddenly, my chair almost crashing to the floor. Bennett caught it and grimaced at the sudden movement, making my heart squish again. But I was too focused on what I was thinking to stop now.

"The photos Mama said she had for me. I think I know where they are." I almost ran to the back door, aware of the three of them following me. The back-porch light lit my way to the detached garage. I threw open the door and flipped on all the lights. They were small, leaving the outer edges of the interior in darkness, the hulking shadows of the stacked desk drawers huddled against the walls. My granddaddy's desk sat in the middle of the space, its thin legs casting shadows across the concrete floor like a spider, waiting to pounce.

I sat down on the ground in front of it, wishing

I'd brought a flashlight. As if reading my mind, Bennett reached into his back pocket for his iPhone, then squatted next to me, shining the phone's flashlight into the dark hole where a chair would go.

"Thanks," I said, giving him a brief smile. I remembered all the times he'd been there for me, reading my mind, it seemed, always having what I needed. And because his face was so close to mine, I leaned forward slightly and kissed him gently on his swollen lips.

Despite his injuries, he pulled my face to his and gave me a real kiss. The kind of kiss that created fireworks behind my closed eyelids, that made me forget everything except for his lips on mine, and made me wish we were somewhere more private. I sat staring at him, my limbs rubbery, my breaths coming very fast.

"That hurt, but it was worth it," he said, wincing slightly as he grinned. "Promise me that there's more where that came from."

"Maybe," I said, my voice thick. Clearing my throat, I turned my attention back to the desk. "The cigar box had a hidden bottom, with a secret spring." I slid my hands around the bottom edges of the desk, pressing every time I thought I felt an indentation in the wood. "Mama discovered the hidden bottom in the cigar box, and I think that might have given her the idea that the desk had a hidden compartment, too." I continued to run my fingers over the old wood, now sanded almost completely smooth.

Bennett remained by my side, patiently holding the light and moving along with me.

"Really, Larkin. Can't this wait till morning?" Bitty said, her voice dry and raspy. "We'll have more light."

"I agree," Ceecee chimed in. "I'm tired, and I can only imagine how tired you must be, Larkin . . ."

A loud click echoed in the room as my finger depressed a small outline behind which the second drawer would have been. I met Bennett's eyes, and he seemed as excited as I was.

"Bingo," he said, his smile lopsided.

He lowered the light to illuminate a narrow cutout in the wood. I stuck my finger around the edge and pulled, the panel falling into my hand. An envelope dropped to the floor in front of me, scattering photographs. I looked down, saw a photo of me wearing a tiara and red sparkly shoes, holding hands with my mother, both of us making faces at the camera. Ceecee and Bitty stood slightly to the right, their bodies cut out of the picture, bright smiles on their faces.

I looked back from where the pictures had fallen, spotting a narrow shoebox-sized compartment hollowed out inside the fake back of the desk. My gaze returned to my mother's face. Something was joggling my memory.

The beam disappeared as Bennett shone the light back in the compartment. "There's something else," he announced.

I followed the direction of the light and saw what appeared to be a folded piece of paper pressed against the back of the opening. I pulled it out, feeling the fine linen stationery between my fingers. I flipped it over and read aloud the single word written in bold, black cursive: **Ivy.**

"What does it say?" Ceecee asked, leaning over me.

"It's addressed to Mama." I reached my hand into the compartment one more time to make sure I had everything, then stood carefully, holding on to the envelope of pictures, the photo, and the letter. I felt Bennett's hand on my elbow. "Let's look at these inside. Better lighting and we'll all have a chair." I looked down at the photograph again. "There's something I want to check."

In the kitchen, Ceecee began pouring glasses of sweet tea while I went into the dining room, searching for another photograph. The one of the two men in Myrtle Beach, pretending to be prisoners in the city jail. I went through the album on the sideboard twice, but it wasn't there. I began walking around the dining room, looking on the chair seats in case it had fallen. I was about to give up when I spotted a white square of paper on the floor beneath the sideboard, a corner hidden by the rug.

I squatted and picked it up. It was the photograph I'd been looking for, the two young men wearing similar expressions. Much like the ones my mother and I wore in the photo I'd found in the desk.

On the way back to the kitchen, I took Ceecee's

wedding photo from the mantel. I placed everything on the kitchen table, the unopened letter addressed to my mother in the middle.

"Who's the letter from?" Bennett asked, sliding it closer to me.

Gently, I opened each third of the letter until it lay flat. Before I could identify the signature at the bottom, Ceecee slumped back into her chair, her voice breathless. "I recognize his handwriting. It's from Boyd."

Bitty's hand stretched across the table and took hold of Ceecee's. I looked at these two women, who'd always been like mothers to me, about whom I'd thought I knew everything. But I could tell by their matching expressions of defeat that whatever it was that I'd discovered, they weren't yet ready to share.

thirty-five

Ceecee
1954

Ceecee dreamed she was flying through fog. She was staring at an odd orange glow on the ceiling of her bedroom at Carrowmore, floating toward the door without feeling her feet touch the ground. Billowing fog covered her, choking her, and she closed her eyes, only to feel a jolt that jerked them open again.

Then she was outside, a strong wind tearing at her face and clothes, fat raindrops splattering on her skin. She saw a gray, wet sky in brief glimpses and heard a loud crackling sound that almost obliterated the distant cries of a baby. A strong smell of wood smoke followed her, as did the thud of heavy steps.

She imagined the sensation of secure arms around her, and she smiled, thinking guardian angels must be real. She was so very sleepy, and she didn't want to fly anymore. She wanted to lie down and close her eyes forever. The cry came again, and she tried to open her eyes to look for the source, but she was exhausted, her eyelids glued shut.

Gently, her body touched the ground. She lay on her side in a reclining position, as if an angel had placed her there. The sound of rain hitting leaves came from above her. The crying sounded louder now, a child—not a baby—crying as if it had just been pulled from a deep, warm dream. **Ivy.** Yes, she knew that sound. It was her sweet Ivy.

Ceecee reached out an arm, felt Ivy's soft hair and small body pressed against hers, and kissed the side of the little girl's head, smelling her delicious baby scent. A warm blanket descended over them, blocking out the wind and rain. Ivy quieted as Ceecee held her close, then shut her eyes. Now that Ivy was safe and warm in her arms, she could go back to sleep.

The sound of sirens woke her. The sky had cleared, and the wind and rain had subsided. Her left arm felt numb, and when she went to move it, she saw Ivy's sleeping head resting on it. She started to smile but stopped when she turned her head and saw Carrowmore. Pillars of black smoke rose like angry exhalations from openings in the roof. The smell of wood smoke mixed with the acrid scent of burned carpets, walls, and upholstery.

Ceecee's head felt as if it had been stuffed with cotton wool. She shook it, trying to clear her vision and her thoughts, to make sense of what she was seeing. Trying to remember why she was in the yard under a magnolia tree a safe distance from the house, the small form of Ivy tucked against her body, a sodden blue blanket thrown over them. She stared down at the blanket, blinking, vaguely remembering it from her bed in the blue bedroom upstairs.

As she tugged at it, trying to cover Ivy's shoulders, her fingers brushed against what felt like paper, soft and crinkly. She pulled it out and blinked, her eyes having trouble focusing, her brain slow to identify the brown-and-white Tootsie Roll wrappers.

A fire truck pulled into the drive, and she sat up straighter, trying to get her eyes to focus, to remember where she was and how she'd gotten there. She struggled to stand, her heart pounding as she saw the black smudges of soot like angry hands around the blown-out windows of the white parlor, nearly identical marks marring the wood surrounding the upstairs front bedroom. She stared at the broken window frames, remembering something. A white nightgown. Candles. And Margaret. **Margaret.** In the white parlor, lighting candles while Ivy slept on the sofa. Spots danced before her eyes as she tried to remember to breathe. She needed to find Margaret. She balled up the wrappers and shoved them into her skirt pocket, then gathered Ivy into her arms and began running toward the house, screaming Margaret's name.

She ran like a drunk person, her legs rubbery and numb, her path meandering. The lawn was strewn with storm debris—limbs, leaves, and clumps of sodden Spanish moss—making it hard to maneuver, especially with a child in her arms. When she tripped a second time, one of the firemen noticed her and came running over. Ceecee began shouting before he'd reached her. "Where's Margaret? Did she make it out?"

The man's red face was streaked with sweat and soot, his brown eyes kind and vaguely familiar. "There's someone in the house?"

"Yes—a woman. Margaret Darling . . . Madsen! Where is she? Where is she?" Ceecee was screaming now, and Ivy was crying, but she couldn't stop. She couldn't awaken fully, nor could she completely comprehend what was happening. Or maybe she did and that was why she was screaming.

Another fireman ran toward them. "Chief!" he shouted. The lingering scent of burned rubber and smoke clung to him. He gave Ceecee a cursory nod before turning to the other fireman. "Just the one casualty, sir. On the second floor, at the top of the stairs."

The chief gave a brief nod. Ceecee clutched at the sleeve of his jacket, recognizing him now as one of her father's parishioners. "No, no—that can't be! Please tell me there's been a mistake!"

He put an arm around her and Ivy, quieting them both. "I'm sorry, Miss Purnell. I know you and Mrs. Madsen were good friends." After a moment, he asked, "How did you and the child get out?"

Ceecee looked at Ivy, her head now resting limply on Ceecee's shoulder, her thumb in her mouth. She shook her head, her gaze traveling from the house to the yard and the impassive face of the fire chief. "I don't know. I don't remember. I don't remember any of it."

She could only shake her head, rising nausea forcing her mouth shut. She kept seeing Margaret, wearing the nightgown she'd bought for a honeymoon that never happened. Talking to Ceecee as she lit the candles. **I sometimes think that if I went away, everyone would be better off.** And Ceecee remembered carrying one of the candles through the dark house, up to the blue bedroom above the white parlor, and placing it on her bedside table.

"Are you all right, Miss Purnell?" the fire chief asked kindly. She knew his name, but her head was still foggy, her memory shifting back and forth as if in a dream. Her stomach roiled, from the pills, the smoke, or the sheer enormity of what had happened.

She clenched her mouth shut and held Ivy tightly, her leg pressing against something in Ceecee's pocket. **Wrappers. Two Tootsie Roll wrappers.** She stared uncomprehendingly at the fire chief before shoving Ivy into his arms, then knelt on the soft, damp earth and vomited.

~

Under Boyd's care, Ceecee and Ivy remained in the hospital for three days. They were both physically unscathed, having miraculously escaped any injury from the fire that had destroyed Carrowmore and killed Margaret. But not all wounds were visible on the outside.

Ceecee remembered taking the sleeping pills, although she wasn't sure how many, and she remembered Margaret telling her that she'd given Ivy half of one, although when she'd confided this to Boyd, he thought it had probably been more. Then he'd surprised her by saying that the pills had probably saved both their lives. A deep sleep induced by narcotics lowered their breathing rate, protecting them from smoke inhalation. It's what they'd determined had killed Margaret, thankfully before the fire found her and burned her beyond recognition. Boyd had been able to identify only the platinum wedding ring on her left hand.

He hadn't told her this last part until Ceecee asked him enough times if he was absolutely sure it was Margaret they'd found in the burned building. She'd begun to cry, and Boyd had looked so devastated that she wanted to embrace him. But their grief was still so raw, their unspoken status still so new, they didn't dare.

Despite question-filled visits by the police and the fire chief—who also brought a doll for Ivy—Ceecee could not recall how they had made it out to the lawn. She told them about the candles, but not what Margaret had said, nor did she mention the sleeping pills. Margaret was dead, and knowing either one of those things wouldn't bring her back. The final conclusion was that one of the candles had accidentally been knocked over, and although they were confident the fire had started downstairs, Ceecee had trouble accepting it.

They said she was a hero for saving Ivy. She didn't feel like a hero. She didn't remember carrying Ivy out of the house. Nor could she forget the memory of a guardian angel, the sensation of flying through the air, or of the sound of footsteps that weren't her own.

While at the hospital, Ivy wouldn't be separated from Ceecee, so they allowed her to be in a crib beside Ceecee's bed. At night, Ivy would cry out in her sleep, as if having a nightmare. She'd settle only when Ceecee brought her into her own bed, each giving comfort to the other.

Bitty visited each day, bringing flowers and chocolates for Ceecee, and toys and a new stuffed bunny for Ivy, since the old one had been destroyed in the fire. She brought news of the hurricane destruction in Myrtle Beach and other areas along the coast north of Georgetown. Miraculously, the Ferris wheel at the Pavilion had been relatively unscathed. Georgetown itself had sustained some flooding and wind damage, but had been spared the devastation of beach towns like Pawleys Island, where some buildings stood unsupported over sodden sand. Others had their fronts blown away, displaying an ugly disarray of broken furniture and soaking rugs.

Neither Bitty nor Ceecee mentioned the incongruity of dying in a fire during a hurricane. Nor did Ceecee mention the Tootsie Roll wrappers she'd found in the blanket. She told herself they must have been there before she lay down on the bed, although when she tried to remember, she was pretty sure she'd folded the blanket away because the air was so warm, and she hadn't seen any wrappers. But maybe she just hadn't noticed. And Bitty couldn't possibly have carried Ceecee down the stairs and out of the house.

Still, the wrappers had been there. But Ceecee couldn't bring herself to ask Bitty, and wasn't sure if she really wanted to know the truth.

She kept waiting to see if Bitty would say something, giving her ample time to speak, not bothering to fill in the conversational gaps and silences. But Bitty said nothing, behaving like the same person Ceecee had always known. Except when Boyd was there. She seemed to avoid him, leaving the room as soon as he appeared. Ceecee thought either it was her imagination, or maybe Bitty just wasn't sure how to offer sympathy to a man who'd lost a wife he'd never loved.

The afternoon before Ceecee was due to go home, her mother came for a visit. Ivy lay napping in the crib next to Ceecee's bed, her eyebrows creased in a frown. Since the fire, she had stopped smiling in her sleep, as if the angels weren't sure what to say to her.

"Poor baby," her mother said, taking off her gloves as she leaned over the crib. She tiptoed over to Ceecee's bed. "I've had to throw away all the clothes you wore that night. I couldn't get the smell of smoke out of them. And I couldn't find your shoes."

"I guess I didn't put them on when I left my room."

She looked at Ceecee strangely.

"What?" she asked.

"I met the ambulance at the hospital, Sessalee, so I saw you before you'd been cleaned up. You'd escaped with a child from a burning building, but you didn't have any soot in your hair or on your face. And your feet and legs were almost clean."

Ceecee just shrugged. "I can't explain the soot, but my feet must have been wiped off somehow."

Mrs. Purnell studied her daughter. "I suppose so." She sat down on the end of the bed. "I've borrowed a child's bed to move into your bedroom. Ivy can stay with us for as long as she needs. Boyd agrees it's the best thing right now. As long as it's all right with you, of course."

"Of course it is. I think she'll be as much comfort to me as I will be to her."

After a moment of silence, her mother said, "The Westons have decided to move to Summerville to be closer to their children. They've put that beautiful old house on River Street up for sale. I know it's too soon after . . . after the fire, but I've mentioned it to Boyd. They're asking a fair price, and I'm afraid someone will snatch it up if he waits. It's a big one, right on the river. It's not Carrowmore, but it's still a good house for a single man and a little girl."

"Mama," Ceecee said in a low, hushed voice, looking around to make sure no one could overhear. "Margaret hasn't even been buried yet. Please let it be."

Her mother patted Ceecee's knee and stood. "You're right. I'm sorry. I won't mention it again." She kissed her forehead and left. Ceecee fell asleep and dreamed of fire and rain, of candy wrappers pressing against her leg as she flew across the lawn at Carrowmore, the flames bright against the storm-darkened sky.

Life returned to normal after a while. Ceecee worked in her mother's garden and organized the flowers for the services at her father's church. Bitty graduated from art school and took a teaching position in Charleston. She called almost every day, and visited Ceecee and Ivy every chance she had.

Everything stayed the same except that Margaret and the great house at Carrowmore were both gone. Ceecee went back with Boyd about a month after the fire, to see if anything could be salvaged. They managed to extract some pieces of art and furniture, even some of the Darlington sterling silverware, which had escaped the worst of the fire. But what remained was the shadow of a house.

The martins had returned to those gourds strung from trees undamaged by the storm and the fire, and the Tree of Dreams remained. Standing under the branches, Boyd took Ceecee's hand, and she knew they were both thinking of the ribbon he'd put inside the tree the day he'd told her he was marrying Margaret. **I will love Sessalee Purnell until I die, and will hope every day that we will find a way to spend our lives together.**

"I would never have wished for this to happen," he said quietly.

"I know," she said. "I couldn't love you as much as I do and believe that you did."

His eyes brightened as he regarded her. "Does that mean there's still hope for us?"

Ceecee smiled, looking out at the autumn marsh, the Lowcountry's only sure indicator of the change in season. The green spartina grass had mellowed to shades of gold and saffron, the color of the seeds the fall breezes would spread to ensure new grass in the spring. It was the only guarantee in life, the constant cycle of seasons, the ombré color scheme shifting from greens to golds to browns before going back to green.

"Yes," she said, meeting his eyes and remembering

the day they'd met. How she felt about him hadn't changed.

"Good," he said, squeezing her hand before leading her back to the car. She stared at the blackened hull of the house as they neared, her heart tightening with grief. She imagined it always would when she thought of Margaret. The old Margaret. The girl she'd grown up with and loved, not the bitter young woman who'd unexpectedly discovered life's sharp edges, who'd learned that dreams and wishes weren't guaranteed.

As they approached the house, a ray of sun shone through a hole in the roof, illuminating a swath of the once-elegant staircase, now just a blackened skeleton. A flash of memory hit Ceecee—of Boyd, carrying Margaret up those stairs when she'd heard Reggie had enlisted, his strong arms around her, bearing her limp weight.

Ceecee turned to say something to Boyd, to ask him why her face and hair didn't have any soot on them that night of the fire, and why her feet and legs weren't as dirty as they should have been. Why she'd found Tootsie Roll wrappers on the blanket.

She opened her mouth, but then caught sight of the Tree of Dreams in her peripheral vision and remembered all of her hurts and losses. All the forgiving she had given to others while her own heart shriveled. She had always done everything she was supposed to. Had been a devoted friend, a good daughter. A woman with the strong moral compass her parents had raised her with. And look where it had left her.

She studied Boyd as they walked, gazed at his strong profile, felt his steady grip on her hand, and knew she could never let him go again.

She turned again to see the Tree of Dreams. "Forgive me," she whispered, not sure for what or to whom she was speaking.

thirty-six

Larkin
2010

"Stop." Ceecee reached across the table and put her hand on the letter. "That belongs to Ivy."

"Yes," I said gently. "But Mama wanted me to see it. She said she'd found out something about the fire and wanted to show it to me."

Ceecee pulled the letter toward her, then carefully folded it before laying her hands on top. I studied her hands for a moment, the neat fingernails with pale pink polish; her hands were perfect for gardening, or making comfort food in her kitchen, or soothing babies. She'd done all of those things for me and my mother. I needed to remember that. From the look on her face when she saw the letter, I knew I would need to remember.

"But how do you know this is it?" she asked, the stubborn jut of her chin just like when she'd told the softball coach he should let me play even though I'd yet to prove that I could make contact between bat and ball.

Bennett covered my hand with his, understanding everything that was going on inside my head and heart without a word spoken between us. I glanced at him, hoping to show my appreciation, and in a sudden flash of insight I became aware that what I felt for him was so much more. He gave me a lop-sided grin with his ruined mouth, then winked with his good eye, making me realize that mind reading wasn't necessarily always a good thing.

I faced Ceecee again, struggling to recall what I'd been about to say. "In the e-mail, Mama mentioned she'd found photos of me as a little girl—and I found those, too, with the letter. It's not definitive, but I think it's likely that this letter is what she wanted to show me, don't you?"

"I need a cigarette," Bitty announced, pulling one from her housecoat pocket. She stood to retrieve an ashtray she apparently kept hidden in the pantry, then sat back down at the table and lit up. Ceecee didn't say a word about Bitty smoking in the house, and that worried me most of all.

"You're right, Larkin," Ceecee said. "It's not definitive. I'd rather wait and ask Ivy."

Bennett squeezed my hand, giving me the courage to say what I needed to say next. "She might never wake up, Ceecee. I think we all should prepare ourselves, just in case."

"Or she could wake up tomorrow." Ceecee's voice was thick with tears.

"She could," I agreed. "That's what we're all hoping and praying for. But before her accident, she wanted me to know something, and I think it's in this letter. Wouldn't reading it be a way to honor her even in her absence?"

We sat in silence, listening to the grandfather clock in the hall chime one o'clock. Bitty blew a ring of smoke up to the ceiling, like a protective halo above us, then rested her cigarette in the ashtray. She picked up the wedding photo in the frame, and the loose photograph of the two young men. "We should probably tell her," she said. "About Reggie. And Margaret."

Ceecee closed her eyes as if deciding between the lesser of two evils. "It's not like it matters anymore. There's nobody left who could be hurt. Except perhaps Ivy." She gave a little shrug. "But I don't think even she would care now. Boyd loved her so much."

I opened my mouth to state the obvious, that of course her father loved her. But then I remembered my thoughts when I first saw the Myrtle Beach photograph, and my mother's silly expression in the photograph of the two of us. It so resembled one of the boys in the first photo. "Oh," I said as I looked at the wedding photograph of Ceecee and my grandfather Boyd, then compared it to the one of the young men behind the fake bars. One of them was definitely the man I'd called Granddaddy, with glossy dark hair and bright eyes, his warmth and strength apparent even in the photo of him as a young man.

"Your mother has the same eyes." Bennett tapped on the image of the man standing next to Boyd. He had lighter hair and was several years younger than the other young man in the photo, but they shared a resemblance.

"So, who was Reggie?" I asked, unable to tear my gaze away from his photograph. "Besides apparently being my mother's biological father."

Ceecee drew a deep breath. "Reggie was Boyd's younger brother. They were very close, despite their age difference. Reggie saved Boyd's life one summer. From drowning."

I shifted in my chair, uncomfortable with my guess as to where this was headed. "That's a huge debt to have hanging over your head."

Bitty and Ceecee shared a glance; then Ceecee spoke again. "You could say that."

Bitty continued. "We three girls—Margaret, Ceecee, and I—met Reggie and Boyd the summer we graduated from high school."

"In Myrtle Beach," I supplied.

Bitty nodded. "Reggie and Margaret fell in love at first sight. It was a match made in heaven. She was smart, beautiful, and rich, and he was handsome and smart with big ambitions. The first time he met her, he introduced himself as a future president of the United States." She took another drag from her cigarette. "They weren't the only ones to fall in love. So did Ceecee and Boyd." She looked pointedly at me.

Bennett squeezed my hand again as the implications of this bombshell settled on me like so much fallout. "Oh," I said, amazing myself again at my clever use of vocabulary. Except there really wasn't anything I could say that would adequately express my surprise.

"What happened to Reggie?" I finally managed.

"He died before your mother was born, and before he could marry your grandmother, although he wanted to." Bitty stabbed her cigarette into the ashtray for punctuation.

"So Boyd married Margaret, who was pregnant with his brother's child, claiming the baby was his own," I said slowly. "And then Margaret died in a fire two years later." **Suspicious.** I saw the word on the fire chief's report, underlined in blue ink. The mural my mother had painted that showed all three women, a child, and a **man** inside the burning house. And I saw the ribbon I'd pulled from the tree with the words **forgive me** written down its length. My voice sounded brittle enough to break. "When did you marry Granddaddy?"

Ceecee's fingers were gripped tightly together, still

imprisoning the letter. "A year later. It was the decent thing to do, to wait a year."

Bennett didn't let go of my hand as I nodded repeatedly, trying to process my rampant thoughts. "So, he was in love with you when he married Margaret, and then after his wife dies in a fire, he marries you, and the two of you raise Margaret's daughter as if she were yours."

"She **was** mine!" Ceecee said, her voice raised, but not yet a shout. "I helped bring her into this world, right there in the hallway at Carrowmore. Ivy never lacked for love. Boyd and I raised her as if she were our beloved daughter because she was. We'd hoped for more children, but it wasn't to be. So our lives revolved around Ivy, to make up for both of her parents being gone."

My jaw felt as if it had been wired shut as I asked my next question. "Did you have anything to do with the fire that killed Margaret?"

Ceecee raised her hands to her face, just as Bitty reached over and snatched up the letter. "I think we've all heard enough for the time being," she said. "I'll take this for safekeeping, and we can look at it together tomorrow. I think our emotions are a little too raw right now."

I started to stand, to reach over and grab the letter, but Bennett held me back. "That's a good idea, Bitty. But to be fair, you're not exactly an uninvolved bystander. Why don't you give me the letter until the morning, when we can discuss this with clear heads?"

My gaze moved from Ceecee to Bitty, two women who'd always loved me, even at my most unlovable. They'd raised me, made me the woman I was. There was something in the letter, something grave, something they weren't ready to share. I owed them at least this.

Bennett looked around the table, waiting for each of us to nod our head. Bitty looked down at the letter for a long moment, then handed it to Bennett. "I trust you, young man. Don't disappoint me." She focused on me. "And don't use any of your powers of persuasion on him, either. He's a good man, but I've seen what a man can do in the name of love."

Without stopping to explain, she slid her chair back from the table and stood, making Bennett stand, too. "I'm going to bed. I'll see you all in the morning."

Ceecee turned to watch her go, then faced me again. "We put a ribbon in the tree—the three of us together: Margaret, Bitty, and me. It said, 'Friends forever, come what may.'" She frowned. "I don't think we understood then that even dreams and wishes have to survive in the real world. I don't think Margaret ever understood that. She never had to live in the real world until Reggie died."

Bennett pulled out her chair and helped her stand, then led her to the stairs. To my surprise, she leaned up and kissed his cheek. "You remind me of my Boyd in so many ways. I'm glad Larkin has you."

I wanted to tell her that I didn't technically have him, but I stopped, realizing that wasn't completely true.

"There are pillows and blankets in the chest behind the sofa, and I'll put fresh towels for you in the upstairs-hall bath. New toothbrushes under the sink. You're on your own for a razor, though."

"Thank you, Ceecee. I'll be fine," Bennett said.

"She sleeps like the dead, so she won't hear you if you come up the stairs," Bitty called over the railing.

I wanted to laugh, or roll my eyes, but I couldn't. I kept imagining the mural in my bedroom, the four martins, each carrying a ribbon in its beak. Did Mama imagine them to be Boyd and the three friends, each carrying a separate message to the Tree of Dreams?

"Good night," Ceecee said, and waited.

But I couldn't say anything, couldn't stop thinking about what I'd learned. How so many secrets had been kept from me my entire life. How the man I'd always considered my grandfather, who'd raised my mother, was my grandfather in name only. Not that it really mattered. He'd been my grandfather in all the ways that counted. He'd been kind and loving, and let me sit on his shoulders during the annual Fourth of July parade so that I was the tallest person there. He was the one who'd taught me how to bait a hook, and how to step into a johnboat without tipping it over. In my usual oblivious way, I'd never asked for the details, but I'd always known that the man I'd called my grandfather had been married to my grandmother and then married Ceecee. It had never occurred to me to ask how that had come about. Or how my grandmother had died. I felt a stab of guilt and shame, and wanted to ask Ceecee to tell me everything.

But when I lifted my head to say good night to Ceecee, the words froze in the back of my throat. I remembered the other mural in the ice-cream shop, of the three adults inside the house, the man carrying a child. Without a doubt, my grandfather's identity hadn't been the only truth kept from me.

Ceecee turned, and I listened to her slow progress up the steps, not moving until I heard the snap of her door as it closed. I went into the living room and pulled a pillow and blanket out and began to make up Bennett's bed on the sofa. I felt him beside me before he took hold of the bedding and gently pried it from my hands.

"Sit down," he said gently.

Too tired to argue, I sat, and he settled next to me. "I know what you're thinking," he said.

"Do you?"

He gave me a look. "Yeah, I do. There are a lot of puzzle pieces here, with several possible solutions, some of them easier to swallow than others."

"Would you consider showing me the letter now?"

He didn't dignify my question with an answer. Instead, he said, "Regardless of what's in the letter, there are a handful of givens you need to remember. First is that you have had the undying devotion of Ceecee and Bitty your whole life. They're not perfect, and I'd question some of their mothering skills, but there's never been any doubt that they have always wanted the best life for you, in spite of where you think their motivation comes from.

"Second, I can't see either one of those ladies engaging in a malicious act toward anyone. That's not who they are, even if circumstances might tempt them. Third, I never knew Boyd, but he was my parents' and grandparents' family doctor, and they're full of stories about his generosity and kindness. How he made house calls for the elderly long after most doctors stopped, and how he'd accept eggs or produce from those who couldn't afford to pay. He delivered Mabry and me—did you know that?"

I shook my head. I hadn't. Like so much else I hadn't known, and not all of it because of Ceecee holding back.

"Last, but not least, look at who you are now. You're an amazing woman, and it's all because of how you were raised. If you're brave and fearless, it's because they showed you how." He took a deep breath. "What I'm trying to say is that how devastating—or not—whatever is in that letter might be, those things won't change."

Tears pricked at the backs of my eyes, but I wasn't ready to cry. I had a feeling there would be an opportunity in the coming days. For now, I had to pretend to be strong and see if I liked it enough to keep pretending until I believed it. "Thanks, Bennett." I tilted my head. "How'd you get to be so smart?"

He shrugged, wincing a little bit at the movement and reminding me of what he'd done for me. "It's amazing what years of practice can do." His face sobered. "We're not all born knowing everything. Most of us have to grow into who we're meant to be."

My mouth twisted in a tight smile. "Mabry said pretty much the same thing."

"Yeah, well, we are twins."

"Thank you," I said, "for sharing your incredible wisdom. And for defending my honor tonight." He was very close to me on the sofa, close enough that I could see the dark irises in the middles of his eyes. All I wanted to do was lean into him.

The clock struck again, and I looked at my watch. Two o'clock. "Do you happen to know if Mabry's on the night shift tonight?"

Bennett nodded. "She is—Ellis is staying with my parents because both Mabry and Jonathan are at the hospital until seven."

I stood. "Good. Because I'll need someone to sneak me into my mother's room. The night nurse is a real stickler for quiet hours. But I need to talk to Mama, and I don't feel like I can wait."

"I'll take you," he said, standing.

"No, I'll be all right. But thank you." My eyes drifted down to his cut and bruised lips, and I felt oddly happy that they weren't completely kissable. Because if they had been, I might not have been able to leave. "I'll be back early—tell Ceecee and Bitty to wait until I'm back to open the letter. And to have the coffee on."

"Will do." He walked me to the back door and pulled it open, watching me head down the back steps. "Larkin?"

I paused and looked at him. "Yes?"

"I meant what I said earlier. About the talent show."

Not able to articulate any other word, I said simply, "Oh," then kept walking to the car, mentally beating myself up for my perpetual inability to recognize the truth of things.

Ivy
2010

I know it's nighttime because the sky through the blinds is dark, and the lights in my room have been dimmed. They're supposed to do that so that my body still understands night and day. Not that it matters. Tonight the ceiling is pulsing with bright white light, like it can't hold it all in. I see it seep through the cracks like the laser show on Stone Mountain Mack took me to on our honeymoon in Atlanta. Back when I thought we could be happy.

I keep seeing the flash of a yellow dress, and I

know Mama is waiting for me just beyond the ceiling. I just can't see her yet. And the Mustang is back, the engine idling, Ellis sitting on the side of my bed, smiling his secret smile.

Larkin's here, even though it's too late—or too early, depending on how you look at it. Mabry let her in. And the second Larkin entered the room, it was like somebody hit the floodlights, and I felt myself lift higher off the bed.

She doesn't speak for a long time, and it's nice just to have her there. I feel her warmth and her love, and that's enough for me. There's so much I want to tell her, but I'm beginning to think she's smart enough to figure it all out on her own. Just having that thought brightens the room a notch, the sound of the idling engine getting louder, too.

"We found the letter, Mama. The one hidden in Granddaddy's desk. I found the pictures you wanted to send me, too. The one of us making faces—I love it. I think I'll get it framed and put it on my desk. I hope you don't mind. A lot of women only want the prettiest pictures of themselves on display, but I think you and I are different. We want the pictures that show the real us. So thanks for that."

I lift up higher, closer to the ceiling now, and I don't know if it's my imagination, but the cracks along the edges appear to be getting wider.

"Ever since I've come home, I've had a lot of time to think about my life. I've had to pay attention for the first time. It took me twenty-seven years, but some of us are slow learners, I guess." Her lips twitch into a half smile.

She sits up and takes my hand, and I wish so badly that I could feel it, but all I can do is look at this beautiful creature who's the best thing I've ever done in my life.

"I figured something out recently. You framed my SAT and ACT scores, remember? I'd shoved them in a drawer, but you must have pulled them out. They weren't great scores, were they? But that's not the point you were trying to make. It's not about how well I did. It's about how far I've come, and how far I still have to go. It's about being okay with not being the best, because there are a million and one things out there to try until I do find the thing that I'm good at and that makes me happy. We just need people in our lives who let us be brave enough to try. And I've always had them in spades."

Lights shoot across the room. Ellis is watching Larkin and smiling.

"So, about the letter. We haven't opened it yet. Ceecee and Bitty wanted to wait until morning, when we'll have clearer heads, and I agreed. I know that they're afraid of something, maybe something that's in the letter that they don't want anyone to know. I'm not even sure I'm ready to hear the truth, because I'm afraid I won't want to. Gabriel told me about the little additions you put into the mural in his shop, and I'm scared to death of what they might mean."

She smooths her hand over my fingers, straightening them. She always likes for things to be just so. She was probably the only five-year-old who lined up her Barbies' shoes by color and style. I think that was Ceecee's doing, not mine.

"But that's the thing, isn't it? Whatever is in the letter won't destroy me. I'm stronger than that. You and Ceecee and Bitty made me that way. You made me brave, and fearless, and I'll just keep telling myself that in case I forget. So, don't worry about me. I'll be okay."

She smiles, and I know she's thinking about Bennett, and my heart feels like it's going to burst. Ellis smiles at me and reaches for my hand. I don't take it right away because I know I can't move. But he's not looking down at the bed but up at the ceiling, where I am seeing the room from above again, and when I reach for his hand, I feel his fingers between mine.

We look down and watch as Larkin places her folded arms on the bed, then leans over in the chair and rests her head in her arms. "I'm so tired," she says. "I'm just going to close my eyes for a moment." We watch as her eyes flutter closed. "I love you, Mama. I think everything's going to be okay now."

I think I know why I didn't die at Carrowmore that day. Because I wasn't done. Because I was still angry. Because there were still things I needed to learn. Like how before a person can forgive others, she needs to forgive herself. That love is always messy, whether it's between a husband and wife or a mother and child. But it's still love, in all of its wonderful, complicated, messy ways. We do our best with it, our hearts bruised and bleeding yet still capable of love if we're smart enough to recognize it.

But mostly, I needed to learn that you never know how strong you are until being strong is the only choice you have. All this time I've been worried that I still needed to teach this to my precious Larkin. I see now that I already have.

The anger that brought me to Carrowmore with a ribbon clenched in my fist disappears as peace and understanding lift me higher toward the ceiling. My heart floods with love for my daughter, and a sadness, too, because I know I'm leaving her. But I'm comforted with the deep knowledge that I'm not leaving her alone. She'll still have Ceecee and Bitty and all the people who have always loved her. And she will finally know that her mother has always loved her, even during all those years I pushed her away, believing there was nothing I could teach her.

The ceiling disappears, and I'm standing on Ceecee's porch. I hear the sound of Ellis's Mustang, and I see it coming down River Street, the top down and his gorgeous long brown hair flying behind him. Daddy hates his long hair, but I don't, and that's the only opinion that matters, according to Ceecee.

And then Ellis stops the car in front of the house, the engine idling, and I run down the porch steps and jump in. I smile at Ellis, and he smiles, too, as he leans over to kiss me. Then he pulls away from the curb, and we drive away, and I am happy again.

thirty-seven

Ceecee
2010

That night, Ceecee dreamed of Ivy. Not the woman slowly shrinking in a hospital bed, her bright hair dimming by degrees. She dreamed of her Ivy as a young woman in love, her hair long and parted in the middle, a corsage on her wrist. Ceecee heard the rumble and thrum of an approaching car, and the anticipation and excitement rippled through her as if the feelings were her own.

And then Ellis in that bright red Mustang pulled up in front of the house, and Ivy turned to Ceecee and smiled. "I love you, Mama," she said, kissing her on the cheek. "I'll be all right now." She turned and ran down the porch steps toward the car, her hair catching the light and showing off its red highlights. As Ceecee watched, Ellis leaned forward and kissed Ivy on the lips. The Mustang's engine whined as it pulled away from the curb, taking Ellis and Ivy down the street, and Ceecee stood still, watching until the car disappeared. Her heart took turns filling and emptying, an odd mixture of happiness and grief coursing through her as she watched Ivy leave, knowing in her mother's heart that Ivy was telling her good-bye.

Ceecee awoke to the sound of the telephone by her bed, and knew without picking it up that Ivy was gone. She touched her cheek and smiled, feeling Ivy's kiss, then answered the phone.

After she hung up, she sat on the edge of her bed, waiting for the thickness in her chest to go away. She was too sad for tears. They couldn't express the grief that filled every vein, every artery, every part of her. Tears would make light of the darkness that edged toward her heart, threatening to overtake it. She forced herself to remember her dream, to know that Ivy had come to say good-bye. Mostly, she needed to remember that Ivy was happy again.

When she thought she was ready, Ceecee walked out into the hallway to tell Bitty. But Bitty's bedroom door was already open, her bed empty. The smell of cigarette smoke drifted from outside. Gripping the banister and feeling much older than her seventy-seven years, Ceecee made her way to the back porch.

Bitty wore baby blue pajamas with colorful uni-corns dotted all over them. Her feet were bare, her red hair sticking up at all angles, and her face was de-void of makeup. Ceecee stopped in surprise. Without the multihued eye shadow and outrageous eyelashes, Bitty was the same girl Ceecee had known all of her life. And had always loved like a sister. They'd weath-ered so many storms together, somehow emerging intact. Ceecee fervently hoped they could weather one more. Sharing the good and bad times with a lifelong friend made the business of living a lot more bearable.

Bitty looked up, her face expressionless. "Was that the hospital?"

Ceecee nodded. "It was Larkin. She went to visit Ivy last night after we went to bed. She said she'd fallen asleep at some point, and while she was sleeping . . ." She stopped, feeling the tight ball in her throat.

Bitty nodded. They were like an old married cou-ple, finishing each other's thoughts and sentences. Ceecee found a great deal of comfort in that. She was getting too old to have to explain things.

"I dreamed about her," Bitty said. "I saw her drive away with Ellis in that Mustang of his—the one Boyd hated so much."

Ceecee smiled softly. "I saw her, too. She came to say good-bye. To let us know that she's okay, and with Ellis. I find it almost hard to cry, because that would be too selfish of me."

Bitty rolled her eyes. "One of these days, Ceecee, you've got to stop worrying about being selfish. You're one of the most giving people I've ever known." Bitty pressed the sleeve of her pajamas into the corner of her eye. "Our sweet Ivy."

Ceecee waited, but the word "our" didn't sting much anymore. Ivy's presence in their lives had been too brief, like the moon passing in front of the sun during an eclipse. Short, yet intense. They had both loved her, and her absence would be equally felt. Grief, Ceecee had learned in her long life, wasn't something that could be measured or apportioned. A person felt as much as they could handle, and then more if it could be shared.

"Are you going to be all right?" Bitty asked.

Ceecee nodded. "As soon as I see Larkin, anyway. She's on her way home now. I think she'll get through this fine. She was there when Ivy passed and had the chance to say good-bye, which I know will give her peace. When she called Mack to tell him, he said that same thing." Ceecee looked closely at her friend. "Larkin thinks it will be a good time to read the letter as soon as she gets here. I'll let Bennett know."

"Right." Bitty nodded. "The letter."

Ceecee took a deep breath. "Yes. So, I thought now might be a good time for the two of us to talk."

"To talk?" Bitty said, busily rearranging her ashtray on the coffee table.

"About the night of the fire. I'm too old for secrets.

For a lot of things, really, but especially secrets. They cost a lot of brain cells, and those are in short enough supply as it is."

"Amen," Bitty said, raising an imaginary glass. "I couldn't have said it better myself."

Ceecee took a deep breath, feeling her lungs expand with the morning air, the taste of salt settling on the back of her tongue like a reminder of who she was. "I'll start. When the police interrogated me, I left something out."

Bitty went very still.

"I found Tootsie Roll wrappers folded in the blanket with Ivy and me. I know only one person who eats those."

Bitty put her cigarette in her mouth in a casual way, but Ceecee could see her hand shaking. After a moment, she said, "They must have fallen out of my pocket when I leaned over to cover you both better with the blanket."

"So you **were** there. Ivy's mural showed you in the house." Ceecee took a deep breath, trying to find the strength to say the next words. "Did you set the fire?"

Bitty looked outraged. "Me? No. I never went inside. When I got there, Carrowmore was already on fire, and you and Ivy were under the magnolia tree under the blanket. There was nothing else I could do, so I tried to pull the blanket up higher. That's all."

Ceecee shook her head. "I don't understand. Why would Ivy paint you inside the house?"

"I don't know. Maybe just to show I was there. After the storm passed, I decided to go to Carrowmore to find you. You can't imagine how I felt when I saw the house on fire. The roads had a lot of water on them, and I was afraid I'd get stuck in the mud, so I left my car on the side of the road and ran through the woods—that's how I found you and Ivy. I have no idea how Ivy knew I was there that night—I left before the fire truck arrived. I didn't want them to ask any questions."

"But why?" Ceecee said. "If you had nothing to hide, why wouldn't you stay?"

Bitty's eyes narrowed. "Have you ever wondered why you've kept the secret of the candy wrappers all these years?"

Ceecee didn't hesitate. "No. I never told anyone because you're my friend. My sister. And if you had set the fire, I thought you might have done it for me."

"But I didn't." Bitty was watching her closely, as if waiting for Ceecee to ask the right question.

"It was an accident," Ceecee said. "From a candle. There were lit candles down in the white parlor, and one in my bedroom. I don't remember if I blew out my candle before I went to bed." She paused for a moment. "I took some sleeping pills. That's why I don't remember."

"And you don't remember how you got outside."

Ceecee shook her head. "No. Just . . . flashes. A memory of flying."

Bitty continued to look at her, willing Ceecee to say the next thing. Finally, Bitty said, "I called Boyd at the hospital that night. I told him that you'd gone to Carrowmore."

Ceecee closed her eyes, nodded. "Ivy's mural. She painted him in the house, too. So he was there."

"He was," Bitty said. "I saw him. In his car, driving away just as I arrived. He didn't see me—or at least he never mentioned it, so I assumed he hadn't."

Ceecee remembered the sensation of flying, of strong arms around her, the sound of footsteps. Of course it hadn't been Bitty carrying her out of the house. She was too small, too slight. Ceecee had never really believed it, but it had kept her busy enough that she hadn't had to consider the truth. It had been Boyd who tucked her and Ivy safely out of the way of the fire. And then left before anyone could know it had been him. There was only one reason why he would have run away. Ceecee had to search to find her voice. "You never told anyone."

"Of course not." Bitty sounded almost angry. "For the same reason you never told anyone about the candy wrappers." She blew smoke up toward the ceiling and laughed. "It's kind of funny when you think about it. We've both been keeping secrets from each other all these years, holding each other at arm's length just in case the other sniffed too close to the truth."

Ceecee glared at her friend. "I'm glad you find this amusing. Because I find it upsetting that the man I loved just about my whole life was probably a murderer."

Bitty sobered. "Or not. We have no proof, nor do we have proof of what candle may or may not have started the fire—although the fire report did say they thought it started downstairs." She leaned forward. "And isn't that what love is? Giving someone the benefit of the doubt?"

Ceecee thought of the gentle man she'd married, the doctor with the warm and sincere bedside manner, the man who'd never raised his voice to anyone. She couldn't believe he'd committed murder. She wouldn't believe it. "You're wrong," she said out loud. "Love isn't about doubting. Love is knowing something is true deep in your heart despite all evidence to the contrary. I never believed you could have done something to Margaret. Lord knows you've got a mean streak a mile wide, but I could never see you killing someone, no matter how much you thought it was justified."

Bitty started to laugh, but it turned into another racking cough, making her whole body shudder with the effort.

Ceecee stood in front of her friend, waiting for it to subside. "It's not just acute bronchitis, is it?"

For a moment it looked as if Bitty would deny it

before she realized that it was pointless to lie to the one person in the world who knew her better than she knew herself. She gave one short nod. "Lung cancer. Stage two."

Ceecee looked at her matter-of-factly. "And you're still smoking."

"Yep. I've tried giving it up, but I can't."

Ceecee reached over and snatched the pack of cigarettes, crushing it in her hand. "You can now. I'm going to help you quit. And then I'm going to help you get better."

Bitty sat up. "Give those back."

"Nope. They're going in the garbage. You're quitting today."

"You can't stop me."

"Yes, I can. You're going to move in here with me so I can take care of you and take you to your doctor's appointments and make sure you never smoke another cigarette."

Bitty just stared at her openmouthed.

"I'm glad we agree." Ceecee sat down next to Bitty, putting her arm around her shoulders. "See? I can be selfish. I'll be lonely now, without Ivy. But with you here, I won't be."

Bitty let out a long, shuddering breath, as if a world of worry had been told to leave. She leaned her head on Ceecee's shoulder. "I guess I was the one who said you should learn to be more selfish, wasn't I?"

"You sure did. And you might as well tell me now

where you keep the rest of your cigarette stash. I'll find them eventually, so I'd appreciate it if you'd save me the trouble."

"I'll think about it." Ceecee felt Bitty's smile against her shoulder. "Do you still miss Margaret? The way she was when we were girls?"

"I miss the way we all were when we were girls. What was it that my mama used to say? Something about Margaret suggesting something outrageous, me cautioning against it, and you goading us all into doing it anyway."

"Sounds about right," Bitty said. "And I wouldn't change any of it." She felt Ceecee look at her. "Except for one or two things."

Ceecee watched as an egret perched on one of the dock pilings, looking out at the smooth water of the Sampit, happily oblivious to the cycle of life and death that took place beneath its beautiful wings. "Maybe Larkin can fill in for Margaret when she moves back home."

"She's moving back?" Bitty sat up with surprise.

"She hasn't said so yet, but of course she is. Like Boyd used to say about our Ivy, she's got salt water running through her veins. I don't know what she's been surviving on in New York, but I say it's time for an infusion."

They heard a car pull up at the front of the house. "Larkin's here," Ceecee announced as she stood. She gave her hand to Bitty and helped her stand. "Whatever's in the letter, we'll be okay, won't we?"

Bitty squeezed her hand. "Of course. Friends forever, remember?"

Ceecee squeezed back, remembering the day they'd put their ribbons in the tree the first time, wishing that they'd simply told Margaret no. "Friends forever," she repeated with a smile as they entered the house together.

Larkin
2010

Bennett met me at the front door. All the tears I'd been holding back found their way to my eyes as I faced him, feeling the burden of my sadness shift from my shoulders because he was there. Like he'd always been when I'd needed him. Before I could say anything, he'd wrapped his arms around me, making me feel comforted without the benefit of words. "I've got the coffee on, as promised," he said, kissing the top of my head. He smelled of soap, and his skin was still damp from the shower. I had the oddest sensation that I could get used to that.

"Thank you," I said, my tears leaving a wet patch on his shirt.

When I got to the kitchen, I watched as Ceecee and Bitty walked through the back door, holding hands and looking like coconspirators. When they saw me, they each hugged me as we cried together, and it was a little like having Mama back.

Ceecee went immediately to the fridge and began pulling out eggs and cheese and other breakfast fixings. "We'll need to start making phone calls and begin with the arrangements for your mama, but we can't do that on empty stomachs, can we?"

I closed the refrigerator door. "Breakfast and phone calls can wait. We need to read the letter now. I know that's what Mama would want." Knowing this was the only thing keeping me from shrinking into my grief.

Ceecee and Bitty exchanged a glance, then sat obediently at the kitchen table. "I'll get the coffee," I said, bringing the pot over, along with four mugs and cream from the refrigerator.

Bennett excused himself, then came back with the letter. "Who'd like to read it?"

I looked at Ceecee, but she shook her head. "Your mama would want you to. Go ahead."

Bennett slid the paper in front of me, and I looked down at the small, neat handwriting that filled the front and back, took a sip of my coffee to clear my throat, and began.

October 10, 1993

My Dearest Ivy,

I've already spent too much time deciding to whom this letter should be addressed, and have decided on you. You're a mother now,

more prepared to understand what it means to love someone more than yourself, to make choices dictated by your heart, and not your head. Life is full of choices, and it's up to us to decide what part will guide our actions.

My doctors tell me that my time is limited, and this is the last task on my list of things I need to take care of before I'm gone. It wasn't a long list, but I took my time, dreading this part even though my intent in writing this letter is more to clear my conscience than to confess. I made a choice long ago, a choice that affected so many lives, and I've never regretted it for one second. Still, it has haunted me for four decades, visiting me in my dreams. You and I have both been suffering through the same nightmare, it seems. Dreams of fire. Which makes sense since we were both there the day your mother died.

The day of the fire, I knew your mother and Sessalee were with you at Carrowmore, preparing to ride out the storm. But despite the hurricane, it was Margaret's state of mind that worried me most. Knowing that Sessalee was with you gave me what little consolation I could find, allowing me to stay at the hospital through the long night, focusing on my work.

After the storm passed us in the early morning, I couldn't wait anymore, and I headed to

Carrowmore, frantic with worry. It took me a long time to get there, having to stop and remove tree limbs and other debris from the road, and to navigate around flooded parts. I remember looking through the woods as I approached the house, searching for the flash of white through the trees. Instead, I saw flames shooting up and turning to thick smoke in the driving rain. I don't remember stopping the car before the long driveway, although I must have been aware of the heavy mud. I don't remember running toward the house and entering. I only remember seeing you in the threshold of the front door, fast asleep, as if someone had just dropped you there. I picked you up, calling Margaret's name and Sessalee's, hoping against all hope that they were safely outside. I must have known that couldn't be the case, because Sessalee would never have left you behind.

I brought you to the large magnolia tree in the front yard, its thick branches giving you shelter from the wind and rain. You were still sleeping, and I realized Margaret must have given you something. She'd done it before, and I'd taken the pills away from her. But she must have saved some, because you didn't even open your eyes.

When I came back to the house, the flames had consumed the white parlor, the smoke billowing out into the foyer. A shout came from upstairs, and I took a deep breath before running up the steps two and three at a time, desperation making me faster and stronger. I went into the first bedroom, the one I knew Sessalee usually stayed in. She was sound asleep in the bed, the same kind of dreamless dead sleep you were in, and Margaret was beside the bed, trying to pull her out and coughing in the smoke.

I picked Sessalee up, throwing her blanket over her face to protect her from the smoke, then shouted to Margaret to hold her breath, and follow me. As we got to the top of the stairs, Margaret collapsed. And that's when I had to make a choice. Should I listen to my heart, or my head? I knew I couldn't safely carry them both down the stairs and out of the house. I had to choose between my wife and the woman I loved.

I stopped reading, and glanced at Ceecee. Her head was bowed, her fingers clasped together so tightly that her knuckles were white. Bitty saw it, too, and placed her own hand on top. "The fire was downstairs," she said. "Not in your room. So you couldn't have started it."

Ceecee nodded, but it didn't erase her expression of misery. I took another sip of my coffee, barely aware that it had grown tepid, and continued to read.

I placed Sessalee next to you beneath the tree, then ran back to the house to get Margaret. But it was too late. The fire had reached the bottom of the stairs. I swear to you that I tried, but the flames and smoke beat me back. There was no other access to the upstairs, and there was nothing I could do.

I returned to where I'd left you and Sessalee. I checked your pulses and breathing to make sure you were both all right. And then I heard the fire truck. That's when I made my second choice—I could either stay and tell them the truth, or I could leave and let them believe that Sessalee had brought you out of the house. I didn't want Sessalee to know the truth, that I had saved her life over Margaret's. She couldn't have lived with it. But I could. So I made the choice to leave.

I saw Bitty as she was parking on the side of the road, and I knew she'd seen and recognized my car. I've waited nearly forty years for one of us to say something about how we knew we were both there that day, and never told anyone. But we never did. I've thought about it for a long time, and I think I finally understand. Secrets can be used for subterfuge. But secrets kept out of love are different. In their own way, they sustain us; they keep us sane. They tell us that love isn't about doubt, but about believing in spite of it.

We have had a good life together, Sessalee and I, and you, our darling daughter. You have gifted us with a precious granddaughter, and I can only be grateful for the choices I've made. My one regret is that Sessalee doesn't know Margaret tried to save her, or that she saved you by leaving you where I could find you. But I couldn't tell her any of that without revealing the rest.

I sometimes wonder if some of your own restlessness is because you might remember more than you think, that you were aware of the struggles going on around you, of the fire and being carried to safety. Maybe you picked up on the mental turmoil of those who wanted to save you. I hope you can forgive me for not telling you the truth. If I'd thought it could have helped you navigate your life better, I would have. I believe that's why you put Carrowmore in trust for Larkin after she was born. She has no memories of it, nothing to sour her belief that it can one day be brought back to life.

Never forget you are a Darlington, like our precious Larkin. It's a legacy that goes back more than two hundred years, when it used to be said that the Darlington luck was legendary. But I don't believe in luck. I believe that love creates good fortune and builds empires, and it's doubt and envy that destroy both. My dream has always been to rebuild Carrowmore, but my health has other plans. My hope is that one day Larkin will decide to reclaim her legacy, to start anew, building on a foundation of what we have learned and the choices we have made. It can be a new legacy, born of love, not fickle luck.

I've thought about placing this letter inside the Tree of Dreams, but instead I'll leave it in the secret compartment of my desk. Fate can decide whether anyone reads it. Like I said, this isn't a confession. Just the final words of a dying man trying to set the record straight.

Ever since the day of the fire, I have had a recurring dream that haunts me into my waking hours. I dream of four martins flying home to Carrowmore, a ribbon in each beak. Maybe wisdom does come with age, because now that I'm facing death, I think I understand what the dream was trying to tell me.

Each bird represented one of us—Sessalee, Margaret, Bitty, and me. We each had something to say, a message to bring back to our nest. Mine was of peace, for the choices I'd made and learned to live with. Bitty's was one of constancy and faith—not blind faith, but faith born from wisdom and a deep friendship that knew no boundaries. Sessalee's was one of unselfish love, for all of us lucky enough to be in her circle. And the fourth was Margaret, whose message was one of forgiveness. Not just for me, but for herself.

I like to think that the nest they're bringing the messages to is where we will find you and Larkin. A wise man named Atticus once said, "We are made of all those who have built and broken us." We have all made mistakes. Just remember that you are loved.

I love you, darling daughter. I know you and Larkin will be a great comfort to my Sessalee once I am gone. Be well.

Love,
Your devoted father

I pulled a tissue from the box in the middle of the kitchen table and handed it to Ceecee, who delicately blotted her eyes—rubbing caused wrinkles—and blew her nose; then I grabbed one to dab at my own eyes. I leaned across the table toward her. "You put the ribbon in the tree, didn't you?" I asked. "The one that said, 'Forgive me.' Because you always thought you'd left Margaret behind."

Ceecee clenched her eyes shut. "That's why Ivy was so angry with me and questioned the trust. Because Boyd chose to save me instead of her mother. And she died feeling that anger toward me, waiting for me to ask for her forgiveness."

Bitty squeezed her hand. "No, Ceecee. She didn't.

She came back to tell you good-bye in your dream. Remember? Then she kissed you. I think that means she's at peace and not angry anymore. I think she understood."

Ceecee looked at her friend, her face softening as she realized the truth of Bitty's words. "Yes," she said, "I think you're right." She thought for a moment. "So, who's been tending the martin houses?"

Bitty smiled softly. "I have." She looked around sheepishly. "I don't believe in luck or legends, but there was something about the story of the martins and Carrowmore . . . I wanted to help it survive. For Larkin."

I leaned over and hugged Bitty and Ceecee, realizing for the first time in my life how very lucky I'd been to have three very different women play the role of mother in my life. **We are made by those who have built and broken us.** So very true, I thought, grateful that my entire past, warts and all, had brought me to where I was now.

A knock sounded on the door. Bennett stood to answer it, and we saw Carol Anne and Mabry, both carrying casseroles, my father arriving behind them.

"Bennett called us about Ivy, so we've brought food."

I wanted to laugh at the Southern equivalent of grief counseling, but found myself crying instead, being comforted by the people I loved most in this world. Mabry hugged me, accidentally snagging her wedding ring on my necklace, breaking a link and sending the three charms scattering to the floor. The arrow fell close to my feet, and I picked it up, feeling the smooth gold between my fingers, the tip pointing toward my heart, and I knew at last what it meant.

thirty-eight

Larkin
2011

I sat next to Bennett in the middle of the front seat of his truck, my head on his shoulder and his arm around me, embracing with a vengeance being back in the South. My lipstick and nail polish matched, and my hair was pulled up into a ponytail beneath a USC Gamecocks baseball hat to protect my skin from the bright May sun.

A song came on the radio, and I leaned forward to turn it up. "Ha! 'We Rode in Trucks' by Luke Bryan. How appropriate."

Bennett chuckled, and I could feel the rumble beneath my cheek. "I sometimes think you're just dating me for my truck."

I pulled back to look at him. "Is that what we're doing? Dating?"

He gave me a half grin, then returned his gaze to the road leading to Carrowmore. "Well, that certainly sounds better than being your contractor with benefits."

I slapped his chest, then tilted my head to kiss him on his jaw right below his ear, where I knew he liked it. "Just be glad I hired you to do the restoration. Otherwise it might have been awkward."

He raised his eyebrows, placing both hands on the steering wheel to navigate the rutted road, still strewn with debris from the previous night's storm. "Speaking of awkward, Mabry keeps on teasing me with snippets from your manuscript in progress but won't let me read it. When are you going to let me see?"

"When it's done. Mabry has sworn to be honest in her critique. I'm afraid if I let you or Ceecee or Bitty read it, I'd be met with undeserved and unending praise. And that's not what I'm looking for."

"Fair enough," he said, pulling around the side of the house. "Because you're right. I can't see myself being unbiased about anything you write. Or say or do." He grinned. "Maybe I just need to spend more time with you."

Before I could retaliate, my phone beeped, and I glanced at the screen. It was Josephine in New York, reminding me of our conference call at one o'clock.

I'd been able to negotiate a remote working arrangement with Wax & Crandall. It was fewer hours, and less pay, but it was a sweet deal. It gave me time to work on the novel Mabry had reminded me that I'd always wanted to write, as well as to oversee the restoration of Carrowmore. Josephine kept threatening to move down to Georgetown so she could see for herself what it was that had pulled me away from New York.

Bennett climbed out of the truck, and I slid over so that he could help me out. I loved the way his arms felt around my waist as he swung me around before gently placing me back on the ground. It was the main reason why I loved riding in his truck so much.

"We're the first ones here," he said. "Want to take a stroll?"

He reached out his hand, and I took it, never tiring of the warm jolt of electricity every time we touched. We walked slowly down toward the tidal river, the edge at low tide showing its bald spots of pluff mud and spiky spartina grass. I took a deep breath, loving the scent, which always reminded me of home. We passed under the martin houses strung among the branches of the old trees, swaying in the river breeze and causing the sunlight to wink at us.

My daddy was maintaining them now, but only until Bitty regained her strength. She'd survived radiation and chemotherapy, which had successfully shrunk the tumors in her lungs, and now we were just waiting to see how permanent her recovery would be. She kept insisting that she was strong enough to move back to Folly Beach, but Ceecee and I wouldn't let her. I think she was secretly pleased, but her independent nature had to fight us, if only for show.

"Do you think Donna will come with your dad?" Bennett asked.

It had taken my daddy almost six months after my mother's passing to ask my permission to start dating Donna. I'd seen her a few times at the hospital where she worked as a nurse, and I knew she was the woman with whom my father had had the affair. He'd asked for my forgiveness, and I'd told him he didn't need it. As my granddaddy Boyd wrote in his letter, we all make mistakes. To survive them, we have to learn to live with our choices.

I think my new understanding of my mother helped me see that, to know that my parents had loved each other, but sometimes love isn't enough when it's not given from a heart that's free. I know Mama is with Ellis now, so it's only right that Daddy find his own happiness.

"Probably. I hardly see him without her anymore. They both like to garden and brew beer, so they spend a lot of time together. It's nice to see," I said, surprising myself by how much I meant it.

We stopped beneath the Tree of Dreams, the hole now sealed courtesy of the National Forest Service, the recipient of the land donation made in my mother's honor. It wasn't that I didn't believe in the tree's power. But I believed in the power of human imagination more, of projecting our dreams and wishes into a safe space where we could place our disappointments if they didn't come true.

"Just think—this could all have been a golf course community with condos," Bennett said.

I gave an exaggerated shudder. "Please stop, or you'll give me nightmares."

"You'll have them soon enough when you start getting the invoices for the house restoration."

"I'm sure—although I know you'll cut a deal. I mean, Meghan Black is practically ecstatic. It's going to be her thesis work. I think the title's going to be something like **From the Brink: Restoring a Nineteenth-Century Rice Plantation Home While Bankrupting the Owner.**"

"You should suggest that," Bennett said, laughing. "Though didn't Meghan say she'd planned to exhaust all grant possibilities first?"

I nodded. "She has a leg up on that since Carrowmore is going to be used for field study by graduate students during the work in progress."

"It's a good thing Ceecee agreed to spend funds for the restoration," Bennett added. "As executor, she could have shut this all down."

"All true. I'm just hoping that we can come through with support from the Land and Water Conservation Fund before I deplete the money in the trust." I bit my lip and sighed. "Meghan says Congress has fully funded the LWCF only twice in its fifty-year existence, though, so I'm not going to hold my breath on that one."

"You can use some of that legendary Darlington good fortune and wish it to be so."

"I do love your optimism," I said, kissing him softly on the lips.

His eyes stared into mine for a long time, as if he was waiting for me to say something else. When I didn't, he said, "You know, for someone who's so good with words, your vocabulary is sadly lacking."

I stood back. "Please don't tell me that Mabry read parts of that old manuscript."

"You mean the one with 'purple-headed love dart'? Nah—she didn't have to. It's been etched in my brain since I first read it ten years ago."

I frowned. "Then what are you talking about?"

"After my fight with Jackson, when you were putting ice on my eye, I told you that I loved you, and all you said in response was, 'Oh.' I haven't said it again, because I'm not good at rejection, but I guess being here and standing under this tree, I'm feeling optimistic."

I stood on my toes and placed my arms around his neck, then kissed him in a way I hoped showed how I felt. "I love you, Bennett Lynch. I wish I'd realized it sooner, but know that I have every intention of making up for lost time."

"Me, too," he said. When he kissed me back, I imagined the ground trembling beneath my feet, my hands clutching at him tightly so I wouldn't fall over.

He looked back toward the ruins of Carrowmore. "You know, this is going to be a lot of house for just one woman to live in all by herself."

"You think?" I asked.

"Yep. I think maybe adding a guy who's handy with a hammer and maybe a passel of kids would fill it out nicely."

"A passel, huh? How many is a passel?"

"Not sure, but just so you're forewarned, twins run in my family."

"Oh," I said, and we both laughed while a white-hot shard of longing shot through me at the prospect of raising a family with Bennett at Carrowmore, sitting on the front porch, and watching the seasons pass just as generations of my family had.

He stepped back, but his gaze was focused on something behind me. "Hang on a sec," he said, then walked toward the marshy edge of the river and leaned down to pluck something from the sucking mud. "Look what I found." He placed it in my outstretched palm.

"A shark's tooth," I said. "Aren't those supposed to be good luck?"

Bennett nodded. "Even as a kid, I was always surprised to find them in riverbeds and marshes. It's crazy how far they can travel. I guess the pull of the marsh will always bring the outcasts home eventually."

I looked up at him, meeting his eyes. "Are you calling me an outcast?"

With a smile, he said, "No. I'm calling you mine."

He kissed me again, until the sound of arriving cars pulled us apart. We left the tree and the river behind us as we walked hand in hand back to the house.

That night, I dreamed again of falling. But this time I wasn't afraid. I allowed myself to enjoy the feeling of weightlessness, almost as if I were flying. And when I awoke, I understood that I hadn't been afraid, because I finally knew where I would land.

Throughout our lives we are all falling. Falling down, falling out, falling away. Falling in love. The trick is finding someone to catch us. And sometimes we surprise ourselves by finding out that person is us.

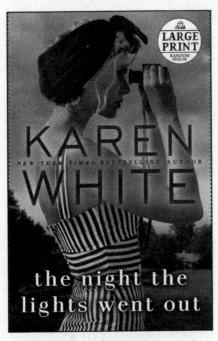